T0367526

Wyatt's
Obsession

NOVEL ONE
OF THE
STRIVE 1
DUOLOGY

W. L. Lyons III

iUniverse

WYATT'S OBSESSION
NOVEL ONE OF THE STRIVE 1 DUOLOGY
Revised Edition of Strive1

iUniverse books may be ordered through booksellers or by contacting:

iUniverse
1663 Liberty Drive
Bloomington, IN 47403
www.iuniverse.com
1-800-Authors (1-800-288-4677)

ISBN: 978-1-4917-7483-0 (sc)
ISBN: 978-1-4917-7484-7 (e)

Library of Congress Control Number: 2015914671

Print information available on the last page.

iUniverse rev. date: 10/2/2015

Acknowledgements

While it may seem trite, I owe the existence of this book to my wife, Darleen. Her patience, understanding and editing skills freed me to evangelize about the passions lurking in the engineering world and the ever-increasing roadblocks to their fulfillment. Thank you, Darlin' Dar.

As a fledgling novelist, I relied on new friends in my writer's group, particularly Toni Floyd, Tom Tucker and John McKenzie. Determined to rescue future readers from the agonies of shoddy plots, they literally took me to school.

With pride, I thank my son, W. L. Lyons IV for the cover design.

Prologue

The police radio crackled: "Foothill Units: 16Adam 81 handle, 16Lincoln 11 and 16Lincoln 22 assist. 211 now. Stratton and Lemont. Code three."

A figure in the dark patrol car reached for the mic and responded, "16Adam 81. Ten-Four in two to three from Stratton and I-5."

Lights flashing and siren howling, the LAPD black-and-white skidded around a corner, tricked by streets greased by the season's first rain. The car regained its footing and raced to a ramshackle industrial area just north of the Burbank airport.

To prevent tipping off possible suspects, the driver hit the kill switch turning off the lights and siren well before reaching the crime scene. The rain's sheen obscured the white lines and curbs as the car crept past a shuttered liquor store and an all-night laundry. Its spotlight probed for a victim.

"There, under the awning," The car jerked to a halt and both men jumped out. They glanced left and right for suspects, but saw only trees and parked cars blurred by the drizzle. Both men bent over the bulky form that sprawled against the peeling paint of a concrete block wall.

"God, blood everywhere," exclaimed the older man. "He's breathing. Big gash on his head. Arm looks funny. Bet it's broken." He snapped on latex gloves and took a compress from the first-aid kit and applied pressure to the man's forehead. The bleeding controlled, he leaned to check the derelict's waistband and pockets. His nose rebelled against the reek of booze and dried vomit that clung to the man's clean-shaven chin.

The other officer, young and slender, keyed his shoulder microphone. "16Adam 81 advising code 4 re: the 211 at Stratton and Lemont. Suspects are GPA; victim unconscious, bleeding head wound, possible broken arm. Request paramedics." Flashlight in hand, he strode a short way along the sidewalk searching the area. He squinted as the bright beam prodded into the gloom, but there was nothing.

The first officer tugged his belt over his middle-age girth and mentally cataloged the scene. *Date: December sixteenth. Time of day: 0140 hours. Light rain. Apparent mugging. Injuries severe but don't seem life threatening. Torn Izod polo shirt. Signs of a struggle. Debris on the right sleeve. Dockers, pant legs show a crease.*

Gently, he searched the man's clothes, looking for identification. *No wallet. Robbed.* Inside a shirt pocket, along with a peculiar mustard-colored mechanical pencil, he found a folded piece of paper. He opened it and read the headline of a newspaper clipping from the *Burbank Leader*.

Start-up Company Folds

Shrugging, the officer slipped the clipping back into the victim's shirt.

Two more police units hissed around the corner and stopped. An officer rolled down a window and called, "Whatcha got?"

Turning from the victim, the policeman replied, "Guy's

unconscious. Paramedics coming. No gunshot or knife wounds evident. Check the neighborhood."

The two black-and-whites crept down the street, their spotlights lancing into dark alleyways and between forlorn houses.

The younger cop, a few steps away, stepped around a puddle and knelt by the curb. "Hey," he called. "Here's a broken fence post. Wonder what it's doing in the street."

"Come and check the guy's arm. Here on the sleeve—might be chips of wood from the decayed end of that post. Take a photo and tag it as evidence."

A shrill siren wailed in the distance. Moments later, the lights of an ambulance spattered the scene and the screech of its siren echoed off the walls.

Both officers flagged the ambulance with their flashlights. Two figures, clad in yellow turnouts, stepped into the rain, pulled on gloves and knelt alongside the fallen man.

"Breathing's okay," said one. "Watch that right arm—broken for sure."

The second paramedic trotted to the ambulance. "I'll get the B.P. cuff and a splint. We'll stabilize his arm before moving him."

The men worked silently, applying the cuff to the left arm. "Ninety-five over sixty. Good enough for transport."

Together, they applied the splint with slow, delicate motions. "Let's check for other injuries." They eased the man away from the wall and swept their hands over his back and legs. "Nothing obvious. Get the gurney, 'C' collar and backboard." With well-practiced moves, the EMT's fitted the collar and slid the backboard under the heavy form.

The two police officers, their uniforms glistening from

the somber drizzle, steadied the gurney as the paramedics grunted, lifting the victim.

A paramedic flung open the ambulance doors and strained as he shoved the man into the interior's bright lights. Swirling mist sparkled as it floated past and the chrome gurney threw stark reflections onto the ambulance doors.

"We'll follow you guys to ER," the older cop said. "We'll warm up in the staff lounge and take a few notes for the crime report. I want to question the guy if he comes around."

Both paramedics nodded in unison. One climbed alongside the unconscious man and started an IV while the other slammed the rear door and leapt into the cab. The ambulance disappeared into the gloom, an apparition of blood-red lights and a haunting yowl.

The two policemen clambered into the dry refuge of their vehicle where the senior man wiped his hand across his mouth. "I've seen hundreds of bums in the ghetto, but this one is odd. Notice his clothes? Muddy, but not ground-in filth of our career alkies. His shoes fit, like he bought them—didn't steal 'em. Pants were creased. No sores, no lice, different from our regular clientele. Seems like a young clean-cut guy."

"I don't give a shit," the other grumbled. "Maybe his old lady ran out on him. Maybe he lost a fortune when the stock market tanked. Who knows? Why's the asshole in the ghetto at one in the morning anyway? In my mind, he deserves what he got."

"That's kind of harsh," admonished the older man, shaking his head. He took off his hat and brushed off the water droplets. "Let's get our butts over to ER. At least we can grab a cup of mud and dry off."

Chapter 1

"**N**ow what?" Wyatt Morgan sputtered as his office phone rang. His fingers danced on the computer keyboard as he grappled with a stress analysis problem, but the telephone was insistent. Aggravated, he snatched the handset from its cradle and grumbled, "Wyatt here. Yeah, Brian...so what's the problem? There's a new DCMA inspector? But I'm busy... Well—okay."

Irritated, he hoisted his tall husky body from the chair and bolted down the stairs from the engineering office two steps at a time. A scowl painted his clean-shaven face, spoiling his usual boyish visage. Wyatt shouldered his way through the double-swinging doors into the machine shop and strode along the yellow striped aisle that sliced between the screeching machines. The air was hazy with cutting oil flung from the lathes, mills and grinders. He drew a breath and smiled. Wyatt loved the smell of cutting oil.

The sudden squeal of a lathe yanked Wyatt from his reverie. He pushed through another set of doors into the comparative quiet of the assembly area. He approached his boss, Brian Simmons, who stood beside a hulk of a man—short, but with a neck resembling a fire hydrant. The stranger's muscled body looked stuffed into worsted wool slacks and his blue blazer bulged like a kielbasa, dwarfing Wyatt's own broad shoulders.

"This is Karl Leechmann from DCMA," Brian said. "He's taking over the quality surveys for the government. It seems he's uncovered a problem."

The new inspector fingered a heavy gold chain that dangled across his hairy chest and said, "This damaged part isn't red-tagged." He handed Wyatt a clevis from a Cessna shimmy damper. "These threads are buggered up. The inspection department didn't catch it and there's no paperwork. The company should'a been all over this like stink on shit."

Wyatt nodded. "I'll check the paperwork once the assembly people pull it together."

Leechmann took a deep breath, his sports coat stretching across his chest. "Discrepant materials *always* gotta have a non-conforming material report and corrective action plan. Can you explain how a bad part got into the assembly area?"

Wyatt bristled. "Maybe it was good when the stockroom issued the kit. Perhaps the assembly technician dinged the thread. Who knows?"

"Could be," Brian nodded.

"Unacceptable," Leechmann pronounced. "You guys can't have junk adrift in the factory. DCMA is crystal clear about the procedures. You'd better shape up."

"Look," Wyatt said, his hazel eyes glittering in anger, "This clevis isn't 'adrift.' It's obvious the part wouldn't assemble properly––that's when we'd reject it."

"Once again––unacceptable. What do I have to do? Pull out the regulations and point out the page number?"

Wyatt clenched his fist and stared down at the man. "We know the regs, but it's impossible to fill out the forms the instant there's a problem. We'll catch up with paperwork as soon as there's time."

"Time to lay the cards on the table. You can't identify

who screwed up the part or when. The assembler could have forced it together without proper disposition through the Material Review Board. This so serious that I can shutter your operation unless you square things away. Am I clear?"

"Easy, easy," interjected Brian. "No need for that. Wyatt will drop everything and dig into it. We'll write up the NCMR within the hour." Turning to Wyatt, he said, "Get this part over to bonded stores. Collar Sid in Inspection and check the remaining parts in the stockroom. Make sure they're okay."

Wyatt spun and marched off. *Why do I have to wave the flag for this world-class idiot? DCMA inspectors go through life finding fault with other people's work—what kinda life is that? The jerks can't keep a real job, so they take refuge at the tit of mother government.*

Wyatt found Sid, gathered up the thread gages and verified the parts in stock were good. He figured the clevis was dinged moving from stock or in Assembly, so he filled out a corrective action form requiring future threads be covered with a plastic sleeve.

Later, still fuming about the muscle-bound government troublemaker, Wyatt sat at his desk and picked up a stack of calculations. As he wrestled with a stubborn analysis, the intriguing challenge displaced thoughts of Leechmann, and he grinned.

He was immersed in thought when Brian strolled over to his desk and said, "Finally got rid of him."

Another dang interruption, Wyatt sputtered to himself.

"You gotta watch your mouth, Wyatt. Leechmann was

serious when he said he could close our doors. Humor the man; kiss his butt if you have to."

"I suppose, but I just can't deal with the mindless sloths of the regulation world. In my book, they're a total waste."

"They've got us by the throat," Brian growled. "So you'd better get that temper of yours under control. This guy's gonna be all over us until he's satisfied we're playing by the rules. We've got to stop the screw-ups."

Wyatt nodded. "Yeah. Sure."

Brian turned and started toward the stairs, paused and returned to Wyatt's desk. "Say, how's the new filter design going?"

Wyatt clenched his jaw. "Fine," he snapped. He looked into the florid face of his employer. Brian was middle-aged with a belly that rolled above his belt like dough rising over the edge of a bread pan. He wore rumpled pants and a wrinkled shirt, only half tucked in. As always, his flyaway hair needed trimming.

Proud of his work, Wyatt set aside his irritation. "The new filter holds much more dirt than the old ones and I've come up with a smaller filter bowl to save weight. Working on stresses, though."

Brian looked through his glasses at the stack of papers scattered over Wyatt's desk and then at the computer screen displaying a complex graph and shook his head. "Don't go off on tangents, Wyatt. This isn't rocket science. We've been making filters for years and they work fine. I think you're taking too much time with these simple jobs." As Brian spoke, spittle collected in the corners of his mouth.

"There's plenty of time," Wyatt contradicted. "There are too many interruptions. For instance, it took two hours to schmooze that iron-pounding gorilla from DCMA. Hank should have tagged the part or maybe Sid missed it. Bottom line: I had to fix their screw-ups."

"Simmer down, Wyatt. They've been with us for years and know their stuff. All these new regulations and complicated drawing standards are confusing. Hell, I don't understand them myself. Try backing off from this hi-tech crap, okay?"

"You're the boss," replied Wyatt, "but technology isn't the problem, it's the paper mill. Remember two months ago when the FAA surveyed us? Said our configuration management procedures and logbooks didn't conform to international standards. The only thing they said that made sense was our metal fatigue database was obsolete. You gotta let me buy the current one."

Brian shook his finger like a second grade teacher reprimanding a rambunctious child. "SAC's been in business over thirty years and got along just fine without a damn expensive database. You've been with us only three years, right? So your perspective might be a wee bit premature." With a scowl, he stalked from the room.

Wyatt sighed. He'd suffered Brian's scolding before, and nothing ever came of it. Wyatt knew both the FAA and DCMA avoided any risk fostered by innovation, no matter how small. Every airplane crash or near miss brought volumes of new regulations administered by plodding, cautious administrators. Precedent, not progress, drove their policies.

Wyatt took a mustard-colored mechanical pencil from his shirt pocket, jotted a note and turned to his computer. The analysis he'd been working on was complex and it took a moment to gather his thoughts. It wasn't long before a smile returned to his face as he grappled with a new thought. "Yesssss," he whispered.

With fresh enthusiasm, he breezed through the hoop stresses but struggled with the concentration factors. At last, the design came together as he'd hoped. As the final analysis streamed from the printer, Wyatt pushed back from his desk, stretched, and glanced at his watch. *Wow! It's one-thirty. Where did the time go?*

Ravenous, he went downstairs to the lunchroom where he saw his friend Bernie sitting in the corner. Wyatt retrieved his sack lunch from the wheezing refrigerator and poured a cup of coffee from the ever-present pot. He went to Bernie's table and pulled out a chair. "You mind?"

"Nope. Sit. How are things?" Bernie, the machine shop supervisor, was in his sixties and moved with quick, nervous gestures. Bald and slender, he resembled a stick figure school children drew. His chronic wide smile and mirthful gray eyes always put Wyatt at ease.

"Made real headway this morning on the new filter," Wyatt bragged. "I also had a new idea to measure contamination levels. I'll whip up a few sketches and see if Brian will okay some development work."

Wyatt extracted a sandwich from his paper sack, peeled the bread slices apart and studied the contents. "I sure get tired of the daily grind of copy-cat engineering. There are dozens of fresh ideas I'd love to gnaw on, but Brian always nixes every new thought I come up with."

"Well, you're not alone," said Bernie. "I've been trying to get his okay to buy a new computerized machine center." Bernie rapped the table with a fork to emphasize his point.

"If we don't upgrade our equipment, good old Simmons Aircraft Components will go out of business and my livelihood will get flushed along with it."

"Good point. Brian knows my computer software is out of date, but he isn't looking at the future. I realize the economy is terrible, but in our business, you have to stay current."

Bernie nodded. "There's no way we can change him. I just keep putting one foot ahead of the other and focus on hitting the month's shipment goals. I'd hoped to retire in a couple of years, but the stock market is in the tub and my 401k has taken a big hit. With no pension at SAC, money will be tight. Guess I'll just have to hang tough and humor Brian."

"I'm frustrated too," said Wyatt, swallowing a bite of sandwich. "If I could develop that contamination monitor instead of cranking the same old garbage, I could make a mark on our industry. Sometimes I feel I'm a racehorse pullin' a plow." Wyatt stared at his half-eaten sandwich and sighed.

Bernie squinted and set his chin on his bony fist. "I know what you're saying. I had ambition once, but over the years, I lost my passion; it just evaporated. It was easy to let go; it's hard work to hang on to a dream."

The two sat in silence for a few minutes. Wyatt eased his bulk back into his chair and thought back to his Navy days, the master's degree in engineering from UCLA, his marriage and the birth of his daughter. "Where does the time go? I'm thirty-two with a career locked up by a stubborn boss and a miserable economy. Sounds as if both our dreams are dead in the water. I need to do something about it."

Bernie rubbed his nose. "I'm the same age as our boss and I try understand how he feels. Brian has a successful, but stagnant company. But now, the world is changing too fast for him. Modern airplanes are all electronics, exotic analyses and paperwork. He doesn't understand these things so he's holding onto what's worked in the past." Bernie snapped his lunch box shut. "Did you know that that you intimidate the hell out of Brian?"

"Intimidate him? No way."

"You do," insisted Bernie. "All your schooling and energy scare him. Brian can't figure how to manage your skills. You threaten him."

"Bull," grunted Wyatt. "I just don't believe that."

Bernie shrugged and let the subject drop.

Wyatt fiddled with the saltshaker. *No matter what Bernie says, I'm trapped between Brian and the insane government maze.* His gaze wandered around the room and then settled back on his friend's face. *We share a passion for engineering and manufacturing, but we're stymied.*

An old song, "If I Had a Hammer" by Peter, Paul and Mary crept into his mind and the saltshaker danced on the tabletop. Wyatt grinned, thinking of a Navy buddy who played 50's and 60's music aboard the destroyer four years non-stop.

"Time to launch," Wyatt said as he rose from the chair. "I have a big meeting with King Aviation tomorrow. Brian's on a short fuse and I'd better man up to this." As he tossed his lunch bag into the trash, a small piece of blue paper fluttered to the floor. He bent, snatched it up and threw it in the bin. He refilled his perennial coffee cup and headed toward his office.

Chapter 2

Early the next morning, Wyatt wore a confident grin as he carried a thick manila folder and a laptop computer into the SAC conference room. He was looking forward to seeing Madison McKenzie again and showing off his new design. She was the lead electrical engineer at King Aviation and it had been ten months since they worked together on the actuator job. An extraordinary talent, she'd been demanding and Wyatt had felt challenged to keep up with her. Today, he was ready. *This will be a great meeting.*

Brian Simmons and the King engineer were already in the room. Madison wore close-fitting jeans, high heels, a smart silk blouse and matching scarf. She exuded a trim, classy look as she sat, ankles crossed and a pencil in her hand. Her flashing green eyes, framed by cascades of long auburn hair, completed an image of a fashion model rather than a stereotypical engineer.

Wyatt nodded to his boss, then reached across the table and shook hands with her. "Hi Madison, how are you doing?"

"Way better than spectacular," she replied, her smile bright and friendly.

Wyatt chuckled and booted up his laptop. "Spectacular? In a meeting about a filter?"

"No. Better than spectacular," corrected Madison. She nudged a strand of hair away from her eye and said, "Dave, our filter specialist couldn't make it, so I'm standing in.

We've set tough design goals on this filter and I'm curious to see what you've come up with."

Wyatt touched his brow with two fingers in a mock salute.

"Let's get this rolling," Brian said, "Why don't you start, Madison?"

"Sure." She uncrossed her legs and tapped her pencil on the conference table. She opened her laptop and punched a few keys. "Okay, Wyatt, our Request for Quotation lists the requirements for a new hydraulic filter for executive jets. In particular, we're looking to maximize filter life." Madison beat a tattoo on the table with her pencil and looked at Wyatt. "If I know you, I'm betting your design is impressive, right?" Madison grinned and fluttered her lashes, looking coquettish. "Hmmm?"

Wyatt smiled and keyed his laptop. "We developed a new filter cartridge that's dynamite." With a flourish, he brought up a graph on his computer and spun it around to show Madison. "Here. The dirt capacity is twice that of conventional filters––should cut way down on maintenance." Wyatt leaned back in his chair and rubbed his chin, feeling smug. After working long hours on this project, he was jubilant his design exceeded King's specification by a wide margin.

Madison studied the graph, scribbled a note on a pad and compared Wyatt's data with her paperwork. She nodded.

"One hell of a design, don't you think, Madison?" interjected Brian. "I hardly believed the test results myself."

"Looks good," Madison acknowledged, turning to

Wyatt. "You used glass beads as a contaminant in the tests. Any data for actual hydraulic oil?"

Wyatt pointed at the computer and said, "Hit the 'sheet two' tab on the spreadsheet and you'll see curves on oil; it's even better. Still, these are laboratory tests. Is there any way to install our filter on a plane and gather actual airborne data?"

"I might be able to arrange that with our customer, Maddox Aviation. They fly two experimental airplanes all the time." Madison said.

Brian stood, went to the credenza at the end of the room and picked out a glazed donut from a platter. "We could have a test filter ready to go in a day or two, right Wyatt?" He took a bite and specks of sugar fell on the front of his bulging shirt.

Wyatt scowled. "Possible, but I want to try one or two design changes before cutting chips."

"Forget it. I want to wrap this up," insisted Brian. He turned to Madison. "Let's push for flight tests. There's no reason to wait." As he settled back into his chair, a fine spray of spittle settled on his donut.

"There's a potential problem," said Madison. "Aircraft maintenance technicians change filters at the regular annual inspections, so they'd replace it, fully contaminated or not."

Wyatt interlaced his fingers. "I came up with a crazy idea for an electrical sensor that tells when the element actually needs replacement. What do you think, Madison? Something King might consider?"

"No way," protested Brian. "We're not going off on tangents. We've never done anything like that."

"That might be a thought, Brian," cautioned Madison. "The whole industry is on a maintainability kick and will pay big money for equipment that saves work on the flight ramp." She drummed her pencil on the table, knitting her brow. "Is it costly, Wyatt?"

"The mechanical parts would be inexpensive. You'd need a transducer and some electronics. That's your field, Madison, not mine, but I'd guess the components are pretty cheap."

"Perhaps, but we'd have to modify the aircraft wiring to power the device and record data."

Brian waved his hand and said, "Whoa, whoa. This is nuts." His cheeks were red and his jowls jiggled.

Wyatt, ignoring Brian's fluster, rubbed his short cropped hair and said, "Why not an internal battery? Suppose we transmit the data wirelessly like Bluetooth?"

"Sounds plausible," Madison said. "If it's wireless, the FAA will balk, but with your new high-capacity filter, there'd be real incentive to try." She paused, halting the pencil tapping. "You and I would need to coordinate closely on this."

"Okay, Okay," sputtered Brian, glaring through his glasses. "Enough of this. Can we get back to business? The question is, does the SAC design meet King's specification? We're ready to assemble test hardware, Madison; we just need your go-ahead."

"I'll have to check with Maddox," replied Madison. "You know, I think we should give serious consideration to the electronic contamination indicator. It sounds like a slick feature."

Brian scowled. "SAC isn't in the electronics business.

You're taking a real simple problem and making a big deal out of it. This is a great filter, let's not screw with it."

Frustrated, Wyatt squirmed and considered arguing with Brian, but yesterday's encounter over the DCMA inspector had been brutal. *You need to control your temper— no more screw-ups* Brian had threatened. Still, the indicator was an elegant concept, a design challenge that he'd hate to abandon.

Madison resumed rapping on the table with her pencil. "The problem is the extended service interval. A contamination sensor could be the answer. It might turn out to be a windfall for SAC."

"Making shoes could be a windfall," retorted Brian. "SAC's not in the shoe business nor are we electronic designers. We sell straightforward hardware at low cost. That's our niche."

"That's a good point," Madison conceded. "But modern aircraft designers are jumping into the computer and electronics world, same as cars with their electric throttles and GPS. To stay competitive, King has to pursue new ideas. We rely on suppliers like you to help push the state of the art."

Mute, Wyatt slumped in his chair, fearing he'd further antagonize his boss. He sided with Madison, but knew he couldn't change Brian's view. His stomach churned with resignation.

Brian fidgeted with a napkin, dislodging the last of the donut debris from his lips. "Do what you have to do, Madison. Just remember we've been supplying filters to King for years and they've done a good job."

Madison stacked her papers and said, "I'll keep that

in mind. Seems like there's nothing else to discuss. The filter design looks great; we'll just have to sort out the service issue and look into the electronic indicator." With a snap, she closed her laptop and slid Wyatt's computer back to him.

They stood and walked toward the door. Wyatt extended his hand to Madison, who took it warmly. "Good ideas, Wyatt. Someday you'll make a fair engineer," she quipped, tossing her head so that her hair fell away from her eyes. After a pause, she released Wyatt's hand and left with a nod and a jaunty bounce in her step.

Brian spun to face Wyatt, his face splotched red. "Damn, you sure blew that, Wyatt! Now we've got a mess. You keep going off on these crazy tangents. Why won't you just settle down and do your job?" He took off his glasses and scrubbed them on his tie.

The cords of Wyatt's neck bulged as he stifled a surge of anger. Exasperated, he took a deep breath.

Brian shook his finger at Wyatt. "Okay, here's what you do. Call Madison, daily if you have to. Convince her that the electronic gizmo is stupid. Tell her we don't have the capability to engineer it. Tell her you were wrong to bring it up."

"Suppose we bring in a consultant to help us?" ventured Wyatt.

"What?"

"You know, hire an engineering consultant to work out the circuitry. Maybe Madison would do a little engineering for us at night."

"Enough! No more! You phone Madison tomorrow— don't put it off. While you're at it, buckle down and clean up the DCMA mess. Leechmann has us by the balls and you're dinking around with nutty ideas." Brian stormed off, leaving Wyatt standing alone shaking his head.

Acid rose in Wyatt's throat and he swallowed, grimacing at the bitter taste. Slowly he walked toward the stairs to his office. *Even our customer thinks the sensor is a good idea; why won't Brian at least consider it?* Disgusted, he detoured to the lunchroom where he bought a soda from the machine, sat and stared at the clock on the wall.

If Brian had been Gustave Eiffel's boss and Leechmann the inspector, there never would have been that tower to put Paris on the map. Wyatt drained the can, crushed it and flung it into the trash.

Chapter 3

Sweat dampened Wyatt's forehead as the late August heat asserted its authority. As he walked to Brian's office, he fought an unsettling mixture of excitement and apprehension. He took a deep breath to settle his nerves and went in.

Four months earlier, he'd conceived a new approach for cabin pressurization on executive jets and wanted to discuss the idea with his boss. All high-flying jets required heating and pressurization to overcome the minus forty-degree temperature and semi-vacuum encountered at cruising altitude. Wyatt's new design would make passengers and crew more comfortable, minimizing ear discomfort. Although Wyatt's career involved day-to-day innovation, this was a real breakthrough. The more he mulled it over, the more his enthusiasm evolved into an obsession.

"Come and sit. You wanted to talk?" asked Brian. "Boy this heat is bad; we gotta fix the air-conditioning someday."

"Yeah, thanks," said Wyatt, taking a chair. "I've been playing around with an idea for a new cabin pressure control system. For months now, I've spent almost every night at home working on it."

"I'll bet that's popular with the wife," Brian joked.

"Oh, no problem. Lauren knew what she was getting into when she married an engineer." Wyatt paused, wondering if that were true. He recalled her frowns when he passed up their nightly glass of wine and retreated to the backroom office and computer. *Well, she knows how important my work is to me. At least I hope so.*

Wyatt resumed. "Current pressurization systems involve dozens of independent valves and controls. My idea is to integrate the components and eliminate wiring between them."

"So?"

"Well, it'd revolutionize pressurization, but I'd need a lot of time to work out the details and get it certified. I was hoping you'd block out a chunk of development time. SAC could support a complex job, including a good machine shop."

Brian folded his arms across his chest. "Machine shop we got, but except for you, Engineering has the sophistication of a teenager in heat. This sounds like another of your tangents, Wyatt."

"I guess it is," Wyatt admitted. "But it's a dynamite way to pressurize an airplane. So far, my work is strictly broad-brush. I figured we might bring in an outside consultant to check out my ideas. I'll bet King Aviation and AirEnvironment might help. Both companies sell sub-contracted pressurization systems, so they'd have valuable insight."

"Come on, Wyatt. We make filters, small actuators and other simple stuff. I'm smart enough to realize pressurization is complicated as hell, right?"

"Yeah, it is. My design has a lot of electronics and computer software. I'm a mechanical guy, so I'd need help with that stuff. It would be a stretch for SAC, but there's tremendous potential."

"No way, Wyatt. How many times do I have to remind

you we're not in the electronics business? Besides, the FAA keeps expanding their requirements––exhaustive analyses, tests and documentation––crap which makes qualifying new equipment almost impossible. It's too risky. Let's not forget our new DCMA guy either. It's clear he doesn't think much of you. Bottom line––I'm not going there."

Nervous, Wyatt gulped. He figured he was losing the battle, but refused to give up. He leaned forward and squared his shoulders. "You're right. The FAA has insane barriers to innovation, but I can work around that. If we focus on general aviation and avoid military contracts, we wouldn't have to futz with DCMA. Mechanically, This is a blockbuster concept. The electronics should be straight forward and a clever programmer could easily blend the valve functions together."

"No."

"I'm just asking for a bit of help to verify the fundamentals, just to see if I'm on solid ground," persisted Wyatt.

"No. I'm not committing resources in this lousy economy and invite more trouble from our government friends."

"Dang it, Brian, this is a-once-in-a-lifetime opportunity," Wyatt asserted, his face getting red. "Can't you see? Let's get out of the box. Let's create a legacy. It's there for the taking."

"I said *no*. We're wasting time, so let's get back to work." Spittle collected at the corners of Brian's mouth as he drew his lips into a thin line. He swiveled his chair to the reference table and began typing on his computer.

With sagging shoulders, Wyatt stared at Brian's back

and jammed his hands into his pockets. *I don't understand him. The man's mad.* Wyatt turned and walked from the office, disheartened.

Back at his desk, Wyatt slouched in his chair and tried to focus on work, but his thoughts wandered back to when he was six years old, watching older boys launch toy rockets in the park. He'd been enthralled as the missile rode a hissing plume into the sky. In seconds, it became a speck, lost in the puffy summer clouds. At its apogee, an International Orange parachute blossomed and caught the breeze, carrying the spent rocket downwind. The boys shrieked as they ran after it and the biggest kid managed to snag it before it struck the ground. Breathless, he held the rocket aloft and brandished it like a trophy.

Wyatt wished he were bigger so he could join them. He'd walked away, scuffing his tennis shoes in the dust, sensing a mystery in the rocket, perplexing and bewildering. Goose bumps had sprouted on his arms even though the breeze was warm. Sequestered in the crannies of his youthful mind, he suspected he'd seen something significant. Something important.

Wyatt spoke to his father about the rocket that night, wanting to know why it flew on nothing but smoke. He asked how the parachute came out and wondered if there were rockets that could go higher. His father, a plumber, didn't have the answers, but hugged his son and promised to get their own rocket at the hobby store.

The next weekend at the park, Wyatt and his dad set up the launch platform, connected two lantern batteries and inserted a propellant cartridge into the rocket. At his father's urging, Wyatt removed the safety key, jabbed the red button and yelled with joy as the missile whooshed aloft.

That was the day he decided to be an engineer.

Wyatt shook himself from his reverie and despondently pecked out an email. He couldn't concentrate and made silly typos. At last he hit "send" and sighed. *I can't go on letting Brian smother my ideas. I'll quit—find a job where I can do good engineering.* Wyatt turned in his chair and looked out at his small group: draftsmen coaxing drawings from their computers and engineers debating designs. With a shake of his head, he thought, *Land a new job when everyone is laying-off? As I told Bernie, I'm stuck.*

He swiveled back to his computer screen and noticed a sticky note saying, "Madison." He'd forgotten to call about the filter sensor, so he picked up the phone and dialed.

"King Engineering. Madison speaking."

"Hi, Madison. This is Wyatt. Have a minute?"

"Sure. What's on your mind?"

"Remember the contamination sensor we discussed? Brian wants me to talk you out of it. Trouble is, I'm convinced he's wrong. I'm not sure why I..." Wyatt's voice trailed off,

"What's going on?" Madison asked. "You sound in the dumps. Talk to me."

Wyatt shuddered, squeezed his eyes shut and tried to compose himself. "No, I'm fine. Well maybe just okay. Just had a major run-in with Brian. I have an idea for a new product, but he wouldn't hear of it. I'm rowing against the current, you know?"

"Everyone has bad days, Wyatt. Was it about the filter sensor?"

"No. I've been working on a new design for a cabin pressurization system and tried to explain it to Brian, but he literally turned his back to me. It's a phenomenal concept—the proverbial earth-shaker. Brian can't see that."

"He's always accusing you of going off on tangents; isn't this another one? What prompted you to work on pressurization? You nuts?"

Wyatt winced. "I don't know. The idea just jumped into my head. I was flying back from Phoenix on a business trip and when my ears began popping on descent, I started wondering how there might be a better design. Bang! There it was. Happens to me all the time."

"I do that too," Madison chuckled. "I call it lightning in the cranium. Is your brainstorm a really good one?"

"It's a lot better than good," Wyatt said, mimicking Madison's turn of phrase.

"Take a few milliseconds and explain it to me," she teased.

"Okay," Wyatt laughed. "Pressurization systems take hot, compressed air from the engines, use it to heat the cabin and then exhausts the air while precisely regulating pressure. My concept computerizes the main valves and ties them into the aircraft's primary flight computer. Similar to the filter sensor, the various components would 'talk' to each other wirelessly."

"Hold on, Wyatt. Let me think this over. You're saying that 'smart' valves will get on 'the cloud' and chat, right?"

"You got it."

"What about weight and cost?" Madison asked. "New designs go nowhere without big reductions on both counts."

"I've driven down the weight by eliminating a bunch of components. With far fewer parts, the costs will fall enough to bring a Scotsman to orgasm." Breathless, he said, "Of course, I'm not up to speed with the electronics and software, but I'm positive the mechanics are solid." He paused and silence hung in the air. "Madison? You there?"

"Yeah—just thinking. It sounds like you're on to something."

Once again, Madison fell silent, but Wyatt could hear her habitual tap-tap-tap of a pencil.

"I know it's a half-baked idea," Wyatt ventured. "But what if…"

For thirty minutes, Madison's pointed questions parried Wyatt's zeal as they debated design problems, laughing as they went.

"I guess you'll need serious electronics and software expertise to get this off the ground," Madison said, sounding playful. "Have any plans to investigate those areas, hmmm? I don't suppose you need a top-drawer electronics consultant, hmmm? Software too, hmmm?"

Wyatt blinked, unsure if Madison was toying with him or considering lending a hand. He bit his lip, trying not to stutter. "Are you offering to help?"

"Why not? King paroles me at five every night."

"Great! Let's get together on this."

"Sooner the better."

Wyatt gulped and poked at his smart phone, bringing up a calendar. "How's your schedule looking this Saturday night? Dinner at my house? We could dig into this a little more."

"Love to. What time?"

"Say seven?"

"Perfect."

Wyatt was laughing. "Okay. I'll clear this with my wife, Lauren, and email directions. You'll meet Timmie, my daughter too. I can't wait."

"See you then," Madison said as she hung up.

Wyatt leaned back in his chair and put his hands behind his head. A sense of contentment settled over him and he kicked his feet up on the desk. Madison sounded enthused and wanted to talk more. He marveled how easily the two of them tackled crazy engineering ideas while he fought bitterly with Brian.

Wyatt rose and went downstairs to the coffee pot, a habit ingrained by his Navy days. His thoughts turned again to Brian and searched for ways to deal with him.

But, as always, Wyatt struggled with social issues. He felt much safer nesting in the absolutes of science and avoiding the vagrancies of people. As a youngster, he'd always been much bigger than his classmates, but in contrast, was very shy. As kids do, they teased Wyatt incessantly calling him a baby, a lummox or dweeb. Consequently, like a tortoise pulling its head into its shell, Wyatt sought sanctuary in the sciences. Even years later, he had no qualms about keeping others at arm's length and dwelling in an analytical world. The only exception was Lauren, his wife.

As Wyatt walked to his desk, he felt a twinge of sympathy for his boss, yet realized he faced a block wall at SAC. The thought rankled him but then he smiled and visualized Madison working beside him.

"Saturday," he chuckled.

Chapter 4

Late that night, Wyatt rubbed the back of his neck as he climbed into the car. The day had been a long, frustrating one and the memory of Brian's tirade churned his stomach. As he threaded through Burbank traffic squinting at oncoming headlights, he punched the radio preset for the station that played his favorite music: old pop songs. He hummed along with Simon and Garfunkel's "Bridge Over Troubled Water" and reminded himself that all was not lost.

He was thrilled Madison wanted to explore his idea. Twice now, she had gone into battle on his side: first, the electronic contamination sensor and now the pressurization. Wyatt drummed on the steering wheel in time with the music. *I wish Madison ran SAC instead of Brian. Together we could rock the airplane biz and wage war on DCMA.*

Fifteen minutes later he pulled into his driveway, parked and started up the short walk where the porch light cast stark shadows. Wyatt bent and plucked a small bouquet of snapdragons that lined the walkway, one of many pleasant touches Lauren did around the house. It was a nice place, he thought, a modest stucco tract house, but inviting, like the warm ski jacket he wore on cold mornings. Lauren seemed happy in the nest she'd created, a thought that pleased him.

"Hi, Darling," Wyatt called as he dropped his brief case next to the bookcase in the entry.

"Hi, Honey," Lauren responded from the kitchen. She wiped her hands on a dishtowel and welcomed her husband with a hug and kiss.

With a gallant bow, Wyatt presented the flowers. "Specially grown just for you by Jack, that beanstalk guy."

"You have no sense of reality, but you're a love anyway." Lauren was only three years younger than her husband, but looked much more youthful, almost child-like. While nearly as tall as Wyatt, her slender figure made her look tiny when she stood alongside his heft. Lauren kept her blond hair very short, but had a curious habit of brushing it back from her face, a carryover from her teen years when she had long hair. Bright blue eyes and fair skin, sprinkled with tiny freckles, enhanced her fresh pixy appearance. A perennial smile bathed Lauren's face making people think she was going to break into laughter.

As usual, Lauren was home from work long before Wyatt and had changed into shorts and a sleeveless white blouse. As she often did at home, Lauren was barefoot.

She patted Wyatt's shoulder and said, "You look pleased with yourself. Did things go well at the zoo?"

"Well, yes and no. I'll explain over wine. Is it too late for a glass? I know it's past seven."

"Really? It's not eat and run to the backroom office?"

A sheepish grin spread across Wyatt's face. "I've interesting news. Thought we'd talk if it's no trouble."

"No, no, it's okay. We're having sautéed scallops and pasta for dinner. Everything is prepped, so dinner will be quick."

A shout came from the bedroom and their daughter, Timmie, raced out and flung her arms around Wyatt's legs. "Daddy, Daddy!" she shouted. Resembling many five-year-olds, Timmie was on the plump side. Her disheveled shoulder length hair was captured in a haphazard ponytail and an abundance of her mother's freckles speckled her nose and cheeks.

"Not so loud, Timmie," Wyatt admonished, giving her a hug. "How's my little girl?"

"Danny hit me," she scowled.

"Danny at after-school care?"

"Yes. He's mean. I hate him!" Her face screwed into a gargoyle pout and tears welled in the corners of her eyes. "Hate him, hate him, hate him," she chanted, clenching her chubby fists at her side and stomping her foot.

Wyatt rolled his eyes and glanced at Lauren.

"Honey," intervened Lauren, "come here." She gathered the child in her arms and almost instantaneously, Timmie recovered and demanded, "I'm hungry. When's dinner?"

"First, Daddy and I want a glass of wine, okay? Why don't you go to your room and play? We won't be long."

"You always talk or Daddy works. Every night. It's not fair."

"It's just one glass, Honey. We haven't had time to visit lately."

Timmie crossed her arms as if trying to force new tears, but gave up and went to her room.

Wyatt sat in his new leather recliner, one of a matching pair he'd purchased for Lauren and himself. The pleasant clatter of goblets came from the kitchen as Lauren prepared a small tray of smoked Gouda cheese and soda crackers alongside a bottle of inexpensive Zinfandel. This was a tradition they called the Sunset Ritual, where they tried to set aside an hour every evening just to be together and catch up on the day's events. However, Wyatt's long, erratic hours at SAC cannibalized his time and now pressurization intruded further into his hour with Lauren.

"Here you are," said Lauren, setting the tray on a small table between their chairs and lighting a scented candle. "It's nice to have a moment with you for a change. Tell me. What's the news?"

"Want the grim part first?" Wyatt picked up his glass and held it aloft in a silent toast. "I told Brian my ideas on cabin pressurization. No surprise, he shot me down. Said new government regulations and terrible economy made it too risky. I hoped to convince him I'd come up with an incredible opportunity, but he kept accusing me of those 'tangents' he finds so aggravating."

"You've been known to go off on peculiar ideas, Hon," grinned Lauren. "We knew Brian wouldn't listen, so that's no news bulletin. That it?"

Wyatt took a sip of wine and nibbled a slice of cheese. "Nope. After my war with Brian, I noticed a sticky I'd left on my computer to call Madison McKenzie. Do you remember me mentioning her? She's that electrical engineer over at King Aviation. I've worked with her from time to time."

"Yes, you've said she's a good at her job."

"That's her. I was supposed to convince her the contamination sensor was a stupid idea, but we got to talking about pressurization––she got really excited."

"Does she think it has promise?"

"She says it has real potential."

"So now what?" Lauren asked.

Wyatt grinned. "I've invited her to come to dinner this Saturday to talk––if it's okay with you."

"Of course!" Lauren said. "You *know* I love to entertain.

Besides, I want to meet this 'Wonder Woman' to see if I should be jealous." Lauren winked at her husband and smiled.

"Jealous? Not a chance. She's just a dynamite engineer, and a customer at that." Wyatt sipped his wine and thought a moment. "I hope something comes of this pressurization thing. It'll be fun to kick around a few thoughts with her." He took the last chunk of cheese. "When will dinner be ready? I'm so hungry I could eat road-kill."

"Let me finish my wine. I'm exhausted. Today at after-school care, the teacher complained that our daughter's attitude was poor, said Timmie throws a tantrum if she doesn't get her way. I guess I was shocked. It's not fun to listen while someone runs down your kid." Lauren drained her wine glass and stared across the room. "I wish she were a happier child. She whines all the time."

"It's probably just a phase," Wyatt said. "She'll outgrow it soon enough."

"I hope so," Lauren sighed. "Mother is right––I should be a stay-at-home mom, but we need the money. Guess I'll slog along until you find a better paying position."

"Well, at least I have a job. Trouble is, the economy is getting worse––the airplane business in particular."

Lauren nodded, went to the kitchen and put on a pot of water to boil. Returning, she said, "I don't want to complain, but lately you seem preoccupied. Tonight, for instance, all you talked about was work and pressurization. I think our Sunset Ritual, when we get to it, has gotten a little lopsided."

Wyatt frowned. "You're right. Guess I get too focused on little airplanes and calculus. I'll try to turn it down, but I've big hopes the pressurization may lead somewhere."

"We'll see." Lauren gathered up the tray and half-empty wine bottle and asked, "More wine?"

"No thanks. You know me; strictly a one-glass guy."

Lauren went to the kitchen and started the pasta and scallops. Wyatt followed her and gently rubbed the back of her neck.

"Humm," she breathed.

"I have a few calculations I want to review," he said and retreated to the bedroom office.

He was fully engrossed when Lauren called, "Wyatt, Timmie, dinnertime!" Reluctant to interrupt his work, he left his computer on, planning to return after dinner.

Wyatt settled in his chair and glanced at Timmie. "Napkin, Little One."

The child flashed her father an irritated look, snatched the napkin from the table and thrust it into her lap.

As Wyatt reached for the saltshaker, Lauren said, "Suppose you and Madison decide the pressurization justifies more work? How will you find time? I never see you now."

"Not true. We're pretty good with our Sunset Rituals."

"Sure—if you call once a month 'pretty good.'"

Wyatt frowned. "Well, no need to worry yet. The idea isn't even in the starting blocks."

"If I know you, you'll live in the backroom until you've slain the dragon. I already feel widowed."

"Dragon? It's not even a sow bug," Wyatt said with a dismissive wave. "Let's cool it until Madison and I get our arms around this thing."

Timmie was silent except for occasional comments about her battle with Danny or how she hated the Power Rangers on TV. "Stupid," she called them.

Lauren rubbed her temples like she did when a headache was coming and said, "We done here? Timmie, let's clean up...no arguing now, come on."

Absently, Wyatt mumbled, "Thanks, Darling. Good dinner. I'll be in my office working on the new pressurization idea. I might be real late, so don't wait up for me."

Chapter 5

Lauren loved to entertain, not lavish parties as her mother did, but intimate gatherings to exchange ideas and talk about books. *I'm amazed how different Mom and I are,* she mused.

As a teenager, Lauren found her home empty and sterile; her parents' life revolved around money and status. Buoyed by youthful idealism, she embraced thoughts of a simple, wholesome existence. When not quarreling with her mother, Lauren retreated to a world of books and became an accomplished student. After high school graduation, Lauren escaped her mother's clutches by touring Europe for a year before starting college.

Things changed when Lauren met Wyatt in the university's student union where she was enrolled in an accounting curriculum with a minor in English literature. It had been a rare rainy day, and the room was swarming with people smelling of wet wool. Lauren managed to find a vacant seat and as she wedged in, she knocked over a cup of coffee––Wyatt's.

He was majoring in engineering and his zeal for technology amazed her. Not the science, but his passion. She'd never met anyone so focused, so driven. Above all, Wyatt possessed the most brilliant mind she'd ever encountered. His fervency complimented her reserved, introspective personality. Long before Wyatt became serious about their relationship, Lauren set her sights on him. Once begun, courtship was swift.

Before they married, Lauren's mother, Liza Bromwich,

scolded her daughter, saying Wyatt couldn't provide the comforts of upper class life. Liza, a staunch elitist, complained that Wyatt "isn't our breed of cattle. You're too young and should take time to discover yourself."

She ignored Liza's stern lectures and married Wyatt anyway.

Her independence suffered when lack of money forced the newlyweds to move into the luxurious agonies of Liza's mansion. Wyatt struggled with the pervasive anger that flavored every glance and every conversation. Even Lauren's father, Earl, fled from his wife by working endless hours at his law firm.

Halfway through Wyatt's graduate studies, the couple discovered Lauren was expecting and Wyatt welcomed the news. A year later, Lauren holding a brand new daughter in her arms, happily watched her husband march to "Pomp and Circumstance."

Right after graduation they paid cash for an older, nineteen-sixties house in a modest neighborhood of Burbank. Lauren silently thanked Wyatt's deceased mother for the generous inheritance that freed them from Liza's bile.

Lauren was excited about meeting Madison and showing off her hostess skills. With a bounce in her step, she scurried from the kitchen to set the dining table.

In a festive mood, she'd abandoned her usual shorts in favor of a sleek polished cotton skirt and an embroidered white blouse giving her a fresh, wholesome look. A well-used apron, imprinted with bright yellow smiley faces, accentuated her slender frame with images of happiness.

Still barefoot, Lauren glanced at her watch and dashed to the kitchen to fill the coffee pot, ready to turn on when Wyatt or Madison wanted a cup. She hoped their guest would enjoy the evening's menu: steamed edamame, grilled salmon and a mixed green salad with her special Asian dressing.

"Wyatt!" she yelled. "Madison's due in fifteen minutes."

"I know," called Wyatt from his bedroom office. After a long pause, he added, "Can I help?"

The tone of his voice told Lauren he wasn't the least bit interested in helping. Irritated, she shouted back, "No, everything is under control." *I hope.* She hurried back to the living room and set out coasters and then paused to inspect the kitchen, the dining nook and the living room. *Everything is ready,* she thought. *I'm done. Oops, shoes!*

Flinging aside her apron, Lauren hurried down the hall, slipped into her black pumps and then stuck her head into Timmie's room. "Did you brush your hair, Honey?"

Timmie turned from her TV and nodded.

"Let me see how you look."

Obediently, the child stood and pirouetted, displaying her freshly pressed blue dress. "I hate dresses," she blurted.

"But you're so pretty." Bending to pull back Timmie's hair, Lauren wrapped a scrunchie around her daughter's ponytail. "You want to look nice for Madison, don't you?" Timmie shrugged and turned back to the television.

>< >< ><

Meanwhile, Wyatt worked, dashing off a rough logic diagram for the pressurization's software and made copy for Madison. As he gathered several documents into a manila folder, the doorbell rang. "I'll get it," he called.

He sprang from his chair, feeling encouraged, even validated, knowing Madison wanted to work with him. He snatched his laptop and several folders.

As he marched down the hall, Timmie bolted from her room and ran close behind him. Lauren joined them as he opened the door.

"Hi, Madison. Come on in," invited Wyatt.

Madison stepped inside and said, "Hi, Wyatt. Your directions were perfect. I brought a bottle of wine—hope you like it."

Wyatt took the gift. "Thanks. We'll have it with dinner. Introductions are in order. Lauren, this is Madison McKenzie; Madison, my wife, Lauren."

>< >< ><

Lauren, with a measured glance, assessed their guest, saying, "Pleased to meet you."

Unlike her stereotypical expectations of a dumpy, dowdy engineer, Lauren was surprised to see that Madison was young, slender, and stylish. She wore a navy knee-length skirt, high heels, a red silk blouse and a floral scarf that complimented her crimson top. Other than a utilitarian digital watch, she wore no jewelry. Lauren found Madison's sparkling green eyes disconcerting and thought that her raven hair, draped over one eye, radiated a distinct coquettish flavor. *She looks as if she just stepped out of the pages of "Vogue" magazine.*

In turn, Madison's brisk glance seemed to appraise Lauren. With an easy smile she shook hands.

"Oh," Wyatt interjected. "We forgot the most important part of the family. Madison, meet our daughter, Timmie."

Timmie clutched her mother's leg and stared at the ground. "Hi."

"I've heard so much about you," said Madison, extending her hand. "Shake?"

Timmie rubbed the toe of a shoe against her ankle. After a moment, she held out her hand and Madison gave it a firm tug. "My, you're certainly as pretty as your daddy told me."

"Say thank you, Little One," Lauren prompted.

Madison drew her eyebrows together. "Timmie is an unusual name for a girl. Is it a nickname?"

"Come sit," said Wyatt. "Lauren will explain while I pour the wine."

Timmie scowled. "Why can't I have wine too? You're *always* drinking wine."

"I'll get you a Coke and you can visit for a while," Wyatt suggested. Rewarded with a grin and a nod, he left to prepare the beverages.

Lauren sat in her recliner and began. "Well, I'm a voracious reader and one of the best books ever written is John Steinbeck's *East of Eden*. Have you read it?"

Madison shook her head. "No. I spend whatever leisure time I have on trade magazines and technical reports."

"Everyone should find time to read it. The novel was so inspiring that I told Wyatt I'd stop cooking for him unless he read it too. His well-nourished physique is testimony that he did. In the book, a very wise Chinese servant explores the translation of the Hebrew word 'timshel' in Genesis. The word evolves into the central theme of the novel, paralleling the story of Cain and Abel. We thought the story was incredibly profound, so we agreed; our daughter's name became Timshel. Timmie for short."

"Goodness, what a tale," said Madison. "That's an incredible name, Timmie, you must be very proud of it."

Timmie slunk closer to Lauren, clutched her mother's arm and said nothing.

Wyatt returned with an apologetic looking smile saying, "She's a little shy."

Timmie scowled, looking unsure, and grasped her Coke, nearly spilling it.

Conversation, at first stilted, became comfortable, and Madison, with an engaging sense of humor, proved easy to befriend. Lauren's role as hostess was going well, and enjoyment displaced her earlier anxiety.

Wyatt, after a few minutes of small talk, tried to steer the conversation to the pressurization system. He didn't seem to notice that Timmie, with a bored expression, rose and walked to her room.

"Hold off on the shop-talk, Wyatt," Madison said. "Let me get to know Lauren. Sit back and listen to some girl-talk—you might learn something."

Wyatt shrugged and crossed his arms.

Madison, Lauren learned, was a graduate of Cal Berkeley majoring in electrical engineering. Like Wyatt, she obtained her master's degree, but in computer science. Only twenty-nine, she already held six patents and had risen to lead engineer at King Aviation.

On the personal side, Lauren was astonished to hear that Madison had married very young. "I had to prove to my mother I could conquer a man," Madison admitted.

"I divorced after a few months. At least I didn't have a kid with that dummy."

This surprised Lauren. "You seem to enjoy children. Why is that?"

"I *do* like children. I was the only girl of four siblings. Years ago, mom suffered a bad back injury from a fall; she's still using a walker. Dad, a salesman, was away most the time. Consequently, I became vice-mother and discovered that I enjoyed being the boss. The boys, even though one was older, got used to it."

When Lauren asked about Madison's hobbies, Madison said, "None. I work sixty-hour weeks leaving little time for anything else." She paused. "I do, however, have a cat named Galileo Galilei––G-G for short. And I love hummingbirds––I've feeders on my balcony."

"We have a cat," interjected Wyatt. "But it's Timmie's. As far as I'm concerned, hummingbirds are cat food," he joked. He started to say more, but lapsed into fidgety silence.

Effusive, Lauren commented on the challenges of raising a child while juggling a fulltime job as an accountant and household duties. She became more and more animated and her face beamed as she described her love of fiction and her monthly Scrabble party.

With smiles and fun patter, they summoned Timmie and sat down for dinner. Although pleased, Lauren blushed when Madison complimented her on the oriental dressing. Even Timmie shed her shyness and joined in. The youngster seemed infected with her mother's effervescence and giggled as she arranged her silverware the way her mother had shown her.

Madison declined seconds, saying, "Delicious, but I couldn't eat another bite."

Wyatt, on the other hand, attacked his third helping of salmon, emptying the platter. "Good stuff, Darling." He scrubbed his mouth and dropped the napkin on the table.

Wyatt and Madison adjourned to the living room while Lauren coerced Timmie into helping clear the table. After putting the dishes in the sink to soak and the meager leftovers in the refrigerator, Lauren joined the two engineers who were having a serious-sounding discussion.

"Another glass of wine, Madison?" she asked.

"Sure. Wyatt, are you having another?"

"No thanks. My normal default is to coffee, a habit I picked up in the Navy where everyone drank it by the gallon."

"I'll have another with you, Madison." Lauren said. Moments later, Lauren returned with two wine glasses and a tray of small chocolates.

Wyatt handed a packet of calculations to Madison. "This will prime the idea pump."

Madison took the folder. "Is there a bunch of crazy ideas in here?"

"You decide. Fresh ideas are an engineer's trade. Our thinking isn't limited because we aren't captured in everyday reality."

With a studied look, Madison thumbed through the papers. "I'm intrigued with your logic diagram, Wyatt, particularly by this anticipator circuit. Good ideas here."

"Wyatt is always coming up with good ideas," Lauren said, trying to follow the conversation.

"This is much better than good," Madison said. "It's very clever."

Wyatt puffed up like a rooster courting a hen. "Well, I haven't worked out the details yet. There might be a major hiccup in there."

"Modesty does not become you, Honey," scolded Lauren.

Madison glanced up from the diagram. "I'd guess the electronics would be straightforward––it's the programming that will be challenging."

Wyatt nodded.

Seeing the empty plate, Lauren asked, "More chocolates?" When they shook their heads, Lauren collected the dish and soiled napkins. She felt a sense of uneasiness return. Wyatt and Madison were ensconced in their own world, a foreign place where she couldn't enter––banished to the kitchen. Water hissed as she rinsed the plate. *They've bonded like Steinbeck and his dog Charley, but instead of traveling the States, they're exploring a nerd world.* Lauren tossed the napkins in the trash and took a deep breath.

When she returned, Madison was saying, "And you've done a reliability analysis?"

"I've calculated a mean time between failures of approximately thirty-five thousand hours, three times current standards."

Madison's eyes widened. "Wow! How'd you do that?"

Wyatt rummaged through a folder and extracted a small bundle of papers and handed it to her. "Because there're fewer parts to break, it translates directly into reliability."

Madison studied the materials, pausing once or twice

to examine details. She set aside the analysis and picked up the logic diagram again. Minutes passed. "Wyatt, this is like an orchestra," she said. "The transducers, valves and heat exchangers work in perfect harmony." Madison crossed her legs and set the diagram in her lap. "This is too complex for a quick going-over. Can I take it home for a day or two?"

"You bet. Take your time. I'd hate to give up my brainchild without your best shot."

"You're right," said Madison. "I don't know the mechanics, but I need more time to see if the software and electronics are practical."

Wyatt nodded. "I'd sure appreciate your help with the electron stuff. They're way beyond me." He glanced at his watch. "Eleven fifteen! Where did the time go?"

"Goodness," gasped Lauren. "I forgot the coffee. It could be ready in a few minutes. Any takers?"

Madison looked at her watch. "I think I'll pass. Thanks anyway, Lauren. I'll be on my way"

They rose and went to the front door. Feeling hesitant, Lauren gave Madison a tentative hug.

"Great fun, Wyatt," Madison said, shaking his hand. "We did good science, didn't we?"

Wyatt bobbed his head. "Yup."

"Lauren, great dinner," Madison said. "Thanks again." She walked down the sidewalk, turned and waved, then drove away.

With a nervous laugh, Lauren picked up the empty glasses. "Madison seems nice. I had no clue what you two were talking about, but it was interesting to eavesdrop. It's like mental sparks fly between you two." Lauren snatched her apron from the pantry and tied it around her waist. "You seem to hit it off. Should I be jealous?"

Wyatt rinsed the glasses and set them in the dishwasher. "Jealous? What for?"

Lauren wiped the counter. "I don't know."

"We seem to click, I guess. Madison has big-time talent and gets me thinking. When I jump into far-out ideas, such as pressurization, I get nervous, like walking a tightrope. Madison gives me a reality check." Wyatt dried his hands on a towel and said, "All that aside, designing airplane stuff is riding a rocket––a mega-blast."

"You'd think I'd know you after all these years, but I've never seen you actually working––in action. Tonight I saw an enigmatic side of you and I'm convinced you're *addicted* to engineering. I never realized that."

Wyatt chuckled as he turned on the dishwasher. "Addiction is a strong word, but maybe you're right. Back to your original question, are you jealous of calculus? Did you know it's the other woman in my life?"

She laughed. "I hope so. I can't worry over calculus."

"There you are." Wyatt gave Lauren a quick hug and winked. "Madison raised a few good questions, though. I think I'll do a little work on that logic diagram before coming to bed. Do you mind?"

Lauren frowned. "Well, if you have to."

Wyatt kissed her, patted her shoulder and went to his office.

Lauren, finishing in the kitchen, weighed the events of the evening and wondered where her nascent jealousy came from. *Madison was thoughtful and appreciative. Okay, she's damn pretty, but it was all sterile science talk that has the sexiness of my accounting ledger.* Lauren sighed. *I'm worried over problems that aren't there. But still....*

Chapter 6

Wind rushed through Madison's hair as she pushed her Miata, top down, past eighty miles an hour. The cool late night air scrubbed her cheeks and the full moon bathed her with a soft glow. The deserted freeway and vacant lane stretching before her beckoned for more speed. But Madison yielded to her prudent nature and lifted her foot, slowing to seventy-five, a speed she judged immune from speeding tickets. She glanced up at the night sky where stars glistened. *No smog. Unusual for L.A. summers. Beautiful.* Cradled in the satiny arms of the evening, she smiled, propped her left elbow on the car door and draped her right hand over the steering wheel.

Her thoughts turned to Wyatt. *The man has a ton of shrewd ideas.* Mentally, she began to catalog the design innovations he'd blithely revealed. *Fully integrated. Wireless. Reliable. Lightweight. Smooth pressure transitions. Low cost.* Excited, she began to understand the immense potential of the design. As she subdued her fluttering scarf, Madison realized that Wyatt, in spite of his obvious brilliance, was a foreigner in the world of electronics and software. If his ideas were to go forward, she'd have to pair with him, same as Hewlett and Packard or Jobs and Wozniak. *Where could I find time? I'm buried.* Even so, the thought was intriguing and, she shivered.

Soon, she glided from the off-ramp and picked her way through the surface streets. Moments later, Madison parked, raised the convertible top and walked up the stairs to her second-floor apartment. At the door, a large gray cat greeted her and rubbed against her ankles, rumbling loudly. "Hi, G-G," she said. "You're up late, aren't you?" The purring became more sonorous as the cat flopped on his back. Madison, setting her briefcase on the floor and tossing her silk scarf aside, bent and scratched his tummy.

Madison's apartment lacked dainty feminine touches, but still exhibited flair where she'd arranged portraits of Tesla and Edison on the wall, intermingled with Japanese woodblock prints by Hiroshige. In the corner, G-G's sheepskin bed hunkered beneath a large photo of a sculpture of Galileo Galilei that Madison had taken in Italy. A large bookcase housed a vast collection of technical journals and well-worn reference books. Her bulky computer crouched on the dinette table, surrounded by neatly stacked papers, books and a mug of pencils. A large vase of supermarket flowers, fresh and fragrant, stood at attention on the kitchen counter.

Madison stepped out on her balcony to watch the moonlight play on the nearby mountainsides. She noticed her hummingbird feeder was empty and walked to the refrigerator to fill the feeder with sugar-water. After re-hanging it, she returned to the fridge searching for a diet tonic. It was bare except for an apple with the complexion of a raisin, the container of sugar-water and a half-empty carton of non-fat milk. With a shrug, she poured a glass of milk and settled into an overstuffed chair where G-G leapt into her lap.

Madison took a sip and reflected on Wyatt.

Her attraction to him was physical, but only partially; it was his mind that turned her on. First on SAC business, and now with the pressurization, she found their technical discussions exhilarating and intense—pure jubilation. *I'm in a special place with Wyatt*, she thought.

Madison knew she was awkward in social settings outside the workplace. Ever since grade school, her love of math and science cast her as a pariah. By high school, her beauty drew dozens of boys into her orbit, but second dates were rare—pubescent males hate feeling inferior. Even now, she had few true friends.

Wyatt's image came to mind. *He has the build of a linebacker. Hard muscled. I'll bet nobody messed with him in college.* His boyish face, round cheeks and long lashes made her want to hug him. "My urges may even go beyond hugging," she confided to G-G. Looking indifferent, the cat glanced up and licked its paw.

Madison recalled Lauren's cute freckles and sweet demeanor, which reminded her of old film clips she'd seen of Shirley Temple. Madison smirked with contempt for those who were "science-challenged" and thought that naming a child Timshel was silly. It was obvious Lauren was lost in Wyatt's engineering world. Madison wondered if the woman saw the chasm and if it mattered to her. She wondered if Lauren noticed her bond with Wyatt as they delved into the mysteries of design. She wondered…

"Enough, G-G. I've work to do." Madison, ignoring the late hour, pushed the cat aside and went to the dinette. There, she shoved the papers and books aside and dove into the intricacies of Wyatt's logic diagram.

Hours later, the sun began its tentative conquest of the darkness. Dim at first, the light probed through the kitchen window. A bright patch crept across the desk, painting

Madison's keyboard. Startled, she looked up, rubbed her eyes and glanced at her watch. "Damn! Six-twenty!" She stood and stretched, realizing that fatigue had hijacked her. Madison's neck and back ached and her eyes felt bloodshot. She turned off the computer, kicked her shoes into a corner and went to shower. *Thank God it's Sunday. I've all day to sleep.*

After showering, she toweled off and turned back the tidy bedcovers. Naked, she slipped between the cotton sheets and closed her eyes. G-G jumped up and wiggled against her. Madison turned onto her back and lay motionless for a few minutes, then blinked and stared at the ceiling light fixture. Her mind darted back to the logic diagram. She sat up and said, "There has to be an elegant way, G-G. I just have to figure it out."

G-G, looking indignant the way cats do, batted Madison's hand as she threw back the sheet and clambered out of bed, reaching for her bathrobe.

Soon, the clacking of her computer keys dueled with the morning songbird serenades beyond the balcony.

Chapter 7

Lauren's arm ached from vacuuming. The old upright machine, a hand-me-down from her mother, wheezed as she tugged it back and forth across the living room carpet. Although Saturday was her normal house-cleaning day, she was extra thorough because today was also her monthly Scrabble party.

Earlier, she'd had cleared the kitchen counter of soiled dishes, wiped hazy fingerprints from the stove and hid the bills in a drawer. Dusting was easy, but when she asked Timmie, starting kindergarten in two days, to put away her new clothes tossed on the coffee table, the child became defiant.

Fists on her hips, Lauren growled, "Timshel, *now.*" As Timmie stumbled off with an armload of clothes, Lauren noticed that Garfield, their cat, had left several stuffed mice scattered on the floor. With a rebellious grunt, she deftly kicked them under the sofa.

Lauren brushed back a stand of hair and went to Timmie's room. "Good— you've hung up your new clothes. Let me brush your hair; we can't have you going next door to play looking like a Doctor Seuss character."

The duel with her squirming daughter finished, Lauren plopped exhausted in her armchair. A moment later, the doorbell rang. *Ah. Mother,* she thought. They had a routine on Scrabble days––Lauren's mother arrived an hour before the others to help set up. Lauren was grateful for her help, but she often found herself at odds with Liza.

Liza had been a wealthy stay-at-home mom and Lauren's

early childhood had been bright and secure. Liza showered her only child with every possible comfort and Lauren adored her mother. Friction between them began when Lauren entered puberty. A dominating woman, Liza scheduled inflexible study hours, forbade make-up and insisted on tennis lessons at the club. By the time Lauren began dating, their relationship deteriorated from uncomfortable to combative. Vehement arguments arose over curfews and dress, solidifying their mutual resentment.

College and her European tour with two girlfriends freed her for a while, but the feud resumed when the newlyweds had to move into the mansion.

Once Lauren and Wyatt moved out of Liza's house, the only time Lauren saw her mother was on Scrabble days. Lauren sensed an obligation, a filial duty, to spend time with her mother. Although Liza never spoke of it, Lauren knew her mother was lonely. After Lauren's father died of a heart attack, Liza threw herself into charities, community functions and politics. It seemed she was trying to compensate for the loss of the elegant social life of her late husband's business dealings. Guessing this, Lauren's sympathy seeped to the surface—once a month.

Lauren forced a smile and opened the door. "Hi, Mom. Come in."

Liza stepped lightly into the room, her sun-burnished body lithe from twice-weekly tennis. She strode into the kitchen and slipped a container of grocery-store shrimp into the refrigerator. "There. My contribution," she said, sitting in Lauren's chair while smoothing her designer dress. "It's scorching out; the usual September oven. Do you have any iced tea, Dear?"

Lauren darted to the kitchen and returned with two glasses of tea.

"Do you have the air conditioning running?" Liza asked. "My, I thought I was past this hot-flash madness years ago."

"It's not menopause, Mother; our little window air conditioner can't keep up. It's not too bad is it?"

"Oh, I'll be alright, I guess." She took a sip of tea and said, "Shouldn't we get busy?"

"I think so. We have only forty-five minutes."

They followed a routine honed by dozens of sessions. Liza dragged a card table from the entry closet while Lauren wrestled folding chairs into place. They set score-pads, pencils and coasters on the card table and extracted shrimp from the refrigerator.

"Where's Timmie, Dear?" inquired Liza.

"She's next door playing with Jennifer."

Liza scowled. "I hoped to spend some time with her. She's my only grandchild after all. Perhaps after Scrabble. You think?"

"Perhaps." Lauren busied herself with the shrimp, arranging them on a plate. *This isn't as nice as the elegant creations mother's maid does.*

"I suppose Wyatt is working as always." Liza said.

"Yes. He has plenty of work to do at Simmons and besides, he feels in the way on Scrabble days."

Liza put plates on the end of the counter. "Does he get paid overtime on weekends? I know you could use the extra cash."

Lauren grimaced. "No, Mother, he's salaried. We get along fine."

"I suppose, but you shouldn't be working. Timmie

needs a fulltime mother. We've been over this before. I wish Wyatt weren't a common worker. You should have married a lawyer or business owner."

Exasperated, Lauren said, "Wyatt is an engineer, a professional. He'll look for a better paying position when the economy gets better." She crossed her arms. "I wish you'd warm up to Wyatt. Ever since I split with Don in high school, you've hated every guy I dated. Just because Don went on to become a Harvard lawyer..."

"No need to scold. It's just my opinion."

Silently, they pulled dewy cans of soft drinks from the refrigerator, plunked glasses by a large bowl of ice and opened two bottles of wine, red and white.

Lauren put out a can of spicy tomato juice and a bottle of vodka. "Can you get the celery from the crisper?"

"Sure," Liza said. "Remember, Marge likes Tabasco in her Bloody Mary, lots of Tabasco."

"Of course." Lauren snatched a bottle of hot sauce from the pantry and looked over the preparations. "Yup. Everything looks ready. Just in time—Marge and Betty are due any moment." Making light conversation, Lauren continued, "I just finished a great book with a crazy title: *The Guernsey Literary and Potato Peel Pie Society* by Mary Shaffer. It's written as letters, an epistolary. It's extraordinary."

"Epistolary? Where do you get those fancy words? No wonder you're the Scrabble Goddess. I haven't time to read, so don't bother explaining it. Let's relax until the girls get here. Let me tell you about my new bridge club."

A short time later, Marge Taylor, clutching a box of cookies under her arm, and Betty Jenkins rang the doorbell. Both were acquaintances from Lauren's work.

They'd become good friends and had played Scrabble every month for three years.

The foursome strolled into the kitchen where they poured drinks and gathered snacks. Marge was complaining of the heat wave when Betty interrupted, exclaiming, "Oh, Liza! What a lovely bracelet! Where did you get it?"

Liza, with a proud look, shook her hand so everyone could see her elegant, glittering jewelry. "Real diamonds, girls. My husband gave it to me two months before he died. A nice going away gift, I'd say."

The women laughed, but Lauren was uneasy with the jest.

Back in the living room, they scooted their chairs to the card table and drew tiles. Lighthearted chitchat flavored the air where gossip was peppered with lively political squabbles. The soft clatter of the wooden Scrabble tiles seemed to keep cadence with the conversation.

"Who's that new movie star?" Click.

"The Republicans are in big trouble." Click.

"Your turn, Betty." Click.

An hour passed, then two, then three. Banter was easy and laughter bubbled among the words. After a play, Lauren drew three tiles and moaned, "Still no vowels." Marge plopped four tiles onto the board and exulted over a double word score play, her joy clearly enhanced by a third Bloody Mary.

Lauren delighted in Scrabble day, an indulgence to her passion for reading and words. The easy friendship, lighthearted conversation and feigned skirmishes over scoring warmed her. Lauren was proud of her home and liked hosting her friends because it fulfilled her need for affable companionship. Sometimes, she thought her life took second place behind family demands, but Scrabble day was her time—not Wyatt's, not Timmie's, not even Liza's.

As the shadows lengthened, the women tallied their points. Betty looked at the score-pad and saw she'd won. "There, I've proven that Lauren isn't invincible," Betty chortled, and the others joined in the mirth. They gathered up their plates and glasses and ambled into the kitchen. Once the women tidied up, they went to the door and exchanged quick hugs. As Marge and Betty walked into the stagnant September air, Betty called over her shoulder, "Lovely time, Lauren. My turn to bring the cookies next month. See you then."

Lauren closed the door and turned to Liza, "That was great fun."

"Yes, very nice. I enjoy Betty. She's the sales manager, right? Sharp lady. Marge can get boorish when she drinks." Liza shook her head. "She should go easy on those Bloody Marys."

"I suppose, but she brings spice to the table. Piquancy."

"Another big word."

As they put away the card table and chairs, Liza said, "Timmie still hasn't come home. Should we call Jennifer's mother? I'd like to say 'hi-bye' if nothing else."

"Why not." Lauren phoned next door and asked that Timmie be sent home. "Sharon says the kids are in the middle of a video game. Timmie will come in a bit."

"I've been aced again," Liza snapped, glancing at her watch. "Regardless, I have to go."

Lauren noticed the irked look that darkened Liza's face and tried to ignore the tension in the air. "Well, I guess that's everything. I'll load the dishwasher after I start dinner for Wyatt. Are you sure you won't stay?"

"Love to, Dear, but I have a committee meeting tonight about a big fundraiser for the Boys and Girls Club. One of our city councilwomen will be there, so I can't possibly miss it." The two walked to the front door and Lauren brushed a kiss on her mother's cheek. "Can we connect before the next Scrabble session?" asked Lauren. "I have errands to run Wednesday night; maybe you could drop in and hold down the fort. Wyatt will be out of town on business and Timmie would love to see you."

Liza's rigid expression softened. "That's a thought. I'll check my calendar. Timmie and I might try out that new board game she has." She smiled, struck an imaginary tennis backhand and bounced down the steps to her car.

Her mother gone, Lauren collapsed in her chair and took a deep breath. *I wish mom could understand how I feel about Wyatt. Even though he says he needs to catch up at work, I know mother's antagonism drives him away. She doesn't see he's an incredible engineer.*

Chapter 8

The California summer heat waned as October marched across the calendar. Lauren, with Timmie's help, took advantage of a bright Saturday afternoon and thumbtacked a cardboard skeleton on the front door. *I hope Madison is into Halloween*, she thought.

Although Wyatt and Madison had talked by phone, more than a month had passed since they'd met to work on the pressurization system, so Wyatt invited her for an encore. Lauren hummed and draped the dining table with a bright orange cloth, saying, "Timmie, set out these paper napkins while I get the Halloween centerpiece. Madison will be here soon."

The table finished, Lauren admired the holiday touches: plastic tombstones and goblins, red and orange sycamore leaves from the neighbor's yard and a handful of hard candies scattered on the table.

Lauren loved holidays—any holiday. She embraced celebrations as a way to bring warmth and togetherness to her home. Along with Valentine's Day and Christmas, she took particular pleasure in Halloween and its decorations, sugary cookies and Timmie's cute costumes. Tomorrow she planned to go with her daughter to Halloween Village to buy a pumpkin.

The Halloween Village sat on a nearby vacant field commandeered every year by an ambitious Mexican family. They scattered hay bales around, erected small tents filled with ghoulish merchandise and arrayed hundreds of pumpkins in precise rows. The family brought a touch of excitement into their operation by painting faux blood on their brown faces and tucking plastic fangs into their mouths. In a few weeks, the hay bales would disappear, replaced by Santa's Workshop. The staff would discard fangs, don Santa suits and bellow "ho-ho-ho" through their gleaming white teeth.

Lauren chuckled under her breath, remembering how last year her daughter was wary of the strange vampire people. At first, Timmie had cowered alongside her. Then, shrieking with joy, she'd scampered among the endless pumpkins shouting, "This one! No, this one!"

Wyatt never had an interest in holidays, which disappointed Lauren. Nevertheless, she planned to pry him out of his bedroom office in the morning to accompany his family among the rows of future Jack-O-Lanterns.

Lauren jumped when the doorbell rang. "She's here," she called to the bedroom door.

"Coming!" Wyatt shouted and hurried to the living room where he found Madison and Lauren chatting.

Timmie stood next to her mother, staring at Madison's long flowing hair.

"Say hi to Madison," Lauren said.

"Hi, Madison." Timmie squirmed and looked at Wyatt, as if needing direction, but Madison had captured his attention. "Can I go now?" Not waiting for an answer, she scampered to her room.

"Have a seat," Wyatt said indicating the sofa.

Lauren had already set out a pot of coffee, cream and sugar along with Halloween cookies on the coffee table.

Madison poured a cup and added a dash of creamer

saying, "Your Halloween decorations are great, Lauren. These Casper-the-Ghost cookies look home made."

"They are. I love to bake." She looked at Wyatt and said, "Our little girl will be out of the house before we realize it. Right, Dear? We'd better treasure these holidays while she's a kid."

"I guess." Wyatt grabbed a handful of cookies and faced Madison. "I'm glad you could break away. I want to talk over lots of things."

"Sorry. The boss sent me on a long business trip," Madison said, sipping coffee. "While I was on the road, I studied your logic diagrams and one thing is certain, you've come up with a startling concept."

"There are times when I find him *very* startling," Lauren said with a playful grin.

Wyatt apparently missed the flirtatious remark and asked Madison, "I'm worried about the link with the main aircraft computer. What did you think?"

"Well, I struggle with the idea that all control commands would be wireless. The FAA will have a coronary."

Wyatt nodded. "I know, but we can encrypt..."

Lauren's head bobbed back and forth as if she were watching a Ping-Pong match. The jargon was a mystery, and she felt left out. She poured a cup of coffee and sat back, watching the conversation become more and more animated. *Wyatt doesn't even know I'm here.*

"Will control hysteresis be a problem?" Madison asked.

"No. The design uses flexures to minimize it."

"Could that result in high-frequency harmonics?"

Wyatt slapped his forehead. "I hadn't considered that. I

have a program that calculates natural frequencies. Let's go to my office and check it out. You mind, Lauren?"

Lauren frowned. "Go ahead, you two. I'll clean up here."

>< >< ><

Wyatt was excited as they walked to his office. Madison gasped as she entered. "This looks like Times Square on New Year's morning! I hope your thinking isn't this cluttered."

Embarrassed, Wyatt mumbled, "Well, you know... man-cave and all that. It's like an old shoe."

Wyatt's computer monitor dominated the desk while the CPU, tucked in the kneehole, was buried beneath a pile of tattered manila folders. A harsh overhead light fixture and a gooseneck desk lamp glared against the walls, bare except for a calendar turned to last month's page. A coffee-stained mug stood sentinel beside a grungy percolator while metal castings, push rods, ball screws and filter bodies were scattered around, trophies to past designs.

He sat, and with a wave of his hand, offered the folding chair to Madison. "Now, let's look at those harmonics."

Time flew. The lamps cast sharp shadows on the clutter of spreadsheets and graphs. The computer screen threw a sickly glow on Madison's squinting face as she perched on the edge of the hard metal chair, seemingly oblivious to its discomfort.

Everything outside the cramped room was banished from Wyatt's consciousness and he saw only technical challenges, the computer and Madison. His mind blended with hers and ideas flashed between them, needing few words.

"Suppose…"

"Possibly…"

"Maybe it's over damped."

"Damn! That's it!"

"Almost. Try a third order curve fit…"

>< >< ><

Once the coffee table was cleared, Lauren worked in the kitchen preparing dinner for Wyatt and Madison. *This pressurization thing is a cancer. Between that and his real job, I hardly see him.* As she worked, she strained to hear the goings-on in the office, but it sounded all business. No giggles, no innuendoes, no silliness. Just science.

Soon, one of her specialties, a carnitas dish, was ready. Lauren went down the hall and as she approached, Wyatt and Madison's conversation became clearer. She paused, thinking their deliberations popped and snapped like high voltage power lines in the mist, intense and crisp.

Lauren stuck her head through the door. "Do you two know it's seven-thirty? Dinner is ready."

"Seven-thirty! Darn! Yeah, I'm starving," said Wyatt. "Can we eat in here? We're in the middle of a tough calculation. Okay with you, Madison?"

Madison hesitated and then said, "Why not?"

Fuming, Lauren returned to the kitchen, threw together a tray of food and took it to the back room. Then she summoned Timmie and plopped a plate and a glass of milk in front of her.

"Mommy, is Daddy going to eat with us?"

"No, Honey. He's busy with Madison."

Timmie pouted, but settled down and ate. Lauren ate too, but the pork seemed to stick in her throat. She felt a huge hole in the room. *Get over it,* she admonished herself. *He's in engineer heaven. Give him a little slack.*

When the meal was finished, Timmie grumbled and balked when Lauren asked her to help with the dishes.

"Come on, Little One. Give Mommy a hand."

She worried about her daughter. Once a cheerful toddler, Timmie had grown into a fretful recluse, with few friends except Jennifer. Now five, she'd become a chronic whiner. When Wyatt worked late, dinnertime without him was especially exasperating. Lauren knew girls Timmie's age formed strong bonds with their dads and she sensed a widening gap between them.

She pushed the thought aside and said, "Come, Honey, jammy-time. It's late."

"No!" shouted Timmie, stamping her foot.

"Tim-*shel.* Jammies. Now!"

Lauren wheedled and cajoled Timmie into bed. At last, the house was quiet except for the murmuring that drifted down the hall. Weariness crept over Lauren, so she sat in her chair and closed her eyes. Her mind wandered: *I need to get Timmie interested in new activities. Draw her out of her shell.*

Her brows knitting in concentration, Lauren inspected her fingernails. Her glance fell on the morning's stack of newspapers and she remembered Timmie seemed interested in the article on the new girls' AYSO soccer team. *She might love meeting new girls and playing in a sport. Maybe Wyatt could go to the weekend games.* Lauren fished through the pile and found the article. She reread it and thought,

I'll call first thing. Pleased with her decision, she picked up a novel from the end table, turned to a bookmark and began to read. The soft rustle of the turning pages marked the passage of time and the hands on Lauren's watch ticked past midnight.

>< >< ><

Wyatt squinted at the image on the computer and rummaged in his mind for a solution. Madison leaned forward, her face nearly touching his and twiddled with a strand of hair. "We need to fit the altitude sensor in here," she said, pointing her pencil to a spot on the screen.

"Right. I could move the flexure a bit higher to make room." He made a quick note on his pad. "That'll be easy, but the real challenge will be developing software."

Madison nodded. "Let's work on the logic diagram some more."

At first, the problems were insurmountable, but Wyatt and Madison persisted. Impossible evolved into plausible which became difficult and finally straightforward.

"I need to stretch my legs," declared Madison. "God, it's after two in the morning! Let's wrap this up, okay?"

"You bet. I'm beat." Wyatt grinned. "What a session. We worked through some ugly stuff, didn't we?"

"We did. It seems as if we catalyze each other. It's weird, but I'm becoming a believer in telepathy." With a toss of her head, she reached over and patted Wyatt on the leg. "Agree?"

Startled, he flinched under her touch. Madison's winsome smile and twinkling green eyes made Wyatt catch his breath. The sensation was uncomfortable, and he pushed it away. With a shrug, he said, "Yeah. We're in tune for sure."

Madison gathered up her belongings, and they tiptoed through the living room where Lauren slumbered in her chair; chin resting on her chest and the book sprawled on the floor.

Wyatt held his finger to his lips. "Shhhhh. Thanks, Madison," he whispered. "You've been a big help. Let's get together again, soon, okay?"

With a nod, Madison left.

Wyatt stood over his sleeping wife and watched her gentle breathing. *God almighty, how I love her,* he thought. He reached down and shook her shoulder. She stirred, looked at him with sleepy eyes and smiled. "What time is it?"

"Nearly two-fifteen."

"No way!" Lauren rubbed her neck and complained, "You're crazy. I'm full of kinks and aches. Well, tomorrow's Sunday. We can sleep in. Did you accomplish a lot?"

"We did. Really did. Still a few big questions, but we wrestled two big problems to the ground. What a blast!"

Lauren shook her head soulfully. "My engineer. You never cease to amaze me. Let's go to bed."

Chapter 9

Lauren bustled about, feeling harried. "Timmie, let's go—it's getting late."

"I'm coming," shouted Timmie, running from her bedroom wearing maroon shorts and a white tee shirt emblazoned with "Burbank Bombers." In her arms, she cradled a brand-new soccer ball. She shivered with apparent excitement and cried, "Where's Daddy?"

"Right here, Timmie, in the kitchen," Wyatt called.

Lauren glowed seeing her husband's eyes crinkle with mirth when their daughter catapulted into the room.

"Are you ready?" Wyatt asked.

"Oh, yes!" Then, a devious looking grin creased her face. "Can I take my Halloween candy?"

Candy was bad for kids, Lauren knew, and she didn't want to deal with Timmie on a sugar high. Even so, she capitulated to avoid another confrontation. "Okay, Dear, but just two pieces."

Timmie dashed to her pillowcase of Halloween treasures, snatched two pieces and followed her parents to the car.

Because Timmie was joining the team mid-way through the Fall season, Lauren worried her daughter would feel out of place. But the child's excitement about the sport prodded Lauren to make arrangements.

The team played at the high school just two miles away. As the car crept along busy streets, Wyatt said, "Traffic seems worse on Saturday mornings than during weekday rush-hours." Lauren nodded. "Everyone is shopping, I guess, or going to soccer." With a grin, she whispered, "It's nice you took time to watch Timmie. I'm sure you're totally buried in pressurization."

"Well, I gotta be a father sometimes."

A smacking sound emanated from the back seat as Timmie demolished a Tootsie Roll and the sickening-sweet smell of chocolate filled the car.

A thoughtful look crossed Wyatt's face, and he said, "I realize I haven't spent much time with you two recently. This new idea just takes over. It's nice to take a break today––get some sunshine." He flashed one of his boyish grins, the kind that melted Lauren's heart.

They parked in the student lot near the gym and walked to the small bleachers alongside the field. Timmie's mouth was ringed with chocolate and her fingers had smeared dark brown smudges on the soccer ball.

A lanky, middle-aged man walked over and introduced himself. "I'm Andy Kotzar, coach of the Bombers. Is this little fireball going to be our star player?" he asked, indicating Timmie.

Lauren offered her hand. "I'm Lauren Morgan. We've talked on the phone. This is my husband, Wyatt and our daughter Timmie."

Timmie clutched her ball and said nothing. Lauren sensed her daughter's zeal for soccer had evaporated in this strange place with this strange man.

Andy nodded at the adults and then put his hand on Timmie's shoulder. "Pleased to meet you, young lady. You won't be needing your ball, so leave it with your parents."

Timmie handed the ball to her father and Andy nudged

her toward a group of young girls jostling and chatting near the sideline. "Come—time to meet some new friends."

Wyatt and Lauren joined a few other parents perched on the hard slats of the bleachers. Timmie, they noticed, stood on the perimeter of an animated cluster of girls. They could hear Andy explain the rules of soccer and virtues of teamwork. "Seems like a capable coach," Wyatt commented.

"He's very nice. I've talked with him twice by phone concerning the team, the schedule and, of course, uniforms. Andy's been coaching AYSO girls for six years. He had an interesting insight: claims that soccer tugs self-centered children out of their shell and introduces them to that weird thing called *others*."

"Makes sense," chuckled Wyatt. "Maybe Timmie will get more confidence."

Lauren smiled, reached out and took her husband's hand. She tucked a strand of hair behind her ear and drew a deep breath of the crisp fall air, savoring the sharp smell of leaves. Contented, she settled into the nest of Wyatt's arm, squeezed his hand a little tighter and gazed at her daughter.

Wyatt squirmed on the cold aluminum seat. "Next time we'll bring cushions." He looked across the field at the cloudless sky. Lauren noticed the usual thin lines in his face were gone and an easy smile had settled between his freshly shaven cheeks, giving him a relaxed look.

"Oh, look, Wyatt. They're splitting up into sides. Timmie's team is on the right. Over there."

"Yeah, I see."

Then, Lauren saw Wyatt's eyebrows draw together, forming little furrows above his nose. "I've been thinking," he said holding her hand. "I've been stewing over my job: the god-awful work environment and what it's doing to me."

Lauren turned from the field and looked at her husband. "Go on."

"Engineering is a creative thing, same as an artist sitting in front of a blank canvas or a composer with a symphony bouncing around in his head. I can't describe how it is to have my boss stomp out good ideas; to be denied your mind. Every morning I drag my butt to work and stare at the computer, knowing the day will be filled with frustration and lost possibilities. Like a whore, I show up every day in exchange for a paycheck."

A roar came from the field. "GOALLLLLLLLLLLL," cried a cluster of parents. Wyatt and Lauren looked up briefly, and then Wyatt continued.

"First, it was the filter sensor and next the pressurization. Leechmann, the government guy, came again yesterday and raised Cain––trying to get me fired. There's one roadblock after another. This isn't how I want my life. It's not bright anymore. When I stood beside you saying, 'I do,' I saw a path to glory. But now, SAC drives me crazy and I'm eaten up by the pressurization. So I've kinda ignored you and Timmie. Guess you noticed."

"Sure have," Lauren said with an edge in her voice. "A few months back, I thought our 'Sunset Ritual' had turned stale. Lately, when we talk, it's about Madison and the pressurization. It's nice that you're enthused, but..." Lauren stared at her feet, then looked into Wyatt's eyes. "I want you to back away. You've been working more and more on the pressurization and less at SAC. What if Brian notices?"

Wyatt winced. "I can't figure a way out. This idea is burning a hole in my head—I can't let it go. Madison said we catalyze each other. She likes my ideas—feeds them. Better than that, she expands on them and challenges me."

As Lauren listened to Wyatt's accolades for Madison, she felt her throat tighten. A specter of jealousy flashed in her mind, hurt she couldn't compete on the playing field of science. It was a crack in their relationship. Would it become a chasm?

Wyatt pivoted and straddled the bleacher's plank and faced Lauren. "At first, pressurization was a wild, half-baked idea, but it's growing. Madison has filled many gaps in my thinking. These last few days, I've reviewed the whole concept. It can work, dang-it. Just jump in! Even if Brian took it on, I figure the project is way beyond SAC. One solution is to partner with Madison and start our own company."

There was a long pause. Children's shouts, intermingled with Andy's directives, drifted over them. Wyatt stared at Lauren with raised brows while she fiddled with her wedding band.

Lauren was not surprised and knew of Wyatt's struggles long before he did. She understood that SAC was a grim trap baited by their need for money. Brian's conservatism and rejection of risk were the antithesis of Wyatt's love of innovation.

She also saw Wyatt's transformation in Madison's presence. When the woman threw out a new idea, he'd become ebullient; his excitement became glowing fireflies on a summer night. For Lauren, it was like listening to an Italian opera; she had no idea what they were saying, but it was beautiful. And that was troubling.

Lauren ignored the big issue in her mind and said, "How can we do that? You say the system is complex. It could take years to design. Where would you find the time?"

With a shrug, Wyatt said, "I haven't made an estimate yet."

Lauren put her elbows on her knees and leaned toward him. "Wyatt, you're talking to your wife who's lonely enough now. You have to think of your family. There's just no way."

Wyatt cradled his chin in his hands and peered through the planks of the bleachers to the ground below. "I'm just trying to think of alternatives."

"What alternatives? Look at us, Wyatt. We came to watch Timmie play soccer, and what are we doing? We're talking about pressurization." Lauren noticed one of the other parents glance over, eavesdropping. She lowered her voice and continued. "Timmie needs us, and I need you, Honey. Launching a company is a twenty-five-hour-a-day effort––is it worth it?"

"No way of knowing," Wyatt conceded. "But I'm up against the wall. Should I resign myself to mediocrity? Should I grow old and watch my aspirations go the way of my hairline? I'm blessed with a creative talent. How can I stand by while Brian wraps it up in butcher paper and drops it in a trashcan? You married an enthusiastic man with a gift and direction. Do you want him back, or do you want to settle for a run-of-the-mill, nine-to-five washout?"

Lauren felt sickened by Wyatt's prediction of a dismal future. An image of a wildflower filled her mind. Years ago, Wyatt had pressed a California poppy in her hand while walking together in the Verdugo Mountains. Then he proposed, an awkward, stumbling proposal, but for her, it rang like Sarna Bells. Lauren foresaw a warm, loving life and knew they complimented each other same as violins and oboes in an orchestra. She had a passionate love of his integrity, his ambitions and his brilliance.

Yes, she'd married a man of excellence. His mind towered above everyone—a genius. While people might discount Wyatt as a geek, a nerd, a disconnected eccentric, Lauren saw his sparkling imagination and skill in his craft with unimaginable potential. Liza and others might find Wyatt bizarre, but Lauren felt compelled to support him in his quest.

Lauren's eyes misted, and she reached over and touched Wyatt's cheek. "When you proposed, an apparition appeared, kind of like the Ghost of Christmas Future. You inspired me and I saw an exciting, fulfilled life, brimming with achievement." Lauren took a deep breath. "There must be a way to circumvent Brian and SAC. I want the man I married."

"Thank you." Wyatt took his wife's hands and stammered, "If we work together we'll have the life we imagined." He swallowed hard, his Adam's apple bobbing. "I love you."

"Oh, Wyatt."

He rubbed his chin. "I don't know if starting my own company is the only answer. The company can't get underway without Madison. I haven't said anything to her because the basic design isn't sorted out. Without her, the whole idea would be scuttled."

Madison. What about Madison, wondered Lauren. She swallowed the lump in her throat and decided the "other woman" wasn't going to run her life. "Yes. I want the man I married," she repeated. "You must go ahead with the pressurization."

A shriek of pain shot across the field and Wyatt and Lauren turned to see Timmie crying and holding her elbow. Coach Andy jumped to console her, "Just a little owie, not bad at all. Okay?"

Wyatt and Lauren started across the field toward their daughter, a very different couple than the one that brought Timmie to soccer.

Chapter 10

Wyatt mulled over his talk with Lauren at soccer practice. He'd felt awkward trying to explain his hatred of SAC, yet figured she understood. He realized his career—and in a way, his marriage, were at a turning point.

Encouraged by his wife's words, Wyatt made a list of things needed to start his company. Most importantly, he worried how to approach Madison, because the project was doomed if she balked. Wyatt knew she had a promising career at King and tried to anticipate her objections. She'd be reluctant to jump into a risky start-up requiring a huge amount of time and vast sums of money—both in short supply.

Before leaving for Kansas to attend a convention in Wichita, Brian handed Wyatt the final Statement Of Work on the hydraulic filter. "Take this to Madison," he said. "Have her check the technical stuff and get her management to sign it."

Wyatt decided to parlay the SOW into lunch with Madison. That way he could broach his proposition to start a pressurization company as well as do Simmons Aviation business.

Madison readily accepted.

The night before, Wyatt tossed in bed for hours, rehearsing his conversation with Madison. While Lauren slumbered beside him, he struggled with phantom arguments and parried imaginary rebuttals.

It all came down to a few words over a sandwich.

Darkness still ruled when Wyatt staggered from bed,

showered and drove to work. An hour early, he detoured to the lunchroom to make a pot of coffee and went upstairs to his desk. He tried to focus on work, but his mind kept wandering. He stared into space and fingered the list he'd made for Madison, making sure he hadn't forgotten anything. Wyatt, feeling guilty of cannibalizing SAC's time, tried to reread Brian's Statement Of Work. As the morning crept by, he slogged through a few phone calls and a boring meeting where a draftsman asked, "Wyatt? Are you with us?"

Flushed from his daydreaming, he'd replied, "Yeah. Sure."

At last, Wyatt's appointment with Madison was twenty minutes away. He slipped his laptop and several file folders into his well-used briefcase, hurried down the stairs and told the receptionist he'd be gone for lunch. He worried as he drove, and distracted, drifted from his lane. He was rewarded by a blaring horn.

Wyatt parked in the restaurant lot and hurried inside. He realized his armpits were damp and hoped the sweat didn't show through his shirt.

"Just one, sir?" asked the hostess.

"No, I'm meeting a lady. There will be two of us."

"Oh. You must be Mr. Morgan. I seated your friend just moments ago. Follow me."

She ushered him to a booth where Madison sat, wearing a dark gray turtleneck sweater and a bright floral scarf that highlighted her emerald eyes.

"Hi, Wyatt. Right on the dot I see."

Wyatt slid into the booth and set his briefcase on the seat. "I try to be on time; it's a fetish of mine."

"Got that." She picked up the menu and said, "I'm not sure if I've recovered from the marathon session at your house."

Wyatt chuckled. "Me neither."

"Be sure to thank Lauren for a lovely evening. I really enjoyed it. At least she had the sense to get a nap while we were knocking heads in the back room."

A young waitress, brandishing her order pad, interrupted them, "Have you folks decided?"

"Coffee for now. Give us a few more minutes," Wyatt replied. Nervousness tugged his belly as he scanned the menu. Nothing sounded good. "Guess I'll have a burger. You?"

"Caesar salad for me."

A few minutes later the waitress returned and took their order. "Well, I guess we could take care of this while waiting for our food," Wyatt said, pulling a folder from his briefcase. "Brian has approved the Statement Of Work. He wants you to double-check the engineering arrangement between us and get your management's signature. There are two copies, one for King, and one for us."

"Right," Madison said. "Our lawyers have gone over the draft you emailed, so there shouldn't be any problems."

"Lawyers, always lawyers," fumed Wyatt. "It seems like they dictate design more than engineers. They're demons looking over my shoulder."

"Isn't that the truth?"

After their food came, they talked about the faltering economy and its impact on the general aviation. Nervous, Wyatt tried to bring up his proposal, but wavered, unsure how to begin. They finished eating and, when the waitress cleared the dishes, Wyatt ordered more coffee, a delaying tactic rather than a desire for more caffeine.

After the waitress topped off Wyatt's mug, he grunted. "Madison, this pressurization thing is exciting. We solved a couple of real problems the other night. The software worried me, but you filled in a lot of blanks."

With a nod, Madison formed a pyramid with the tips of her fingers. "It was fun."

"I need to work out a bunch of details." Wyatt hesitated, trying to organize his thoughts.

"Are you going somewhere with this?"

Wyatt wiped his palms on his pant legs. "This thing is incredibly complex: pneumatics, electronics, software…" He clenched his fists. "Dang-it, Madison, this thing has huge potential. It's a once-in-a-lifetime opportunity."

Madison laced her fingers and looked at Wyatt. "And you're thinking you can't do this alone, right?"

"Well, I was hoping…"

With a smile, Madison leaned back in the booth and tapped the tabletop with a spoon. "You need a little help, hmmm? You need a good software person, hmmm? You need someone crazy enough to team with you, hmmm? Now who could that be?"

Wyatt laughed—a big, nervous laugh. "Madison, you can be downright devious." He felt giddy. "Yes, let's join forces. Perhaps you saw that old movie where Rocky Balboa said, 'You got gaps. I got gaps. Together, we fill gaps.' I can do the mechanical stuff and you can handle the electronics and software. Like Rocky might say, 'it's a knockout.'"

"You're quoting a punch drunk boxer as if he's a management guru." Madison propped her chin on her fist and said, "Regardless, you're right; we *can* do this. Suppose we sketch out the basic concepts and write a few lines of sample code. Then, we could approach an established company to see if they'd develop it. There are at least two firms that make pressurization systems that might consider a licensing agreement, Randel for example."

"Actually, that's not what I was thinking."

Madison's brows furrowed. "No?"

"No. I'm thinking we should start our own manufacturing company, part-time at first, evenings and weekends. Perhaps in a year go full-time. The concept is unique, patentable for sure, but there are a lot of unknowns. If we farmed out our design, we'd have no control of the final product. It's better if we do it ourselves."

"That means we'll have to quit our jobs," Madison grunted.

"Well, yeah, but not right away. Sure, you have a great job, but ask yourself: is King a true innovator that can challenge you? My concept is break-through stuff. We can set the bar in the aircraft industry."

"I hear you." Madison paused, studied her hands and fiddled with her spoon. She looked up, and said, "It's one thing to have an idea and make a few drawings, but another to design, troubleshoot and manufacture hardware and PCB's. Plus, we're looking at miles of code. That adds up to tera-hours and mega-bucks. Then there's the FAA and their certification obstacle-course."

"Can't argue, but what you want from life? Get comfy and chill forever? Mellow out in mediocrity? Or does your destiny include mind-bending adventure? If we really want it, we'll find time; money will come."

Madison tossed her head, her hair shimmering in the light. "That's a bold vision, my friend; you've guts. We're good engineers, but what do we know about running a business? In a bad economy?"

Wyatt pressed his lips together. "We both are experienced with small aviation companies—it's not like we're moving to Mars. Lauren can help with finances and we could outsource the actual machine work."

The tap-tap-tap of Madison's spoon increased in tempo as she scrunched up her face in thought. "It can't hurt to dip our toe in the water...part-time just to see how it goes. This may be my only chance to rock the business." She reached over and patted Wyatt's hand, "I guess you have a deal."

This time Wyatt didn't flinch. He couldn't decide whether to yell with joy or cringe at the prospect of a huge commitment. "Great!" he exclaimed. "First thing, we need a plan." He reached into his briefcase. "Take a look at my list of action items to launch the ship. I'll bet we can move much faster than you think."

"I can't believe this," Madison gasped. "You had this list all along? What if I turned down your craziness?"

"You had no choice. I'm irresistible, you know," Wyatt quipped. Pointing to the list, he said, "First, we'll have to finalize the basic designs then generate detail drawings and code..." He breezed through the list, finishing by saying, "I'll get my banker and tax guy to help out with the business stuff. Look over my plan and call me tonight."

Madison folded Wyatt's list and tucked it into her purse. Her green eyes sparkled, drawing a grin from Wyatt. "Let's get back to work before we're fired."

Wyatt went to pay the check, but Madison insisted

paying half. "It's precedent," she said, handing him a few bills with a wink. "Fifty-fifty."

They walked to the parking lot where Wyatt unlocked his car.

"Is this machine yours?" Madison asked, scowling at the grubby Ford.

"It gets me around," he said, a little ashamed.

"I'd think the world's greatest engineer would drive a Ferrari or a sixties muscle car." Pointing to his vanity license plate, she read, 'STRIVE1.' What's this?"

Wyatt tipped his head to one side and said, "It's my philosophy of life, for everyone to see."

"The essence of your being in one word? Well, it certainly fits you, Mr. Morgan," she said, rubbing his arm. "To a tee."

With broad smiles, they shook hands as business partners do, and drove to their respective jobs.

Chapter 11

Timmie attacked her plate of spaghetti, painting her mouth and spattering the table with red sauce. Irked, Lauren scolded, "No, Timmie. Use a spoon and fork, like this." Demonstrating, she wound the limp strands of pasta on her fork, continental style. Timmie, trying to imitate her mother, spilled a blob, but undeterred, fingered the pile onto her fork and sucked the mess into her mouth. The corners of Wyatt's lips turned up as he watched his daughter while Lauren shook her head in exasperation.

"Yummy," Timmie grunted.

"Salt, please," Wyatt said.

"That's bad for you, you know."

He shrugged, laced his spaghetti and speared a big wad.

Frustrated, Lauren gave up on both her husband and daughter. "What happened at your lunch with Madison? You said she's decided to get involved with this project. How's that going to play out?"

As he scoured his mouth with a napkin, Wyatt said, "We're thinking it will be more than a project. I plan to start a company to design and build the pressurization."

"Build? Weren't you just going to design the thing?" Lauren tried to digest this new revelation, but her thoughts wouldn't jell. "I don't understand how you can start a manufacturing company. You have a job and a family. Where will you find time and money?"

"Madison and I will make a formal business plan to

figure out those things. It'll be part-time at first, evenings and weekends. I'll be more certain after we talk."

"Part-time *at first?* Are you suggesting this will become full-time someday? What would happen to your job?"

"It'll be at least a year before I'd quit. We'll have plenty of time to see how it goes before I bail out."

"You're just placating me." Lauren swallowed the last of her spaghetti, mopped Timmie's mouth with a napkin and watched as the child scurried to her room. Lauren felt duped. With a clatter, she stacked the dishes, took them to the kitchen and shoved them in the dishwasher.

Wyatt dropped into his easy chair and turned on the table lamp. A soft pool of light pushed the darkness into the corners, creating an island of warmth. Softly humming, he fingered through the day-old newspaper.

Lauren finished in the kitchen and joined him. Her stomach cramped with anxiety and she shook. "Come on, Honey, level with me. It's obvious we had a misunderstanding at soccer practice. I didn't realize pressurization would turn into an obsession. Start a business? I can't believe you're serious."

"Very serious. There's a big idea buzzing in my head, filling my mind so much it could explode. The designs need to be turned into hardware, something functional and tangible. That takes a manufacturing company. Madison wanted to farm out the whole project once we finished the preliminaries, but I can't have a bunch of strangers screwing around with it. If we can clear a few hurdles, I hope to start within a week. She wants to take a more cautious path, but I'm anxious to get going."

Irritated, Lauren crossed her arms. "Knowing you, you

won't clear the hurdles, you'll kick them down. You'll start this damn company no matter what. This pipedream could take tens of thousands, perhaps hundreds of thousands of dollars. Where, Wyatt? Where do we get the money?"

Wyatt's brows wrinkled. "Well, we have a little saved. Maybe Madison has some money. Maybe we could get a loan from the Small Business Administration—the SBA."

Her mind churning, Lauren asked, "And if you can't get a loan?"

Palms up, Wyatt spread his hands and shrugged. "Who knows? I guess we might consider taking equity out of the house. It's the only other asset we have."

"Hold on! This house is our only security! It was you who insisted we pay cash for this place using your inheritance. You were emphatic saying it would be a solid backstop. Think of Timmie, of our financial future."

"You're right. I'll find the money somewhere." He jabbed the chair arm with his finger. "I'll make it happen somehow."

Lauren could see Wyatt's anger percolating to the surface, but persisted. "You read the paper. You realize how bad the economy is. New federal regulations force the banks to hold huge reserves, so money is scarce. The SBA doesn't loan money; they just guarantee bank loans. It's still up to the banks."

"There's gotta be a way. Give me a little time to figure."

"I wish you'd put this company idea out of your mind. I know how you are about SAC, but you should ride it out a while longer."

Wyatt slumped in his chair, lines creasing his face.

"Didn't we resolve that at soccer? I thought you understood. SAC is not an option."

"I *do* understand. But now you're talking about our savings, a mortgage and business loans. You didn't mention those at Timmie's soccer game. Think of the time you'd squander. We don't see much of you as it is."

Wyatt rose and stood in front of Lauren, feet wide apart, and glared. "Squander is not a word I'd use," he growled. "This isn't a casual thing, Lauren. Sure, it will take a lot of time and require money, but I'll find them. The pressurization is a baby in my belly. It has been conceived and I will not abort it. I want the joy of seeing its first step. It's my destiny, and in time, my legacy. You have to understand. You *must* understand."

Lauren reeled. Wyatt's eloquence startled her. Usually stolid and unemotional, his outpouring revealed a consuming contagion. Wyatt stood like a dark rock, motionless. He held her gaze with fierce looking eyes.

Conflicting thoughts swirled in her head. *Timmie. Time. Money. And Madison.* Turmoil ravaged her as the threads of security and comfort of a predictable future unraveled. She tried to speak, but all she could do was stare at her husband.

Lauren felt a tug from Wyatt's glare, a giant magnet that burrowed into her consciousness. Abruptly, like fog dispersed by a breeze, her confusion evaporated and she decided. "I understand, but you need to understand something, too. You and Madison are ignorant of the business world. I'm an accountant, so I know finances. Should we do this, I'll take over the business side. Design is your thing; I'll write the checks. Deal?"

Wyatt's shoulders sagged and he reached down, took her hands and drew her to him. "Lauren," he whispered.

"Honey," Lauren began. "I... We..." Tears trickled from her eyes, sparkled among her freckles and collected at the corners of her mouth. She embraced him and kissed him; her tears dampened his cheek.

Wyatt yielded to her touch and slipped his arm around her.

"We'll figure this out, okay? Try to be patient with me," she said. "This is a huge step."

As the couple drifted toward the bedroom, the solitary table lamp cast their soft shadow on the wall. Lauren's tension dissolved into the grayness of the night and she sighed.

"Come," Wyatt said.

Chapter 12

Crud, *Wyatt was supposed to take out the trash last night.* Lauren yanked the straps of the plastic trash liner and heaved it to the floor. She always felt rushed this time of year. The Christmas decorations were finished the day before, but several gifts needed wrapping and she wanted to finish baking gingerbread cookies for the Scrabble party that afternoon.

All morning, Timmie had been underfoot, teasing Garfield and scattering dollhouse furniture on the floor, adding to Lauren's anxiety. She was grateful when Jennifer came over and the children went next door to play.

Better hurry, Lauren worried. *Mother is due anytime.* When the oven timer buzzed, she snatched a hot pad and removed a sheet of cookies. She wiped her brow with the back of her hand, set the cookies on the counter to cool, then returned to the trash bag and dragged it outside.

"Hi, Dear," called Liza as Lauren returned to the kitchen. "You didn't answer the doorbell, so I let myself in."

"Hi, Mother. I was taking out the trash. I'm glad you're here because I'm running way late. Will you start the coffee? I need to finish the cookies."

Lauren rolled out a sheet of dough and liberated another batch of little gooey Christmas trees with a cookie cutter while Liza filled a carafe with water.

"Just wondering, Dear," Liza began, "is Wyatt still flitting around with that Madison creature? Didn't you say they had lunch together?"

"Wyatt doesn't flit, Mother," laughed Lauren. "Besides, Madison isn't a creature, she's an engineer. Can you imagine two engineers flitting?"

"You know what I mean."

"Don't be silly. Now that you mention her, I have news. Wyatt and Madison are thinking of starting a company. It's not certain, but they've begun putting together a plan."

"What?" Liza gasped. "Is he crazy? He can't provide for you now. How can he consider starting a company? How can you let him?"

Lauren squared her shoulders. "Wyatt says he has a serious advance in technology and wants to design and manufacture it. He's very excited. We've talked it over and his enthusiasm is as contagious as a cold."

"You have to stop this, Lauren. A new company takes money, big money. I ought to know. When your father began his law firm, we were paupers for years. We had nothing! Wyatt has to think of you and Timmie. He should concentrate on finding a better-paying job, not jumping into a crazy scheme. And we both know he's not equipped to run a business."

"You did okay starting a business—we can too." Angry, Lauren slapped a small holly centerpiece and matching napkins on the card table while Liza set out coffee cups. Although livid, Lauren realized Liza was right about the money. There would be money problems, plus myriad predicaments as the business developed, but that did not sway her commitment to her husband. She saw herself arguing with Wyatt over money, time and risk—but as a peer and a helper—not an adversary.

But money wasn't the complete picture. While Liza

judged Wyatt solely on his income, Lauren loved her talented, impassioned man. Liza, she knew, always dug, poked and criticized Wyatt, and in a roundabout way, her. The thought squashed her spirits.

"Besides," Liza said, "You need to watch out for this Madison. From what you tell me, she's damned attractive. Men wander, Dear, and for all his shortcomings, Wyatt is handsome. Any woman would be tempted."

"Mother, you haven't even met her. She's very nice." Still seething, Lauren thought, *Okay, I'm a little worried.* "Sure, she's pretty, but that doesn't mean she's looking to shag my husband."

Liza rubbed her nose and said, "Madison is divorced, right?"

Lauren nodded.

"Well, don't be naive, Dear. Keep a close eye on them."

The doorbell rang and Lauren welcomed the interruption saying, "I'll get it."

Marge and Betty burst into the room chattering like sparrows on a wire. Liza shed her scowl and joined Lauren to welcome the newcomers. The four women strolled into the kitchen where they gathered warm cookies, hot coffee and a hefty Bloody Mary.

They settled into their chairs, drew tiles and began to play. Soon, the holiday mood flavored their chitchat with witticisms, chuckles and gracious compliments. Lauren decided to say nothing about the new company, let go of her wrath and embrace the bonhomie of her friends.

"Great word!"

"Love your centerpieces, Lauren. You're sooo creative."

"Damn, I have the 'Q' and no 'U'. Just my luck."

Laughter. The tiles clicked and the mellow afternoon drifted toward evening.

"Mommy, Mommy!" screeched Timmie as she burst through the front door. "Jennifer gave me one of her Barbie dolls!"

"Not so loud," Lauren admonished. "Did her mother say it was okay?"

Timmie nodded and held out the doll.

"Let me see," Liza said, beckoning. "Oh, she *is* pretty. Have you named her?"

Timmie puckered her lips and stared into the doll's face. "Jenny calls her Barbie, but that's yucky. Abby Cadabby is better. Abby's on Sesame Street. She's funny. She has blond hair just like my new doll. Abby Cadabby, that's what I'll call her."

"That's lovely, Dear," Liza said. "I'm sure the doll will love her new name."

Lauren noticed Marge, looking impatient, stirring the ice cubes in her glass with a celery stalk, while Betty, waiting to resume play, rearranged her tiles. "Run along, Timmie," Lauren said prodded by her friend's restlessness. "Why don't you introduce Abby to your other dolls?"

Liza frowned, ignoring the others. "Well, I guess you should run along, Little One. After we're done here, I'll come to your room and we can look at all your dolls, okay?"

Timmie hugged her new possession, smiled at her grandmother and skipped down the hall.

The Scrabble party was breaking up when Wyatt strode through the door. He nodded to the ladies, pecked Lauren on the cheek and went to his office. The door clicked shut, and a faint "bong" announced that Wyatt had turned on his computer.

Liza put her hands on her hips, thrust out her jaw and stared at the closed door. "I don't suppose he'd take a moment to say hello to his mother-in-law. What brings him home from work this early?"

"He isn't spending as much time at SAC as he used to," Lauren explained. "He used to work on Scrabble Saturdays, but today he went with Madison to Starbucks to draft their business plan."

"Humph," breathed Liza.

While Lauren and Liza engaged in their terse exchange, Marge and Betty busied themselves with their handbags, getting ready to leave. With a hurried nod, they thanked their hostess and left.

Lauren, waving at her friends from the front porch, felt her Christmas cheer evaporate.

Without stopping to help clean up, Liza went back to Timmie's room.

Lauren, tiptoeing as she cleared dishes, eavesdropped on her mother and daughter, catching snippets of the conversation coming through the open door.

"Hi, Grandma."

"Your hair is so pretty, just like your mommy's when she was five. I wish I could take you home with me."

"Yes, yes," Timmie giggled. "Can I swim in the pool?"

"No, Darling, it's much too cold. You can come over this summer. You deserve a swimming pool."

"Shit!" The sailor-like expletive exploded through Wyatt's door and boomed down the hall.

There was a long moment of silence and Lauren cocked her head, listening.

"Yes, Little One," Liza said. "You deserve better."

Chapter 13

It was Wyatt's thirty-third birthday and Lauren was certain he'd forgotten it; he always did. She'd secretly taken the day off to prepare for a surprise party, and to fool him, dressed in her normal work clothes.

He'd rushed around, getting ready as usual. Wyatt grabbed his jacket and briefcase, reminding her that Madison was coming over that night to help with the business plan. He stepped into the pre-dawn chill, waved to Lauren and drove away.

Lauren allowed herself a satisfied smirk knowing Wyatt had fallen for her ruse. She had searched for a clever way to surprise Wyatt, but there was a problem. He and Madison worked every night and weekends on the new company. With no alternative, Lauren had to scheme with Madison to arrange a phony work session at the house. So a week ago she called, and the two agreed to con Wyatt. Lauren hoped for a nice, easy-going social gathering to soften the incessant grind of the business.

Lauren pulled a box of cake-mix from the pantry and poured its contents into a mixing bowl. Besides baking, she wanted to decorate the dining table and hang decorations from the overhead light. That meant a trip to the party store after dropping Timmie off at school. She did a little dance move, her hands waving above her head. It promised to be a fun night.

With the cake in the oven, she wrested Timmie from bed to get ready. The child whined while Lauren tugged on her daughter's socks and helped with her shoes. "You're old enough to do this yourself," she scolded.

Once dressed, however, Timmie dashed into the breakfast nook and devoured Froot Loops and a glass of milk while Lauren jabbed the cake with a toothpick. Finding it done, she slipped it from the oven to cool. Together, they lugged a lunch box, heavy jacket and a backpack to the car and drove to school.

Lauren, feeling smug with her clandestine plot, went shopping for rolls of crepe paper, balloons and a package of beef jerky—Wyatt's favorite.

Late that afternoon the sun was low, and the temperature had plummeted. In the front yard, fronds of the Palmetto palm rustled in the cold wind as Madison trudged up the walk, grasping her coat collar around her throat.

Lauren, hearing the doorbell, hurried to the door and greeted her fellow conspirator. "Come in, come in. Thanks for helping."

Madison handed Lauren a bottle of champagne and said, "Anything for Wyatt." She slipped out of her coat and shook her head. "I realize Wyatt's a serious man, so it's hard to understand how he forgets his own birthday."

While juggling the champagne and Madison's wrap, Lauren laughed, "He doesn't pay attention to such things. I suppose it's because his birthday falls in the middle of the holidays. Everything gets jumbled together: Thanksgiving, Christmas and New Year's. It's crazy."

"I still don't buy it. Wyatt doesn't forget calculus, Euler's formula or the tensile properties of steel. Nothing wrong with his memory." Madison looked around the room. Half a dozen helium balloons with "Happy Birthday" printed on their flanks tugged on their strings. Bright streamers cascaded from the ceiling light and the tablecloth was strewn with hard candies. A white-frosted cake, glistening with sprinkles, stood proud in the center of the table. "This is beautiful, Lauren, but how did you hang the crepe paper from the ceiling light?"

"Teetering on a chair. I worried that Wyatt would find me on the floor with a broken neck." Lauren glanced at her watch. "He's picking up Timmie at after-school care—due any moment. I didn't tell my daughter we were having a party because she can't keep a secret."

It was nearly dark when Wyatt pulled into the drive. They heard him coming up the walk chatting with Timmie. As he opened the door, Lauren and Madison jumped out shouting, "Happy birthday!"

Startled, Timmie shrieked and Wyatt's face was smeared with a befuddled look. "What's going on?"

"Welcome to your birthday party, Hon," Lauren giggled, giving him a big hug. "It's time for serious relaxation; you've earned it."

Wyatt grinned and looked at his feet. "Guess I forgot," he muttered.

"So what's new?" Lauren laughed. "We'll have champagne, a nice dinner and pleasant conversation." Turning to Timmie, she said, "We're having ham. That's your favorite, right?"

Timmie nodded. "Daddy's birthday? Will he get presents?"

"Of course, Dear," said Lauren. "Go put your school things away, okay?"

"Is Grandma coming?"

"No, she's going to a meeting at the country club tonight," explained Lauren.

Timmie shrugged and dragged her backpack to her room.

Lauren went to the kitchen, wrestled with the champagne cork and thought: *Why can't Mom give up one little committee meeting for Wyatt's birthday?* With a towel, she wiped the foam from the side of the bottle, gathered the glasses and returned to the living room.

There, Madison brushed back a strand of hair that had fallen across her eye and said, "Congratulations, Wyatt. You've survived another year. Not to rain on your parade, but I've uncovered a serious algorithm problem. We'd better do some work as well as celebrate."

"Okay by me; I'm lousy at birthdays," Wyatt smiled.

Madison tilted her head toward Lauren. "I hope you don't mind."

Anger flashed in Lauren's mind. "I hoped we'd forego work tonight," she grumbled, filling three chilled flutes. "It's a party, not a labor camp." They settled in the living room to talk. Miffed, Lauren sat with her arms crossed, saying little.

An hour later, her wrath somewhat abated, Lauren served dinner. Wyatt ate with enthusiasm while Madison nibbled at her sparsely covered plate. Even Timmie jabbered between huge mouthfuls of ham.

"The glaze on the ham is delicious, Lauren," Madison said. "It's perfect."

"Would you like the recipe?"

"No. Don't bother. It's rare day when I cook, you know."

Lauren smiled. "I'm jealous."

"Well, two of us are *thrilled* you cook," Wyatt said. "Right, Little One?"

Unable to speak, her cheeks bulging like a chipmunk, Timmie nodded.

Lauren felt herself blush; delighted that Wyatt was obviously enjoying himself.

The meal over, Wyatt declined a second glass of champagne and graciously unwrapped a birthday wallet from Lauren. "Is that all?" complained Timmie.

"No, Little One," Lauren said, handing a gift sack to Wyatt. "Here's the piéce de résistance."

Wyatt looked self-conscious as he fished through the tissue. "Wow! Jerky. My favorite brand."

Madison reached for her purse and pulled out an envelope. "This is for you, Wyatt. Happy birthday."

He slipped the card from the envelope and mouthed the inscription.

When he showed it to Lauren, she saw it was signed, "Yours, Madison," in purple ink. A big, scrawling signature. A spark of irritation jabbed her—the card was far too intimate.

"Now that dinner is over, let's do some work, Wyatt," said Madison. "Back to your alleged office?"

Timmie wrinkled her nose in apparent disappointment and fled.

Lauren resented Madison's pushy suggestion—that wasn't their agreement. With business set aside, it had been a pleasant gathering so far. She was about to intervene, but Wyatt's eagerness made her realize that pressurization had captured the evening. Lauren, fearing she'd be excluded, suggested, "I want to listen in, so why don't you work on the coffee table? Three people will never fit in Wyatt's office."

"Good idea," Wyatt said. "I'll get my laptop and papers."

Lauren went to the kitchen and poured three cups of coffee.

When Wyatt returned, Madison said, "Look, we've already spent dozens of hours on the business plan. We'd better get to that design oversight I mentioned."

"Why not?" Wyatt asked.

"I have a better idea," Lauren said. "Let's pick a company name––that'll be more fun. How about 'Wyatt's Magic Factory?'"

"No way," Wyatt said, grinning. He thought a moment. "A good name should relate to airplanes; include the word 'systems.'"

A hint of satisfaction nuzzled Lauren. She'd pre-empted Madison and her funk evaporated.

They threw out many suggestions, saying them aloud to hear how they sat on the tongue. All were discarded after an Internet search showed other firms had taken the name. At last, one stuck: Optimal Aviation Systems.

"Even the initials, OAS, sound good," Lauren said. "Another thing, the company where I work is a Limited Liability Company, which shields personal assets. I think we should set Optimal up as an LLC."

The two engineers, looking confused, nodded.

"We'll have to create a formal operating agreement," Lauren went on. "Check the State default rules for conflict and define the financial structure. It gets very involved."

Wyatt moaned, "I need simple, Darling, not involved."

"I'll take care of everything," reassured Lauren. "Remember? I'll handle the business part, okay?"

"Crazy legal paperwork," Wyatt complained. "Help yourself, my Love. Madison and I are techies, not accountants."

"That leaves the tough part: money," Lauren said. "We should decide how much capital we need and how to get it."

"The first few months will be mostly design work," Madison said. "That takes time, not money. According to our schedule, it will be six months before we order prototype hardware. Any idea what it will cost, Wyatt?"

Wyatt tapped the keys on his computer and found the list he sought. "Parts are expensive. There are four valves, two checks, a logic module and a heat exchanger. Each valve will have forty to fifty machined parts. The others will be simpler. That's about two hundred pieces averaging three hundred dollars each, so we're looking at sixty thousand dollars. A very rough number."

Lauren coughed. Wide-eyed, she exclaimed, "Good Lord, Honey, that's huge!"

"Prototype circuit boards will add another fifteen thousand dollars," said Madison. "Software certification will run into several thousand more. So initially, we'll need a total of around eighty thousand."

"Then there's production tooling," Wyatt added. "I'd guess it could set us back around five hundred thousand, but that comes much later."

Lauren gasped and stared at Wyatt and then Madison. She wondered if they realized the figures were outrageous—much more than she'd been led to believe. She wrestled with her thoughts. *What is he thinking? All these years we've tucked away a bit here, a snit there, putting together a prudent nest egg. Timmie's college, maybe a Caribbean cruise someday. He's risking everything we've worked for.*

Wyatt continued, "Also, in a year we'll need assembly space."

"I agree," Madison nodded.

"Are you both crazy?" Lauren exclaimed. "Where can we get that kind of money?"

Wyatt sat back in his chair and crossed his arms. "I've been thinking. Between our savings account and my 401k, we can turn up with forty or fifty thousand, but that's it. What about you, Madison?"

"Not much savings, but my 401k might match yours. Too bad I rent. I wish had a house with equity; take out a mortgage…"

Wyatt rubbed his forehead. "No matter. Sounds like we have enough money to start full-scale development and do a little testing, but we'll have to keep our jobs for a while. Lauren, what do you think?"

"You're not going to mortgage our house like Madison mentioned, are you?"

"No. Our savings and 401k's alone will keep us running at first," assured Wyatt.

Lauren's frown eased. She was used to dealing with much larger sums at work and was relieved knowing that funding for the next six months was in hand. She shrugged. "It could be worse, I guess. What happens when the money runs out?"

Wyatt leaned forward, elbows on his knees. "By then we'll have a working prototype and patent protection––something to chum potential customers."

"I think we should talk to our bank about a line of credit to make sure we have money to build the prototypes," Lauren suggested.

"Good idea," Wyatt said. "Once we line up clients, we'd go to the bank for a larger business loan, maybe through the SBA."

"Right," Madison said. "King Aviation could become our first customer."

"There's also AirEnvironment," Wyatt said, tapping the business plan folder.

"Say, I'm tight with Ed Morales at AirEnvironment," Madison exclaimed. "I've done a lot of business with him and their buyer, Nick Nolan. I could connect with them––give them a pitch."

"Sounds good," Wyatt said.

Lauren cradled her chin in her hand as resignation engulfed her. "Well, I guess we go with this. I'll get online and dig up the standard business forms. We'll iron out the details then. I'll check into filing as an LLC and opening a bank account in OAS's name. We'll need a tax I.D. number from the IRS, too. You two focus on design. I'll deal with paperwork."

Wyatt laughed. "It seems, Madison, that we just elected the president of our company."

"President Lauren is fine with me."

Lauren grinned, feeling smug.

"It's late, Wyatt," Madison said, looking at her watch. "Let's dig into my software problem tomorrow night."

"First, a toast to Optimal Aviation Systems," Wyatt said, raising his coffee cup. "May it prosper and grow." Solemnly, Lauren and Madison joined him.

"To the future," Madison said.

"To the future," chorused Wyatt and Lauren.

Lauren tried to swallow a sip of coffee, but it wouldn't go down. *Yes. To the future—not just ours, but Timmie's too. I hope we haven't created a catastrophe.*

Chapter 14

It was an hour and a half past normal quitting time and Wyatt was concerned that Lauren would worry where he was. That afternoon, Brian had fussed over the upcoming Critical Design Review for the new Gulfstream jet and demanded to go over all preparations. Wyatt dropped everything, completed the plan and compiled the drawings, thus mollifying his boss.

As he drove home, Wyatt recognized that Optimal interfered with his work at SAC. A sense of guilt weighed on his mind, but he pushed it away, remembering it was Brian who'd rejected the pressurization.

When he got home, Lauren agreed to give up their Sunset Ritual to prepare for tomorrow's meeting at the bank. After a quick meal, Wyatt and Lauren cleared the table.

"It's Timmie's bedtime, Honey," Lauren said. "I'll tuck her in while you gather up the paperwork, okay?"

He went to his office, collected a jumble of documents and sorted them into neat piles on the dining table. As Wyatt waited for Lauren, he thumbed through each stack, taking a mental inventory. *This is insane. Reports, forms, applications. Good science strangled by paper.*

Sounds of Timmie's evening ablutions and Lauren's firm guidance emanated from the back room. A sudden silence indicated that mother and daughter had come to terms. Lauren looked disheveled when she joined Wyatt. "Well, she's down. Do you have everything?"

Wyatt waved his hand over the piles of paper. "I think

so. You're the accountant, suppose you explain why the bank needs our life history."

"What if you lent *your* money to a stranger? Wouldn't you want to be sure you'd get paid?"

"We've been doing business with them for five or six years, we're hardly strangers."

"This is different," Lauren reminded him with a stern look. "We're asking for a hundred thousand dollar line of credit."

With a grin, Wyatt reached out and squeezed his wife's hand. "I love you when you put on your accountant face."

She grinned and said, "Stop that, Honey. Let's finish this. It's getting late."

Wyatt stood, took both of Lauren's hands and leered. "I'd rather forget this bank madness. What do you say?"

"Wyatt!"

With a forlorn shrug, he dropped her hands and picked up Optimal's business plan. "I added detailed schedules, capital requirements and even a list of equipment we'll need. The LLC is the tough one," Wyatt said, fingering another pile. He shook his head. "I suppose we should hire a lawyer help sort this out, but we can't afford the huge fees."

"Stop grumbling, Honey; we need to finish this." Lauren fished out several sheets of paper. "These résumés will show we have the training and experience to start a new company. The bank should be impressed."

"Is that everything?" asked Wyatt.

Lauren's eyes swept the tabletop. "No, there's more. Here's the paperwork for the eighty-five thousand dollars I deposited into our new business account last week.

Lee Wong was the banker who helped me. He seemed very capable and will be a big help. You meet with him tomorrow?"

"Yup. I have an appointment over my lunch hour. I'll explain our plans and lay the groundwork for a loan."

"Well, that's that. I wish I could go with you, but I'm in the middle of month-end at work. Call me if you hit a snag." Lauren gathered the papers and put them in a folder. "Our Sunset Ritual tomorrow should be interesting."

"You bet. Now that business is taken care of, perhaps we can move on to other things?" Wyatt winked as he slipped his arm around her waist.

Lauren giggled and pecked his cheek. "Oh, Wyatt. You can be a pest."

Wyatt pushed through the security doors of the bank and looked at his watch. *Twelve-ten. Exactly.* He grunted with satisfaction and walked across the foyer toward the executive desks, his freshly polished shoes glistening. Workers were removing ornaments from a Christmas tree and the air was pungent from disturbed pine needles. He brushed past the seasonal bustle and searched for Lee Wong. Because it was lunchtime, only one of the four desks was occupied.

He strode over, set his briefcase on the floor and extended his hand. "Mr. Wong? Wyatt Morgan."

The banker stood, and using both hands, gave Wyatt a firm shake. Wong was fastidiously dressed in a tailored dark suit and his French cuffs were bound by small, conservative links. "Very pleased to meet you, Mr. Morgan. I've had the pleasure of helping your wife. Exceptional lady." He gestured to a chair saying, "Please have a seat."

"Thanks. Are you ready for the New Year?" Wyatt asked.

"Yes," Wong said, rubbing his small parchment-colored hands together "The first week after the holidays is always refreshing. It's invigorating to start the year with a clean slate."

Wyatt chuckled. "Me too. I always reflect on the past year and hatch new ideas for the coming one. Last year I decided to review my skills with differential equations. Came in handy." Wyatt leaned forward. "But this year will be *really* exciting. As you know, I'm launching a new company. Gonna be a blast."

Wong nodded. "Your wife briefed me on Optimal Aviation Systems. Catchy name." He pulled an elegant looking fountain pen from his suit pocket and laid it on his tidy mahogany desk. "Now then, how can I help?"

"Our new checking account should cover our needs for a few months, so I want to go over our financial needs for the longer term." Wyatt flopped his briefcase on the floor, opened it and removed the business plan.

Wong tilted his head to one side. "What do you have in mind, Mr. Morgan?"

"Please, just call me Wyatt."

"Fine. And I'm Lee."

Wyatt turned to the funding section tab. "The first year will be mostly design, but in nine or ten months we'll need specialized test equipment, software and prototype hardware. By year-end we'll rent office space. Altogether, I expect we'll need another hundred thousand dollars for the first year. Further out, I'm looking at five hundred thousand for production tooling."

Lee frowned. "That's considerable money."

"I know. Once Optimal develops a viable system, I hope the bank could consider a larger loan."

"You mentioned a system, but I'm not clear what Optimal does. Can you explain?" asked Lee.

Wyatt smiled as he spread several engineering drawings and a packet of detailed calculations in front of the banker. He was explaining the FAA certification process when Lee held up his hand saying, "Excuse me. This is far too technical." With a bewildered look, the banker nudged his fountain pen. "Let's go back to the money. To set up a line of credit, the bank requires a cash-flow analysis showing projected earnings. Guarantees from your customers would help."

"We don't expect to sign any customers for at least a year, although two firms have expressed an interest."

Lee pushed his pen an inch to one side. "Do you have any assets for collateral? A house, perhaps?"

"I have a house, free and clear. But I don't want to mortgage it. It's a big issue with my wife."

"I understand." The banker studied the pen and prodded it another half inch. "Without actual purchase orders from customers, collateral or concrete evidence of income, lending becomes very difficult."

Wyatt twisted in his chair and stared at Lee's pen. He hadn't anticipated this problem. *Was I clear about the workings of the pressurization? Perhaps the jargon confused him.* Looking up, Wyatt said, "Lee, I don't understand. This thing has super potential, and the risk is small. What proof do you need?"

"Government regulators have made the banking environment very tight," said Lee with a shrug. "To proceed, we need a comprehensive business plan, notarized contracts between you and your partners and background checks on the principals. Then there's a list of major suppliers and a tabulation of assets and liabilities. You'll be filing as an LLC, so we'd need Articles of Organization, too."

"Here's what I have." Wyatt handed Lee several folders. "But I'm not sure it meets all the requirements."

Lee accepted the materials saying, "I'll look these over, but to be honest, the best option is to pursue a government-backed loan. Washington has established a new SBA division aimed solely at stimulating the economy by funding new companies. However, they have special qualifiers."

"Such as?"

"Are any of your principals a minority?"

"My partner is female."

"The new SBA regulations don't consider that significant unless she's disadvantaged. Does she have any physical handicaps?"

Wyatt shook his head. "Actually, she's a knock-out."

Lee smiled. "How many people do you plan to hire this coming year? The government endorses firms which lower the unemployment rate."

"Ha! There's just three of us with no plans to employ anyone else."

Lee frowned. "Do you expect to locate in a disadvantaged neighborhood: a HUBZone?"

"What's a HUBZone? No matter, we'll work from my

home for now. I hadn't even thought about disadvantaged areas."

"A major emphasis of the government is to promote green energy. Does Optimal's system incorporate or enhance solar, wind or bio-energy in any way?"

"It keeps people alive at high altitudes. Does that count?"

"Afraid not," sighed Lee. "The SBA sets aside a large percentage of their awards for new firms that meet these criterion, not exactly Optimal's profile."

"Sounds like social engineering," Wyatt grumbled.

Lee scowled. "Maybe friends or family could buy in, stockholders, so to speak. Otherwise, you might reconsider using your house as equity."

Defeated, Wyatt slumped in his chair. "Well, we have six months to find more money. The SBA sounds like the best bet."

Lee nodded and took a crisp new folder from his desk drawer. He slipped Wyatt's paperwork inside and said, "I'll review your material and contact the SBA. Because of the struggling economy and terrible unemployment, they're under intense political pressure to fund new firms, so we have a chance. Here is our Loan Request Form. Fill it out and fax it back. I'll get back to you within a week."

Resigned, Wyatt took the paperwork. He'd wanted to discuss a five hundred thousand dollar loan for production tooling, but knew it was useless. He needed to prove to Wong that pressurization could earn millions. *I'll get with Lauren—figure a way to convince the bank that Optimal will be a moneymaker.* "Fine," he mumbled.

Lee stood. "Funding may take months. I'll do

everything possible to help. Our bank is always interested in building long-term relationships."

"Thanks, Lee. Call me if you make any headway."

With a nearly imperceptible bow, Lee took Wyatt's hand with both of his. "Don't be discouraged. We'll find a way."

As he drove back to SAC, Wyatt tried to shake off his doldrums. The session at the bank had been ruinous, and he awakened to the fact that his engineering skills were useless in the business world. Worse, he saw no course of action. Wyatt thought of Lauren and Timmie, sensing a profound responsibility for his family, but sagged under the realization he could never match the affluence of his wife's childhood. A melancholy mood settled over him and he rubbed his temples, trying to push his despair away.

Stop this, he thought. *My part is design. Lauren will know what to do.*

Chapter 15

It was an early January morning when Wyatt shouldered his way through the doors of SAC an hour before regular starting time. He pocketed the key, flipped on the lights and settled at his desk. He had only two hours before the Critical Design Review on the Gulfstream flap hinge. Wyatt expected a long, rigorous session.

Uncharacteristically, he was unsure of his preparations. In service, the hinge would experience thousands of cycles, and like people, could fatigue and weaken over time. Brian turned down his requisition for the latest database on properties of aluminum, so Wyatt feared his predicted fatigue limits were inaccurate. Also, he usually checked every drawing for correctness, but he'd gotten tangled up for hours with DCMA again. Out of time, Wyatt delegated the drawing review to a junior engineer.

Wyatt labored in the harsh fluorescent lights and scowled, drawing creases across his forehead. The silence was punctuated by clicking computer keys and the scratch of his pencil. Hunched over his keyboard, Wyatt didn't notice when one, two and then three other employees appeared and rustled at their desks. "Morning," offered one. Wyatt waved him off and continued working.

"They'll be here in fifteen minutes," Brian announced, poking his head into Wyatt's office.

Startled, Wyatt looked at his watch in disbelief. "Right. I'll get my stuff and meet you in the conference room."

"All right," said Brian, trying to tame his unruly

shirttail. "This is an important meeting. I should have insisted on that dress rehearsal yesterday."

"Yeah, but I wasn't ready. Came in early to clean up a few things."

Brian glowered. "It had better go okay. Gulfstream is sending Paul Gerber and Don Moody. They're tough cookies who put us through our paces when we did the CDR on the access door last year."

Wyatt remembered. They'd been demanding, but it went well. *However, I was prepared––today is iffy.*

Wyatt hurried downstairs to the conference room and plugged the projector into his laptop. He took a deep breath and looked around the room. The coffee urn was steaming; a platter of donuts filled the air with their sweet aroma and an iced carafe of water sweated at center table.

Brian rushed in with copies of the agenda. "They're in the lobby. Bring them in, will you?"

Wyatt tried to look relaxed as he greeted the two engineers. "Hi, Paul, Don. Been a while."

"It has, it has," Paul said. "A year, right? Access door, right? You guys came out clean as I remember."

"Yup," Wyatt said. "Don, how's things?"

"Fine." Don looked at Paul as if seeking instructions.

Paul patted his briefcase and said, "Lots of stuff in here––much more involved than that access door. Boy, I could use a cup of coffee. Have any?"

Wyatt beckoned and led the way.

While Wyatt poured coffee, Brian renewed acquaintances and directed his guests to their chairs.

"Okay, let's get going," said Brian. "Wyatt has a PowerPoint summary of the design status. It's okay to ask questions as we go." Brian dimmed the lights and Wyatt began the slide show.

In the semi-darkness, Wyatt fell into a smooth rhythm, stressing SAC's experience with similar products, the fundamental aspects of the design and the project schedule. The Gulfstream engineers squinted in the flickering light and stroked comments into their laptops. Wyatt fielded two or three questions and forty-five minutes later, he turned on the lights saying, "Well, gents, that's it. Any comments?"

"A few," Paul said. "About the schedule. The hinge is a safety of flight item so the FAA will look hard at it, right? Did you allow extra time?"

Brian and Wyatt explained how the schedule had been prepared and Paul nodded.

The discussion continued, clarifying the loci of the hinge pins, inspection criteria and load testing procedures.

It's going well, thought Wyatt, crossing his legs. Paul and Don looked pleased as they checked off items in their notes. Brian said little and munched a second donut, licking his fingers.

Paul leaned over and murmured to Don, who pointed to a copy of a slide in Wyatt's presentation. Paul cocked his head and said, "Let's take a look at the stress analysis. The levels seem high, right? Walk us through your computations, will you Wyatt?"

Wyatt winced. He handed a packet of calculations to Paul. "Here are the numbers." His hand trembled and Wyatt hoped Paul didn't notice.

Paul ran his finger down a page and then shook his head. "You can't exceed the fatigue limits, Wyatt. Your software should have flagged that. Are you using the current FAA database?"

Wyatt swallowed before replying, "We used the same figures as always. I didn't have a chance to dig into the new numbers."

Paul frowned. "Well, you'll need to redo the analysis."

Brian stared at Wyatt. "He'll get right on it. It can't be a big deal, right Wyatt?" Spittle gathered at the corners of Brian's mouth and he wiped his lips with a napkin. "It's just a simple oversight," he mumbled, fidgeting in his chair.

Humiliated, Wyatt pretended to busy himself with his papers. It wasn't an oversight as Brian claimed. Wyatt knew the numbers were hokey before presenting them. He'd tried to crunch the numbers manually, but ran out of time. He grimaced, knowing the shoddy work was not up to his standards.

"Okay, okay." Paul said. "You'll just have to add a little meat to the hinge and re-run the analysis. But watch the weight, right? The whole airplane project is over-weight."

Wyatt and Brian nodded like bobble-head dolls.

"Let's keep moving. There are still detail drawings to go over," Paul said. "Don has already checked those you emailed last week. We have a few thoughts."

Time crept as they examined the drawings one by one. "Why did you pick 6061-T6 aluminum? Is this pin heat-treated? I'd prefer electroless-nickel plating on this part. Won't this sharp bend induce stress risers?" Wyatt felt harried, although his answers were articulate.

Brian ordered pizza and soda and they worked through lunch and the questions streamed between the pepperoni and Coke without pause.

Paul went on, "You need a concentricity call-out here, right? Don, do you think this dimension is okay? Wyatt, can you explain..."

It was dark when the Gulfstream engineers collected their papers and laptops. On his way out, Paul turned. "You fumbled this one, Wyatt. A screwed-up stress analysis and several drawing errors. You've lots more work, so make it fast or you'll fall behind schedule. Our purchasing people are pushing for a go-ahead by the end of next week. If you can't clean this up, they'll place the order with your competitor."

Brian, lurking over Wyatt's shoulder, blurted, "Right away. Wyatt will jump on it. We'll have the revisions in a day or two."

Wyatt rubbed the back of his neck, trying to subdue his tension. Although it was his fault for the errors, he resented Brian for making promises he, Wyatt, would have to keep. "Yup," was all he said as Paul and Don left.

"Crap, Wyatt," stormed Brian. "That was one hell of a mess. They nailed your butt on the stress analysis. We looked like morons."

"Come, on, Brian. I asked for that software update months ago, but you shot me down."

"Cost a fortune! You could have done it by hand."

"It's too complex," retorted Wyatt. "It'd take days to calculate. Besides, Leechmann hammered me for hours last week screaming that I filed our data sheets wrong. I just ran out of time."

"Well no wonder! I see you sneaking out at five o'clock every night. You should spend extra hours on such an important project. Gulfstream already has a vendor for the hinge; we're second source and could lose the contract this fast," Brian yelled, snapping his fingers.

He's right. Before Optimal I'd work whatever hours were needed. Wyatt shrugged, palms up. "I'll take care of everything. Give me a day or so."

Wyatt collected his materials and started toward his office with a knot in his stomach. *If I keep going this way, I'm gonna get fired.*

As Wyatt passed the lunchroom, he saw Bernie, looking red-eyed and haggard, holding a mug. Exhausted from his daylong meeting, Wyatt smiled and joined his friend. "I see you're working late."

"Yeah," said Bernie, caressing his bald spot. "Sixty hours a week. More, sometimes. We're way behind on the Cessna job; the material for the parts was late. I put on a second shift in the machine shop to catch up. It's a bitch trying to cover two shifts."

"Hear you," Wyatt said.

Bernie waved his bony hand at the coffee pot. "Fresh. I just made it. Help yourself."

Wyatt found a clean cup, filled it with coffee and sat. He took a sip and flinched. "Dang! It's hot!"

"Surprised? It's coffee, isn't it?"

Wyatt chuckled. "A scalded lip is a fitting end to my day. The Gulfstream boys tore me apart. I'd tried doing stress analysis by hand, but I was a sailor rowing a destroyer. Never finished. That, along with a few hitches on the drawings, made for an embarrassing day." Wyatt slumped, cradling his cup in both hands.

"Strange," commented Bernie. "Your drawings are

usually spot on. What's with you? Distracted? Got a honey on the side?"

"No way. I can't handle what I have at home." An image of Lauren flashed through Wyatt's mind and he grinned. "I just can't find enough time."

"I noticed your work hours took a dip awhile back. We used to get together late at night—fixing problems. Not anymore. Now, your office goes dark at five. What's changed?"

"I hoped it wasn't so obvious. Yeah, I've cut back. I'll admit I have something going outside SAC, but it's not a woman." *Not entirely true*, he said to himself, thinking of Madison. "You remember our talk about my frustrations, copy-cat engineering and Brian's rejection of fresh ideas?"

Bernie nodded.

"Well, I'm doing a little outside engineering. Sure, I'm not doing overtime like before, but, as the Navy says, it's general quarters—battle stations."

Bernie rubbed his eyes with his knuckles and said, "Go for it, Wyatt. You have dreams; a young guy has to reach for his dreams." His thin smile drew wrinkles across his face. "Do me a favor, will you? Stop by first thing every morning and help with whatever problems that popped up the night before. Sometimes I get stuck and need your advice. Okay?"

"Deal." Wyatt felt a surge of affection for Bernie. He was connected to the old guy, bound by their devotion to manufacturing and airplanes. He stood, reached across the table and shook Bernie's hand. "Yes sir. It's a deal."

Chapter 16

The weak winter sun had set and darkness blanketed the kitchen window as Lauren uncorked a bottle of Zinfandel and cut thin slivers of provolone cheese. She set the wine and cheese with two wine glasses on the table between their recliners. When she heard Wyatt's car pull into the driveway, she smiled, thankful that he'd called saying he'd be home early.

"Hi, Darling," Wyatt called as he hurried through the door. He dropped his heavy briefcase and peeled off his jacket. "Dang," he shivered. "It's cold out."

Lauren took his coat and hung it in the entry closet. Turning, she gave her husband a warm hug and kissed him. "The sunset's gone, but our wine is ready," she said pointing to the chairs. "Zin and provolone are the evening's starters."

Wyatt pecked her cheek and shrugged. "I really shouldn't. Madison called Ed Morales at AirEnvironment and he's interested in our stuff. But there's a design problem on the altitude limiter and Ed wants an update ASAP, so I want to tackle it tonight. Mind?"

The words extinguished Lauren's smile, and she recoiled as if slapped. She glowered at the wine glasses, and then turned her stare at Wyatt, speechless.

Just then, Timmie hurtled into the room in noisy pursuit of Garfield. Lauren thought of scolding her daughter but instead, snatched the wine and stalked to the kitchen. "I'll start dinner," she hissed over her shoulder.

With a pat on Timmie's head, Wyatt grabbed his briefcase and marched to his office.

A cabinet door banged, silverware clattered and a saucepan clanged on the stovetop. Lauren hurled three potatoes into the sink and peeled them like an Apache scalping a wayward settler. She yanked a leftover roast from the refrigerator, plopped it on a plate and thrust it into the microwave. The kitchen maelstrom continued for thirty minutes while Wyatt worked in the back room.

"Call your father to dinner Timmie," commanded Lauren.

Obediently, the child strolled down the hall to her father's office. When she returned to the kitchen, she said, "Daddy says he'll be here in a minute."

"In a minute? Well then, if his dinner is cold, it's cold." Lauren filled the serving bowls and put them on the table.

After a few minutes, Wyatt came and sat. He sliced a piece of roast and grumbled, "The fool altitude limiter is driving me crazy. There's no room for the pressure sensor."

Lauren said nothing.

Playfully, Timmie made a tall pile of mashed potatoes and then smashed it flat with her fork.

"Timshel," growled Lauren, "Don't play with your food."

The child made one last rebellious splat and flashed a defiant look at her mother. She finished her meal, slid off the chair and spotted Garfield playing with the shoelaces of her soccer shoes. With a coy smirk, she sauntered next to him and lunged, snaring the cat. With a proud looking tilt of her chin, Timmie hauled the wide-eyed feline off to her bedroom.

Wyatt helped clear the table and fill the dishwasher. Lauren rubbed her tired eyes, draped a dishtowel over the oven handle, and collapsed in her chair.

"You look beat," Wyatt said. "How about that glass of wine? I'm burned out on the limiter problem and need to get away for a while."

Surprised, she said, "Thanks. It's been a long day."

Wyatt rattled around in the kitchen and reappeared with two glasses. He sat, gestured a silent toast and sipped. Lauren raised her glass and drained off a big gulp.

"You know," Wyatt said, "The altitude limiter is tough. I'll get it though. It's the business part that worries me. I thought common sense would float the ship, but the fiasco at the bank proved me wrong." He swirled the wine in his glass and sipped. "Wong called today and he scheduled a meeting for us with the SBA. That'll be fun."

Lauren nodded, "Hmmm."

"You've been working on the LLC application. How is it going?" Wyatt asked.

"So much for our tardy Sunset Ritual," she whispered.

"What?" Wyatt asked.

"Nothing." Despondent, Lauren emptied her glass and held it out to Wyatt. "Another," she directed. When he returned with her filled glass, she said, "There's no time. I worked on the Articles of Organization, wrote checks to the California Secretary of State and the Franchise Tax Board. That's a thousand dollars right there." Overwhelmed, she sank in her chair and closed her eyes. "I'm buried in legal paperwork. I want to throw up my hands."

Wyatt pursed his lips. "Well, you have to stay with it.

I'm relying on you to finish it up. Madison and I don't have time."

Trembling, Lauren snarled, "When, Wyatt? When do *I* have time?" Her voice soared. "I work fulltime, take care of Timmie, cook, clean house and now, wrestle with Optimal. You're either at SAC or holed up with Madison. If that isn't enough, Timmie is turning into a pill and needs a major dose of attention." Lauren shuddered. "I'm tired, very tired—I don't know if I can hang on. I hoped we could start the New Year on a better foot." Lauren wiped a tear and sniffled.

The chords of Wyatt's neck bulged. "Dang it, Lauren, we've been through all this. We knew pressurization would hog our time. You have to hang in there."

Her body tensed. "You're crazy," she spat. "Timmie and I are not sacrificial lambs to be slaughtered on your altar! While you and Madison are in your fanciful world, I'm stuck in the backwater. It's not fair." With tears streaking her checks, Lauren stood and wobbled down the hall. She glanced into Timmie's bedroom and saw her daughter cowering on her bed where the crashing sounds of the argument had penetrated. The child was sobbing—small silent sobs.

Ashamed her quarrel with Wyatt had caused Timmie's anguish, Lauren laid down beside Timmie and put an arm around her shoulders.

)( )( )(

Wyatt stared at his glass. *Stop being a self-centered nut job, dummy. It's gonna cost me a marriage if I'm not careful.* He ran his fingers through his hair, took a deep breath and struggled with his dilemma: how could he nurture his marriage while building a new company? He relied on Lauren—her knowledge of finance, her sage common sense. But she was burned out. What would happen?

He rose from his chair, followed Lauren's path and found her sitting beside Timmie who'd been conquered by restless sleep. Wyatt took Lauren's hand, wet with tears and looked into her eyes. "I love you," he whispered. "I'm sorry." He lifted Lauren to her feet and hugged her. Tenderly, he led her to their bedroom.

Lauren wiped her cheek on the sleeve of her blouse and smiled weakly "Oh, Wyatt. I'm so tired." She dabbed her eyes with the back of her hand, clutched Wyatt's neck and kissed his cheek.

"I didn't understand," Wyatt said. "I'm too caught up in Optimal. Too focused. I'll be more help from now on—you'll see." He closed the bedroom door with a click. "Come," he said, slipping his arm around her waist. They came together and embraced. Wyatt caressed Lauren's back and the gentle curve of her bottom. As he kissed the her neck, she yielded in his grasp, her body melding with his. She clung to him as he began undressing her. Soon, the floor was littered with clothes. They eased between the cool sheets and made love, not a violent, impassioned love, but a gentle, knowing love.

"You'll try to spend a little more time with us, okay?" Lauren whispered as she slipped into fitful slumber.

And the altitude limiter languished in solitude.

Chapter 17

For months the newspapers had been rabid about the bank crisis and the economy's decay. Wyatt knew that Washington created an independent division of the SBA to juice employment—especially startup firms. Hopeful, Wyatt had taken the afternoon off to join his banker at the new SBA offices. They met in the shabby-looking lobby and Lee, as usual, clasped Wyatt's hand with both of his and smiled.

"Thanks for helping, Lee," said Wyatt. "I'm lost in the world of finance. Lauren did most of the preparation for our meeting. She wanted to come, but had to attend a business seminar for her work." Then he remembered the ruckus he'd had with Lauren and added, "Besides, she needs a break from Optimal's madness."

"No problem. I don't often meet clients outside my office, but the new SBA mandate has my interest."

Wyatt chuckled, happy to confront the SBA with an ally.

A clerk escorted them to Mr. Garner, who pulled two shabby side chairs alongside his desk and introduced himself as their Personal Ambassador. "Ignore the mess. Our new Emergency Stimulus Division is just moving in." Garner keyed his computer. "Let me check your submittal. The computers are slow today; it'll take a moment."

Impatiently, Wyatt watched a large wall clock where the second hand stalked an unwary fly creeping across the glass. Time dragged. His gaze wandered over the cluttered office. A dozen desks were crowded in rigid ranks, their gray Formica tops shiny and fresh. Each had a black telephone and an In/Out basket peeking from heaps of paper. Swivel chairs squeaked as staffers pivoted, yakked on the phone or talked with worried looking clients. Two desks flaunted red Valentine's cards, the only color in the room. Wyatt looked up at the clock again. The fly was gone.

At last, the official looked up and said, "Lots of omissions." He leaned his thin body back in his chair and crossed his legs, flashing wingtip-clad feet. "Lots," he repeated.

"Mr. Garner," began Lee Wong.

"Please. Just call me LaMarr, okay?"

Lee nodded and asked, "Omissions?"

LaMarr pursed his full lips and stroked his trim goatee. "You know, missing information. We can't process your application without more information."

Wyatt raised an eyebrow and looked at Lee. During the past month, Lauren had meticulously combed through the forms and briefed Wong, who'd confirmed everything was in order.

Lee asked, "Can you be more specific?"

"Sure. I need sales history to prove this pressurization thing has a future." LaMarr spun in his chair and tugged a black loose-leaf binder from a bookcase. "These are the new regulations." He turned to a page. "See? Section 7.71.4a."

Lee studied the paragraph. "We don't have sales figures yet; Optimal is just starting. Although we know who our customers could be, they haven't signed any agreements. The product is in the conceptual stage and working models are months away."

"That's right, Mr. Garner—I mean, LaMarr," Wyatt said. "Here's a detailed analysis showing its feasibility." He lifted a thick folder from his briefcase. "Want to go over it?"

"Pointless. Analysis isn't sales." LaMarr inspected his fingernails. "Understand?"

"Yeah," muttered Wyatt. *Pompous little twit,* he thought.

Lee nodded and asked, "Any other issues?"

"Many. There are no staffing plans that list titles, description of duties and pay rates. We also need plans for identifying and training disadvantaged workers. We have to document every new job and payroll growth. There are targets to meet, you know."

"Staffing?" Wyatt growled. "There are only three of us. We don't plan to hire anyone for at least a year. As for disadvantaged workers…" Wyatt crossed his arms and clamped them against his chest, trying to check his anger.

Lee turned to LaMarr, "What he means is we'll be happy to work with you." He raised his eyebrows and looked at Wyatt, who sighed in exasperation.

LaMarr replaced the black binder and pulled out another. He thumbed through the book and found what he sought. "Here—Section 4.8.3, third paragraph. It requires the address and square footage of any facility you plan to occupy. You haven't addressed that."

"For now, we're working from my home. We don't expect to have a place for a year," Wyatt said. Rankled, he stared at LaMarr's bookcase and counted eighteen loose-leaf binders. He thought of tombstones, black tombstones. "Now look," he began.

"Hold on, Wyatt," interrupted Lee. "I wasn't aware of these new regulations. Are they online?"

"Of course. They were posted last week. As soon as we complete our move, we'll offer seminars. I took a two-week training course on the new procedures myself." With a smug look, LaMarr fingered a heavy class ring. "You might look into these services."

Lee nodded. "I'll do that."

"Back to your location," LaMarr said, "We strongly urge development in needy neighborhoods. They're called HUBZones or Enterprise Zones."

"Yes, we're familiar with HUBZones," Lee said.

"Good. Although the government offers tax incentives, the most important benefit is to aid poor areas in the city. This goes hand-in-hand with training unskilled people—bringing them up."

Wyatt boiled over. He leaned forward and thumped his fist on the desk. "Optimal is just starting! I can't worry about curing poverty when every ounce of my energy goes into engineering. I need a loan, not feel-good social baloney."

LaMarr scowled.

Lee glared at Wyatt. "Easy, Wyatt," he purred. "LaMarr is just trying to explain these new regulations."

"Okay, okay. I'm sorry I popped off," Wyatt grumbled.

LaMarr rubbed his hands and smiled. "Fine. It's simply the way it is. We can't change our new rules just because you think they're inconvenient."

Subdued, Wyatt stared at his shoes.

"Another thing—the new rules say that OSHA has to review all potential hazards. Your system could be dangerous or emit toxic fumes. Who knows?"

"It's air," sputtered Wyatt. "A small valve that controls air flow."

"No matter. It's in the book. An OSHA report is mandatory."

Wyatt shook his head. He remembered OSHA had inspected SAC several times, but looked for uncovered solvent cans or extension cords on the floor—never anything like this. Once more his gaze fell on the bookcase. *Tombstones*, he brooded. *Dang tombstones.*

"We'll need time before getting back to you," Lee said. "A week or two. Is that okay?"

LaMarr smoothed his tie and stood. "No problem. You'll find all the forms online, a dozen or so. Follow the instructions to the letter, or there could be delays."

Lee thanked LaMarr for his time and shook hands while Wyatt jumped to his feet and strode toward the lobby. Lee scurried after him, catching up in the parking lot.

"Wyatt, if we fight with LaMarr, he could make trouble," Lee scolded. "The guy is just a small time administrator who has to follow procedures."

"What are we supposed to do? Genuflect? He's a bonehead. The guy's surrendered whatever brain he had to a stack of black books. I ought to forget the whole thing!"

"Wyatt, you need funding. My bank's lending constraints are tighter than the SBA's, so LaMarr is our best path."

Wyatt peered through the gathering darkness and jammed his hands into his pockets. "You're right." He worked his jaw. "How is it a mental midget like LaMarr has Optimal by the throat? You saw the books. Thousands and thousands of rules. From where? For what? Do I have to kneel and kiss LaMarr's feet?" Wyatt walked to his car and idly kicked the tire. Feeling contrite, he said, "Sorry I lost my cool. You're a big help. I guess Lauren and I will be seeing more of you these next few weeks."

Lee looked embarrassed and fiddled with his cufflink. "Yes," he nodded. "I'll work with you, I promise. We can win over LaMarr."

Wyatt placed his hand on Lee's shoulder. "Thanks. I really appreciate your help." He shook Lee's hand, glanced at his watch and groaned, "Dang, I'm late for Timmie's soccer match."

Chapter 18

Traffic was heavy and car lights glared in the early evening darkness as Wyatt raced from the SBA offices. "Idiot!" he yelled as he jerked the wheel, avoiding a motorist sneaking through a stop sign. Wyatt zipped around a bus and accelerated up the freeway on-ramp, only to tromp the brakes, trying to merge into an interminable string of creeping cars. A small, gift-wrapped package slid off the seat and plopped on the floor.

"Dang it!"

For the next fifteen minutes, Wyatt kept a running conversation, venom-laced, with drivers blocking his way. Muttering, he checked his watch and jockeyed closer to a crawling pickup.

At last, he gunned off the freeway and flew along the street toward the school where Timmie was playing. His tires squealed as he spun into the parking lot almost clipping a trashcan. The old Ford skidded to a halt. Wyatt leapt from the car and sprinted toward the bright lights of the soccer field.

"Darn!" He ran back to the car, yanked open the passenger door and picked up the package from the floor. Hampered by darkness, he patted the car seat until he found the envelope he sought. Wyatt slammed the door and bolted once more toward the lights.

He was gasping as he reached the sparsely populated bleachers. He spotted Lauren and trotted to her. "Whew! Sorry I'm late. Got tied up at the SBA." Wyatt felt like a naughty child and scrunched up his face, expecting a scolding.

"Hi," Lauren smiled. "The game is just starting. Timmie's not in yet. See her on the bench?"

Surprised by her amiable greeting, Wyatt grinned and looked where Lauren pointed. Timmie wasn't watching the game and fiddled with an unruly strand of hair. Her teammates, resembling beads on a string, were arrayed on either side. A few girls followed the play, but most chatted.

Wyatt dropped on the cold bench next to Lauren and took a deep breath to slow his pounding heart. Lauren slipped her arm through his and pecked him on the cheek. Warmth coursed through Wyatt and he snuggled closer.

Lauren lifted an eyebrow and pointed to the package in Wyatt's hands.

"Oh yes," stammered Wyatt, handing the envelope and package to her. "For you."

Like a scholar turning fragile pages of an ancient text, Lauren opened the envelope and pored over the Valentine card as a slight breeze stirred her fine hair. Rapt, Wyatt watched.

"It's lovely, Honey. Thank you."

Embarrassed by her praise, he prodded the box on her lap and blurted, "Candy."

"I guessed. I'll get fat, you know. Is it See's Candies—my favorite kind?" Lauren's eyes shimmered in the field lights as she grasped his hand.

"Yup," Wyatt grunted with pleasure. Yesterday he'd bumped into Bernie who'd reminded him that Valentine's was coming. Wyatt, knowing his absent-mindedness, dashed off a sticky and stuck it in the middle of his computer screen. He had second thoughts and peeled it off, jogged to his car and slapped it on the speedometer.

Predictably, he'd forgotten all about Valentine's until he started the car that afternoon to go to home. It was a short detour to the drug store to buy a card and truffles at the nearby See's candy store. That night, in the secrecy of his bedroom office, Wyatt jotted a note in the card, thankful that the store had wrapped the candy. As he did with the sticky, Wyatt smuggled the card and package to his car so he wouldn't forget them.

Lauren cuddled closer, fending off the nighttime chill. "Timmie seems to enjoy her teammates. Look—she's playing Rock, Paper, Scissors with one of the girls."

Wyatt bobbed his head. "She likes soccer and has made a few good friends. It's too bad the season is nearly finished."

"Mmmm," Lauren nodded. She shielded her eyes from the bright lights and watched her daughter. "Timmie had a good day at school. She drew a crayon picture of a farm and the teacher showed it to the other kids. Timmie was sooooo excited. I put it on the refrigerator. Be sure to compliment her when we get home."

"You bet."

"Things are better at after-school care too. Timmie was actually cheerful tonight when I picked her up. Even the teacher gave me a friendly wave."

"No fights with…what's his name?"

"Danny."

"Right. Danny."

Lauren chuckled. "No news is good news. But I'm not asking either."

Contented, Wyatt wrapped his arm around Lauren's

shoulder and gazed at the frenzy on the field. His mind wandered back to the mess at the SBA. "Had big trouble today. Thought we'd done a good job with the application, but the 'Personal Ambassador' was a jerk. He sprung a huge set of new regulations on us. Even Wong didn't know of them. I teed off on this LaMarr guy. Wong had to rein me in."

"LaMarr is the 'Ambassador?'"

"Yeah."

"What was wrong with our application?"

Wyatt spread his hands wide apart. "Long list. The new division's policy is to make it easier to qualify. They've changed everything. It's not worth raking through the muck right now. Tomorrow, I'll jot down a few notes for you and Madison."

"Good enough," Lauren glanced at the field. "Oh look! Timmie's going in!" Jumping up and yelling, they watched their daughter sprint onto the field. The coach bellowed, positioning Timmie on the flank and pumped his fist. The girls screamed and swarmed like wasps as the game resumed.

"I wish she'd move that fast when I ask her to clean her room," snickered Lauren. A frown crept between her freckles. "What happens if the SBA falls through?"

Wyatt shrugged and huddled against his wife, seeking a warm spot on the metal bench. "Guess we could take out a personal loan, but that would get us just a couple thousand dollars. The only other option is a mortgage on the house."

Lauren stiffened. "You promised me! Personal loan, maybe. A mortgage, never."

Wyatt loosened his grip on Lauren's shoulders and faced her. "Relax. That's down the road. Our bank balance should hold up until we need to buy prototype hardware. Worry when we get there."

"No. That's not what you said. We agreed. No mortgage ever," Lauren insisted.

Wyatt grinned. "You're sexy when you put on your business face. You're right—no mortgage. I'll just make sure we get the SBA loan."

"You sure? You hate government, but now you're betting Optimal's future on a Washington program."

"No alternative. I'll work with you and Wong until the loan application's right. I'll even kiss the Personal Ambassador's butt if necessary."

Lauren drew a deep breath and nodded. "Okay. It's settled."

"Settled," he echoed.

Wyatt wished he were as certain of getting the loan as he sounded. Finance was a mystery to him and government always pushed his buttons. He knew Lauren, with Lee's help, would step up. *They know their stuff. They'll make it happen.*

Wyatt turned back to the game and watched Timmie lunge after the ball. He drew Lauren closer and kissed her ear.

"Stop that. People might stare."

"So? We're married. I have my conjugal rights."

Although an indignant looking expression swept her face, a giggle betrayed Lauren's real feelings. "You're silly," she teased. "Engineers aren't supposed to enjoy…" She leaned close to Wyatt and whispered, "sex."

"Ha! Rumors spread by horny lawyers. It's Valentine's Day after all." He pointed to the box. "Think of the chocolates as a bribe. Get my drift?"

The referee's shrill whistle interrupted Lauren's boisterous laughter. The game was over; Timmie's team had won, two to one. Timmie, flushed with excitement, rushed over calling, "Did you see me? I dribbled a long way. See me?"

Lauren mopped her daughter's sweaty face and said, "Sure did, Sweetie. You were great."

Timmie beamed. Wyatt gave her a quick squeeze and helped Lauren off the bench. He gathered up Timmie's ball and guided his family back to their cars. Lauren had parked a few slots away and Timmie, bubbling about the game, clambered inside.

Wyatt, holding the door for his wife, flashed an exaggerated wink, saying, "I'll see you at home. We have unfinished business, I believe, beginning with a glass of Zin."

"Only if you're good," teased Lauren.

"I thought you said I'm always good," Wyatt boasted as he turned and walked to his own car.

Chapter 19

Wyatt cradled the phone between his chin and shoulder and tried to organize his thoughts. "No, Madison, the default has to be fail-safe. The FAA will clean our clocks if we do it that way."

"I'm confused," complained Madison. "I wish I had your revised schematic. Designing by phone is insane; things are too complicated. We need a spot to work together. My apartment is too small; can we work at your place?"

So, in late February, Madison and Wyatt decided to cohabitate, so to speak, meeting nearly every night in the jumbled backroom at Wyatt's house. He was pleased when Lauren went along. It was only a little irritating when she interrupted by bringing coffee and cookies as the evenings dragged into late nights.

For a while, Wyatt and Madison managed, but the mess in the office cloned itself. Books, calculations and hurried sketches spread like lava, first engulfing the hall and then the living room. Wyatt guessed that Lauren, trying to hold back the deluge, stacked papers into neat piles and propped the books in tidy rows against the sofa. She even tiptoed around, hushing Timmie. The arrangement was awkward, but work progressed.

One evening, a week before Scrabble day, Lauren stood with hands on her hips and looked at the tornado-like devastation.

"Wyatt!" she yelled.

Later, looking back, Wyatt drew a humorous parallel

between the Scrabble cleanup and the logistics of the D-Day landing at Normandy. Lauren, usually a sweet, supportive wife, morphed into a battle-hardened sergeant. Sidetracked from their usual work, Madison and Wyatt cringed as Lauren lobbed instructions.

"Find a way to keep his mess in your office," commanded Lauren.

"There's no room," protested Wyatt.

"Come," Lauren ordered. "Let's start with your closet. What's in those boxes?"

"I don't know. Tax records?"

"Out to the garage. Move those filing cabinets in there. Chuck the TV tray and get rid of all those gadgets from SAC. They're just junk."

"Junk? No way," Wyatt whimpered. "Those are a history of my old designs ––fossils, you know?"

"Wyatt…"

"Okay." He reached for a casting, caressed it and deposited it in the trash basket. He made the sign of the cross and said, "Rest in peace."

Lauren picked up a small stack of books, her head swiveling as she tried to find a place for them. "You've a few boards in the garage; build another bookcase. Today."

"Next, you'll be putting pretty pictures on the wall," Wyatt complained.

Thus, spawned by a Scrabble party, they whipped the first office of Optimal Aviation Systems into shape. Over the next few days, Madison and Wyatt managed to work without stepping on one another. The office was cozy, like eggs in a carton, but when heads come together in thought, little space is needed.

March flew by and the spring sunlight lingered in the small window. Wyatt settled into a comfortable routine and looked forward to evenings filled with new challenges and Madison's insight. She, in turn, threaded her way through the maze of code writing and PCB design, pre-occupied and intense. In a grudging way, Lauren seemed to accept her new role as innkeeper.

It was late April and Wyatt rubbed his eyes, stumped over a troublesome stack-up analysis. Nearby, Madison, her forehead wrinkled, underlined two lines of code with brash strokes, scrolled through the program on her computer and turned to Wyatt.

"Does Delta P have precedence over the cabin pressure setting or the other way around? I'm having trouble with the logic."

"Delta P, always," Wyatt replied. "If you exceed Delta P, you risk structural failure of the aircraft hull." Wyatt rummaged in the file cabinet and produced a folder. "Here's the new FAA specification. See if this helps."

Madison took the folder and went back to her computer. Silence settled like fog on a lake. The air was stuffy, but neither took the time to open the window to admit the fresh breeze.

Hoping for an extra hour or two of work, Wyatt asked Madison to stay for dinner. Like wisps of smoke, sounds of Lauren's dinner preparations drifted over their calculations and across the face of the computer monitor. Timmie and Jennifer were playing a computer game in the living room and the girls' joyous laughter blasted through the door.

Wyatt twisted in his chair, trying to concentrate. Madison stirred, glanced over her shoulder and returned to work.

"Hush, kids. Daddy's trying to work," Lauren scolded. A while later, she bustled down the hall and stuck her head into the office. "Dinner will be ready in ten minutes, okay?"

Both nodded without looking up.

Lauren sent Jennifer home and dished out rice, peas and pork chops. "Wyatt, Madison, Timmie, dinner's ready!"

They gathered around the table and Lauren passed a platter and serving bowls around, everyone helping themselves. "Is everything going okay?" she asked.

"Fine," answered Wyatt. He glanced at his wife and noticed a quizzical tilt of her head as if she expected more than a one-word answer.

Two nights ago, they had a tiff about the Sunset Rituals, which had been pre-empted by work. Wyatt had promised to dedicate more time to his family, but Optimal was a narcotic; he simply lost track of time. And Madison's chronic presence was a persistent itch—an irritation that derailed any chance for private moments with his wife.

Guilt crept into Wyatt's thoughts, so he continued, "Things are coming along. I'm cranking through a new analysis and Madison is cleverly conjuring code. How's that for alliteration?" he chuckled, pleased with his wit.

Lauren smiled. "Good, Wyatt. Just wonderful. With your talent, you'll grow up to be a novelist."

"Yeah, sure," Madison said. "I think Lauren is being satirical. Are you familiar with satire, Wyatt?"

"Sure. A satyr is a little guy with horns."

The adults laughed, but Timmie looked mystified.

"Can I get down, now?" she asked. Lauren nodded and Timmie slid off her chair and skipped back to her room.

"Kinda off the subject, Dear," interjected Wyatt. "Have you heard anything from the SBA?"

"Not a word. They were supposed to get back to us two weeks ago. I'll touch base with Wong in the morning to see if there's any news."

"Better yet, see if the government has a pulse," Wyatt said. "I hope our cash holds out. There's a bill for new computer software coming due. Don't want to run short."

Lauren frowned. "How much money is involved? You didn't say anything about that."

Wyatt shrugged. "Madison? Any idea?"

"Sorry, Lauren. I should have said something." Madison set down her fork. "The invoice is in the office. I can get it in a flash."

Wyatt tossed his napkin on the table. "We're done with dinner anyway, Madison. Let's go find it. Can we help clear, Hon?"

"No. Go ahead."

When Wyatt returned with the paperwork, Lauren dried her hands on a dishtowel and read it, scowling. "Over six hundred dollars? How do you expect me to keep tabs on the money if you can't even give me invoices? You'd better get a leash around Madison's neck. She's out of control."

"Sorry." Wyatt slunk back to the claustrophobic office, threading past the resurgent clutter in the hallway. Spellbound by a new approach to the troublesome analysis, he soon forgot Lauren's anger.

"Garfield!" Timmie shouted, chasing the petrified cat down the hall. Garfield, wielding a bottle brush tail, burrowed under Wyatt's desk. The child dropped on hands and knees and tunneled after the cat, spilling books onto the floor.

"Timmie!" roared Wyatt.

"Easy, Wyatt," admonished Madison. "They're just doing what kids and cats do."

Near tears, Timmie slunk from the room. Garfield crouched in the corner and surveyed the room with saucer eyes.

Wyatt bent to shoo the cat, but Madison pushed him away. "Just leave him be," she said. "He won't make any trouble."

Infuriated, Wyatt clung to his anger. "Yeah? What do you know about cats?"

"I have one. His name is G-G."

"G-G? What kind of name is that?"

"You'll appreciate it. It's short for Galileo Galilei."

He laughed, his frustration dissolving. "Galileo Galilei. Figures." Wyatt shook his head and waved at the chaos of their office. "Look at us. Junk everywhere. On top of that, we have a hyper kid and a paranoid cat. I'm thinking it's time we leased a small office somewhere."

"Expensive, Wyatt."

"I know. Around two and a half, three dollars a square foot." Wyatt jotted a few numbers on a scrap of paper. "We need only three hundred square feet, at most."

Madison pursed her lips and leaned back in her chair. "Maybe you're right; it's tough to concentrate. We need room to spread out. Besides, I feel I'm encroaching on the Morgan castle."

Wyatt nodded. "Okay. I'll start looking for a place, Maddy. See what's out there."

Madison reached over and patted Wyatt's hand. "Agreed."

Lauren was standing in the doorway with two cups of coffee. "What's this? You're not thinking of leasing office space, are you?"

"I know it's much sooner than we planned," Wyatt said, "but it's crazy around here and we need more room."

Lauren gritted her teeth and set the cups on the desk. "It's late. I have to get Timmie to bed. We'll talk about it later."

>< >< ><

She stroked his hand

Lauren tried to hold her troubled thoughts at bay as she coaxed Timmie into her jammies, wheedled through the tooth-brushing ordeal and finally prodded the fussy child into bed.

Lauren walked into the dark living room and sat. A sudden chill made her shiver, and she pulled her feet under her.

Maddy. Now she has a nickname.

For some time, Lauren feared the day when Wyatt and Madison moved into an office where they'd be alone together. She wouldn't be able to watch over them and Timmie would be an anchor, tying her to the house. Things could get out of hand. She considered confronting Wyatt, but didn't want to appear as a jealous witch. True, she hadn't seen any overt flirtations; everything seemed professional—engineer-to-engineer. Then again:

She stroked his hand.

Chapter 20

The last two weeks had been frantic. Nearly every evening Christine, the real estate agent, trundled the Morgans from office building to industrial facility searching for Optimal's new home. Thankfully, Sharon had watched after Timmie. Lauren gasped in relief when they settled on a modest business location in a run-down area. Although Wyatt had agreed to repair the hot water heater, replace the stained ceiling tiles and do ongoing maintenance, the landlord lowered the rent only ten percent. Cash flow was tight and concern gnawed at her.

Lauren hurried into Wyatt's backroom office after he'd left for work and tapped her foot waiting while the computer booted up. After updating the budget to reflect the office rent, she rushed to clean the house—it was Scrabble Saturday and much remained to be done.

With Timmie's help, Lauren had dyed Easter eggs the previous night and bowls, half full of vinegary liquid dotted the kitchen counter. Dried red, blue and yellow blotches languished everywhere and green paper grass from the Easter basket littered the floor. She swept, wiped the counter with jerky motions and whirled a dust rag over the coffee table.

The doorbell startled her.

Breathless as she opened the door, Lauren said, "Hello, Mother. Don't mind my looks. I'm bouncing off the walls this morning."

"I can see. You seem tired. Are you getting enough sleep, Dear?"

"Not really. Wyatt and Madison decided to look for an office and these last few days have been crazy. We signed a lease on Optimal's new office just yesterday."

"A lease? Is Wyatt crazy?" snorted Liza, tossing her alligator handbag on the sofa. "Didn't he plan to work on this silliness at home?"

"It's not silliness, Mother. He and Madison don't have enough space and it's impossible to concentrate with Timmie and Jennifer running amok. We found a nice place, a little larger than we wanted, but it has room for future test equipment."

"I don't understand how you allow him go on with this…this *company*. How can you afford it?"

"It's not that bad. I'll just have to keep my job a while longer."

"Wyatt needs to get his head on straight so you can stay home with Timmie, that's what."

Lauren rubbed her temples. "I know, Mother. It's just not in the cards." She flopped into her armchair. *I'm exhausted. No energy to fight with her.*

The doorbell rang again. Weary, Lauren went to the door and greeted Jennifer and her mother, Sharon. "Hi. Come in." She ushered her neighbors across the room and made introductions.

They shook hands and Lauren continued, "Sharon is kind enough to take the kids to the movies this afternoon—early birthday celebration for Timmie. Should be fun, right Jennifer?" She playfully tugged on the child's braided hair, then called to her daughter, "Jennifer's here!"

Timmie came running. "Hi, Jennifer!" she yelled. Then she turned and asked her mother, "Can I have some Easter candy?"

"Not until tomorrow," Lauren said.

Timmie brooded, then suddenly brightened. "Can I have popcorn at the movies? Please?"

"Well...okay. I'll get a little money for you. Come along; you'll be late."

Sharon collected the youngsters saying, "We'll be back around five or so. We're seeing the new Disney film, or DreamWorks. I forgot. The girls will enjoy it."

The two girls jostled through the doorway and ran next door to the car. Sharon laughed and called out, "Wait for me!"

Lauren closed the door and turned to her mother. "That's nice of her. It will be a fun outing."

Liza nodded. "I can't believe Timmie is six already. I hardly recognize her anymore." She walked to the sofa and sat. "You know, I had an idea."

"Yes?" Lauren said. *Now what?*

"Suppose I arrange my schedule to free up a day or two during the week. Perhaps I could pick up Timmie at school and spend occasional afternoons with her. Besides, it'd save you money on after-school care."

"But you're always so busy."

With a wistful frown, Liza looked at her hands. "Sure, tennis lessons are fun, but––I mean––how important is it to perfect my backhand? What's the point? I just wondered what it would be like to become good friends with my granddaughter."

Lauren shook her head in disbelief. This was a side of her mother she'd never seen.

Then Lauren had an epiphany. Without having to pick up Timmie from after-school care, she could pop in on Wyatt and Madison right after work––unannounced, of course. "Mom, that's a *great* idea. Timmie would *love* it."

Liza smiled, her first since she arrived. "Really? Would Timmie be happy playing with…with an old person?"

"You're her Granny! Of course!"

Liza stood and smoothed her dress. "Well, I'll think it over. Let's get to work; the girls will be here before we're ready." Her smile lingered as she went to the closet for the card table.

"About the company, Mother," Lauren said. "Wyatt isn't pushing me. He's very passionate about the company and I believe in him. I'm committed to it."

"At what cost, Lauren?" Liza sputtered as she set up the table. "Timmie fights with her classmates and spends most of her time in front of the television. And those urchins at after-school care? They're probably a terrible influence."

Lauren turned to Liza, her fists on her hips. "She's just young, Mother. Timmie is doing well in school and has a nice friend in Jennifer. Besides, if you'd spend an afternoon or two a week with her, maybe you'd nudge her along the right path."

"Ha!" Liza snorted, wrestling the folding chairs. A grin returned to her lips. "Say, are you going to help?"

"Sorry. Let's get the beverages."

They bustled into the kitchen, where Liza scooped ice cubes into a bowl and rummaged in the refrigerator for dip. Framed by the open refrigerator, she turned and pursed her lips. "You love him, don't you?"

Surprised, Lauren raised an eyebrow. "Very much."

Liza let the refrigerator door swing closed and after a long pause, said, "Okay. I'll do it."

"What?"

"Spend a few afternoons with Timmie."

Lauren reached to give her mother a big hug, but the doorbell rang, interrupting her.

With a broad smile, Lauren greeted her friends. "Hi, girls. Come on in. Are you ready to duel with Webster?"

They trooped into the kitchen where Liza was slipping a stalk of celery into Marge's glass. While chatting, they lingered around the counter sharing Betty's cookies and pouring wine and soda.

Betty forked a slice of bologna onto her plate. "Lauren, is your husband still playing around with that invention?"

"Not exactly *playing*, but yes he is. Wyatt's been at it for five months, now. We've signed a lease for a small facility and hope to move in this week. It's scary, but exciting too."

"Wow, that *is* exciting," exclaimed Marge. "I'll bet there's a lot to do in starting a business. Where do you find time?"

Lauren shrugged. "It's involved. First we have to refurbish the new office. Every alteration has to be to code, so we have to pull permits. Wyatt's trying to get a loan from the SBA and I've started setting up the books, ordering equipment, paying bills and all that."

Lauren glanced at her mother, whose face brimmed with skepticism.

With a nervous laugh, Lauren invited everyone to the living room. Clutching drinks and snacks, they strolled to the table and drew Scrabble tiles. Honed by dozens of sessions, they fell into an easy conversation as the tiles began to click.

"Is that a word?"

"Look it up."

"Did you read the article about that congressman fooling around with his secretary?"

"His wife said she had no clue. They're the last to know."

Last to know? Lauren wondered. *Do I really understand what's going on with Wyatt and Madison?*

The afternoon shadows were long when Lauren smiled and totaled the scores; she'd won again.

"You're a word savant, Lauren," Betty chided. "It's not fair."

Marge and Betty gathered their belongings and Lauren escorted them to the door saying, "It's been fun, girls. Drive safely."

They started down the walk and Marge giggled, "The nice thing with carpooling with Betty, I don't worry if I'm sloshed."

After the girls had left, Liza folded the card table and slipped it into the closet, saying, "I'll call once I look at my schedule. I hope to drop in on Timmie early next week. Okay?"

"That will be great, Mom."

"We could stroll in the park or visit the library. I don't suppose a first grader has much in the way of homework, but I could help if she needs it."

"Oh, you might be surprised." *Mom can be a dream when she chooses.* Lauren gave her mother a warm hug and kissed her cheek. "Thanks. You're wonderful."

Liza picked up her purse and jacket, twisted the doorknob and said, "I still wish you'd rein in Wyatt. This Optimal thing is a pipe dream. He should have never signed a lease, and I'd be very careful with that female engineer, too. Madison, right? Damn pretty, you said. Better get a tight leash on that husband of yours." Without looking back, she went to her car and drove away.

Stunned by her mother's abrupt about-face, Lauren sank into her chair and stared at the wall, near tears. *She can be so vicious. How can she love her granddaughter and hate Wyatt?* Melancholy devoured her and she wrung her hands.

Garfield, apparently realizing that the boisterous two-footed animals had left, came out of hiding to rub on Lauren's ankles. She absently leaned over and scratched behind the cat's ear. "Garfield, I'm overwhelmed. Maybe Marge is right. I'm trying to do too much. She stood and rubbed the back of her neck. Then, the nagging thought returned. *Maddy.*

Bang! The door flew open and Timmie propelled herself across the room and threw her arms around Lauren's legs. "There was a dragon in the movie! A nice dragon that took kids for a ride on its back! It was green! And it could blow fire from its nose!"

Tenderness overwhelmed Lauren and she sank to her knees and swaddled her daughter in an immense hug. With her eyes squeezed shut, she rocked back and forth, then leaned back, gripped Timmie's shoulders and gazed at her with moist eyes. "Timmie, you're beautiful."

Timmie squirmed and squinted at her mother. "Mommy? Are you okay?"

"Yes, Dear. Mommy's okay."

Chapter 21

"I hope this will be easy," Madison said as they walked through the parking lot toward the city offices.

"Me too." Wyatt had laid out the modifications to the new office with care so the permit people couldn't trip him up. With Madison's help, he'd planned exactly where every electrical outlet had to be, where he'd spot the desks and benches and what additional lighting was needed. Even so, he was nervous.

"The Planning website mentioned they've hired a bunch of young people called Liaison Clerks," Madison said. "Seems odd."

"Yeah, I noticed that. Something about training unskilled people. They've waived the usual qualifications." He gripped his file folder tighter as he stepped over a curb. "Because of insane unemployment rates, the voters are shelling Sacramento. I'm guessing they leaned on the county and city governments to hire anybody so long as they're warm."

"Did you see the new CALgreen standard?" Madison said. "A hundred and eighty pages!"

Wyatt cringed at the thought. "Yeah. California always tries to lead the green revolution, dumping useless regulations on us," he said. "No wonder businesses are leaving the state."

They walked past a waterfall and entered the door marked "Burbank Department of Planning and Zoning." The spacious room teemed with people jostling along an

L-shaped black granite counter. They clutched bulging folders and binders and talked on cell phones as they waited to be served. "Look at the lines," Wyatt groused. "Same as the DMV."

"You'd think with more employees things would move faster," Madison said. "Look at the kid behind the counter—looks like we get to deal with one of those young liaison what-evers."

Wyatt nodded. "Yeah, he looks twelve years old."

The line inched forward. Wyatt looked at the wall clock, checked it against his watch and fiddled with the keys in his pocket. Madison rocked back on her heels and gave Wyatt a thin smile.

Twenty minutes later, the clerk beckoned. "Name's Brandon. Brandon Hess." Like nails to a magnet, his fingers sought a fiery pimple on his jaw, which he scratched and pinched. Almost as an afterthought, he continued, "Name?"

"Wyatt Morgan and Madison McKenzie, with Optimal Aviation Systems."

"Opti... Is that a word?"

Wyatt rolled his eyes. "Yes, of course."

"Spell it." Brandon's hands abandoned his face and hovered over his keyboard.

"O. P. T...."

"Slow, okay?" Brandon, using his index fingers, ferreted out each key and verified every prod on the monitor; his head bobbing like a skiff at sea.

Why can't this guy type? It's his job, Wyatt thought, doing his best to stay calm.

Brandon reviewed his entries, dragging his finger down the screen. "Got your application?" Taking the paper, he looked it over. "You're a business, right? You need to talk to Zoning first. Line's around the corner."

Wyatt stepped back and saw a rotund woman confronting a line of weary-looking people. "You mean I gotta stand in another line?"

"Yup. Zoning first. New procedure. Speeds things up." Brandon handed the paperwork back to Wyatt. "Get this stamped and come back here."

Wyatt glared at his adversary, seething. Madison tugged on his elbow saying, "Come on. Let's check Zoning."

It was another fifteen minutes before the clerk banged a rubber stamp on the application leaving a smeared red declaration, "ZONING VERIFIED." She shoved the paper across the desk and said, "Check back with Planning."

"Patience is not my strong suit," Wyatt said as they took their place at the end of the first line.

"Somehow I'd already figured that out," Madison said, brushing a strand of hair away from her face. "At SAC, you work with the FAA all the time. Is this any different?"

"Both are a pain in the butt," Wyatt muttered. "Government monopolies." Once more, he jingled the keys in his pocket and then gave Madison a sheepish grin. "You're right. My frustration won't move this line any faster. I'll try to chill."

"Good. We're at Brandon's mercy."

At last, the clerk beckoned them, asking "Name?"

"Morgan and McKenzie, same as before," Wyatt growled.

A glimmer of recognition flashed across Brandon's cratered face. "Oh. Right. Opti...something?"

Wyatt nodded.

Brandon took the stamped application and scrutinized each line, grunting to himself. Finally he looked up. "You're adding electrical stuff, right? Got plans?"

Wyatt slipped a CAD drawing from his folder and spread it out. "For now, we're just adding four electrical outlets on the wall and hanging a few overhead lights. The landlord said we'd need permits."

"Yup. That's right. Anything electrical." Brandon pulled the drawing closer. "How far off the floor are the new outlets?"

"Does it matter?" Wyatt asked.

"Yup. The code defines that. Get your contractor or architect to add that to the drawing."

"We're doing the plans ourselves," Wyatt said.

"That's not a good idea on electrical stuff."

Madison interceded. "I'm an electrical engineer and Wyatt is an aerospace engineer. I'm sure we can handle it."

A hurt look clouded Brandon's face and his fingers searched for a pimple on the back of his neck. "Suit yourself, but our inspectors will check your work very, very careful." He studied the application again. "You gonna put a sign on the building?"

Wyatt blinked. "I haven't thought about that. I suppose we should, right Madison?"

She nodded.

"Well, you gotta have a permit for a sign, so I'll need to see your plans."

Wyatt scowled. "Suppose we buy transfer letters and put the company name on the front door?"

Brandon shrugged. "That's okay." He poked the

computer. "Now, a different subject. There's a new law called CALgreen."

"Saw it on the website," Wyatt said.

"First, whenever a rental changes hands, all faucets and toilets gotta be upgraded to low flow standards. Did your landlord do that?"

"I don't know. I'll check with her," said Wyatt.

"It's a requirement. Can't approve the permits until the building is up to code."

Wyatt jotted a note on his manila folder. "Seems like a lot to do."

The clerk tapped a tattered checklist. "Also, I need a list of the electrical appliances you plan to use. They gotta be Energy Star qualified."

Wyatt scowled and scratched another note.

"You mentioned some future work?"

"Yes, within the year. While I'm here, I figured to get your input—head off any problems. Here are a few preliminary drawings. Take a look." Wyatt said, spreading out the documents. Brandon frowned, looking confused.

"Let me help," offered Wyatt. "Outside, we'll install a vacuum pump and an air compressor, both about fifty horsepower." He quickly explained the general layout of the future test rig. "I've more detail, if that would help," Wyatt said, patting his folder.

"Industrial stuff," Brandon grumbled. "Let me call my supervisor."

Wyatt leaned impatiently on the counter while Madison gazed around the room.

After several minutes, an older man appeared wearing

glasses that dangled from his neck on a cord. "What's up, Brandon?"

"Hi Jeff. This is Mr. Morgan and…" His voice trailed off. Brandon's eyes skittered over the application, jerking from line to line. Abruptly, he resumed, "and this is Mrs. McKenzie."

"Miss," Madison corrected.

"Right. Jeff Hunzaker, my boss." He turned and showed him Wyatt's layout.

Jeff slipped his glasses on and asked, "The pump and compressor discharge into the atmosphere, right?"

Wyatt and Madison nodded.

"You'll have to contact the AQMD," Jeff grunted. "Needs special permits."

"How could my equipment affect air quality?" asked Wyatt. "The exhaust is just air."

"Could be oil mist or ozone from the motor. Who knows? The AQMD requires an analysis of the effluent—it's a new environmental regulation. Also, the electrical service needs upgrading. Contact Burbank Water and Power for that. We'll need much more detail on all breaker boxes, cable conduits—you know."

Wyatt scribbled more notes. "This is turning into a major deal," he muttered.

Jeff grunted. "Well, Mr. Morgan, it's the code. You have to follow code."

"Sure, sure, I know. It seems a lot for such simple stuff."

"On the web," Jeff went on, "you'll find templates for the standard plan, called 'Details.' Just fill them out and file on-line."

"How involved are they?"

"Oh, they cover everything. There are several lengthy forms."

Wyatt leaned over and rapped his knuckles the counter. "You don't understand. I have *real* work to do. There's no time to fiddle with bureaucratic guff. There has to be an easier way."

"I'm sorry, Mr. Morgan," Jeff said through clenched teeth. "This is the process. There are no shortcuts."

"This is nuts," growled Wyatt. "How long does it take to get a permit?"

Jeff flashed an angry glare. "We can't say until we go over your corrected plans."

Madison patted Wyatt's hand. "Let's just get the information. It won't take long, okay?"

"Yeah. Sure. Let's get out of here." He spun and strode toward the exit.

Shrugging, Madison gave a tight-lipped smile to Jeff and Brandon and scurried after Wyatt.

In the parking lot, Wyatt turned to Madison. "Government! Codes! They'll drive you crazy!"

"Simmer down," Madison said, tilting her head. "We'll just pull together the information and turn Brandon into a pussy-cat." She laughed and her eyes sparkled in the sun.

Wyatt had to smile. "You're like taking a drag on some wacky-weed, Maddy. You put me in a mellow place." He saw the light play across her face and her playful posture—a hand on one hip. A puff of air stirred her hair. *Dang, she's pretty*, he thought.

>< >< ><

Madison slapped her forehead with her palm. "Damn, we left the folders inside. Be right back."

Inside, she found the papers where Jeff and Brandon were murmuring. They had their backs to her, so they didn't seem to notice her presence.

"Every so often," Jeff was saying, "we see these assholes. They make big trouble. That Morgan is the kinda guy who'd sue our ass if we made the slightest mistake. Put a cautionary note in the computer. When he comes back, nitpick his paperwork to death. No oversights of any kind, understand? Even typos." Jeff pivoted toward his office, then turned to Brandon again. "Oh, yes, just thinking about it, I wouldn't be surprised if his application found its way to the bottom of the stack. Know what I'm saying?"

Brandon grinned. "Gotcha."

"Good."

With a wince, Madison snatched the file folders and fled.

Chapter 22

Wyatt was in trouble.

"I'm gonna have your job," Leechmann yelled, his neck bulging, straining his tie. "How many times do you have to screw up the paperwork to figure out I'm serious?"

"You're right," Wyatt said. "I'll sort this out right away." He knew the inspector could lean on Brian with the weight of government authority to cancel contracts. He could be fired if he didn't placate the gorilla glaring at him.

What Leechmann didn't know, was Wyatt's time was stretched like taffy between SAC and Optimal. Desperation, an increasingly frequent emotion, brought bile to his throat. "Tell you what, by the time you have a cup of coffee, I'll have the forms filled out."

"So jump, Morgan. I'm tired of kicking your butt."

Within fifteen minutes, Wyatt gave the delinquent paperwork to Leechmann who stormed out of the building trailing a stream of livid oaths.

Back at his desk, Wyatt took a deep breath, relieved he'd appeased the government, at least for a while. He keyed his computer bringing up a CAD drawing of an actuator housing. Unsure how to machine the raw casting, he phoned Bernie, the "Sage of the Shop," for advice.

Bernie stepped into Wyatt's cubicle, wiping the back of his hand across his forehead. "Those stairs up to Engineering aren't getting any easier, my friend. I ought to put in a requisition for escalators."

"Lots of luck," Wyatt laughed. He scooted back his

chair and pointed at the computer monitor. "Take a look at this part. Any thoughts about the machining sequence and datum locations?"

Bernie pulled up a side chair, settled his lanky body onto its thin cushion and studied the computer model. He slipped a tooth-pocked pencil from behind his ear and tapped the screen. "I'd face this surface first. That'd be the primary datum. Next, turn the O.D."

Within a few moments, Bernie outlined the complete machining sequence. He glanced once more at the monitor and, wielding his pencil like a fencer's foil, pointed again. "Wyatt, you came up with a damned clever core-pull on the casting––saved a bunch of machine work."

Wyatt blushed with a surge of affection for the old man. "Thanks. It comes from listening to guys like you."

Bernie rose from the chair. "That it?"

"Yup. As a matter of fact, it's quitting time and I have to go. I have a busy evening ahead of me."

It was a short drive from Simmons Aviation to the new office. The springtime air was warm and fragrant as Wyatt unlocked Optimal's front door. With a grunt, he set down a box of books he'd brought from home and returned to his car for a load of tools. Soon, cartons cluttered the floor. Wyatt smiled with pleasure as he began categorizing the texts and setting them into a second-hand bookcase.

Benefiting from the weak economy, an office furniture re-seller had been amply stocked with a large selection commandeered from failed companies. Wyatt purchased the bookcase along with an array of desks, benches and chairs at bargain prices.

Yesterday, anxious to get started, Wyatt had plugged his computer into an extension cord and set up a table lamp borrowed from home. The room still smelled of fresh paint. Scrubbed windows sparkled and Wyatt had replaced the stained ceiling tiles. Even the hot water heater, once teetering to one side in violation of the earthquake code, stood erect, looking proud in its new military posture. These repairs, plus the new low-flow toilet he'd installed, allowed Wyatt to submit a revised permit application. Madison had told him what she'd overheard at the Planning desk when she'd returned for the folders. *Turkeys,* he'd fumed. Still, he hoped Brandon would process it without delay.

"Anybody home?" called Lauren, scurrying through the door.

"Over here, Darlin'." Wyatt dropped an armload of books and greeted his wife with a big hug and warm kiss. "You're early."

"Mother picked up Timmie from school, so I came straight from work. There are a few things in the car. Help me with them?"

"Sure."

The clutter grew. "This is worse than your home office," Lauren joked.

"Not to worry. I'll have it tidied up tonight." Wyatt glanced at the window and saw Madison drive up, park and begin gathering boxes from her back seat. "I guess we should help."

They went out and lugged in more cartons, adding to the swelling disarray.

"Thanks, guys; these are heavy," Madison said. "This is most of my stuff. I'm glad we set up the computers yesterday. No fighting spaghetti tangles of wires tonight."

"How about lending a hand with the books?" asked Wyatt. "Want to fold yours in with mine, or do you want them separate?"

"Together. If we're partners, it's gotta be together, same as the Three Musketeers."

"Actually, there were four Musketeers, if you count d'Artagnan," Lauren corrected.

Wyatt, looking up, thought he detected a hint of a sneer on his wife's lips.

"Four? Whatever," Madison shrugged. "Maybe we can put Timmie to work. That would make four," she snickered.

Wyatt felt an air of excitement as he stocked the bookcase. *It's happening. Really happening.* While Madison helped him alphabetize the books, Lauren stuffed supplies in the cabinet, stashed copy paper beneath the printer and set coffee, powdered creamer and plastic spoons alongside a spare percolator.

Slowly, the jumble diminished, tucked into drawers, thrust into files, aligned in bookcases.

"Sorry, guys, I have to bail out," said Madison. "I'm on an early plane tomorrow for Wichita. Business meeting with Cessna. I have to pack and get a few hours' sleep. I'll be back in two days."

Lauren looked at her watch. "Wow! It *is* late. I'd better get home, too. Mother has a committee meeting of some sort. You coming, Wyatt?"

"Don't think so. I promised myself this place would be neat and tidy by tonight. Need an hour, no more."

The two women walked to the parking lot and paused, exchanging a few words. They nodded, slipped into their cars and left.

Wyatt returned to his desk, unearthed a small notepad and listed things he'd need the next day: number-ten envelopes, toilet paper and the disk on stress analysis. He paused and rubbed his chin. *Something else. Software for turbulent airflow?* Wyatt wiggled in the chair to ease his aching back, a consequence of lugging heavy boxes. His glance fell on a stack of calculations and his mind jumped. *I wish I could sort out the pressure balance problem on the outflow valves. Maybe if I...*

He switched on his computer, abandoned his intent to organize the office, and attacked the design problem. Hunched over the keyboard, he jabbed his thoughts into the machine. The computer's maze of transistors and intricate circuits melded with Wyatt's thoughts. Time stood still and pedestrian reality receded, leaving only the engineer and his problem.

This phenomenon wasn't new to Wyatt. Once, during a lunchtime chat with Bernie, he tried to explain the fervor, the fire in his gut, but Bernie couldn't grasp the idea.

When Wyatt tried to explain his passion to Lauren, she'd smile as a mother might at her child. But he knew this part of him puzzled her and the thought saddened him. This isolation in his craft, this solitude, made him lonely, and he realized that, in many ways, he marched alone. He sought solace by seeking technical challenges, same as an athlete searching for the most formidable adversaries.

So Wyatt worked. The hour became late and the intrusive outside noise of traffic softened. The only sound was the tap, tap, tap of Wyatt's fingers dancing on the keyboard.

Numbers aren't right. His thoughts stuttered as he fought disturbing conflicts in the data. He crouched closer to the computer. *Something's wrong.* He rubbed his burning eyes and reviewed the mathematical formulas he'd entered in the spreadsheet. *Reynolds Number. Looks funny. Viscosity?* "Dang!" Wyatt bellowed at the empty room. "Wrong exponent! Crap!" He banged on the table and jumped from his chair. "Gotta re-do everything!" He paced back and forth trying to calm himself. He felt exhausted and sank into his chair rubbing his eyes. Wyatt sighed and turned off the computer. *I'm beat. Besides, Leechmann's back at SAC again tomorrow and I should follow up with Bernie on the housing.*

Wyatt tucked his 'To-Do' list into his shirt pocket, tugged his key ring from his pocket and stepped out. Turning, he locked the door, smiled and patted it. "Optimal, be happy in your new home," he whispered, "We'll give them hell tomorrow."

Traffic was light. Wyatt rolled the window down and sucked in the cool evening air. He reflected on the day's work and realized that the mistake was a serious setback. To quell his agony over the blunder, he turned on the CD player and listened to the Everly Brothers singing *Let It Be Me.*

But insistent thoughts overruled the music, prodding Wyatt's mind back to the design problem. Then it happened—lightning! "I got it!" He yelled and slapped the steering wheel with joy. "Hot dang!" Laughing, he pulled up to a red light and looked around, hoping nobody heard his outburst. *Wait 'till I tell Lauren. Madison too.*

Chapter 23

It was past nine at night when Lauren finished loading the dishwasher. She dried her hands, took a final glance around her tidy kitchen and flipped off the light. Weary, she trudged into the living room where Timmie was thumbing through a children's picture book.

"Nice to see you reading, Timmie."

Timmie turned a page without looking up. "It's the Easter book Grandma gave me. About rabbits and things." She snapped the book shut. "Can I have a cookie?"

"No, Dear. You had one after dinner. That's enough. Besides, it's way past your bedtime. Come get ready."

"Where's Daddy? I want Daddy to put me to bed."

"He's still working. I don't know when he'll be home, so I'll tuck you into bed."

"He's *never* home." Timmie pouted, her lower lip quivering. "Jennifer's daddy comes home every night. He's nice."

Lauren kneeled and took her daughter's hand. "Your daddy's nice, too; he's working very hard for our future, that's all."

Her face puckered, Timmie looked at Lauren. "He doesn't love me, does he?"

Lauren's throat clamped off her breath., her heart pounded and her eyes misted. "Of course he loves you, Sweetheart," she stammered. "He'll be home soon and I'll have him give you a kiss, okay? Now let's call it a night. It's late."

Timmie stood and kicked her book half-heartedly. "I'm not tired."

"Tell you what. Get into your jammies and I'll get a cookie for you. Deal?"

Timmie smiled. "Okay."

Lauren had been in bed for three sleepless hours and was still wide-awake. The red eye of the digital clock blinked, heralding the passage of yet another minute. She turned on her side and tried to sleep, but couldn't. The distant hum of the refrigerator crept through the bedroom doorway and pried into her consciousness. Garfield, snoozing at the foot of the bed, stood, stretched and turned around. With a yawn, he flopped back down and curled into a ball.

Lauren heard Wyatt's whistling as he unlocked the door. Angry, she rolled over and squinted at the clock. *One-fifteen. He promised one hour at most. Can't the man tell time?*

She heard a plop when Wyatt dropped his briefcase, a grunt as he peeled off his jacket and the soft clump-clump when he walked toward the bedroom.

"You awake, Honey?" he called softly.

Lauren pretended to sleep.

Wyatt sat on the edge of the bed, scratched Garfield's back and repeated, "Honey?"

She remained motionless.

He reached over and shook her. Lauren stirred, pulled her pillow closer and feigned slumber.

Wyatt shook her again, more vigorously. "Lauren, Honey? I have great news. Can you wake up?"

Lauren abandoned her charade and propped herself on an elbow. "What?" she hissed.

"Had a great night. Remember that problem with the pressure balance on the main diaphragm?"

"No."

"Well, it was the last remaining conceptual problem on the outflow valves. Bang! Out of nowhere, the solution came to me." Wyatt kicked off his shoes. "What a breakthrough. It's a huge load off my mind."

Even in the dark, Lauren sensed the joy in his voice, but her anger wedged between them. Tight lipped, she looked at the clock. "Wyatt, I go to work in a few hours. Go kiss your daughter." She rolled over and pulled the blanket over her ear.

"Sure." He stood and started toward Timmie's bedroom, shaking his head.

)( )( )(

The next morning, Wyatt was puzzled. *Why was Lauren mad? Heck, I'd crushed the pressure balance problem!*

Wyatt fumbled with the coffee pot, spilling grounds on the counter. He ran his fingers through his hair, still damp from the shower, and went out into the chilly darkness for the newspaper. Returning, he sat at the dinette table and saw the headline,

Congress Plans New Regulations

Wyatt clenched his jaw and began to read the article, but the crash of a cabinet door boomed from the bathroom interrupted him. The thunder of slamming drawers and the rattle of shampoo bottles shattered the pre-dawn stillness.

Bewildered by his wife's anger, Wyatt thought. *Okay, I was late, so she had a reason to be mad. But I'd solved a huge problem. She never gave me a chance to explain.*

Lauren stormed into the kitchen, took two boxes of cereal from the pantry and dropped them in front of Wyatt. The pantry door banged shut. She snatched a carton of milk from the refrigerator. Smack went the door. She rummaged in the drawer for spoons and silverware clattered as she threw them on the table.

Wyatt fought to control his temper. Slowly and deliberately he poured a heap of Frosted Flakes in his bowl, added milk and sprinkled a heaping spoonful of sugar on top.

"It's already sweetened," scolded Lauren. "Sugar's bad for you."

"You've sung that tune dozens of times. What's going on? All this mayhem?"

"Mayhem? Maybe I should show you *real* mayhem." She sat in her chair and said, "Milk."

Wyatt passed the carton. "Well?"

"Last night. You said an hour at most. It was after one in the morning when you finally blessed us with your presence."

"I know—got caught up in the design problem. Should have called."

"Darn right. Know what Timmie said last night? She wanted you to put her to bed, but you weren't home. So she asked, 'Does Daddy love me?' Nice, huh?" Lauren's face was rigid, and she clamped her arms taut against her chest. "How do I deal with that, Wyatt? How?"

"She said that?"

Lauren nodded. "Broke my heart."

Wyatt set his spoon on the table. "I had no idea."

"There's more to life than work. Timmie's our legacy. She's the fruit of our love and you've abandoned her."

Humiliated, Wyatt stared at his cereal bowl. "Guess so."

Lauren caught her breath. "I think you believe engineering is more important than your family."

The accusation stunned Wyatt and frantically, he tried to explain. "That's not true. I'll admit there's a demon inside me––like last night. Sometimes it takes over." He held up his hand as Lauren began to interject. "No excuse. I'm not making excuses."

"Look, we're bouncing off the walls," Lauren said. "Full-time jobs, Optimal and family. We're worn out. We have to cut back."

"I don't understand. Yesterday you seemed excited about our new office. I thought you were having fun."

"Okay," Lauren said. "The new company *is* exciting, but we're drowning; our family is hurting. We have to put more distance between us and the business."

Wyatt gazed across the table into his wife's glittering blue eyes. His gut tensed as he realized he could never back away from Optimal; he couldn't do what his wife wanted. He thought of lying, telling her what she wanted to hear, but rejected the idea. No question he worked long hours, but it was for his family.

Or is it? Like always, he searched for a solution. Perhaps he could spend more time at home if he hired an engineer or quit Simmons Aircraft, but there wasn't enough money. There wasn't an easy way out.

"Tell you what," he said, "I'll try to be home for dinner, even if I go back to the office later that night."

Lauren nodded, but was silent.

"Something else," Wyatt said. "I miss our Sunset Ritual. Let's start again. Even if we talk about Optimal business, at least we'd be together for an hour or so."

"Without Madison, I hope?"

"Without Madison."

"Every night?"

"As often as I can."

"That's not very definitive," Lauren said.

Wyatt rose and went to Lauren and rubbed her shoulders. "We'll do what we can do."

Lauren stood and gathered an armload of dishes. "I have to get Timmie to school and you need to leave for work. I expect to see you tonight for a glass of wine. Later, you can go back to the office for an hour or so. Agreed?"

"Agreed." Wyatt smiled and swallowed the last of his tepid coffee. "Suppose we invite Timmie to our Sunset Ritual. Give her a wine glass filled with milk. What do you think?"

Lauren looked at her husband with a raised eyebrow and then pecked him on the cheek. "Go to work."

Chapter 24

Her day at King Aviation over, Madison journeyed across town and parked her Miata, top down, in front of Optimal Aviation Systems' new office. At last the morning's overcast had burned off, and the sun was high, even at five-thirty in the evening. The springtime air was warm and puffy fair-weather clouds brushed the nearby mountains. She stepped from the car and ran her fingers through her hair, untangling the wind-blown snarls.

Madison walked into the empty office, flicked on the lights and booted up her computer. She ignored the glaring table lamp and snaking extension cords strung across the floor because a miracle had happened—Brandon couldn't find more excuses and approved their application. Wyatt planned to work on the electrical outlets and partitions over the next few days and then call for inspection.

She pulled a sheaf of papers from a drawer, scrutinized a logic diagram and began typing code. After a few moments, she leaned back in her chair and laced her fingers. Alone in the office, Madison was uneasy. In an older industrial area, the building was plastered with flaky stucco and had a seedy appearance. Out front, the pot-holed street was lightly traveled, emphasizing her sense of isolation.

Madison knew the source of her anxiety. Three years ago in September, she'd attended the IMTS trade show in Chicago. She'd spent the day at the convention center, visiting booths, talking with garrulous sales people and gathering literature. After the show closed, she dropped into a hospitality room hosted by a prominent software firm. After several glasses of wine, she decided to clear her head by walking the two blocks to her hotel. Madison had stepped out into the dark, blustery night where a leaf-laden gust of wind tugged at her coat and blew hair over her eyes.

Suddenly, a pair of muscular arms yanked her into an alleyway. A scream rose in her throat, but was stifled by a hand clamped across her mouth. A gravelly voice said, "You make a sound and I'll break your fuckin' neck." The man shoved her deep into the dark chasm and pinned her to the wall. Holding Madison by the neck, he seized her purse and growled, "You a rich bitch?" The assailant stared at her and sneered. "Hey, you're a sweet piece of ass." Dropping the purse, he grabbed her breast. Madison, gasping for breath, tried to knee him, but couldn't. With a frantic twist, she yanked free, stumbled out of her high heels and dashed toward the bright lights of the street. Hoarse laughter followed her. Desperate, Madison ran to the hotel, staggered through the lobby and flung herself on the front desk, sobbing. The clerk called the police, who launched a broad search for the man—although a futile one.

Come on, Madison; stop this. Settle down and write the damn code. She scooted closer to the keyboard and closed her eyes, concentrating. Her anxiety eased, and the work swept her into a comfortable world of zeros and ones.

It was almost eight o'clock when Wyatt strode through the door. "Hi, Madison. You making any progress?"

"Yup. Working on that algorithm we talked about yesterday." She turned and faced him. "It sure is lonely without you here."

A scowl clouded Wyatt's face. "It isn't fair, I guess, you working while I'm at home. It's just that my family life could use a tad of maintenance work."

"Perhaps being single has its advantages." Madison gave him an appraising glance and his burly build, easy smile and hazel eyes set her at ease. "Well, it's not dark this time of year. Winter will be worse. I don't like being alone in the dark."

"Didn't the real estate lady say they had security patrols?" Wyatt asked as he turned on the computer and flopped in his chair.

"I've never seen a car. Have you?"

"No. Tell you what, I'll call the security company and a see if they'll patrol when I'm not here."

"That'd help." Madison rose, went to the coffee pot and filled it with water. "You're not in trouble at home, are you? Maintenance, you said?"

"No, not really. Lauren and I bumped heads because I'm working all the time. Timmie's the age where little girls go crazy-nuts over their fathers, and I'm not around much. And there's the Sunset Ritual, where Lauren and I have a glass of wine every night. Been decommissioned for a while, but we're starting again. That's why I can't get here until late."

"Sounds like the tail wagging the dog." Madison returned to her computer, but her mind wasn't on code. She felt unsettled. Was it because she was frightened of being alone at night? Did she think Wyatt wasn't holding up his end? Or was she jealous of his family life?

Click, click, click, she entered a line of code, looked at it, grimaced and hit "Delete."

Jealousy, she decided. More and more, she dreaded going home to a vacant apartment. Optimal had filled big chunks of empty time, but dark, silent rooms still confronted her every night. Although Madison didn't want children, she understood how Timmie brought meaning to Wyatt's life.

Her fondness for him had grown as the weeks passed. Madison acknowledged she was drawn to him physically, but as they worked together, the brilliance of Wyatt's thinking pre-empted her carnal urges. Intoxicated with science, they connected on an esoteric level she'd never thought possible.

"Coffee's done. Want a cup?" Madison asked.

"Sure."

She filled two cups and returned to her desk. "Here. Cream?"

Wyatt shook his head.

Madison added a dash of creamer to her cup and took a sip. She rubbed her chin and said, "Wyatt, here's a philosophical question for you. We're burning hours like a California brush fire on this project. Does it matter in the broad scheme of things?"

Wyatt looked up from his monitor. "Heavy question. You're not getting cold feet, are you?"

"No, no. Not at all."

"What's the alternative? Mediocrity? Dang right, it matters." Wyatt looked fierce as he continued. "You and I have a gift, Madison; we have a way with engineering. But gifts come with an obligation. Suppose Mozart or Einstein just hung out at the beach, drank beer and dropped out? The world would be smaller. Maybe we're not Einstein, but our idea could benefit millions. It's immoral to squander our skills chasing mindless pleasures."

"Interesting thought," Madison said. "But in a few years, our work will be obsolete anyway. Worthless."

"Never worthless! When men came down from the trees, they started a long trip toward knowledge and understanding. In a sense, you and I are in harness pulling toward the future. Others will build on our efforts and perhaps be appreciative as we are of Newton or Bill Boeing. We've been given a noble calling, Madison. Our work, and Optimal, matters in every sense of the word."

Madison nodded, astonished at Wyatt's homily. He'd flashed a bold light into her thinking, bringing new significance to her life. *This man has a soul*, she thought. Tears welled in her eyes and she turned away feeling embarrassed and silly. She gulped.

It was then she realized that she loved Wyatt.

"Enough of these mental gymnastics," joked Wyatt. "Let's get some work done."

Madison laughed—too loudly. Giddy, she nodded and turned to her computer. The work stalled and the program rambled without discipline. She struggled with revisions, but the code fought back, stubborn. Wyatt's words swelled in her mind, *we have an obligation, Madison*. She ground her teeth and concentrated.

Wyatt, too, seemed engrossed as he juggled an open book, a sheaf of graphs and twitched his mouse back and forth. Silence, punctuated by clicking keyboards and an occasional grunt, plodded onward.

"Wow!" Madison cried. "I got it! Wyatt, look at this."

Wyatt scooted over in his chair. "What?"

"I changed the logic diagram, here and here," she said pointing. "Half the code is eliminated. The thing becomes elegant. Beyond elegant."

Wyatt studied the revised diagram. His smile spread and his eyes crinkled with glee. "This is beautiful. Have one of your lightning strikes?"

"What?"

"You know, 'lightning in the cranium,' Remember?"

Madison laughed. "Yeah. I do." Wyatt's praise was a warm blanket, comforting and secure. With a contented smile, she dropped her hands into her lap. "Hey, it's eleven thirty; want to buy me a drink to celebrate?"

Chapter 25

Madison sat in her dark apartment and struggled with her love for Wyatt.

In high school, Madison's parents fretted over her passion for math and science. They saw their daughter as a social outcast and prodded her to give up technology, hoping she'd become a cheerleader or star in school plays. But Madison rejected family pressure, joined the astronomy club and pestered the algebra teacher for extra help.

As graduation approached, her mother, fearing her daughter's looming spinsterhood, pushed Madison into a relationship with a star football player of a local college. Madison yielded to her adventurous nature and married that summer. Her new husband was a gorgeous, easygoing man but an intellectual dolt. Divorce came swift and painless. Without breaking stride, she enrolled in college, majoring in electrical engineering.

Madison was wondrous over the ardor she felt for Wyatt. Her days sparkled, and she hummed tunes as she designed circuit boards. On an impulse, she bought expensive gourmet cat food for G-G and a toy mouse, stuffed with catnip, for his playing pleasure. The checkout clerk at the grocery store, seeing her effervescent smile, asked for a date. A colleague at King Aviation, hearing her laughter, asked if she'd won the lottery. In the mornings, as she put on lipstick, Madison knew the image in the mirror had changed. Tenseness had yielded to girlish freshness; her skin glowed and her hair glimmered in the light. Spring had arrived in Burbank and in Madison's heart.

She cherished the evenings with Wyatt as they worked. Optimal became the center of her life. Although King Aviation consumed her days, Optimal and Wyatt, devoured her nights. Madison couldn't express her love for Wyatt in bed, so she became fervent in making the company a success. When she wrote code and designed printed circuit boards, it wasn't science as much as vicarious lovemaking.

But Madison knew the relationship couldn't go anywhere and suspected Wyatt had few feelings for her except professional respect. But she didn't feel rejected. Rather, she was pleased to share his passions, even if platonically. But a spark of trouble edged into Madison's mind. *Would that be sufficient tomorrow? Next week? Next year?*

Spring eased into summer and the mountains shed their green cloak and donned a mantle of bronze. The last rain occurred in March, and typical of the Southern California climate, no more was expected until Christmas. Although afternoon temperatures soared, evenings were cool. Television commentators predicted a horrific fire season and officials began the process of leasing firefighting aircraft from Canada. A 4.5 earthquake jiggled the rides at Disneyland satiating the tourists' expectations, but native Californians brushed it off, far more concerned about dry chaparral on the hillsides.

Madison didn't notice the subtle seasonal changes and embraced her work. At day's end, she bolted from King to the sanctuary of the new office where the summer sun was bright and her fears of being alone receded.

By late summer, the software was ready for testing. She was pleased; the code was exquisite in its sophistication and simplicity––worthy of Wyatt.

Next, she turned her attention to the design of the printed circuit boards. Four complex multilayer boards, each the size of a playing card, connected hundreds of transistors, resistors, logic chips and capacitors. Madison's new PCB design software facilitated the work, and she completed the designs by mid-October. Then, she began constructing jury-rigged cards, called breadboards, for testing.

Like a child thumbing through Christmas toy catalogs, Madison went online and ordered myriad electronic components. They, alongside soldering irons, schematics and a coffee cup crowned with green mold, smothered the bench. Even when a molten drop of solder burned a hole in her jeans, Madison was happy and gratified. The breadboards were a manifestation of her talent and skill. When Wyatt kidded her about their spaghetti-jumble, she defended her work with roguish zeal.

Side-by-side with Wyatt at the bench, they ran through a pre-planned series of checkouts. His closeness warmed her and their banter was spontaneous and often funny. By Halloween, they'd reached a milestone; both the circuitry and software were successful. She confidently anticipated the full-scale system tests yet to come––when her work would coalesce with Wyatt's hardware and consummate their ersatz marriage.

>< >< ><

Time between the Sunset Rituals became longer and longer as the business eroded their earnest commitment to marital harmony. Lauren shivered with the realization that her time with Wyatt had dwindled while Madison commanded his full attention.

Lauren didn't know what to do. Liza's busy social schedule allowed only occasional days with her granddaughter. Twice after work, Lauren picked up Timmie at after-school care and took her to Optimal's new office. But the child became bored and fussed, disturbing Wyatt and Madison. Lauren tried to help, but was as useless as Casanova in a convent because she couldn't contribute to the technical negotiations.

Maybe it would be better, she thought, if she stayed home with Timmie, but that left Madison alone with Wyatt, a troubling situation. Anxious to check the goings-on at Optimal, Lauren made arrangements with Jennifer's mother to watch Timmie from time to time. That way, she could pop in on Wyatt unannounced, pretending errands. Occasionally she took off an hour from work. It was awkward, and Lauren feared, transparent. But she saw no other course of action.

Now that soccer season was over, Timmie became increasingly irascible. With a pointed gibe, Liza told Lauren that a part-time mother could expect little else. Determined to prove her wrong, Lauren devoted her spare time to her daughter. They sang songs and chitchatted about school adventures as they drove home from after-school care. Looking like flour-painted clowns, they baked cookies, and after dinner, read until bedtime.

Thus, with Liza's and the neighbor's help, Lauren found

time to make occasional surprise visits to Optimal while bonding with Timmie.

Lauren grappled with the business and searched online for information on licenses, permits and taxes required for new companies. Most of what she found was solicitations by consultants, but the website for the City of Burbank was useful.

Lauren was pleased when Lee Wong, on one of her visits to the bank, offered his help. "Strictly unofficial," he cautioned. She enjoyed Wong and felt protected as if he'd put a fatherly arm around her shoulders. At the bank, the calmness of soft-spoken tellers, mahogany desks and tradition soothed her.

With Wong's help, Lauren compiled a list:

- Air quality form with emissions fee: State AQMD.
- Burbank fire permit for alcohol and acetone storage.
- HAZMAT disclosure program.
- Form 501EF to State Board of Equalization.
- Form 501LA regarding lead poisoning. Get waiver?
- Pay Burbank City Business Tax.
- Burbank City Business license.
- Look into second hand smoke ordinance.
- Look into noise control ordinance.

The list intimidated her. The complicated government forms seemed to multiply like proverbial rabbits. Lauren dreaded the times when she picked up the bulging folder labeled "Business Filings." The pages blurred into a confusing jumble as she labored late at night with scratchy eyes and aching shoulders.

The hateful folder aside, things went well in May and June. Lauren had little trouble managing Optimal's cash because the he monthly bills for rent, utilities and cable were modest. But as autumn approached, Wyatt and Madison began buying expensive test equipment and data acquisition software. Grimly, she watched the bank balance diminish.

Wyatt, in his own world at Optimal's new office, was unavailable to help, leaving her feeling abandoned and forsaken. A cloud of foreboding hovered over her as she mechanically plodded through her workday and the late night combat with "The Folder."

)( )( )(

Wyatt enjoyed these months and work progressed well. While he chafed at SAC, evenings and weekends were riveting. By divesting the business portion of Optimal to Lauren, he concentrated on the prodigious amount of design. Four major assemblies comprised the system, each requiring up to eighty detail drawings. But Wyatt wasn't intimidated by such enormity; rather he found it fun, roller coaster fun, ice cream fun. He leapt into each analysis with zest, and rapture encapsulated him in a cocoon. Like a chrysalis, his ideas evolved from primitive to wondrous. Time faded from Wyatt's consciousness and fatigue held no sway. With reluctance, he'd crawl into bed at two in the morning and fend off sleep conjuring novel designs.

Often, he and Madison snacked on pretzels or apples, and they put the coffee pot on overtime. Although Madison hovered nearby, Wyatt had little interaction with her; she cranked code, he created drawings. He failed to notice little things Madison did for him. She sometimes left cookies cradled in colorful paper napkins by his keyboard and once gave him a mouse pad with a portrait of Einstein. Oblivious, Wyatt munched and worked, sequestered in his private realm.

By the first of October, Wyatt had completed most drawings and searched for companies to manufacture prototype parts. He'd looked at two or three small machine shops, but they had limited capabilities.

So he sought larger shops that could do everything. The web provided several candidates, and he picked one close by—Precision Tool and Machine, a long-established aerospace house having 175 employees. He sneaked a telephone call from SAC and made an appointment to check them out on the following Saturday.

That Saturday morning at Optimal, Wyatt was in a sunny mood, kidding with Madison as he heaped a hundred blueprints in a bundle to take to Precision Tool. He'd crested a hill and the road ahead looked easy. The physical activity of making copies, collating and stapling pages was a pleasant change from "computer pounding." Lauren lent a hand while Timmie, after pouring coffee for her father, quietly played with a few discarded cardboard cartons, fashioning a house.

Wyatt, taking a break, stepped outside with his perennial coffee cup. The fall air was crisp and the sky bright blue. He sucked in a bountiful lungful of air and watched as birds fluttered in random patterns.

Then he frowned, remembering that although he got permits for the office updates, the Building and Safety office had rejected his third try for the big test equipment.

Also, he had no luck with the SBA. "No HUBZone? Well, that's a complication," they said. Wyatt's anxiety soared when Lauren grumbled that their cash was coming to an end, but there was nothing he could do. Frustrated, he went inside and resumed compiling copies of drawings.

Then his frown morphed into a grin. Precision Tool promised to be a happy diversion from the regulatory bog.

Chapter 26

"I'm Mike Graham. How the hell are ya?" said the short, chunky man in his late-sixties. He sported an immense gray mustache that looked out of place beneath his high forehead crowned by bristly stubble. Bushy eyebrows bridged his flashing coal-black eyes and an unlit cigarette dangled from his lips. Clad in faded jeans and an oil-spotted shop apron, he thrust out his hand and nearly jerked Wyatt off his feet with the handshake.

Mike's gruff greeting surprised Wyatt; he'd expected Graham, the owner, would be a stolid, soft-spoken business executive. With a grin, he said, "Wyatt Morgan. This is Madison McKenzie."

"Sit," Mike commanded.

As they settled into chrome and Naugahyde chairs, Wyatt looked around the room. Mike sat behind a scarred, wooden desk, cluttered with blueprints and metal parts. A broken milling cutter crowned a stack of papers and a soiled keyboard rested in front of a computer monitor. Off to one side, gray metal shelves sagged under the weight of hundreds of sample parts, making the office resemble an auto-parts store rather than an industrialist's bastion. An old coffee table was awash with job folders and trade magazines, well thumbed and dog-eared. A water cooler lurked in a corner, its catch tray full. Through a side door, a shrill squeal pierced the jumble. In contrast, Wyatt noticed an elegant glass display on the far wall, brightly lighted.

Its panes were sparkling clean and inside, glistening metal objects were arrayed in precise rows.

"What's in the cabinet," Wyatt asked, pointing to the case.

"Those are Mars Rover components," Mike said. "*Spirit* and *Opportunity*. Bastards ran forever. Most are titanium. Damn fine stuff, but shitty to machine. Had to develop special tools and techniques. I worked on the new one too: *Curiosity*. Got that award from NASA, there on the wall," he said, pointing. "Big fucking ceremony with a bunch of suits, know what I mean? Put Precision Machine and Tool on the goddamn map." Mike's smile became so wide; the cigarette teetered on his lips.

Wyatt was impressed. "That means you passed NASA's quality survey, right?"

"Fuckin' A," Mike boomed, slapping the desk. His glance fell on Madison. "Sorry, Madison, my language gets a little salty sometimes. My apology."

"That's okay," she said. "with an older brother, my vocabulary matured at an early age."

"Want a quick tour of the shop before we get down to business?" Mike offered. "Got nice machinery out there."

"Sounds great," Wyatt said.

"Okay," echoed Madison. "But remember, I'm an electrical engineer who can't tell a file from a jackhammer, so be patient with me."

They stepped through the side door into the machine shop. Wyatt gasped. "Look at that, Madison. Dozens of lathes."

"Twenty-seven, to be exact," Mike exclaimed, his unlit cigarette bobbing. "Everyone but the tool maker's is computerized. All are painted yellow. You'll notice the lathe people wear yellow tee shirts. The mills are blue and their operators have blue shirts. Grinders are red, saws green and the burr guys are in orange. Fuckin' rainbow," he smiled.

Madison nodded. "Why...the rainbow?"

"Pride. Competition. Allegiance. See the signs over each department? They show rejection rates. Each month, I invite the department with the fewest rejections to my house for a barbecue. Everyone brings their spouse. We get bombed on beer and eat ribs so spicy you fart flames. Check out the banner hanging from the ceiling in the middle of the shop. Red this month. The grinding department was best. See the gold stars on it? That's how many times the grinders won. Guys in red are struttin' today, you can be damned sure."

Wyatt was euphoric. The machines were arranged in cells where a single operator could manage two or three at once. In every cell, computers displayed detail drawings and routing sheets for each part. Racks held dedicated cutting tools and inspection fixtures. Forklifts scurried down the aisles ferrying pallets of raw material or racks of parts.

Wyatt watched Mike stride between the machines, conferring with the operators and fondling parts, still warm from the friction of the cutting tool. With a smile ringed with pride, a machinist in charge of a cell explained his approach to the job.

Wyatt beamed. *Here's a millionaire owner of a big company, dressed same as the workers. I guess he fancies himself as a machinist first, then a businessman. You gotta love it.*

They were moving through the mill department when Mike excused himself, saying, "You guys hang out, okay? I need to make a stop." He jabbed his thumb toward the men's room and walked away.

Madison looked across the factory floor. "Smoke from the machines looks like London fog."

"Noise is bad, too," Wyatt said. "I'm glad I don't work out in a shop, but I'll admit it turns me on. This is industry at its finest, Maddy. In a way, Mike explored Mars, riding his titanium parts. We're aiming high too. Soon we'll be pampering the Warren Buffets of the world at 35,000 feet."

"Sorry," Mike said returning. "Nature called." He set his unlit cigarette between his teeth. "Tryin' to quit smoking. Shitty habit." He grinned, and they continued.

Wyatt had questions, many questions. Mike, bending over a machine where gossamer chips hissed in the mist of cutting oil, explained several innovative processes new to Wyatt.

"Wyatt, check this out," Mike hollered over the skirl of a flexible machine center. "Automatic tool wear compensation. See that sapphire probe? Accurate within 5 millionths of an inch. Wireless transmission to the computer."

"Wireless?" Wyatt exclaimed. "So is our pressurization system."

"Kindred spirits," Madison yelled, grinning.

"Fuckin' A," Mike shouted.

Wyatt, unaccustomed to profanity, had to smile. While there was a chasm between them in age, dress and vocabulary, Wyatt felt a bond with Mike. Here was a man who found joy in sculpting precision mechanisms from formless chunks of metal. Skill seemed to ooze from his pores as he showed off his shop.

They returned to Mike's office where Madison glanced through a trade magazine while Wyatt spread his drawings on the desk. For an hour they studied them, critiquing the designs. In hushed tones, they sketched refinements and tabulated tolerance stack-ups on the prints.

"You have a good head for design, Wyatt," Mike pronounced. "You ought to see the crap people bring in— impossible to make. Why don't you leave your drawings with me so I can work up firm costs? Take around a week, okay?"

"Fine," Wyatt said.

"Madison, come over here—I want to brag on Precision Tool," Mike said. "My father started the company in 1942, during the War. He was a young shit. Ass was on fire, know what I mean? Had my butt haulin' metal chips by the time I was ten. Didn't hurt me a bit! Now, child labor is against the law," He laughed. "It's fucking crazy, but I *love* the chatter of milling machines and chips in the soles of my shoes. Look." Mike swiveled in his chair and crossed his leg, revealing the sole of his shoe. It glittered with dozens of metal fragments, picked up from the floor as he walked in the shop.

"I took over in '82, grew it from 25 guys to over 180 now. Crankin' two shifts. Holding my own, even in this fuckin' economy."

"You probably think I'm nuts trying to start a company these days," Wyatt said. "But my pressurization idea has me by the throat."

"An obsession," Madison chuckled.

"I suppose that's right," Wyatt admitted. "But when a

guy sees a chance to stir the soup of technology, to rock an industry, you have to jump in."

They walked to the door where Mike said, "I don't know where you found this guy, Madison, but he has his shit together. Be a fuckin' pleasure to work with you guys."

"Mike's one big garbage mouth," Madison said as they drove back to their office. "It sounds as if he knows his stuff. Does he?"

"Fuckin' A," Wyatt winked. "In just a few minutes, we cut the cost of the bleed air valve by $200. He's clever and imaginative. Must be sixty-something, but moves like he's my age. Almost a full crew on Saturday. Yup, he's doing well."

"What's with the cigarette? He went into the restroom with a half-chewed butt and came out with a pristine one."

"Saw that," Wyatt chuckled. "He didn't pee at all. Bet he lit up."

They laughed, drove to Optimal's office and worked past midnight.

It was getting dark earlier as October crept toward Halloween. Sycamore leaves swished in the wind and invaded Optimal's doorway when Wyatt and Lauren stepped inside. "Hi, Madison," both chimed.

Madison nodded. "You had something important to talk about?"

"Yeah," Wyatt began. "Mike's quote is mind-boggling. A set of prototype hardware comes to over $70,000."

"Good grief, Wyatt, that blows our cash," Madison gasped.

"Well," Lauren said, "it's obvious we need quotes from other machine shops. We can't commit this kind of money on just one bid."

Wyatt crossed his arms. "You're right, but I have confidence in Mike." He leaned back in his chair. "Remember what you said of Lee Wong? How you connected with the banker? How he gave you a sense of reliability? Well, I feel that with Mike. I'll bet he has cutting oil in his veins."

"Did you expect the parts to cost so much, Wyatt?" asked Madison.

"Well, we have to consider we're buying around two hundred different components—all precision stuff."

Madison stood and walked a few paces, then turned with her hands on her hips. "Look, I'm an electron person, not mechanical, so I'll have to rely on your judgment. I can't help with this decision."

"Me neither," Lauren said. "I'm just shocked about the cost. Like I said, we should get more bids."

"I agree," said Madison. "We haven't looked at the cost of the printed circuit boards yet. That'll add even more."

Lauren shook her head and looked at Wyatt. "Honey?"

Wyatt scowled and rubbed his eyes. "Let me sleep on it. I think I'll go to Precision Tool and discuss the quote with Mike. Do a little negotiating. For now, let's decide not to decide, okay?"

Lauren sighed and dropped her chin to her chest. "Okay," she whispered.

)( )( )(

By Halloween, Lauren agreed with Wyatt's decision to go with Precision Tool. Madison selected a consultant for software certification and found a fabricator for the printed circuit boards.

It was a Sunday afternoon at Optimal, and the three were busy. Timmie was sent next door to play, giving Lauren an hour or two at the office. She shuddered as she wrote the purchase orders to Precision Tool and Madison's PCB house. *At least Wyatt negotiated a discount and got Mike to stretch out payments.* Lauren, anxious about the immense financial commitment, double-checked the bank balance and blanched. But there was nothing she could do.

Wyatt stared at his calendar. "I have to block out a week or two to update the drawings the way Mike suggested. Same for you, Madison?"

"It's not so bad. My challenge will be the software certification. The FAA has to approve my test plan and authorize a third party to review and bless the results. At least I've been through this a few times."

Wyatt chuckled. "Yup. We're making progress."

Madison nodded. "For certain. We're on schedule and there haven't been any big blunders; knock on wood."

"Except money," Lauren grumbled. "No way it can last. These purchase orders are budget busters." She was perplexed. *How can they ignore the money? The business side of things? No matter what they think, it's not all science.* She shook her head again. "Without funds..." her voice trailed off.

Wyatt pushed back from his desk and faced Lauren. "I know. We have to do something. The SBA says it will take more time to examine our application. Maybe we should take out a personal loan to tide us over."

"Let's talk about that at home," Lauren snapped. "You and me."

Chapter 27

Wyatt strode into the SAC lunchroom, anger simmering in his throat.

"I see you're having a late lunch too," he said sitting across from Bernie. "Got tied up with Leechmann again. He was trying to ding me on one of my MRB dispositions. What an idiot."

"Did he nail you?"

"Nope. Had to admit he was wrong. He's clueless when it comes to metallurgical grain structure in a weld zone. The jerk should take a class or something. Better yet, get promoted to a mop jockey."

Bernie grinned. "You're a snob, Wyatt. A goddamn elitist."

"Not so. Government inspectors may have college degrees, but if a problem isn't covered in 'the book', they won't take a risk and make a judgment."

"'Nuff said." Bernie ladled a spoonful of hot soup to his lips and slurped. "I just spent three hours setting up a mill for the Gulfstream job. The machine is thirty years old and is temperamental as a pre-menstrual ballerina."

Wyatt laughed. "Some kinda temperamental. You sure spend a lot of time playing with your machines."

"I don't spend time, I waste it. Most of SAC's equipment ought to be dropped in the ocean to make reefs for fish."

Wyatt thought of Precision Tool and Mike Graham, knowing Bernie would envy the beautiful, modern machines, arranged in efficient cells. Their managers and engineers worked, not to Band-Aid ailing equipment, but to maximize production and quality. "Fish," Wyatt said wistfully. "It's not like that everywhere, Bernie."

"Tell me where they're doing it right and I'll put in my application."

Wyatt hesitated, opened his sandwich and doused it with salt. "There's a company close by. A top-drawer place."

"If it's so hot, why haven't you jumped ship, Wyatt?"

"It's a job shop, so they build to other company's blueprints. Their engineers are manufacturing types, not designers." Wyatt finished his sandwich, wadded the baggie and stuffed it inside the lunch bag, ignoring a piece of blue paper at the bottom. "I'd be out of place there."

Bernie nodded. "If I were younger, I'd check it out, but who'd hire a sixty-something derelict? How did you find this place?"

"Just did." Wyatt shifted in his chair. "Googled it or something."

"Why you lookin' for machine shops? Is my work unsatisfactory?"

"No, no. Not at all."

"A while back, you hinted you were working on something outside. Is there a connection?"

Wyatt picked up the saltshaker and fiddled, spinning it and bouncing it. The conversation had taken a bad turn, but he felt a need to explain things to his friend. More than a friend. It had become natural for them to meet in the lunchroom after-hours to work on problems that had arisen during the day. In the solitude of late night, they'd stare through steam from their coffee cups and wrestle with glitches or huddle around an intransigent lathe. In time, they bonded—not a casual buddy-thing, but a friendship rooted in mutual respect. But lately, Wyatt had been leaving at five o'clock sharp.

So Wyatt smiled and said, "Yeah, it does. Keep this under your hat, but I've started my own company. New product. Been at it a few months, now." The spinning shaker tipped, spilling salt on the table. Without thinking, Wyatt, pinched a few grains from the table and tossed them over his left shoulder. "The machine shop is making a few parts for me."

"You miserable shit. I *knew* something was going on." Bernie rapped the table and grinned. "Good for you, Wyatt. Yes sir. Guess you'll quit SAC?"

"Can't. Not for a while. A thing called money, you know."

"I bet it takes a bunch of cash to start a company. Hope you're rich."

"Ha. I'm scratching together my savings, such as they are. I have a partner, but she's just another poverty-stricken engineer."

"Lawyers and plumbers have money, but engineers and teachers march side-by-side to the poor house," Bernie laughed. "How's your wife taking this?"

"Not great, I guess. The business sucks up my time, so she worries our marriage is suffering. Maybe it is. Lauren's worn out from working full time, taking care of our kid and helping with Optimal too. Oh, that's the name of our company, Optimal Aviation Systems." Wyatt pushed his chair back from the table and crossed his legs. "You're right about the money. The machine shop order blew our bank account. I'm working on the SBA, but they won't lend unless I hire a bunch of dropouts." Wyatt sighed and spun the saltshaker.

Bernie tilted his soup-bowl and spooned out the last noodle. "I remember telling you that over the years, my dreams had slipped away. Hearing you talk, they're not gone, just hibernating." Bernie shook his head. "When you get old, you'll look back and reflect on what you've done, where you've been, and decisions you've made. I've many regrets; one because I always followed the easy path––never took a flyer. I had big visions once, but they were snuffed out by that evil called contentment." Bernie laced his fingers. "You can't appreciate how much I wish I were thirty again, and we were sitting in a coffee shop planning to launch our own company. We'd make a good team."

Wyatt's eyes sought those of his friend, but Bernie was staring at the wall. *He's right; we make a good team.* Wyatt swallowed and resolved that when Optimal got off the ground, he'd find a place for Bernie. He was an honorable man, one who Wyatt would like to stand alongside.

"Darn right, Bernie. Consider yourself a senior consultant for Optimal, unpaid, of course."

Bernie flashed a wry grin. "In a few weeks, or months, you'll set off on your great adventure and I'll plod my way into retirement. I'm gonna miss you."

"Bernie, you're not a plodder. Your work is important and everyone relies on you, me especially." Without thinking, Wyatt reached across the table and shook Bernie's hand. "You're the best."

The moment passed, and they rose to return to work. As Wyatt started up the stairs to Engineering, Bernie called, "If you need an investor, I have a few grand. Okay?"

Wyatt coughed to clear his throat. "You're nuts," he said.

Chapter 28

Wyatt concentrated and clenched his jaw. "Pass the screwdriver, would you, Maddy?"

"Just another Sunday morning at the Optimal sweat shop," Madison said. "I remember when I'd nestle in my favorite chair with the newspaper, a cup of coffee and G-G on my lap. Ah, for the old life."

"Hold this. No. Over here. Gotta align these two flexures. Good." Wyatt smiled as he tightened the screw. "Don't miss it."

"What?"

"The newspaper. I don't miss it."

"Honestly, Wyatt. You have a one-track mind."

He grunted. "Look at these parts. They're perfect. Go together like cream cheese on a bagel." He paused, his eyes searching the bench top. "Ah. There it is." Wyatt took the Allen wrench and tightened a setscrew. "Good." He held the assembly up to the light and squinted as he turned it over, checking every angle. "Okay. Let's see if the electronic pressure sensor tracks the aneroid."

They scooted their chairs to the opposite end of the bench where they'd constructed a crude vacuum calibration station and installed the sub-assembly.

Uncharacteristically, Wyatt felt chatty. "That Mike, for all his rough vocabulary, did a fantastic job. Sets a good example of how a business should run. When we swing into production, he'll be right there, cranking out perfection."

"Fuckin' A," grinned Madison.

Wyatt turned, stared at her with a raised eyebrow and chuckled, "Watch your language, young lady. You're supposed to be a professional."

They switched on a small vacuum pump. "Hope this works," Wyatt said. "That second-hand pump cost a mint. Lauren almost fainted when I gave her the bill."

"You saying the vacuum pump sucks?" Madison giggled.

"Puh...leese. Let's behave like serious scientists, or the ghost of Isaac Newton will sabotage everything."

"Newton? Don't you know that Tesla, Faraday and Ohm rule everything?" Madison joked.

"Second string." Watching the vacuum gage, Wyatt twiddled a needle valve. "What's the electronic sensor reading?"

For more than an hour, they bent over the test equipment, comparing the electronic sensor to the mechanical aneroid while Madison entered data in her laptop. Their occasional words mingled with the soft thumping of the vacuum pump that filled the room like chirping crickets on a summer's night.

"That ought to be enough," Wyatt said. "Let's look at correlation and linearity."

Madison keyed in the last data points and created a graph from the spreadsheet. Wyatt peered at the screen while Madison chewed on her pencil.

"The sensor tracks right on top of the aneroid. It's a virtually perfect correlation," Wyatt said.

"Linearity not so hot though. The graph curls up, start to finish." Madison took her pencil and tapped the screen.

"I could fix that with a simple algorithm. I don't think it's a problem."

Wyatt studied the curves and stood, turning ideas over in his head. "You sure?"

"I'm *positive*." She marched over to Wyatt, grasped his arm and beamed. "I can make it perfect. We've hit a major milestone!"

Wyatt thought her smile could have lit up the Rose Bowl stadium. "Positive? Coming from you, that's gold. I guess that's one small step for Optimal, one giant leap—you know the rest."

Madison waved her arms excitedly and cried out, "And one giant leap for Wyatt and Madison." Laughing, she threw her arms around him.

Wyatt was startled, but slipped an arm around her waist. She was bouncing with joy, infectious joy. Wyatt laughed and put his other arm around her and squeezed. The hug lingered and Wyatt suddenly felt traitorous, so he pushed Madison away and held her at arm's length. She gazed at him and drew her hair back. Madison's green eyes didn't waver from his and an easy smile lit her face.

Wyatt's heart clattered in his chest and he made a conscious effort to start breathing again. *Good grief. She's something. Like hugging a piece of heaven.*

The ringing of the telephone jolted Wyatt. He welcomed the distraction saying, "Optimal Aviation Systems, Wyatt speaking. Oh, hi, Darlin'. Of course I didn't forget; time just got away from me. No, I'm on my way. Sure. Bye."

He turned to Madison. "Seems I'm late to Timmie's soccer practice. Forgot all about it."

"That isn't what you told her."

Embarrassed, Wyatt grimaced. "Little white lie. I'm not in the habit, but sometimes..." Needing something to do, he switched off the vacuum pump. *Gotta put some distance between me and Maddy. Things are getting out of hand.* "Sorry I have to leave. Paternal duty calls, okay?" he muttered.

"Not a problem." A frown swept across Madison's face. "I'll tidy up the documentation and lock up. Go be a daddy."

Chapter 29

The next morning, back at her apartment eating breakfast, Madison fretted. *I shouldn't have hugged him, but it was wonderful.* She set her newspaper on the table and swallowed a spoonful of muesli. Her mood matched the November darkness lurking outside her dinette window. G-G jumped on a spare chair and whined for his morning treat of milk. Madison finished her cereal and set the bowl on the floor where the cat leapt to lap the lingering drops.

With furrowed brows, she strained to think of a way to rein in her passion for Wyatt—after all, she'd stumbled into forbidden territory. *How did such an impetuous thing happen? I'm a rational, disciplined engineer.* Madison worried it might happen again; only in daydreams could she make sensual love to Wyatt in thatched beach huts or walk hand-in-hand in Griffith Park.

Wyatt, she suspected, must have noticed something different. Although notorious for living in his engineering fog, he couldn't fail to see her stares, hear her unseemly giggle or sense her love when she patted his hand. He'd pushed her away when she hugged him and looked puzzled. He'd said nothing, but Madison felt his distress.

If she were to remain at his side and if Optimal were to survive, she had to squelch her desire for him. Depressed, Madison stared at the newspaper; the print blurred by tears, and vowed that there would be no more hugs. Ever.

Madison's morning at King Aviation was typical: a meeting to discuss a new electronic package for Raytheon, an hour on a troublesome computer program and a debate with the Sales Manager over a pending customer. At noontime, she walked into her office and closed the door. She opened her insulated lunch bag and set yogurt, an apple and a can of diet cola on the desk. As Madison ate, she assembled her thoughts, jotting a few lines on a yellow quad pad. Then she placed a call to AirEnvironment in Massachusetts.

"Eduardo, mi amigo. ¿Como esta?" Madison said.

"Estoy very tired today, Madison. You know damn well my Spanish is rusty. Why do you always slaughter such a nice language every time you call?"

Madison, hearing humor in his voice, laughed. "Because it annoys you, Ed. You always rise to the bait. Don't belittle my Spanish. I took two years in high school, right?"

"You slept through the classes, I'll bet. Say, isn't it lunchtime in California? Shouldn't you be swimming in a three-martini lunch?"

"No, Mr. Morales, I am an engineer, not a lawyer. I take my professional obligations seriously. And speaking of serious, I want to chat about something. Can you spare a moment?"

"Sure. Fire away."

"Don't mention this to anyone because my partner and I might get into trouble at our jobs, Okay?"

"Lips are sealed," Ed said.

"A friend and I have started a company to develop a new pressurization system that would play right into AirEnvironment's business. I'm hoping to pick your brains."

"Wow. Pressurization? That's an ambitious undertaking," exclaimed Ed.

Madison spent the next few minutes explaining how the system worked and the advances Wyatt had conceived.

"Is this a paper design, or do you have hardware?" Ed asked.

"Both. We've prototyped and tested key sub-assemblies. So far, so good." Madison tingled as her enthusiasm swelled. She gripped the phone and continued, "Our drawings are finished and we've placed orders for the parts."

"You sound as if you've witnessed the Second Coming, Madison. Is it that good?"

Madison took a deep breath and held it for a moment. *I can't sound too evangelical. Easy does it.* "We think so, Ed. There's work to do, but we plan to start system tests by the end of March. We'll know more by then."

"Sounds interesting. What do you want from me?"

"I'm hoping that we could meet and go over our ideas. Our ultimate aim is to do business with AirEnvironment."

"Crap, Madison. You should realize that mere engineers aren't allowed to talk business. I'll have to get Purchasing involved. We got to make them feel important, you know."

Madison chuckled. "Same at King. Would you do that? Pull them in for a presentation?"

"Let me get Nick Nolan on the line. He's the buyer for hardware like yours. I'll put you on hold for a second, okay?"

"Sure." Madison picked up a pencil and drummed impatiently, waiting for Ed to return.

"Madison? Nick's on the line. Nick, this is Madison

McKenzie. You'll recall we've worked with her before. King Aviation."

"Yeah. Hi, Madison," Nick purred, his voice as smooth as a trained actor. "What's up?"

"This is confidential, okay?" Ed interrupted. "Madison's working on a hot-shot pressurization system. Her own company. She wants to make a presentation to explain the thing."

"Wish I could, but I'm tied up until late next week."

"No, no," Madison said. "We won't be ready until March."

"Oh. That's okay. Ed, what's your thinking? We're buying good pressurization equipment now from Randel Products. Any reason to change?"

"Could be," Ed said. "What did you say, Madison? Way better than spectacular?"

"I was just being modest," Madison quipped.

"Wouldn't hurt to listen, I suppose," Nick said. "Nobody is developing fresh products anymore because the complicated FAA protocols snuff out innovation and drive certification costs out of sight. Even the big guys such as Cessna, Maddox and Raytheon have cut back on product development. Fact of life."

"True," Ed said. "But Madison may have something special. Like you said, it can't hurt to listen."

"Well, if you think her ideas have technical merit, I can arrange a meeting. Give me a week's notice, okay?"

Everyone agreed and Nick signed off.

After a pause, Ed said, "I want you to deal with me on this, Madison. I'll coordinate with Nick. Sometimes

I suspect he has fingers in more than one pie. Makes me nervous."

"Okay, and thanks for everything. We really appreciate your help."

"What's all this 'we' stuff? Do I know your partner?"

Madison felt the blood rush to her cheeks. "Yes. Wyatt Morgan, over at Simmons Aircraft Components."

"I've bumped into him, but we haven't done much business."

"Well, he's very good. This whole idea's his."

"Sounds like you have the technical bases covered. Do you have good financing?"

Madison flinched. "Not very. Savings, 401k, that sort of thing."

"Nick will dig into your money situation," Ed cautioned. "He'll want you to share the expenses for qualification. Be ready to discuss that."

Inwardly, Madison groaned. "We'll work on it."

It was five-thirty when Madison pulled into the gloom of Optimal's parking lot. She gathered her purse and papers and started to get out of the car, but hesitated. The office was still dark; Wyatt hadn't arrived. She set her stuff on the seat, locked the doors and waited, her eyes searching the deep shadows beyond the window.

Twenty minutes passed before Wyatt appeared. Madison greeted him at the door.

"Been waiting long?" he asked.

"Where have you been?" Madison demanded. "You said you'd be here by five-fifteen." Seeing Wyatt's quizzical look, she cautioned herself. *Simmer down. No big deal.* "Just a few minutes," she lied.

Once inside, they turned on the lights and settled in their chairs.

After Madison set down her purse and laptop, she sat on the corner of Wyatt's desk. "I've good news. This afternoon I talked to my friend at AirEnvironment. They've agreed to let us present our design sometime in March."

Wyatt glowed. "Fantastic, Maddy! A coup. How'd you do that?"

"When pressed, a girl has ways," she said, fluttering her eyelashes. "I had my friend Ed Morales begging to see our stuff. He pulled in their buyer, Nick Nolan, who'll want to go over our phantom finances."

"Maybe we can win the lottery," Wyatt laughed. "One thing is certain; AirEnvironment is a major supplier to the primes. You've landed a big fish."

"Please, Wyatt, give me credit. It's a whale. We're making real progress at last."

"If we land a biggie like AirEnvironment, it would help pry a loan out of the SBA." Wyatt rubbed his hands together. "Plus you've said King Aviation is interested, so that's two potential customers. SBA, here we come! Tonight, I'll ask Lauren to call Wong with the news—see if we can get that loan moving."

Madison nodded happily. "Call Mike too. I'll bet they're one of his customers."

"Yup. In the meantime, we have to finish the test stand for the inflow valves." Wyatt thumped his fist on the desk. "March, you said?"

"Right."

"March has 31 days, correct?" Wyatt said. "We'll need every minute we can get."

"Shift into overdrive," Madison chuckled.

Wyatt pumped his fist. "No, we'll light the afterburners."

Madison reveled in Wyatt's happiness and a smile creased her face. *Look at him. The airplane angels sit on his shoulder. He dances with them and they are joyful together. I envy the little bitches.*

Chapter 30

In spite of the late hour, Lauren tried to mellow out as she set a wine glass next to the Thanksgiving-themed candle twinkling between their chairs. She was looking forward to a rare moment with her husband.

"Here you are, Honey."

"Thanks, Darlin'. I'm glad you stayed up. It's been a crazy day."

"To be honest, I dozed after you called––around ten I guess. I'd put Timmie to bed long before that." Lauren shook her head. "Your daughter was a holy terror today; threw a screaming fit when I told her you were coming home late. So I bribed her with macaroni and cheese. I guess it's my fault she's chubby."

"Sorry," Wyatt said. "Got behind at work, so I stayed to finish two critical drawings. Got to Optimal around five-thirty. Madison was waiting in her car. She tried to hide it, but she seemed put-off. Then we wrangled with a bunch of new ideas; lost track of time. That's when I called you." Wyatt reached over and took Lauren's hand. "I miss our Sunset Rituals. I know I promised to do better, but time just evaporates. Today, I guess sunset is at midnight." Wyatt looked at his watch. "Correction. Twelve-forty-five."

Lauren made a soft purring sound and squeezed his hand. Wyatt's face shimmered in the candlelight. *He looks worn out.* "No matter," she replied, setting aside her irritation over Wyatt's tardiness. "Let's enjoy the moment."

Lauren reflected on the tumultuous year and couldn't

decide if it had been enthralling or troubling. Often Wyatt seemed possessed, preoccupied and remote. But other times he was affectionate and considerate. Mostly a mix; tonight for example. He'd called, sounding contrite, to cancel yet another Sunset Ritual. When, at last, he appeared at the front door, he gave her a warm kiss and hug and asked if she'd sit with him. Now, seeing him slumped in his chair with that boyish grin playing across his face, Lauren felt bonded to him, an intimate part of his life. Lauren enjoyed the thought and sipped her wine. "Fill me in on your day."

"Good news and bad news. The bad news first. Called LaMarr Garner, the SBA dork, who said they're still processing the application. Reminded me for the tenth time it would go easier if we'd locate in an enterprise zone. I stopped short of telling him to shove it, but..."

Lauren flinched, remembering their cash reserves were scant. "Wyatt, you have to placate those people. Remember what I said about the honey-vinegar thing?"

"Sure; honey catches flies. The problem is I'm dealing with life forms more primitive than flies. Same thing when I called Planning and Zoning––still no permits for the big test equipment. It's late November already, and I should have ordered the pumps and tanks by now."

"They're just doing their job, Honey."

"*Do* is a foreign word to them. I swear the guy at Planning is trying everything to sandbag us. Madison overheard a conversation at the Planning office––said they'd nit-pick me to death. Bet they're torqued because I argued with them."

"Planning wouldn't do that intentionally. They're just following the law."

"Well, I'm tired of waiting around. Gonna write emails to the Labor Department and the Burbank Mayor. Twist some tails."

"Settle down, Honey. We can't fix the government tonight. Let's change the subject. What's the good news for today?"

Wyatt sat straighter in his chair. "Ah yes, Madison contacted a friend at AirEnvironment."

"Is that the big airplane contractor you've mentioned?"

"Yeah, that's the one. Madison has a friend in Engineering there and convinced him to listen to a presentation describing our system. They could be our first customer."

"Wonderful," exclaimed Lauren. Thrilled, a tingle swept up her spine. "It sounds as if they're taking Optimal seriously. You also said King might follow soon. That'll raise our adrenaline levels."

"It's a kick to have your dream turn into something tangible. I feel like I've found my place in the universe."

Lauren leaned over and patted her husband's cheek. Swept up in the grandeur and scope of Wyatt's vision, she shivered with excitement. Settling back in her chair, she touched her breast. "Your place is right here, in my heart."

Wyatt laughed. "You're nuts."

Lauren paused and took a sip of wine. "Did you say Madison was stuck in her car?"

"Not stuck. She was waiting for me."

"She has a key. Why didn't she go inside?"

"I'm not sure. A while back she mentioned getting mugged in Chicago; perhaps that has something to do with it. It's funny that a confident woman like her is afraid of the dark. Stayed in her car until I showed up."

"Maybe she's not Wonder Woman after all," Lauren said smugly. "The neighborhood may be on the seedy side, but it's not Skid Row."

"Well, I called the security company. They have a patrol car in the area and they'll try to re-route it to cruise our street around five-thirty. That's when Madison usually arrives."

"I don't know why you take time to coddle her. You have better things to do."

"It was just a phone call––no big deal," Wyatt said. "Say, I have a great idea. Suppose you lure me to bed and give me a good old-fashioned back rub. My shoulders are as tight as Sherlock's."

"Shylock, Honey. It's Shylock. Shakespeare, you know."

"Sherlock, Shylock, same. Only my high school English teacher would care."

"I care," she winked. Lauren stood and extended her hand. "Come. Your accountant-turned-masseuse beckons."

Chapter 31

Liza sat cross-legged on the floor, playing with Timmie. She enjoyed these times with her granddaughter, a welcome respite from the loneliness of her house. Although Liza had never been close to her husband Earl, his death created a void. There was the money, of course. The law firm had been immensely successful, affording a spacious summer home in Montana and a fifty-five-foot cabin cruiser docked in Marina Del Rey.

But status is what Liza missed most. When the firm branched into international trade law, Earl vaulted into global prominence. Liza's social circle sprang from stuffy bridge gatherings to Parisian dinner parties hosted by ambassadors. Conscious of her image, Liza toned up at the gym, frequented her private tanning salon and read three daily newspapers to stay current on world affairs. Her closet overflowed with elegant gowns and hundreds of shoes. Her jewelry box cradled opulent star sapphires and ostentatious diamonds.

Yet there was a thorn in her lavish life. Ever since Lauren's adolescence, friction between them intensified, igniting fires of disagreement. Liza knew her daughter was content with modest endeavors: good friends, thought-provoking books and an orderly life. Lauren seemed awkward at her elegant dinner parties and was reluctant to join even the most casual ones.

Now widowed, Liza's social world retreated to parochial charity work and tennis. She felt life seemed shallow and devoid of meaning. More and more she sought companionship with her granddaughter and welcomed Lauren's invitations to baby-sit.

Lauren had left an hour ago on another errand and Liza suspected she capitalized on these opportunities to check on Wyatt and Madison. *She can't fool me with these phony trips,* Liza smirked. Sure of her convictions, she set aside presumptions of Wyatt's infidelities and handed a crayon to Timmie.

"Here, Darling, red would be nice for the elephant's belt. You think?"

Timmie grabbed the crayon and scrubbed in the coloring book.

"Try to stay inside the lines, Little One."

"Good?" Timmie asked.

"Perfect."

With a gleaming grin, the child bubbled, "I color good, don't I, Grandma?"

"You're the very best." Liza shifted her legs, happy that at her age, she could still hunker down on the floor.

It wasn't long before Liza heard the front door open.

"Where is everybody?" called Lauren.

"In Timmie's room, Dear," replied Liza. "We're coloring elephants."

Lauren stepped through the door. "You two having fun?"

"Look, Mommy, I colored the circus picture. Grandma says it's perfect."

"Beautiful. Grandma's right." Lauren smoothed her daughter's hair. "I talked to Wyatt on my way home.

He'll be here soon and wants a bite to eat, so I'll whip up something. Even though you can't stay for dinner, Mom, how about helping out?"

"Maybe in a while. Timmie and I aren't finished with the picture."

"I've important news about Wyatt and Optimal," Lauren persisted. "I thought we could chat over the stove."

Irritated, Liza wanted to avoid any discussion of either Wyatt or his stupid company. Looking fondly at Timmie, she shrugged. "If I must."

In the kitchen, Lauren took a package of Tater-Tots from the freezer and covered a small cookie sheet with frosty lumps.

"They look like Chihuahua turds," scoffed Liza.

"Mother! Since when do you use profanity?"

"I've been around Wyatt too long."

"He hardly ever swears." Lauren rummaged in the refrigerator and located four pork chops. "Want to grab a frying pan while I find the olive oil? Wyatt loves fried chops." Lauren went to the pantry and extracted a small bottle.

Liza wearied of the idle chatter. "What did you want to talk about, Dear?"

"Oh, yes. We've identified a potential customer—AirEnvironment has asked Optimal to make a big presentation. I Googled them and they're a big firm. Into everything. This is the first big company that's expressed interest. Wyatt's terribly excited."

"Sounds, good," Liza said, "but have they signed a contract?"

"Not yet. But they are definitely interested. It's an important first step." Lauren flipped the chops in the pan.

Liza wasn't impressed. "You may think that's progress, Dear, but nothing is firm. There are still money problems."

"The SBA, with our banker's help, will consider us more seriously knowing AirEnvironment is in our corner. Plus, Madison has been proselytizing at King Aviation where she works. They're interested, too. As an accountant, I know these developments are big."

Although ignorant of the business world, Liza figured Lauren's words made sense. Was it possible that Wyatt could become an important businessman? She'd have to think that over, but it'd be difficult to surrender her image of him as a clueless nerd. *But two big customers?*

Wyatt burst through the front door, strode into the kitchen and kissed Lauren's cheek. "Smells good."

Liza eyed him, trying to envision a successful executive, but he looked like the normal Wyatt—a boyish, clean-shaven face atop a grizzly's body. Yet his easy smile radiated a new confidence and skill. The dichotomy disturbed her.

"Good evening, Wyatt," she said. "Lauren says things at the business are looking up."

Wyatt looked startled. "Why yes, they are. There's a long way to go, but our ship is underway."

Liza pursed her lips. "Yes, I can see that. How big is this potential customer, Wyatt?"

"Around a billion, top line."

"Billion. That's good. Very good." Liza gave Lauren a smile. "Well, I'll say goodbye to Timmie before I leave." She started down the hall, and then turned. "Glad to hear the good news, Wyatt. I wish you luck."

As Liza disappeared into Timmie's room, Wyatt breathed, "She's wishing me luck? What brought that on?"

Lauren shrugged. "I'll never understand her."

Chapter 32

"It's five-thirty in the morning—what a crummy way to start a day." Wyatt rubbed his eyes, trying to focus on the DCMA specification. He slapped the documents with the back of his hand. "Brian was idiotic to take a military contract, but needed business—any business." Wyatt tossed the paperwork aside and slid his chair closer to the dinette table. "Is the coffee ready yet, Darlin'? My blood pressure is zero over zip."

"Almost." Lauren tiptoed to the pantry and slid out a cupcake, pushed a small candle into the crusty frosting while avoiding a piped yellow "34." She shielded the cupcake with her body, placed the treat on a saucer and lit the candle. With a twist, Lauren cradled the dish behind her back and eased alongside Wyatt.

"Here's a sugar jolt to overcome this awful hour." With a flourish, she set the cupcake in front of Wyatt and smiled. "Happy birthday."

Wyatt laughed. "Again? I forgot again? Dang, it seems my last birthday was only a couple of weeks ago."

"Make a wish."

Wyatt paused a moment, considering success for Optimal, health for his family and world peace. *It's all nonsense, anyway,* he reflected, and blew out the candle. "Thirty-four? Where does the time go?" Wyatt grasped Lauren and pulled her onto his lap. He raised his face and commanded, "Kiss me, wench."

Lauren's lips met his and lingered. With a wide grin,

she stood and hustled to the coffee pot. "Here's your coffee," Lauren said, setting a steaming cup on the table. "You'd better review the DCMA stuff before this Leechmann guy gets you fired."

"That bodybuilding turkey has his knickers in a bunch over the interpretation of a stupid clause in the design specification. I wish I could take one of his bar bells and shove it right up his...well, you know."

Lauren grinned. "Right. I remember you said he was a bodybuilder."

Wyatt peeled the paper from the cupcake and bit off a huge chunk. Specks of chocolate fell on the government document and he brushed them away. "Yeah. Big biceps and a microscopic mind. Guy's been after me for over a year just because I crossed him about MRB procedures. The trouble is Brian sides with him half the time. My own boss doesn't have the backbone to stand up to this nut case."

"Honey, not vinegar, Hon."

"Sure." Wyatt finished the cupcake, picked up the specification and thumbed to a page marked with a paper clip. He scowled as he read, then scribbled a note in the margin.

Later, as Wyatt drove to work, he thought of Lauren and smiled, recalling the twinkle in her eyes and the cupcake with a candle. Then he remembered he'd promised to come straight home that night because she'd arranged for a babysitter and made dinner reservations at a fancy restaurant. "Champagne, steak and a birthday celebration," she said. "Just you and me. Tell Madison you have more important things to do."

I better not forget, Wyatt thought. *Or there'll be hell to pay.*

>< >< ><

Feeling mellow, Lauren nodded as the waiter poured champagne. Thick carpeting and flowing white tablecloths muffled the voices of fellow diners. Candles on the tables twinkled in the dim light of the restaurant. A pianist, seated at a baby grand in the far corner, played softly as if fearing he'd intrude into the elegant ambience of the room. *Beethoven's Minuet?* Lauren wondered. *Perhaps.*

"Isn't this special, Honey?" she said, raising her glass. "To you, old man," She took a sip of champagne. "Mom suggested this place. Not too extravagant, is it?"

"No. It's fine."

After they ordered, Lauren continued. "Have you noticed Mother has changed recently? She's backing away from charity work and tennis and spending more time with Timmie."

"I guess."

"It's nice seeing more of her. We're not fighting as much and Timmie enjoys her grandmother." Lauren paused as the server twisted a pepper mill, sprinkling black specks on her salad. "Our daughter is growing fast. I think Mom is a good influence. She has a second chance at parenthood––a chance to do better the second time around. You agree?"

Wyatt nodded.

Lauren gazed across the table. "You're a little pensive, Honey. You're much too young for a mid-life crisis. What's on your mind?"

Wyatt beckoned to the waiter for a coffee refill and said, "Just the usual. Loans and permits. They're scuttling my ship."

"Devilish things, those. I have a toast," she said raising her flute once more. "May we vanquish all roadblocks to our progress. Like King Arthur, our perseverance will prove our hearts are true and the LaMarrs and Brandons of this world will falter and fail."

Wyatt lifted his glass. "Hope so." He sipped and then stared into the candle flame. "Darn good thing we have Madison. She's tough as a bo'sun's mate. She's been arguing with the FAA people about software. I don't know what I'd do without her." Wyatt reached into his pocket for his cell phone. "I'll give her a call and set a time to talk over the problems."

"Don't you *dare!*" Lauren hissed. "I'm sick and tired of her! I came to celebrate your birthday with *you! Not her!*"

Wyatt stared, looking blanched by his wife's outburst.

Lauren trembled. "Put that damn phone away. *Now!*"

The steaks were served, desserts nibbled and plates cleared.

And the waiter padded quietly through the silence.

Chapter 33

Ravenous, Wyatt ripped open his package of French fries and smothered them with salt.

"The cooks salt them in the kitchen, Wyatt," Madison said. "You trolling for a heart attack? Anxious to get to heaven?"

"Heaven is good," Wyatt countered, opening his burger wrapper. He lifted the top bun and laced the patty with more salt. With a satisfied grunt, he took a huge bite, smearing his chin with sauce.

Madison shook her head. "You're impossible. It's unconscionable that a man of science would ignore the fundamentals of chemistry."

"Yup. I know better," Wyatt said, happily stuffing fries into his mouth.

Madison nibbled on a small piece of lettuce. "You might try a salad sometime. This one is great."

"Rabbit food. Not man food."

She laughed. "Salt must trigger memory loss. As proof, I'll bet you forgot your birthday yesterday."

Embarrassed, Wyatt mumbled, "You're right, but salt didn't cause my absent-mindedness. Just old age."

"Right, at age thirty-four." Madison removed a card and a small package from her purse. "Well, I remembered. Happy birthday from me."

Wyatt blushed. "Gosh. Thanks." He opened the card and read it, flustered by its sentiments. Madison had wrapped the package in crisp silver foil and capped it with a small red bow. He tried to open the present without tearing the paper, but gave up and ripped it off. On lifting the box lid, he found a mustard-yellow mechanical pencil.

"Hey. Same as the one I lost a while back. My favorite. Nine-tenths millimeter."

"I know," Madison said. "With HB lead, just as you like."

"You spoil me, Maddy."

"Sure do." A broad smile played across her face. "My partner deserves the best I have to offer."

Wyatt felt his brows pull together. *What did she mean by that?*

They ate in silence for a while. Wyatt was surprised Madison knew his preference for soft lead, but her familiarity with his habits disturbed him. With a quick glance, he saw her sparkling green eyes, half hidden by a cascade of mahogany hair. Her smile danced as she rested her chin on the back of her hand. *Wow, what gorgeous eyes.* Wyatt felt his face flush and feeling uncomfortable, turned his attention back to his burger. He sighed and his thoughts migrated to a more comfortable subject—Optimal.

"I've been thinking," Wyatt said. "Maybe we should quit our jobs and work full-time on pressurization. Our workload is beyond ridiculous. Lauren is tight-jawed because I'm never home and my work at SAC is getting sloppy. I'm trying to do too much."

Madison frowned. "Me too, but we need to buy equipment for the big test stand and a data acquisition system. That's big bucks. Give up our only reliable incomes? How could I pay rent?"

"Guess we'd take a draw against Optimal. The real

problem is the SBA, so I'll ask Lauren to get with Lee and kick their backsides. They've had our updated application for weeks. On top of that, I'm trying to find a few hours to design plumbing for the big vacuum pump." Wyatt sipped his coffee. "We have to find more time—that means quitting our jobs."

"Maybe," Madison said. "But still…"

"Look at us. We'll gobble a fast-food lunch and run to fight another battle with the Planning jerks. We're stealing time from our jobs right and left. It's a wonder we haven't been fired."

Madison laced her fingers and stared at her salad plate. "You're always eloquent, but now you're persuasive too. I remember when we wrote our business plan a year ago; we said we'd quit this month. I guess it's calling our bluff."

Wyatt grinned. "Shit or get off the pot, my mother used to say."

"Very articulate, your mother." Madison drew a deep sigh. "The work load *is* bad—I'm way behind on the PCB revisions. Sooner or later we'll go full-time, it's just…." She pursed her lips and looked at Wyatt. "Suppose we give notice in two weeks, the first day after New Year's. That'll give us time to chicken out, but the SBA loan better be sewed up by then."

Wyatt wiped his mouth and gave Madison a thin smile. A knot formed in his stomach. "You sure?" he asked.

Madison nodded.

"All right," Wyatt said. *This is it. We're throwing away our lifeline.*

Wyatt was strung between two emotions: anxiety and relief. Anxiety over giving up his income, relief knowing he'd have more time for Optimal. The SBA and Building and Zoning people frustrated him and dragged him away from engineering. He hated the dangling thoughts, the niggling chores and sense of ineptitude. Tasks lingered on his action item list week after week and he'd stare at it, trying to pick a job he could finish. But there were few.

Even worse, he knew his family life was deteriorating. Lauren was exhausted and short-tempered and Timmie fussier than ever. Much of the blame rested on his shoulders, but Optimal possessed him; he couldn't escape its grasp. Perhaps his traditional New Year's ruminations would take on a different flavor if he were full-time with Optimal. Wyatt relaxed as he turned the idea over in his mind. *Time. Much more time.* He saw his list wither. He saw triumph.

"Let's head out to Planning and Zoning," he said to Madison. "Get Brandon to turn up the revs."

"Ha," Madison said. "I don't care if he's one of the new 'Liaison Clerks' they've hired, you have to wonder how he got the job. There's no hint of initiative or ambition. His sole motivation seems to be to stay out of trouble."

"And he's got us by the throat."

"Today we turn the tables," she said. "We've done our homework and solved every problem he brought up. Mark my words, tonight we'll have our permit for the big test stand."

Standing in line at the Planning and Zoning office, Wyatt's arm ached from the weight of his briefcase, so he set it on the floor between his feet. He wished the new policy of using Liaison Clerks instead of qualified engineers at the desk would be canceled. Brandon was a dolt even if he was majoring in architecture at college as he claimed. "Been fifteen minutes already," he complained.

"Simmer down, my friend." Madison patted his arm. "Just one guy ahead of us now."

Finally, they faced Brandon, disheveled as always with hazy patches of acne cream on his face, camouflaging the eruptions.

Brandon's eyes flickered with recognition. "Ah yes, Opti...whatever."

"Right," Wyatt began.

Madison jumped in. "That's us. Optimal Aviation. We've incorporated all your comments from last week. There shouldn't be any more problems." She leaned on the counter, brushed her hair away from her eyes and fixed the clerk with a bold gaze. It was obvious to Wyatt that Brandon was unnerved by Madison's beauty.

"Well, we'll see," he said, looking away.

"As you wanted; we sent the vacuum pump specs to the AQMD," Wyatt explained. "They gave us a permit to construct, but wants to take exhaust samples later. They'll issue a permit to operate if we pass."

Brandon took the papers and studied them. His fingers wandered to a nascent pimple, then retreated. "Looks okay, but I'd better check with my supervisor."

"Why don't you have him look at it while we're here," Wyatt said with a sense of pending trouble.

"He's off today. I'll catch him tomorrow."

Wyatt leaned forward to complain, but Brandon continued, "Did you contact Burbank Water and Power like you were supposed to?"

"We did," Madison replied. "I talked to a Mr. Mortensen who faxed the service requirements. Wyatt, show Brandon the new electrical schematics."

Wyatt scowled and spread out the drawing. "Here's the updated wiring diagram."

"Lots of changes," Brandon said. "We'll need time to review it."

"But we just did what you wanted," Wyatt pleaded. "There's nothing new. We were hoping to finish this today."

"Oh, that's not possible. I'll get with my boss in the morning. Got to make sure everything is to code."

Wyatt was about to explode, but a harsh glance from Madison stopped him. His anger disintegrated into resignation. *This jerk has us in a headlock.* "Sure," he said. "I'll call in the morning to make sure everything is okay."

"Don't bother. We'll e-mail our comments when we're done." Brandon slowly folded the schematic, floor plan and other materials and inserted them into a folder.

Wyatt gathered up his remaining papers. "I'll call anyway."

Brandon smiled. "Whatever."

As they walked toward the exit, Wyatt turned and heard Brandon whistle softly as he slipped the Optimal folder into the bottom of the stack in his supervisor's in-box. "Next," he said.

Chapter 34

Lauren had no use for football——none. Curled up on the sofa, she cuddled against Wyatt while he watched the game. Oklahoma and somebody; it didn't matter. She pulled the lap blanket tighter around her shoulders and looked with amusement as Wyatt polished an oxford. She pushed part of her blanket over his legs while he switched to a pair of brown loafers and scrubbed them with a brush, jiggling her.

Just as "Walk the dog" is a euphemism for smoking a cigarette, Wyatt claimed he never followed football, but "shined shoes." He'd grab his shoeshine kit, turn on the TV and smear, scrub and buff his way through the games. "Can't start the New Year with grubby footwear," he'd say.

Lauren wiggled an arm from under the blanket and turned a page in her new book, a Christmas gift from Timmie doubtlessly coached by Wyatt. It was *The Sea Hunters*, by Clive Cussler. "New York Times Best Seller" the dust jacket bragged. Cussler was not Lauren's idea of inspiring reading. She suspected that Wyatt, an ex-sailor, probably figured a book on ships had to be good and "Best Seller" told him he'd picked a popular novel. *At least he didn't forget Christmas,* she chuckled to herself.

In the corner, Timmie huddled with Jennifer, playing Candy Land, a Christmas present from Liza. The two sat cross-legged on the floor, murmuring, drawing cards and tapping markers around the board. Garfield strolled to a patch of sunlight streaming through a window, sat and groomed. Looking smug, the way cats do, he turned around and lay with his belly toward the sun.

The word "tranquil" came to Lauren's mind as she looked around the room. For the first time in weeks, she could set aside the crush of the holidays and relax. She wiggled her shoulders affirming her tenseness had disappeared and returned to the book.

Soon, winter gloom smothered the feeble day, and the television glared in the gathering darkness. Wyatt had finished his shoes plus three pairs of Lauren's and looking restless, propped his feet on the coffee table and stared at the screen.

With scratchy eyes, Lauren looked at her watch. "Almost six, Honey. Ready for dinner?"

Wyatt glanced at her, reached for the remote and snapped off the TV. "Love some." He gathered her in his arms and buried his face in her hair. "You smell good."

"You're not getting fed doing that," she teased.

"Starved men make lousy husbands." Wyatt stood and stretched. "I don't know why I watch that junk," he said. "The announcers make fourth and short sound as if North Korea just nuked Lady Gaga. It's just a game for crying out loud. At least the commercials are for beer rather than the usual ads from lawyers crying about asbestos, drug or implant victims. Where's the tort reform the politicians keep promising?"

"No soapbox speeches on New Year's, okay? Let's send Jennifer home and have a bite."

Lauren hummed as she spooned the potatoes into a serving bowl and sliced the roast.

Timmie shrieked with obvious ecstasy as Wyatt chased her across the living room, playing tag. Her cornered her and swept her into his arms, squeezing so hard that Timmie's face turned red. She squirmed free, tagged Wyatt and flew down the hall, screaming.

"Hey, you two––need help in here." Lauren called.

Gasping, Wyatt puffed up the hallway and set the table, scattering the silverware and dishes haphazardly, alien to Lauren's sense of precision. As they sat at the table for dinner, Timmie looked tired enough to fall face-first into her plate. "Bushed, Honey?" Lauren asked rhetorically. Timmie shook her head and tried to jam an immense slice of beef into her mouth.

"Let me help." Lauren leaned over and cut the meat into manageable portions.

"Did you say your mother is in Mexico?" Wyatt asked.

"Yes, in Cancun with friends. Country Club crowd, I guess." Lauren poured a glass of milk for Timmie. "Odd thing. Mom flew coach. She *hates* coach––calls the people in economy 'the great unwashed.' She made reservations months ago but said first class was booked. It doesn't make sense."

"It isn't like your mother, for sure." Wyatt pushed his plate away. "Say, let me help with the dishes. When I get our darlin' daughter to bed, I'll tap that champagne bottle."

A gentle silence settled into the household and the Christmas tree, now naked of its ornaments, lurked in the darkness, its fate with the trash truck a certainty. Lauren lit her favorite candles and wadded an empty microwave popcorn sack that Wyatt had abandoned. She heard a "pop" in the kitchen, signaling that Wyatt had subdued the champagne cork. With an easy sigh, she dropped into her chair and closed her eyes.

"A little bubbly for the best wife in the world," Wyatt announced, setting two chilled flutes and the sweaty bottle on the coffee table. He poured slowly, watching the hissing bubbles seek the glasses' rim, then recede.

"Here," he said, handing a glass to Lauren. "To us and Optimal. It'll be a great year."

They clinked their glasses and sipped. Contented, Lauren wiggled deeper into her chair. The candles cast dancing shadows, making Wyatt appear ruddy, yet young.

"The neighbors sure had a roaring party last night," Lauren said. "I hope they're not put off because we didn't come. We don't enjoy drunken parties."

"Besides, we had better things to do last night," Wyatt said. "Much better things."

Lauren could see his exaggerated leer in the flickering candlelight. She giggled. "You're right about that." She swallowed a taste of champagne, dwelling on a thought. "Do you ever think that Timmie might want a brother? My clock is ticking."

"Wow! That's an out-of-the-box, New Year's Day question." Wyatt rubbed his chin. "Yes, I have. I don't know where the years have gone. Only yesterday I was changing diapers and now Timmie is pushing seven. But our finances are too shaky. I can't see how we can afford another child."

"Things are certainly unsettled. You've never put down roots at SAC. Been there five years, but I've always worried that you'd blow up and quit."

"Or get fired. This DCMA guy, Leechmann, keeps tearing into me. Insecure jerks like him feel better when others look bad."

"No matter, it's ending. You'll give notice next Monday and Brian and Leechmann will be history. Everything is hanging on Optimal and the SBA loan. It's odd to think the existence of our daughter's sibling depends on this thing called pressurization."

A solemn look clouded Wyatt's face. "Sounds terrible when you say it that way. I could survive at SAC, I suppose, but Optimal would die. Our marriage suffers too. Here we are, sitting in candlelight, drinking champagne and worrying. We deserve a chance to make our mark, to enjoy real security. Optimal will make it happen."

"We'll see."

"It will; count on it," said Wyatt. "I'll pry the permits for the full-scale test stand out of the Planning fools within a week and then work up a list equipment––it'll cost a bundle."

Lauren winced, trying to fend off a sudden feeling of melancholia. She wished Wyatt hadn't brought up cost, but he'd opened the floodgates.

Between Christmas and New Year, Lauren had agonized over Wyatt's decision to quit his job. All at once, two disasters loomed: paring back to live on her meager paycheck and the immense expense of test equipment. They had to get money, and the SBA kept delaying their application. *We're at the end of the road.* With a pounding heart, she thrust aside her doubts. *As they say in poker, all in.*

"I never thought I'd be the one pushing for a line of credit using our house as equity," Lauren said. "When I suggested a mortgage, you sure looked astonished, but we've exhausted every option. If Optimal has any chance, we'll need bridge funding until we get the SBA loan. I'll get with Lee Wong to arrange it." She crossed her arms, straining her shoulders. "We'll borrow only what we need and pay off the loan as soon as the SBA delivers." Lauren gulped, realizing she'd wagered both her house and her way of life.

Wyatt nodded. "Dang SBA and their government 'reforms.' If it's not them, it's Planning and Zoning throwing up roadblocks. A guy can't get *anything* done. We should strangle every one of them."

"Now Wyatt. No soapboxes on New Year's."

"But..." He paused and then grinned. "Sorry, Dear. I promised. No soapbox tonight."

Lauren's hand was cold and quivered when Wyatt reached over and took it. *I hope luck and Optimal become good friends*, she thought.

Chapter 35

As they walked into the dusky entry of Winton's Castle restaurant, Wyatt smelled the scents of dry gin and rare steak. They made their way toward the hostess lurking behind her station.

"Hello," Bernie said. "We have a reservation—Bernie White."

As Wyatt's eyes adjusted to the dim light, the young woman's image became clearer. Her long blond hair contrasted with brown eyes and a contrived-looking smile was a testimony to flawless orthodontia.

"Ah, yes." She picked up the menus and beckoned, "This way."

As they settled into their booth, Bernie grinned. "They didn't look that good when I was in high school."

"The girl? Heck, when you were in school, the women were hairy and walked on their knuckles."

"Ha, ha. I'm not *that* old."

Feeling underdressed, Wyatt looked around the room. "Fancy joint, my friend. Starched tablecloths and genuine china plates."

A waiter, wearing creased slacks and a pressed dress shirt, came to the table. "Gentlemen? Something to drink?"

"Hell yes," Bernie said. "This is an occasion. Bring me a Bud. Wyatt?"

"How about a glass of house red."

The waiter nodded and glided away, his shoes sinking into the plush carpet.

They studied the menus for a minute or two and Bernie slapped his closed. "What did Brian say when you told him you were quitting SAC?"

"He was so tight-jawed he could have bitten through re-bar. Didn't say much except, 'That explains your short working hours.' Brian thought starting a company in this economy was stupid, saying I'd be broke within a year. He laughed when I told him I was developing the pressurization. There was an interesting piece of news about the DCMA guy, Leechmann."

"Yeah?"

"Well, the government gurus figured out he's a world-class idiot and promoted him. You won't be seeing him around SAC anymore."

Bernie shook his head. "Glad to get rid of him, but I'm going to miss you. We've had great times together." Bernie unfolded his napkin and placed it on his lap. "Remember when I accidentally left the key in the chuck of the toolmaker's lathe and turned it on? Key took off like birdshot from a twelve gage. Damn near killed you."

Wyatt laughed. "Missed me by an inch. Poked a hole in the wall that's still there. And you call yourself a machinist. Don't they cover that in *Lathe Operation 101*?"

The waiter returned with their drinks and they ordered.

"To friends," Wyatt toasted, clinking glasses with Bernie. The tart Cabernet bit the back of his tongue. "Remember the Weller Air job? We worked through the night and all the next day. Didn't even break for meals."

"We sure didn't come across as aerospace poster-boys when Weller picked up his parts that night," Bernie chuckled. "The two of us were grungy: oil spotted and smelly."

Their lunch came, and they began to eat. "Soup's good. How's the burger?" asked Bernie.

"Needs salt."

"Burgers and salt; they'll kill you."

"You sound like my wife."

"Smart lady. Setting aside your stupidity, is Brian looking for your replacement?" Bernie asked.

"Not yet. He said he'd run Engineering himself for a while ––but it's not your problem."

Bernie finished his sandwich and ordered another beer. "Is Optimal still fighting the government?"

"Do history majors hate calculus?" Wyatt dipped a French fry into a ramekin of catsup. "Had to take out a line of credit on our house because the SBA keeps making sacrifices to the trivia gods. The building permit morons still have their thumbs up their...nose."

"They'll come around sooner or later. Did you say your prototype is working well?"

"Doin' fine. Some hiccups, of course, but so far we've been lucky."

"You make your own friggin' luck."

Wyatt looked fondly at his friend. "We're just alike, you know. We both eat steel chips for breakfast and guzzle cutting oil."

"Yeah. I think we're born with it. Manufacturing, I mean. Bernie waved his hand. "You were green as limes on your first day at SAC. You picked up a valve spool and petted it, the same way I'd pet a dog. 'What alloy?' you asked. 'Duplex stainless,' I answered. 'That's tough on cutting tools,' you said. Amazing you'd know that."

Bernie buttered a piece of bread. "When I was twelve, my dad tried to change an empty propane tank at a vacation rental. He was yanking on the wrench and the air got pretty colorful. So I said, 'Dad, aren't threads on propane valves left handed?' Gave me a crazy look and jerked the wrench in the opposite direction. Off came the valve."

Wyatt nodded. "My father was a plumber, and he'd take me to job-sites in his big truck. Before I finished grade school, I could ream, thread and plan pipe runs."

"That's what I mean. It's in our blood."

They ate in silence for a while, Wyatt savoring the masculine-style camaraderie.

Bernie broke the stillness saying, "I did a crazy thing yesterday and called the *Burbank Leader* to see if they'd be interested in doing a piece on Optimal. I thought I'd surprise you––go for some publicity. They said articles on new businesses are always popular and they want to send a reporter and photographer out to interview you and Madison? Mind?"

Wyatt chuckled. "I don't suppose it would hurt anything. Why not?"

"They'll drop in Saturday around ten in the morning. I gave them your address."

"What? You already set it up? Suppose I didn't go for it?"

"I guess I knew what you'd say."

"You're something," Wyatt said, shaking his head. "We'd better get back to work. Thanks for lunch."

Without looking at the tab, Bernie slipped a credit card into the folder, waved it at the waiter and turned to Wyatt.

"Here's something for you. I refuse to let you walk out of my life. I'm a believer in you and Optimal and want to be part of it." With a grunt, he reached into his hip pocket, pulled out a check and handed it to Wyatt.

Wyatt looked and whistled. "Ten thousand? Made out to me? Why?"

"Thirty years ago a friend had a hell of an idea for a new surgical instrument. He was a doc and needed help with design and production; wanted to make me a partner. But I didn't have the guts to walk away from my regular job; so he found somebody else. I've regretted it ever since. I want a piece of Optimal and I figure money is tight."

"But I can't accept this. You're nuts."

"Like Warren Buffett. I'm a partner, now—just a small one. I'll worry about my share in Optimal later because I figure you'll be fair."

"Bernie," Wyatt stammered. "I don't know what to say."

"Zip it. This isn't charity. It's business. I have to plan for my future which includes you."

Wyatt laughed and pocketed the check. "You win. I'll make sure you can retire with a Bentley and a chateau outside Paris."

"I'd settle for a Schwinn and a tent. Just make a go of it, okay?"

Bernie signed for the lunch and they walked to the parking lot, stood in the sun and shook hands. Wyatt didn't want to say good-bye and his grasp lingered in Bernie's hand. With an awkward motion, Wyatt hugged and patted Bernie on the back. "Thanks, guy. I'll be in touch."

Chapter 36

Lauren puttered in the kitchen, dreading to tell her mother the news. She realized her industriousness was only a delaying tactic, but she needed time to gird herself. *Why do we argue all the time? Is every mother-daughter relationship this combative? Like walking on eggs.*

In the living room, Liza looked at the Valentine cards scattered on the coffee table and shook her head. "Timmie?" she called. There was no answer. "Timmie!"

"What, Grandma?"

"What a mess," Liza scolded as the child skipped around the corner. "These cards are strewn everywhere. The Scrabble ladies are coming, so take them to your room."

With a scowl, Timmie said, "Mommy told me I could put them there. They're from my friends at school."

Liza took a deep breath. "Okay, let's set them in the bookcase. They'll look nice there."

Timmie nodded happily. They gathered up the cards and set them in neat rows in front of Lauren's books. A satisfied looking grin painted the youngster's face, and she scurried back to her room.

"Oh, that's nice, Mother," Lauren said as she brought in a vase of flowers she'd picked in the yard. "Now we can use the coffee table for chips and dip." She bit her lip. "Say, Mother, I have news."

"What's that, Dear?"

Lauren cleared her throat. "About Wyatt. He's taken a big step."

"Big step?"

Lauren nodded. "Yes. He's...we've decided he should work on Optimal full-time. Friday was his last day at SAC."

"Wyatt quit his job?" Liza snapped. "How can he do that? You and Timmie are scraping by as it is."

"Not so loud, Mother. Timmie will hear."

"He's insane!"

"Not true," Lauren said, clenching her teeth. "Wyatt struggles to find time and Optimal is at a turning point. Madison quit her job too. I still have my job which will help keep us solvent."

Lauren knew the mother part of her wanted security while the wife part in her ached for her husband's fulfillment. The dichotomy scrambled her thinking, but Wyatt's zeal and empty coffers won over. From there, it was a simple step to reverse her adamant opposition to a mortgage.

"There's more," Lauren gulped. "We've also taken out a line of credit against the house."

"You allowed him to do this? You could lose the house."

"For the record, the line of credit was my idea. Sure, it's a big gamble, but we're going to do this." Lauren stormed into the kitchen.

Liza followed, went to the refrigerator and snatched a bundle of celery from the crisper. After snapping off several stalks and splashing them with water, she said, "It's your life, I suppose. I hoped you'd be more responsible about money."

"It's more than money, Mother. Have you seen the

hawks soar above the ridges? Wyatt's mind is like that, effortless, unfettered. Ninety-nine percent of his ideas are a mystery to me. No matter. I'm in awe when I hear a jetliner thundering to the sky, but I don't need to know how it works." Lauren trembled as she spoke. "That's the foundation of my love for him. Sure, Optimal might be crazy, but I'm behind him all the way." She jerked open a package of cheese and slapped the slices on a platter. "Be nice to have a little understanding."

Liza, looking weary, leaned against the counter and shook her head. "I get tired of doing battle with you, Lauren. I tried to be a good mother; to raise you right. You'll discover that money is a slippery thing. One moment, you're flush, and then things turn bad. Earl and I built a life together, a comfortable life. I want that for you. Wyatt has snared you in this frivolous thing without regard for Timmie's future or your own retirement."

"Mother…"

Liza held up her hand. "Hear me out." She removed her glasses and kneaded the bridge of her nose. "Foundation, you said. My foundation was building a financial sanctuary. Even when your father was alive, I was lonely, but money opened doors. People sought me out to support their charities. I wintered in Bermuda and became friends with the mayor. Because of money. But it has a way of evaporating. Without Earl, I feel isolated. I stare in the mirror and wonder where the future will take me."

Lauren was astonished by her mother's admission. Liza looked withered and her robust tan seemed faded.

"So," Liza went on, "The nice things I've accumulated

have brought me comfort, but now I wonder. I haven't been to the yacht in weeks, so I'm selling it."

"But mother, you *love* your boat. You entertain on it all the time."

"Boat's a lot of trouble."

Lauren was confused. She knew her mother often held extravagant parties on the boat with the marina crowd and went on weekend cruises to Catalina Island.

Lauren recalled other recent oddities. *She flew to Cancun—in coach. And now, she's selling the yacht and cut back on tennis. Is it because Mom is getting old, or was there something else, illness perhaps?*

The bing-bong of the doorbell derailed Lauren's train of thought. "Must be Marge and Betty," she said. "I'll get it."

Looking startled, Liza stood, smoothed her dress and smiled. "Don't pay any attention to my prattle, Dear. Let's play some Scrabble."

Chapter 37

The last day of February burst with good news—the Planning Department finally issued permits for construction of the large test rig.

Without delay, Wyatt ordered two large tanks, the vacuum pump, an air compressor and a used gas-fired heater. Madison purchased data acquisition software and dozens of smaller electrical items needed for tests. They hired contractors to pour concrete foundations for the tanks and electricians to run 230-volt, three-phase service.

Even with the new line of credit against the house, the bank balance plummeted, and the SBA remained as balky as ever. Regardless, Wyatt's spirit was bright.

March gave way to April, and then May. A springtime heat wave swept Burbank, pushing temperatures near ninety, but abruptly turned chilly with fog and overcast skies, an early precursor to the traditional "June Gloom" of Southern California.

A large flatbed truck delivered the massive equipment in late May and workers dropped everything in place with two large forklifts. Madison and Wyatt donned tattered work clothes to saw, paint, wire and plumb the test rigs. Wyatt rented a second hand arc welder and installed the large diameter vacuum pipe, but per code, hired a certified welder for the high-pressure plumbing.

Frazzled, Lauren sacrificed weekends to issue purchase orders, update accounting records and pay the Burbank business tax.

Although their days bordered on frantic, Wyatt embraced the chaos and remained happy.

Wyatt grabbed a hacksaw and cut a length of copper tubing and deburred it. As he swaged a flare on one end, he congratulated himself for the sticky he'd slapped on his car's dash three days ago: "L Bda." Otherwise, he wouldn't have remembered. "Great way to spend your thirty-third, isn't it, Darling?" he joked.

Lauren grinned and stirred the goop in a paint can with a wooden stick. "I thought you'd give me my birthday off, but I guess I married a slave-driver."

"Working on these test stands is nothing compared to filling out paperwork for a provisional patent. Now that King and AirEnvironment both are interested, we'll need patent protection before showing them details. Madison and I are drafting the application, but it's a nightmare. Because a provisional expires after twelve months, we'll have to do everything over again. The formal patent will be worse because it requires much more detail."

"Should we get a patent attorney?" Lauren asked.

"No way. Those guys charge hundreds of dollars an hour for something we can do online. It just takes time."

"We have time to burn?"

"More time than money, according to the company accountant," Wyatt cracked.

"Okay, you got me on that one," laughed Lauren. She

dipped her brush into the paint, stroked a white streak across the metal frame of the cabin tank and tilted her head. "Do you think Rembrandt would approve?"

"Is he the inspector from Planning and Zoning?"

"You're silly," she chuckled.

"If you do a good job, I might treat you to a nice birthday dinner tonight."

"You'll need reservations. It's Saturday, you know."

"Paint. I'll worry about dinner."

Wyatt was installing tubing for a pressure transducer when Madison came in, picked up a screwdriver and started wiring a thermocouple. They'd constructed two large instrument panels with gages, switches and digital readouts aligned in purposeful rows. Wyatt jockeyed a length of tubing onto the panel and tightened the B-nut with a wrench. He paused and inspected his work and decided it was neatly done, pleasing him.

Lauren's paint job gleamed, looking fresh and sleek under the new fluorescent lights. Wyatt noticed a white splotch on her nose and he dabbed it off with a rag. "You look like a clown," he chuckled.

The front door swung open, admitting a puff of sweet spring air, along with Liza and Timmie. "Happy birthday," shouted Timmie, running to her mother. "Here!" She thrust a small package into Lauren's arms.

"Happy birthday, Dear," Liza said, stepping in and closing the door. She pecked her daughter's cheek. She set a gaily-wrapped box and a sack of Chinese take-out on the desk.

"What's this?" Lauren exclaimed.

Wyatt laughed. "We got her, Liza." He went over and hugged his wife. "Surprised?"

"Incredulous," Lauren sputtered.

"There you go with your big words," Liza quipped. She looked around the room. "This isn't what I expected."

"First time here, isn't it?" Lauren asked. "It's a mess now, but come back in a few weeks. Then it will be presentable."

Liza froze—her eyes locked on Madison. After a moment Liza's composure seemed to return. "No. That's not what I mean. It's...I don't know...impressive. Scientific looking. I had no idea."

Wyatt's eyebrows arched as he glanced at Lauren, flabbergasted that Liza had anything nice to say about Optimal.

Lauren returned Wyatt's look with a shrug. "Thanks, Mom. We've been working hard, trying to get back on schedule. Things are falling into place though."

Liza and Madison stood staring at each other. "Oh my," Lauren gasped. "Introductions are in order. Mother, this is Madison, Wyatt's partner. Madison, my mother Liza." They shook hands stiffly.

"Party, party," chanted Timmie. "Let's open presents!"

"Yes, let's do that," Liza nodded. "I don't know why I let Wyatt talk me into a celebration at his work. I adore parties, I guess."

"Let's sing '*Happy Birthday*,'" Timmie squealed, and discordant notes filled the office.

Lauren blushed and bowed as the song ended. "You're all nuts."

Wyatt and Madison brought out gifts they'd sequestered behind a stack of cartons. Timmie helped rip the wrapping paper from the presents, shouting and laughing with her mother. Madison sat to one side, her gaze latched onto Wyatt's face. When he happened to catch her stare, she abruptly diverted her eyes.

Odd, he thought. *What's that look about?*

But it was Liza who puzzled Wyatt. Prompted by the sticky in his car, he'd phoned her knowing that Lauren's birthday celebration had to include her mother. Her cool tone seemed to thaw when he explained his plans for a surprise party for her daughter. Liza agreed to babysit Timmie in the morning and pick up Chinese and paper plates on the way to Optimal.

Now, sitting in the building she'd labeled 'stupid,' Liza chatted with Lauren and frolicked with Timmie. Although Liza glanced at Madison through squinty eyes from time to time, she actually had a smile or two for Wyatt.

When the gifts had been opened, Timmie scurried through the wrapping paper and ribbons strewn on the floor and pried open a carton of chow mein.

"Timmie, let me help," Lauren said and began serving.

"Hold on," protested Wyatt. "It's *your* birthday. I'll do the honors." He took soda from the refrigerator, poured foaming Coke over ice cubes and spooned out the chow mein. Conversation gave way to smacks and grunts as they foraged through the meal. Within thirty minutes, only a half-bottle of soda remained.

"It was a lovely surprise, Honey," Lauren said while Madison tossed the empty food containers in the trash.

Wyatt nodded, happy he'd pleased his wife and beamed as Timmie shrieked while he tickled her ribs. He noticed

Liza watching them play, her broad smile radiating across the room.

"Come, Timmie," Liza called. "I'm sure your parents want to get back to work, so let's go home." She escorted her granddaughter through the door and waved goodbye.

"Thanks, Hon," Lauren said to Wyatt after her mother left. "You're getting better. First you remembered Christmas, and now my birthday. Back to work, right?"

"Yup. In our wedding vows, you said you'd honor and obey. So I'm cracking the whip."

"I remember the honor part but you're imagining the obey business." She grabbed his collar, pulled him to her and gave him a kiss. "I'm looking forward to dinner tonight. It isn't IHOP, is it?"

After weeks of work, they'd finished the bleed air test stand and Wyatt summoned the Planning Department for inspection. They'd spent an hour going over schematics and the welder's certification. The inspector decided the blowout plug was undersized and the emergency shutdown button improperly marked.

"The idiot is wrong; I sized the plug myself, and it's fine," Wyatt fumed after the inspector left. "It'll be at least two days before we can get him back."

"It's frustrating, I know," Madison said, rubbing his arm.

"The $270 fee for a 'Pressure Vessel Permit and Inspection' is just a bribe." Wyatt moaned. "This is nuts. Next week it'll be the same thing when he comes to check the vacuum system." As predicted, the building inspector found a dozen shortcomings and required two more audits before he cleared Optimal to operate the vacuum pump.

With the delays, it was July before Wyatt and Madison attempted the first checkout. Wyatt set the hot air flow to his liking and sat on a stool in front of the vacuum system control panel while Madison hunched over the data acquisition computer, looking anxious.

"Ready?" asked Wyatt, his hand poised above a switch on the panel.

Madison looked through the Plexiglass window at the prototype outflow valve on its mount. She typed the altitude settings into her computer and said, "May the Pressurization Gods be with us."

"Here goes." With a churning stomach, Wyatt flipped the switch, and the pump howled like a pack of coyotes. His eyes jumped from gage to read-out and back, looking for problems. *Ambient pressure, good. Cabin pressure, right on. Delta P, nominal.* "Okay here," Wyatt called out. "Madison?"

"We're fine. Take ambient to 2,000 feet. The cabin should hold at 1,000."

Wyatt slowly adjusted a control, and the altimeter crept toward 2,000. He shuddered with excitement as the outflow valve squelched the exhaust air, holding the cabin at 1,000 feet. "It's working!"

Madison beamed at the computer display. "Sure is. Let's go to 30,000 and see if the delta P latches."

Fifteen minutes later, Wyatt had 'flown' the virtual airplane to 30,000 feet. As programmed, the delta P held at eight. "Hot dang!" Wyatt exclaimed. "It's perfect."

"Something odd, Wyatt," Madison said. "My instrumentation seems sluggish. Pressure changes seem damped."

Wyatt wiped the back of his hand across his lips. "Let's see what happens with rapid altitude changes." He simulated an emergency descent at 10,000 feet per minute.

Madison pointed at the computer screen. "It's weird. No hunting or hysteresis in the control loop."

Wyatt stared at the precision pressure gages on his control panel. "Same here. Smooth." He stood and rubbed his forehead. "We're doing this piecemeal. Let's take a complete look at the full range of airflow, altitudes and climb rates, okay?"

The wall clock ticked off another two hours while Wyatt and Madison ran test after test. At last, Wyatt shook his head. "My data is the same as yours. The valve is rock solid, far more stable than we expected. The wireless interaction with the inflow valve must be the reason. They're like the Everly Brothers—singing beautiful harmony."

Madison hooted, "What a fantastic design!" She flung her arms around him. "My man!"

Her hair brushed across his face and Wyatt inhaled deeply, her scent fresh and erotic. His arms crept around Madison's tiny waist and he felt stirrings of passion. *What the hell am I doing? Get back to business!*

"Hold on," Wyatt said, pushing her away. "We have lot's of work before we've checked out everything."

It was well past midnight when Wyatt leaned back and declared, "Done." He felt lightheaded with glee. Everything was perfect. Better than perfect. The tenseness in his shoulders ebbed, but fatigue took command. As he shut down the pumps, he said, "We have a winner, Maddy. I'll sleep well tonight." He took a deep breath and suddenly his eyes welled with tears. Embarrassed, he wiped his cheeks and smiled at Madison.

"Better hurry," Madison said. "Not much left of tonight." She shut off her computer, rose as if to give Wyatt a hug, but paused and stroked his arm instead. "We make a fine team. We're on a roll now."

"Darn right. Lauren will be happy. Our success puts us back on schedule––helps our cash situation. Yes sir! She'll be tickled."

With a scowl, Madison snatched her purse and marched toward the door. "As long as your wife's happy." She glared at Wyatt. "You lock up. I'm done for the day."

Chapter 38

With a critical eye, Wyatt looked over the data from yesterday's tests. Although the compressor delivered enough air to the inflow valve, the temperature was too low. He started a "to-do" list: adjust the air/gas mixture on the burners, add insulation to the lines and calibrate the thermocouple.

Madison, studying a chart on her computer screen, said, "Wyatt, everything worked perfectly: the wireless transmission between the valves, the encoding, the algorithms, everything." She threw her head back and laughed. "We've created a true twenty-first century pressurization system."

Wyatt grinned. "Don't get comfy, there's a lot more to do—qual tests and everything, but today is huge—we finally file for our provisional patent."

For over a month, they'd worked feverishly preparing the paperwork. The application required a written description of the inventions and sufficient drawings to illustrate the claim. The vast scope of the pressurization technology created havoc, resulting in a submission of thirty typed pages and six complex, multi-sheet drawings.

"I can't believe how many hours we burned," Madison said, shaking her head. "The Patent Office's new guidelines are a terror. In the old days, a provisional was just a placeholder, not a full disclosure."

"Well that's behind us," Wyatt said, waving a large thick envelope. "I'll get this in the mail today."

Madison's reply was interrupted when the phone rang. She picked up and said, "Optimal Aviation Systems, McKenzie speaking. Hi, Mike." She clapped her hand over the receiver and mouthed, "Mike Graham, Precision Tool."

Wyatt nodded.

"You're here in Burbank? A couple of blocks away? Sure, we'd love to have you. Five minutes, then." With a chuckle, she replaced the handset. "Mike is coming over to see our place." Her gaze swept the room. "My God, what a mess!"

They scrambled around, shoving hand tools into drawers, coiling an extension cord, piling papers into neat stacks and wiping up coffee-cup rings.

Mike burst into the office wearing a suit and a red power tie. "Afternoon," he boomed.

"Traded your apron for a suit, Mike?" Wyatt said with a playful smirk. "Are you a banker or machinist?"

"It's damned embarrassing, that's what," said Mike, shedding his jacket. "I had to put on my salesman's hat this morning. Pitched Monroe Medical Designs. They're stuffy bastards. Not just suits, but fuckin' *three*-piece suits."

"I'm sure you were right at home," Madison joked. "Isn't Monroe one of the few big manufacturers left in Burbank?"

"Don't light my goddamn fuse. Burbank used to be an aerospace hub—Lockheed, Pacific Airmotive and the rest. They've disappeared, replaced by mini-malls sellin' tacos and hair-do's. It's total crap."

"Wow. Did she push a button, Mike?" Wyatt asked. "Need a soap box? I have one in the back."

"Ignore him," Madison teased. "Wyatt's always on that box."

"Well, I just get fuckin' mad." Mike yanked off his tie. "All that aside, I thought I'd check on what you guys are up to—see my parts in action."

"We just got the system working," Wyatt beamed. "You're in luck."

Mike tugged his mustache. "I make the parts, but they're pieces of a puzzle—I can't figure out the whole picture. How about a demo?"

"Why not?" Madison said. "Let's show him magic at work, Wyatt."

Madison went to a console and turned on the vacuum pump while Wyatt started the bleed air compressor.

"Okay, Mike. Here's the deal," Wyatt explained. "On an airplane, hot, compressed air is taken from the aircraft's engines, cooled and released into the cabin by our bleed air valve. That's for ventilation and heat. The outflow valve, over by Madison, is nothing but a controlled leak, exhausting air and regulating cabin pressure. Without pressurization, you'd pass out from lack of oxygen."

"Didn't Payne Stewart, the golfer, die that way?" Mike asked.

"Exactly," Wyatt said, twisting a regulator knob. "There's much more, but that's the basics. Here we go."

While the compressor grumbled outside, the bleed air valve whistled. Wyatt dialed up the airflow and the flow meter flashed, six, eight, ten pounds per minute. A temperature indicator climbed as Wyatt fiddled with the burners.

Meanwhile, across the room, Madison set the "airplane" altitude at Burbank's elevation. "The computer in Wyatt's valve is talking to the computer in mine—all wireless," she said, turning to Mike. "Each tells the other what it's doing so the passengers don't get big earaches."

Mike, standing next to Wyatt, held his hand close to the bleed valve. "Damn. That's hot".

"Only 900 degrees. Should be 1,050," Wyatt said. "I have to work on the burners."

Mike shook his head, crossed the room and peered through the window in Madison's cabin tank. "That's it?"

"That's it," Madison said.

"It's nothing but a fucking cookie tin."

"Yeah, same as your computerized machine centers look like lawn mowers," Madison taunted.

Mike nodded and stared at the control panel. "I've seen simpler airplane cockpits. Gages, switches, blinking lights. You guys understand this stuff?"

Madison flicked a switch. "We try. We'll do a simulated takeoff, cruise and landing. You'll see how the system controls cabin pressure."

After twenty minutes, Wyatt said, "Well, that's it, folks," and turned off the burners which extinguished with a soft puff. "You're our first witness—a privileged dude."

As the plumbing cooled, popping and moaning, Wyatt and Madison stood side by side, looking smug. It was a proud moment for Wyatt. After two years, he could finally feel good enough to stick his thumbs in his belt and puff out his chest. He basked in his achievement like a marathoner at the finish line or Armstrong taking the first step on the moon. He looked at Madison, who seemed to glow. Her green eyes glittered and a big grin lifted her cheeks.

"You two make a fine looking couple," Mike said.

Wyatt grimaced like an embarrassed kid caught

cheating on a school quiz. "Have a seat. Get you a cup of coffee?"

"Gotta beer?"

"Just coffee or Coke."

"Coffee will do. Black."

"Where's your cigarette?" Madison asked. "You were quitting, right?"

"I did it! Fucking pain in the ass," he grinned, patting his shirt pocket. "Carry a full pack, emergency rations, just in case." His eyes skimmed around the room. "This is a nice place," he said. "Sophisticated, business-like. It's good to see a manufacturing start-up."

"Thanks," Wyatt said. "We're very excited. There's more good news. Today we'll mail our application for a provisional patent." He patted the envelope reverently.

"Hot shit," Mike said. He reached into his pocket and pulled out the cigarettes as if to light up. He saw his hand and looked startled. "Habit has a mind of its own." He passed the pack under his nose and with a dreamy look, put it back in his shirt.

"I watch you guys at work and get to thinking," Mike continued. "We were talking about how the big manufactures are leaving. To me, the good ol' USA is sinking in shit. China and India are whipping our ass and we're doing nothing."

Wyatt frowned. "I don't know, Mike. A lot of people just are cruisin'. Take our schools, for example. They're grinding to a halt, coddling the laggards and holding back kids who try. I don't get this tenure and unions thing...."

"You have a point, Wyatt," Madison nodded. "In yesterday's paper, I read that our local school district negotiated a new union contract calling for even fewer instruction days. Interestingly, the same article also ranked our math skills behind Lithuania and Russia and in science we're behind Slovenia and Iceland."

"No wonder our jobs go overseas," Wyatt said. "That's where the smart people are. I've heard that China and India graduate ten times the number of engineers than we do."

"Yeah, but we kick the shit out of them when it comes to lawyers and political science majors," Mike growled sarcastically. "Fifty years ago, everyone admired a man if he made steel for a living. Today, the sweet job is a union lawyer suing Boeing for building a factory in the wrong fuckin' state."

Wyatt nodded. "The U.S. is full of people with their hand out. I can't save our country, Mike; I can't control anyone but me."

"Not good enough, Wyatt. Our parents gave us the best damn country that's ever been, but it has cancer. We gotta help. For instance, I have an intern program for high school kids where they get a small paycheck and an honest dose of my world. I hope these kids will help America someday."

"Mike, that's great," Madison exclaimed. "You're an old softie at heart."

"Nope, just grateful. For me, sweat is good. Air conditioning is for pussies. Broken fingernails and chips in your shoes are good. After-shave and button-down collars are for wusses. You two have scratched together a fucking dynamite design and assembled a good-looking facility. If your concept is as good as I figure, a wise businessman might want a piece of Optimal."

"Not likely," Wyatt laughed. "Our net worth is two miles lower than the Mariana Trench."

"So?" Mike said. "Hey, enough of this bullshit—I gotta make a living. Back to work. You guys too." He gathered his coat and tie and flung them over his shoulder. "Thanks for coffee and the words of wisdom."

Madison smiled. "Looks as if we needed three soap boxes. We'll have to do this again."

"Right on," agreed Wyatt. "Glad you came. Loved showing off and shooting the breeze."

Mike nodded and strode to his car.

Chapter 39

Here we go again. Wyatt slammed his fist into an open palm. He'd just received a form letter rejecting their application saying it needed clarification and to contact the Office of the Deputy Commissioner for Patent Examination Policy.

Wyatt grabbed his binder with copies of the application and drawings, took a slurp of coffee and dialed the Patent Office.

After being handed off to several people, he finally heard, "Regina Mendoza. May I help you?"

"Yes. I'm Wyatt Morgan calling about a letter I've received rejecting my patent."

"Do you have the application number? It's on the letter. First paragraph."

"Yes." Wyatt read the number and waited.

"Okay," Regina said. "I have it on the computer—Optimal Aviation Systems." After a pause, she murmured, "This seems irregular. My supervisor, Julie Ann Kelly, entered a note on the file saying, 'Extraordinary technology. Requires specialized examination.'"

Flattered, Wyatt grinned as he heard Mendoza's keyboard clicking.

"Before we can approve your submittal," Regina said, "there are a few items we'll need from you. They're listed in the letter."

Wyatt bristled. "I thought my paperwork was complete.

I wasn't clear what your letter meant. Walk me through the problems––step by step, okay?"

"Sure. First, your drawing format isn't correct. Several of the lead lines are wrong and you didn't provide targets for scanning."

Frustrated, Wyatt snatched his mustard-colored pencil. "Hold on; let me write this down. Give me the drawing and sheet numbers where there are problems."

They quibbled for fifteen minutes going through drawing flaws and problems in the sample code. Wyatt's frustration boiled and he slashed the pages with fat pencil lines that resembled a late-period Picasso. "Dang it, Mendoza, is this really necessary? This stuff is piddly."

"Call me Reggie," she said in a soothing tone. "I know these corrections seem trifling, but regulations are regulations."

"Look at the time we've wasted. We haven't spent a second on the technology. Come on, Reggie, is my paperwork that hard to understand?"

Seconds ticked by. "Reggie? You still there?"

"Wyatt? May I call you Wyatt?" Reggie replied in a hushed voice. "I understand your impatience. It's the bureaucracy. My hands are tied."

Surprised, Wyatt set his pencil down and selected his words carefully. "Sorry I got short with you. It's just that I…"

"I know, I know," Reggie whispered. "Our procedures are often petty and I confess I sometimes bend the rules trying to help out. Just this month, congressional committees have issued more new rules––aimed at China,

I guess. It's awful. There are days I wish I never took this job."

"Why don't you quit?"

"Can't. This is my first job out of engineering school. The government was the only one hiring. I have great benefits and good pay, so I can't be particular. There you have it: I'm stuck."

Wyatt flushed with sympathy. This conversation echoed his talks with Bernie. Reggie made him realize there were many conscientious people with similar struggles. "I had a lousy job too. That's why I've started my own company. Guess you and I have something in common."

Reggie's voice boomed through the handset. "So Mr. Morgan, you'll need to forward a corrected application."

Startled, Wyatt yanked the phone from his ear. "Reggie? Oh. I get it. Someone is listening, right?"

"That's right, Mr. Morgan. We'll be looking for it. Thanks for calling."

He hung up and tried to sort out his feelings. As a government employee, Wyatt automatically ranked Reggie below used-car salesmen and pimps. Yet he sensed that she tried to be helpful. He certainly understood the dilemma over her job. "Petty" she'd said. *Same as SAC. We're rowing the same boat. I should have been easier on her.*

Two weeks had passed without word from the Patent Office when Nick Nolan, the AirEnvironment buyer, called to say he'd be in Los Angeles on business and wanted to visit Optimal. Morales would be with him, hoping to see a demonstration of the pressurization. "Could you guys block out Monday morning for us?" he asked.

Nick's words thrilled Wyatt. Suddenly, with a large firm wanting to see a demo, it looked as though Optimal had blossomed into a serious enterprise.

But the facility's appearance was sobering. Over the past weeks, they'd made many changes to the set-ups, and in their rush, abandoned any pretense of housekeeping. Duct tape lashed pressure gages in place, data sheets were scattered like confetti and a brown banana peel gave the appearance of an octopus crawling from a waste paper basket. The bench tops groaned with soldering irons, screwdrivers and calipers. It was Wyatt who elegantly summed it up: "Holy cow."

That Saturday, Wyatt sneezed as dust invaded his nostrils. He turned his rag and wiped another shelf, trying to tune out Lauren's vacuum cleaner that droned in the mid-day heat.

"Six years in the University got me this?" Madison complained, wrinkling her nose while scrubbing the hand basin. "I don't believe the Dean had this in mind when he told us to go forth and be leaders."

Wyatt grunted. "I could be at home watching the UCLA game, sucking on a beer."

"You're both whimpering, snot-nosed babies," Lauren laughed. "This is business-as-usual for me. I wrestle with accounting every day at the office and then come home to housework and cooking. Saturdays are a walk in the park."

They met the next day at seven in the morning to

go through a dress rehearsal. Their first try resembled a "Three Stooges" comedy. They forgot to hook up an electrical connector on a valve and then the burners went out. Even a compressed air line blew a gasket.

It was late afternoon before they managed two consecutive trials in shipshape fashion. Afterwards, they perched on stools and critiqued the tests and planned the demo.

Because Madison was a friend of Ed Morales, Wyatt decided she'd conduct the meeting. To help, Lauren planned to take Monday off work. Sorting through a checklist, she complained, "The last time I had the jitters was just before the curtain went up on the junior play in high school. I was so tense I couldn't swallow. I played an elderly nun."

"Glad you gave up that idea," Wyatt quipped. "I guess we're all nervous. Lots riding on this. We finished?"

Lauren and Madison nodded.

"Back here at six tomorrow," Wyatt said. "Show time."

The next morning, darkness lingered when Wyatt and Lauren came through the door. Wyatt dropped a box of donuts on his desk, looked at his watch and the clock on the wall. *Two hours to H-hour.*

Lauren fed the agenda and handouts she'd written late the previous night into the copier and stapled the bundles. "Where's Madison?"

"She'll be here soon. When it's light."

With a shrug, Lauren rinsed the coffee pot and set it to turn on fifteen minutes before AirEnvironment arrived.

Wyatt had cleared two reference tables and was

pushing them together in the center of the room when Madison came in.

"Morning everyone," she said, slipping out of her coat. "I updated the PowerPoint presentation last night adding the material on our finances that we talked over yesterday. Hope it goes okay." She set the projector on the end of the jury-rigged conference table. "We'll use the wall for a screen. It's freshly painted and shouldn't look too bad."

Madison plugged in her computer while Lauren arranged small note pads, ballpoint pens, coffee cups and napkins at each chair.

"Checked the oil levels on the compressor and vacuum pump," Wyatt said. "Emptied the water trap on the high pressure line. Everything looks fine."

Madison tossed her head. "Let's do a quick run-through on the slide show to see if we agree on my changes, okay?"

Lauren dimmed the lights and Madison began. Bright images from the projector danced on the wall and reflected onto their intense faces. Madison gave a quick commentary on each image as they flashed.

When she'd finished, Wyatt nodded. "Perfect." The clock on the wall said seven-fifteen. *Forty-five minutes to H-hour.* Having finished his tasks, Wyatt was disquieted by the sudden idleness. Even Lauren and Madison wore quizzical expressions and fidgeted.

"Let's do a quick dry run," Wyatt said. "Make sure everything is working."

"It was fine yesterday afternoon, Honey," Lauren reminded him.

"Do you know Murphy's Law?"

"Of course."

"Well, Murphy has a special affinity for engineers. He lives in our pockets, looking for ways to screw us, particularly in front of prospective customers. Let's check again to be sure."

"Why not, we've time," Madison said.

After a frenzied half-hour, they exchanged high-fives; everything was in order. With nothing left to do, they sat at the table and waited.

Wyatt straightened his tie and looked at his watch "They're late."

"Just ten minutes," Madison said, drumming her pencil.

"I've got butterflies," moaned Lauren.

Soon, they heard tires making a soft chirping sound as a car turned into a parking spot. Ed Morales and Nick Nolan squinted in the bright morning sun as they stepped from the car and walked through Optimal's doorway.

Madison greeted them. "Hi, guys. Welcome to Optimal." She made introductions and beckoned their guests to the conference table.

Ed Morales was in his late fifties, skinny with thick black hair, streaked with gray. He spoke with a slight Spanish accent and greeted his hosts with a quick, gleaming smile. He wore a white shirt with rolled up sleeves and a tie that hung loosely around his neck.

In contrast, Nick was much younger, perhaps thirty. On the pudgy side, his slicked black hair was heavy with tonic. He too, wore a tie, but it was cinched around his neck. His suit jacket was buttoned.

Madison cleared her throat. "Before we begin, please sign our non-disclosure statement, the usual legal routine.

Our patent is in the mill, but we don't have it yet." She passed the paper to Ed and Nick who scribbled their signatures.

"First, Wyatt will explain the test equipment and then we'll run the system pointing out its special features as we go. Then, I'll do a PowerPoint presentation and afterwards go over business issues and flight test arrangements."

"Good," Ed said. "When you run the tests, I'll be looking for specific things, such as smoothness of cabin rate of climb, altitude limiting and delta P regulation."

Madison rose. "To start, we'll simulate a normal flight profile and then show altitude limiting under the worst case of explosive decompression."

A sense of confidence buoyed Wyatt as he and Madison went to their control panels. With a flourish, he pressed two buttons and the compressor and vacuum pump growled to life.

Lauren spread her checklist and began. "Wyatt will set the inflow at 9.4 pounds per minute at 1,050 degrees. Madison will 'fly' the airplane to 25,000 feet climbing at 1,500 feet per minute."

Wyatt and Madison adjusted their controls.

Their practice paid off. Under Lauren's prompts, their motions were confident and fluid. Other than Lauren's reminders, few words were spoken, but Ed seemed entranced and Nick typed copious notes into his laptop.

After ninety minutes, Lauren turned the last page of the checklist. "That's it."

Wyatt smiled. "I guess we've covered everything. Before we shut off the pumps and burners, do you want to see anything else?"

"No. I'm satisfied," Ed said. "Impressed, actually. Looks better than any pressurization I've seen."

Wyatt tried to conceal an exuberant fist-pump. "Okay, let's shut her down." The thunder of the pumps and roar of the burners fell away.

"Wow. I didn't notice how loud those things were," Nick said. "My ears are ringing. Ed, you said it looked good. How good?"

"Smoothest pressure transitions I've ever seen. Has to be the software."

Madison nodded. "There's an anticipator circuit that coordinates both valves. A very special algorithm."

Nick jabbed more notes into his computer. "Ed, I'm ready to look at their PowerPoint if you are."

Lauren poured coffee and passed around donuts. Ed and Nick lounged in their chairs as Madison dimmed the lights and took them through the presentation. She looked commanding as she spoke and her voice conveyed a sense of excitement, drawing the visitors into her world. Even Lauren appeared interested, although she'd seen several rehearsals.

Wyatt had little to do. He leaned back and crossed his ankles, more relaxed than he'd been in months. The presentation was flawless. Wyatt had a song in his heart and he reached under the table, took Lauren's hand and winked in the near darkness.

"And so gentlemen," Madison finished with a wave of her hand, "the schedule shows we should complete flight tests and qualification within twelve months. Questions?"

"What do you think, Ed?" Nick asked his colleague. "Is the system technically sound?"

"Yeah. They nailed it. I'll go over the data when we get back to Massachusetts, but judging from what I've seen, they have a dynamite product."

"If that's the case," Nick said, "I want to talk about pricing. Wyatt, do you have any figures?"

"Not yet. Optimal's design has far fewer parts than current products. Every component is engineered for simplicity, so we expect very competitive pricing."

"How much? Ten percent? Fifty?" Nick persisted.

"No guarantees, Nick, but approximately thirty to forty percent below the competition," Wyatt said.

"Sounds good, but I'll need hard numbers," Nick said. "How soon could you get some?"

Wyatt rubbed his chin for a moment. "I'd need to get with my machining house. Hammer out a few details. Might take two weeks. Is that okay?"

"That ought to be fine, don't you think Nick?" Ed said. "I'll need that much time to review today's tests."

"Make it sooner if you can," Nick said. "Let's go over Optimal's financial strength. Your slide show didn't convince me you have a solid company."

Wyatt gulped.

"Let me elaborate on the presentation," Lauren said. She handed out a sheet of accounts to the visitors. "This is a summary of our assets and liabilities. The money is tight, but our plans are..." Lauren explained projected cash flow and dealings with the SBA, painting a viable scenario.

She's spinning our situation faster than a destroyer's propellers, Wyatt mused. *What a gal.*

"Looks shaky," Nick muttered. "I'll think about it. Now, about qualification. Maddox Aviation schedules flight tests on an ongoing basis. If you can get the FAA's preliminary buy-off, we could piggyback your tests with theirs. It could save a bundle. If you could have a qual system checked out and ready to go..."

"Count on it," exclaimed Wyatt.

"That's it. Great session," Ed said as he stood and gathered his papers. "We have a lunch meeting with another supplier, so we better get going."

Nick rose, but settled back. "A word of caution, Wyatt. There's another company that's also bidding. They've sent us information showing they have a great design that takes a similar approach as yours."

Astonished, Wyatt said, "How can that be? Ours is a huge departure from the state of the art. How similar?"

"Obviously, I can't get into details, but I'll say their proposal is very good."

"Impossible," Wyatt stammered. "There's no way."

"Maybe so. I guess innovation can pop up in two places at the same time." Nick paused, his eyes fixed on Wyatt. "Just thinking, I'd like you to send drawings of the key assemblies and a diagram showing the logic behind the software. Something to illustrate the special features of your design."

"That's odd, Nick," Ed said. "We don't usually ask for that level of detail on proprietary products."

Nick scowled. "We've never certified anything as unique as this. It's all about airworthiness."

Ed grunted. "Whatever." Turning to the others, he said, "Great job, guys."

"Stay in touch, Wyatt," Nick repeated and left with Ed.

Dumbfounded, Wyatt collapsed in a chair, looking

with disbelief at Madison and Lauren. He spread his hands, palms up, and said, "You think it's true?"

Both the women nodded.

Wyatt winced and clamped his eyes shut. "I feel like I've been run over by a train."

Chapter 40

Lauren awoke, sensing something was amiss and realized that Wyatt was not beside her. She squinted through sleep-swollen eyes and saw 4:07 on the clock. "Honey?" she called. There was no answer. She rose, slipped into her bathrobe and started down the hall. There was a dim light in the living room where she found Wyatt sitting in his easy chair, dressed in a rumpled sweat suit. "Honey? You okay?"

Wyatt looked startled. "Yeah. Sure," he said with a dismissive gesture.

"Can't sleep?"

"Feels like Nolan stirred my brain with an oar. I can't understand how someone else came up with my idea. I'm stumped."

Lauren went over and rubbed the back of his neck. "It bothers me too, but the Patent Office wouldn't allow two identical applications. Nolan must be confused."

"I don't think so," Wyatt said. "He's a bright guy. Remember what he said? 'Very similar.' Even Morales didn't contradict him." He crossed his arms and scowled. "I can't believe such a complex design can pop up in two places and why is our patent taking so long? Something smells."

"You have a point," Lauren said, looking at her husband. In the pre-dawn darkness, he looked defeated, gray and despondent. As she studied him, a sudden chill swept her. *This pressurization thing has become his identity. It's as if someone stole his life's purpose.*

She leaned toward him, elbows on the arm of the chair. "Honey, we don't know what the other guy has. Perhaps you're upset over nothing. Why don't we have a patent attorney check into it? At least then we'd know."

"Using what for money?" Wyatt mumbled.

Lauren grimaced. "Good point. But we shouldn't dwell on boogeymen. I understand your feelings, but we have no alternative except to keep going."

Wyatt sank lower in his chair.

A pale dawn eased into the room and Lauren could just make out the dim outline of Wyatt's profile. With a sigh, she studied her hands. It wasn't just Wyatt who was snared by Optimal, she was too. The situation reminded her of a NASCAR race she'd once seen on television where several cars bunched behind the leader, sucked along by the draft. *That's it. Not only me, but Timmie, Madison and even Bernie. Everyone is drawn into Wyatt's draft. It must be a huge burden for him.*

"But we've come so far, Hon. The design is proven, test equipment is in place and we have two possible customers. We can't allow a phantom competitor to derail us."

Wyatt stirred. "This whole thing is depressing." He stood in front of Lauren and wagged his finger. "For some crazy reason, Nick wants a bunch of documentation…for what? Even Ed thought it was out of line." He walked to the window and looked at the gathering dawn. "It's hard, Dear. Really hard."

"Lee is helping us with the loan and the patent application is being processed. Everything will be fine, you'll see."

With a faint grin, Wyatt turned and said, "I guess so."

He drew a deep breath and stretched. "Sometimes I think you're a cute little Valium pill the way you calm me down. How about a bite of breakfast? I have to hurry to meet Bernie at work."

Wyatt crept down the rutted street and parked in front of Optimal. His pulse quickened with the thought of seeing Bernie again. It had been months since Wyatt had left SAC and he missed his friend. They'd talked by phone, of course, but had never found a convenient time to meet until Wyatt insisted. "Bernie, enough excuses. You're an investor and entitled to a tour of our facility." They'd laughed and finally set a date: Tuesday, September eighteenth, eight-thirty in the morning.

When Bernie ambled in, Wyatt smothered his skinny frame with a hearty bear hug. His guest gasped as Wyatt pounded him on the back. "Been too long, you miserable old-timer."

"Forever," Bernie agreed.

"Hey, I made fresh coffee in honor of our lunchroom head-knockings at SAC. Want some?"

"You bet," Bernie nodded. "By the way, where's the lady partner you've been bragging about?"

"Across town talking with a software consultant. She'll be gone most of the day."

"Too bad," Bernie said. "I'd hoped to meet her. Another time."

With steaming mugs, they sat at the conference table. "Tell me the latest gossip at SAC," Wyatt said.

"There isn't much to say. Brian is still running

Engineering and the guys are bouncing off the walls. Nobody can pry any decisions out of him and there isn't a single new project in the pipeline." Bernie slurped his coffee. "I'm getting worried."

"How long before you retire?"

"I'm sixty-three, so it's two years before I get Medicare. When I look at my 401k, it's obvious I'll be working for years."

"Yeah. Economy sucks," Wyatt scowled. "Let's hope Brian can hold it together for a few more years."

Bernie went to refill his cup, and said over his shoulder, "He'd better. I can't afford to lose my job. The good news is I've finally caught up. SAC is back to one shift. It's nice to have a day off, I'll tell you."

Wyatt chuckled. "I bet."

"And you? Is Optimal on a roll?"

"Hmmm. Things are okay. Like I said on the phone, I found out that another firm is offering a pressurization system similar to mine. Takes the wind out of your sails. Even so, we're making headway, I guess."

"You *guess*? It sounds like you're off your stride, Wyatt."

"Maybe so. Been a rough few days."

"Where's your usual zip?" Bernie cradled the hot mug in his hand and looked at his friend. With an impish grin, he said, "I'm not a shrink, but if you have a mental bolt I could tighten or a burr to file to bring you back to your normal self…"

Wyatt's mind flipped like flapjacks on a griddle. He realized Bernie had invested in Optimal because his ambition had been revived. Now, late in his career, he still clung to his lust for glory. Veiled in Wyatt's subconscious was the thought that Bernie needed Optimal—somehow his friend would feel diminished if the company failed.

"I'll be okay. Just need a winning lotto ticket," Wyatt joked. "Got one?"

"Hell," Bernie said, looking around the room, "From what I see, you have a modern version of Edison's laboratory. Didn't you say the system is running fine?"

Wyatt nodded.

"You have two customers pounding on your door. Right?"

"Sorta."

"*Sorta?*"

"Well, perhaps better than sorta," Wyatt admitted. "Actually, they seem enthusiastic."

"There you are," beamed Bernie. "Optimal is on a roll just as I said." He stood and swept his arm in a dramatic arc. "Why don't you get off your ass and show me the place?"

Wyatt stood, thrust his hands deep into his pockets and grinned, "You sure are pushy for such an old fart. But you're right. With luck, Optimal will hang tough. Step this way; we've some great equipment in here."

Chapter 41

The telephone jangled, jarring Madison from her work.

"Hi, Madison. Victor Flemming returning your call."

"Hi, Vic," Madison replied, pleased to hear from her old friend and colleague. "I'm glad you called back. How's things at the zoo?" she asked, afraid of the answer.

"King is struggling as you might guess. Nobody is buying airplanes. There was another layoff last week."

"You're okay, right?"

"So far. They've hit Engineering hard. A lot of us have sent résumés out, but fishing's really bad. Everyone is just plain nervous."

Madison bit her lip. She drummed her pencil on the desk and wondered if she should go ahead with the true purpose of her call. "Without contracts, what is Engineering doing?"

"There's a big campaign to cut costs. Management has us reviewing designs, hammering on suppliers to find economies––anything we can think of."

Madison felt a hint of encouragement. "Are you still looking for second source suppliers? Companies with better prices?"

"Affirmative that––checking every possibility, no matter how long the odds."

Good, she thought. "Remember a few months back you agreed to meet with Optimal and talk about our new pressurization system?"

"Sure."

"Well, my partner and I have just run our system. It has everything: low cost, lightweight and high reliability."

"You're singing the Battle Hymn of Aviation, Madison. How do I fit in?"

"Can we go ahead and schedule that presentation?" Madison asked.

"Love to, but things are crazy here with the layoffs and stuff. Tell you what, Madison. Send me a summary of your project. Design details, test data, schedule. I'll wave it under the boss' nose and see what happens, okay?"

"You got it. Give me two or three days."

Madison hung up and leapt from her chair. She whirled imitating a ballerina and cried out, "Wyatt? Did you hear that? Hot damn! King's a go!"

Wyatt looked up from his computer. "What do you mean?"

Madison sat on the corner of Wyatt's desk. "That was Vic at King. He wants a summary of our program so he can brief his management and set up a conference with us. Now we have *two* customers––AirEnvironment and King."

"Fantastic," Wyatt said. "We'd better be careful about giving out design details though. Our provisional patent isn't issued yet. Could lose everything if the drawings and test data fall into the wrong hands."

"Oh, I'll put a proprietary notice on the summary. It's not a patent, but it's better than nothing. What else can we do? King and AirEnvironment will want to see specifics if we're going to sell them."

"It's a problem," Wyatt said. "We have to land the provisional before we can go much further."

>< >< ><

Wyatt poured another cup of coffee and returned to his desk. AirEnvironment had been pressing him for more information and Ed Morales was getting impatient, wanting to gnaw on real meat. Wyatt worried that Ed might move on to more urgent priorities, a disaster for Optimal.

Now, King was showing interest. Because they were close by, he assumed they'd want to see a demonstration right away, a serious, gritty trial run. If he failed to reel in customers, Optimal would die. They had to get patent protection. Simple.

Madison stood, put her hands on her hips and glared at Wyatt. "We have two companies knocking on our door and the government has our countdown on hold. It's time to kick a bureaucratic butt. Call Mendoza."

Wyatt fished in his desk drawer and pulled out a file labeled, "Patent." With a heavy sigh, he punched in Mendoza's number and heard a familiar voice, "Regina Mendoza. May I help you?"

"Hi, Reggie. Your charming friend Wyatt at Optimal Aviation. I apologize for calling, but I'm desperate. I need to follow-up on my application."

"No problem, Wyatt. Hold on while I pull up your file."

Wyatt waited, tapping his foot.

"Got it," Regina said. "I suppose you want to know the status, right?"

"Yeah, I have two potential customers asking for proprietary information. They're pushing hard and if I don't get the patent soon, I'll lose them."

"There's good news, Wyatt. Your application is out of the queue and in the approval cycle. You should see it in a week."

"Thank God," Wyatt breathed, slumping in his chair as his anxiety evaporated. He felt spent, yet joy bubbled in his mind. He turned to Madison and gave her a thumbs-up sign.

"Reggie, you're the best. I *really* appreciate your work. You're the first government employee I've been able to work with. Thanks."

"I may not be in government much longer, Wyatt. I lined up an interview in Gary, Indiana, with a car parts company. With luck, I'll quit this miserable job within the month."

"Super! You'll bless my provisional first, right?" teased Wyatt.

"Of course."

"I'm curious. Does every patent application take so long? It's been six weeks since I filed."

"Odd you mention that. Usually provisionals are processed within a week or so. I remember it got tied up in the Technical Director's office. That's never happened before."

"Well that's behind us," Wyatt said. "Good luck on that interview."

It had been a wild celebration at the restaurant. Wyatt, with Lauren's help, had framed the patent certificate and he waved it proudly as Mike, with his unique turn of phrase, toasted their success. Lauren's face seemed to glow and Madison abandoned her usual seriousness in favor of rollicking laughter. Bernie hid behind a huge grin saying little.

The next morning Wyatt was groggy with sleep. "Dang!" he hissed through his teeth, hopping on one foot. His shin screamed with pain where, in the darkness, he'd collided with the coffee table. He dropped into his recliner and rubbed his leg. As the pain ebbed, he thought back to the evening after last night's party. Images of zinfandel, candlelight and Lauren's soft smile came to mind. Whispers, gentle touches, urgent gasps and blissful slumber had swept aside his plans to finish the preparations for today's meeting with Mike. *No regrets,* he thought. *Sometimes romance should take precedence over work.*

On tiptoes, he stepped to the entry and grabbed his briefcase. Back in his office, he filled it with dozens of engineering drawings. The house was dark in the autumn morning and Lauren and Timmie were still asleep. He crept into the bedroom, touched Lauren's cheek with a kiss, and stole out the door.

By the time Wyatt arrived at Optimal, dawn had begun to dilute the darkness and chattering birds serenaded him as he walked from his car. With a spring in his step, Wyatt went to his desk and set to work.

An hour later, Madison arrived. "Hard at it, I see," she said, dumping her coat and laptop her desk. "Need any help?"

Wyatt glanced at his watch. "There's still time to correlate these prints against the Bill of Material. Do that while I tweak the casting drawings?"

"Sure. It's your big day with Mike, right?"

"Yup. We'll work up pricing on production quantities—up to a hundred ship-sets."

"I'm amazed how expensive our prototype hardware

was," Madison said, checking off drawing numbers with her pencil. "I hope bigger manufacturing quantities will lower the costs."

"Good tooling might cost several hundred thousand dollars, but parts would be cheap. For now, we have to watch the short term expenses and stick with inexpensive tooling. Parts will be more costly, though."

Madison nodded. They worked wordlessly; Madison's scratching pencil and Wyatt's clacking keyboard were the only sounds. Half an hour passed.

"There, I'm done," Madison said, handing the stack of drawings to Wyatt. "Anything else?"

"Nope. I'd better get going. Thanks for your help." Wyatt jammed the drawings into his already bulging briefcase and went to his car.

Thirty minutes later at Precision Tool, Mike bellowed, "Great news about your patent! It's about fucking time! But what's this about hard quotes? You sounded like a Terrier after a cat when you called."

Wyatt pulled out his stack of drawings and cradled them on his lap. "As I said on the phone, things are starting to move."

"You mentioned AirEnvironment in Massachusetts. They're a big company; a good customer of mine."

Wyatt nodded. "The buyer called last night—a follow-up to our meeting. He wants production pricing right away. Also, Madison talked to King Aviation, here in town, and they're interested too. That's why, Big Mike, I need pricing."

"Fuckin' A," Mike growled, drawing out the 'A' sound. "Are they really serious?"

"Sure are. They're pushing hard—I promised AirEnvironment a firm quote within two weeks. I'm not talking to any other machine shop, just you, Mike. So if my customers are going to bite, you've got to give me rock bottom numbers."

Mike shoved aside the clutter on his desk. "Fucking pig sty. It seems to get worse every year." A small patch of vacant desktop appeared and Mike patted it. "Dump your drawings here. Let's get to it!" He keyed his computer and opened a file. "I kept my notes when I bid on the prototype parts, so just point out any significant changes."

Wyatt unfolded the first print.

"On this bleed valve body," Mike said, "we hogged the prototype from a block, but it's better as a casting."

"You're right," Wyatt agreed. "There are ten more parts I'm converting to castings."

"Great. I know a bitchin' foundry right here in Sun Valley."

The morning struggled toward noon. Wyatt's head ached from concentrating, but Mike seemed tireless. One by one, they waded through the drawings, dashing notes on them with red pencils. While Mike updated his spreadsheet, Wyatt softly hummed another Everly Brothers tune, recalling its close harmony. He felt in tune with Mike. Even though they sang different notes, Wyatt of design and Mike of manufacturing, they marched to a precise tempo. Their skills blended to make perfect music. *All I have to do is dream, dream, dream…*

"Damn, I'm hungry," blurted Mike. "Let's grab a bite. McDonald's is fast, or does that violate your allegiance to IHOP?" Mike joked.

"McDonald's is fine. I'm ready to stretch my legs."

"Is that fancy talk for taking a leak?"

"That too," Wyatt laughed.

They were back at Precision Tool within thirty minutes, clutching paper bags in one hand and sweaty drinks in the other. Mike stopped at reception to pick up messages and renew his request to hold all calls. Back at his desk, they spread out another drawing and their harmonious song resumed.

"This is fucking fine work, Wyatt," Mike said. "Over the years I've seen great design, but this is *damn* great. This aneroid cover, for instance. I'll bet it's an extrusion."

Wyatt blushed from the praise and replied, "Figured it's simple to slice off the thin covers same as salami. Tooling's cheap too."

"It seems you're steering away from expensive tooling," Mike observed.

"Well, we're not exactly awash with money. Have to sacrifice profits until this gets off the ground. In a year or two, we could look at re-tooling to reduce part costs."

"Hmmm," Mike murmured. He stood and walked to his display case of the Mars Rover parts, clutching his hands behind his back. Mike stared through the pane and after a minute, turned and faced Wyatt. "Level with me, my friend. How are you fixed for capital?"

Wyatt shrugged. "We're struggling. Same as any start-up, I suppose."

"Thought so." Mike walked back, sat and put his feet up on the desk. "To grow a company like mine, you have to be a good judge of men. I peg you as top-drawer and your pressurization too. I've done my due diligence and figure you have two of the three things needed to kick off a new company: good talent and a great concept. Optimal lacks the third: money."

"Where are you going with this, Mike?"

"Just listen. I have a hell of a good machine shop. But after all these years, I'm still fighting two problems. Customers are the first. They've got me by the balls. When times get tough, as they are now, they pull their work back inside, or they go to a hole-in-the-wall guy in China with two lathes and no overhead. So I have to chop prices to stay in business. As you see, I'm keeping busy, but margins suck. That's the first. You'll never guess my second problem."

Wyatt shook his head.

"It's the fucking boredom. The daily-grind of finding a way to make fifty-one parts an hour instead of fifty. Setting up a mill for the millionth time. You could say that I haven't had a hard-on since the early Mars Rover days, you know?"

"I get the image," Wyatt smiled.

"You might solve both problems." Mike leaned forward and tapped his finger on the desk. "To expand, I need a proprietary product that will give me higher profits and kill the boredom. The bad news is I can't invent squat. That's where you could help. You're good with ideas and product development and I have money. Agree?"

Wyatt coughed and crossed his legs. "You serious? Are you suggesting we team up?"

"Damn right. I haven't thought this out completely, but here's what I'm thinking. You need hardware for qualification tests––I could contribute that. I'd provide the tooling too––save you a fucking pile."

Astonished, Wyatt's thoughts bounced around like a golf

ball in a tile bathroom. "I don't know what to say. Money *is* a real concern. Been trying to get an SBA loan, but it keeps getting delayed. I have serious doubts I'll *ever* get it. Took out a line of credit backed by my house, but that's evaporating fast. It'd be *huge* if you'd put up hardware and tooling."

"Bet I could kick in a chunk of cash, too. Tell you what. Precision Tool has a great financial guy. I'll send him over to go through your books to see exactly what's needed. Then he can draft an agreement; set us up as partners, all that shit. Sound okay?"

Wyatt shook his head in disbelief. "Sounds better than rare steak, but I'd better talk it over with Madison and my wife. Bernie too––he has a small piece of Optimal. Let you know tomorrow."

Mike stood and pumped Wyatt's hand. "You can solve those two problems of mine. I think this deal is written in the stars. Gemini, the twins. Get it?"

"Gemini?"

"The space craft. The one between Mercury and Apollo."

Wyatt's shoulder ached from Mike's energetic handshake, but he nodded with glee.

With one final yank on Wyatt's arm, Mike concluded, "It's late. Let's pick up tomorrow morning and finish these quotes."

Dazed, Wyatt collected his drawings, stuffed them haphazardly into his briefcase and headed home. He hoped Lauren and Madison would welcome an infusion of money knowing they both had profound respect for Mike.

Gemini, he remembered, was the space capsule that

carried two men. Did Mike have a poetic side? Precision Tool and Optimal Aviation blasting into space together?

As he drove, Wyatt worried about working with another partner. Optimal was desperate for money, but he was uneasy that Mike might contaminate the design and interfere with running the company. *By his own admission, Mike has no design talent. He'll stay away for sure. When we draw up the agreement, I'll make sure that Madison and I have the majority stake. Lauren will work it out. She's good with such things.*

Wyatt swerved violently as a car dashed in front of him, grabbing a parking spot on the street. Driving past, Wyatt smiled, a soft easy smile, and nodded to the driver. "Good job. It's your lucky day."

He continued on in a buoyant mood, feeling liberated from an immense burden. Wyatt figured the evening's Sunset Ritual would be especially warm and effervescent.

Chapter 42

Imitating a boxer, Wyatt thumbed his nose and flung a right cross at his shadow on the wall. *It's been an amazing week.* Mike's manufacturing prowess and generosity banished every doubt he'd be a worthy business partner. Madison and Lauren were thrilled with Mike's offer and chortled as if they'd vanquished a Voodoo curse. Already Mike's financial expert had met with Lauren and after a few hours of amiable negotiations, they'd drafted an agreement for Wyatt and Madison's review.

In spite of the overpowering workload, euphoria permeated Wyatt's days. Happy grins and playful pokes in the ribs displaced fatigue and tension. No matter how late, he rushed home for the Sunset Ritual. Once, arriving before Timmie's bedtime, he asked her to join in with a glass of chocolate milk, shocking both her and his wife.

An amazing week indeed.

But this morning, Wyatt was anxious because a survey team from the FAA was coming to go over his quality manual and management procedures.

On learning of the pending FAA audit, Mike had lent Wyatt his two-hundred-page Quality Assurance manual. Although he was familiar with rules such as the Material Review Board, part traceability and corrective action procedures, Mike's manual proved invaluable. Wyatt had labored for hours, adapting it to their small firm.

Wyatt stood alongside Madison at Optimal's conference table and grunted as he punched holes in a bundle of papers.

Thin stacks of typed pages, graphs, photos and drawings smothered the table top. Madison, collating the new manual, stepped—paused—stepped—paused like a bride walking down the aisle. "I hope we finish in time."

"Better," Wyatt replied, binding a sheaf of pages. "You know how government keeps hours; they'll show up at ten and bail out after an hour."

Madison snickered. "I don't think so. They'll hang around long enough to bum a lunch."

"We can't. Government policy says that's a bribe."

"Want to bet?" Madison sauntered over and playfully stuck out her hand. "Shake?"

Wyatt smiled. "No. If I've learned one thing in the two years we've been in business together, it's that you're always right."

"You're a wise man," Madison chuckled.

"That's it," Wyatt announced, looking at the stack of loose-leaf binders. "They're a mini-version of Mike's manual, but it suits a small firm like us." He straightened the manuals in a neat pile. "You know, the FAA is nothing but paperwork. If they were serious about safety, they'd audit design work, rather than grubbing through useless procedures."

"Don't go there, Wyatt. Don't spoil my glorious morning with Libertarian lectures. Airplanes and the FAA are inseparable as Siamese twins. Besides, their mission is to assure airplanes are safe, right? We have a perfect manual, tailored to our needs. The FAA honchos will sprinkle their holy water, then it's throttle to the wall."

With a coltish shake of his head, Wyatt laughed. "You're a hard woman, Maddy, but you're right. Once we get FAA certification, we're official. Free to ship hardware."

"Is that the FAA boys?" Madison said, looking out the window.

Jason Miel and his assistant, Rob Rio, stepped in and introductions were made. Jason was of average height and at least sixty pounds overweight. His thinning hair, bland features and milky complexion reminded Wyatt of the Michelin Man. In contrast, Rob Rio was squat and dark, and as time would show, would never utter a word.

Jason's gaze swept the room like a lighthouse beam. His nose wrinkled and his lips curled into a pronounced sneer. "This it? The facility?"

"Yup, world headquarters of Optimal Aviation Systems," Wyatt said, feeling defensive. After a year and a half of work, he was proud of the neat test panels, fresh paint and bright lighting. Jason's apparent contempt left a sinking sensation in Wyatt's stomach. He ushered his visitors to the table, saying, "We are just starting up, but have a great product. Coffee before we get started?"

"No thanks," Jason said. "Too acidic."

Rio remained motionless.

Wyatt handed copies of the new manual to his guests.

Jason grunted. "To begin, I want to focus on management systems and record keeping. Then I'll survey the facility, checking calibrations and test procedures." He opened Optimal's manual to the table of contents and with pudgy fingers, turned to a page and read.

"Are you ISO?" he asked.

"We're planning to be ISO 9001 compliant, but not third party certified. AS 9000 too."

Jason typed a note on his laptop. "First, let's check your

procedure to control age sensitive items: rubber goods for example."

As the morning wore on, Wyatt and Madison patiently explained how Optimal would process X-rays of metal castings, raw material certs and instrument calibration records. All the while, Jason typed comments into his computer.

"Back to material control," Jason said. "The government restricts imports from certain countries. There's no procedure for that in your manual."

Wyatt gulped. *What does that have to do with airplane safety?*

"You'll have to add a section."

"Okay."

"You're doing electronics, I see," Jason said. "There's no plan to control static electricity during assembly of the printed circuit boards."

"We reference MIL-STD-1686 in the manual," Madison said.

"You're not allowed to use a government standard in place of a facility-specific plan. Same with software."

"We'll do most software certification work in-house to hold down expenses," Madison said.

"Expenses aren't my concern," Jason frowned. "It's best if an independent consultant does the whole thing. I go by the book. No deviations."

"You can't expect our three-man company to write procedures same as Boeing or Raytheon," Wyatt blurted.

"Afraid so."

Wyatt felt his face redden. Once again, his efforts to

conform to governmental regulations were inadequate. He stared at Jason, his anger building.

Soon Jason finished his questions, typing lengthy notes into his laptop. "Let's take a look at the test equipment, procedures and calibration stickers."

Wyatt and Madison showed Jason around, with Rob trailing behind like a puppy. Jason strolled across the room, gave a cursory glance at the bleed air stand and stooped for a critical look at the stickers on the gages. He waved off Wyatt's invitation to check the big compressor and the vacuum pump outside and said, "Okay. Let's do the exit-briefing." They returned to the conference table where Jason poked at his computer and began a litany of shortcomings: data sheets not fully annotated, sketchy development logbooks, no locked bond area for non-conforming materials, on-and-on.

The chords of Wyatt's neck bulged and Madison squirmed, her lips pressed into a thin line. Their eyes met. Wyatt opened his mouth to say something, but Madison shook her head as if to say, "Don't."

Twenty minutes later, Jason said, "That's about it. I'll send a confirming letter listing all corrective actions. Once you've fixed everything, you'll need to schedule another audit. We're very busy, so allow at least two weeks."

Wyatt, with clenched fists, nodded stiffly.

"Rob," Jason said. "Do you mind? I want a private word with Wyatt and Madison, okay?"

Rob bobbed his head, shoved his hands deep into his pockets and stepped outside into the chilly November day.

Jason crossed his arms and leaned back in his chair. "As I said, our backlog has never been higher, undoubtedly because of new regulations resulting from last year's plane crash. We're clamping down on industry, but deep budget cuts keep us from hiring, so we get behind. On top of that, the lousy economy has become a personal problem."

"How so?" Madison inquired.

"My son got laid off from an auto parts store and can't find a job. I'm spending a lot of time helping him get work, time I normally spend working overtime to catch up."

Wyatt grimaced. He knew where the conversation was going.

Jason adjusted the knot in his tie and smoothed it. "You two are buried; it'll take hours and hours to re-write the manual. Maybe Jeffrey––that's my son––could help," he said, waving his hand at the list of action items. "Kill two birds with one stone. Jeffy gets a job giving me extra time to work on Optimal's application, and you get badly needed help."

The bastard, thought Wyatt. *Has corruption migrated from the Third World all the way to Burbank?*

Madison must have sensed his fury and gripped Wyatt's arm saying, "We don't have plans to hire anyone now, but we're anxious to move the certification along as fast as possible. Give us a day or two to think it over, okay?"

Wyatt slumped in his chair, stifling an urge to throw a stapler at Jason's pasty face. Since morning, he'd gone from elation to despair, from a cozy sauna to an ice-choked lake. He shivered.

"Don't wait too long," Jason said. "My son has a résumé of sorts. I'll ask him to email it." He stood and stretched. "Poor Rob. I hope he's not getting cold." He walked to the window and rapped on it, signaling Rob to come back inside.

"Say, do we have time for lunch?"

Chapter 43

Two days later, Madison squinted through the smoke of her soldering iron and asked, "You turned thirty-five today, right?"

"Yeah," Wyatt replied, wishing she hadn't brought up the subject. "To be honest, I dread my birthday party tonight, but Lauren has her heart set on it. She's invited everyone." He felt pulled between Lauren's insistence he spend more time with the family and his own fanaticism over Optimal. Wyatt shook his head.

"Lighten up. It'll be fun," Madison said.

Wyatt pushed back from a pile of drawings he was redlining. "Yeah, sure. Can't wait to see how Liza and Mike get along. Be like waving a lit match at a firecracker."

"Firecracker? I'm guessing dynamite."

Wyatt grinned. "Maybe so. Tonight's party is bad enough, but this thing with the FAA is depressing. Jason's got me by the...well, you know. He's right about one thing though. We're drowning in work."

"Suppose we hire an intern from Glendale Community College," Madison said. "We could look for a part-timer; offer a low wage. It might not be a bad deal."

Wyatt crossed his legs. "You think this Jeffrey could go part-time? If he's a mechanical or electronic type, we might work something out. What's involved in hiring someone? I brought in a few people at SAC, but the HR manager did the paperwork."

"Same at King," Madison said, "I remember seeing

a checklist they used to process new employees. I might have it here in my old papers. Let me check." She opened a file drawer and fingered through the folders. "Here's something. Yup, here it is." She turned and handed two sheets to Wyatt.

King Aviation Hire Checklist

Employee _____

Date of Hire _____

	Form Description	Date Given	Date Filed/Sent
1	Employment Letter/Hiring Confirmation		
2	Employment Application		
3	Pre-Employment Physical		
4	Job Description		
5	Form W-4: Employee Withholding *		
6	Form I-9: Employment Eligibility Verification (INS) *		
7	Workers' Compensation Pamphlet *		
8	Disability Insurance Pamphlet *		
9	Paid Family Leave Pamphlet *		
10	Sexual Harassment Information Pamphlet *		
11	Initial Safety Training		
12	Employee Orientation		
13	Emergency Information		
14	Employee Handbook Receipt		
15	King Property Return Agreement		
16	Direct Deposit Authorization Form		
17	Arbitration Agreement		

18	Vacation Request Form		
19	Confidentiality Agreement		
20	Credit Union Information		
21	401(k) Summary Information & Booklet *		
22	401(k) Enrollment & Beneficiary Forms *		
23	Health Insurance Information & Summary Booklet *		
24	Health Information Release *		
25	Section 125 Notice *		
26	Notice of HIPPA Rights *		
27	General Notice of Cobra Benefits *		
28	Acknowledgement Receipt of Health Insurance Notices *		
29	Waiver of Coverage Form *		
30	Medical Provider Network (MPN) Notification & Receipt		
31	Enroll employee for Health Insurance		
32	Enroll employee for 401K *		
33	Report of New Employees *		
34	Social Security Number Verification *		
35	E-Verify Verification *		
36	Forklift Certificate		

* GOVERNMENT REQUIREMENT

"This is madness," Wyatt exclaimed. "There's dozens of pamphlets, forms and booklets! It's impossible to wade through this stuff!"

"I'd forgotten how complicated it was," Madison admitted.

"We'd blow more hours on this garbage than we'd gain with a part-time worker. Need a consultant to sort this out."

"Or an attorney."

"Oh, sure." Wyatt tossed up his hands. "Isn't there a saying—something about a frying pan and fire? No way. We haven't the money or the time. I'll just call Jason and tell him no dice. I'm not wasting my time on this."

"Be careful. There's a downside. If we turn him down, he has the power to sandbag us. Our certification could take months."

Wyatt stood, walked to the window and stared at the fading day. "We don't have proof he'd do that, but…"

Madison joined him and clasped hands behind her in silence.

Powerless, Wyatt felt his shoulders tense. Without the FAA's blessing, Optimal would wither away. Jason held the key, but demanded a steep tribute. He glanced at Madison, drew up an eyebrow and shook his head.

"You're right," Madison shrugged. "There's no way we can hire anybody even if a corrupt FAA official has our tail in a vise."

Wyatt nodded, picked up the phone and dialed. "Jason? Wyatt Morgan. Yeah. I'm calling about your son." Wyatt shifted the phone to his other hand and sat.

"Be nice," Madison whispered. "Very, very nice."

"We've talked it over," Wyatt said. "As much as we want to interview your son, Optimal isn't in a position to hire anyone, even part-time."

"Very nice," Madison breathed. "Doing good."

"Well sure. I understand," Wyatt said. He gritted his teeth and shook his fist in the air, aimed at the voice on the other end of the line.

Madison slowly waved her hands, palms down, like she was petting an alligator. "Easy. Go easy," she murmured.

"Yes, I know what you're saying, Jason." Wyatt released his pent-up breath with a hiss. "If anything changes, I'll call. Sure. No problem. Be in touch." He banged the phone into its cradle. "Why do I have to be nice to that conniving jerk? I wouldn't hire his son if he were the Second Coming. This is horse-pucky!"

"Calm down. You're going to get an aneurism." Madison scooted her chair toward Wyatt so their knees almost touched. "What did he say?"

"Exactly what I expected." In a singsong whiney tone, Wyatt imitated Jason. "Ohhhh. That's too bad. I'm sooo busy. I hope, you know, maaaybe I'll find some time to work on your application. I just don't knooooow." Wyatt slapped the desk. "This guy's so dumb, he can't even spell FAA."

"Suppose we turn the tables? What if we called back and explained that if we had certification, Optimal could hire Jeffrey?"

"He'd never go for that. As soon as we get his go-ahead, he loses leverage."

Madison shrugged. "You're right. No matter. You did good. We'll just wait and see what comes."

"Waiting is not what I do, Maddy. I'll push hard; talk to Jason's boss if I have to." Resigned, Wyatt patted Madison's knee and swiveled back to his computer. "I'm calling it a day. It's my birthday and I'm going to take off an hour or two. Okay?"

Madison winked. "You deserve it. I'll see you tonight at the party. It starts at seven?"

"Right." Wyatt gathered his belongings and went to his car.

The afternoon sun was low as Wyatt drove home and

he slapped at the visor. Disconsolate, he recoiled from the prospect of a raucous party. He pulled into his driveway, feeling so weary that it was an effort to turn the wheel. Wyatt turned off the engine and sat a moment, trying to force a smile on his face for Lauren. *Chill. It's just a few hours.*

>< >< ><

Lauren whisked out her cell phone and snapped a picture of Wyatt scowling under his conical party hat. "Smile, Honey. This photo is destined for the family archives, an image your grandchildren will revere, a record that historians will treasure as they chronicle the ascendancy of the most brilliant engineer ever."

"It's a dunce hat, Dear. I look like a fool."

Liza turned to Bernie saying, "There she goes with her big words." Then addressing Wyatt, she went on, "If the hat fits…oh dear, I'm mixing metaphors."

Mike laughed. "Lauren's not the only one with big fucking words, Liza."

Liza grimaced at Mike's profanity and walked over to her granddaughter. "Be careful with your ice cream, Timmie. Don't get it on the floor. That goes for you too, Jennifer."

"We won't," chorused the children.

Lauren joined her mother, putting her hands on Timmie's shoulders. "When you two finish the ice cream, perhaps you could watch cartoons. SpongeBob SquarePants?"

Both youngsters raised their chocolate smudged faces to Lauren and smiled.

"I don't think he's on, but we'll check," Timmie said.

When the girls finished and ran off to the bedroom, Lauren went to the kitchen and with brisk motions, rinsed the ice cream dishes. Mike's financial guy had drafted the new business agreement. It added Mike as a partner and affirmed that Wyatt and Madison would retain control of Optimal. Mike was allotted twenty-five percent of the company, which accommodated Bernie's interests. Thanks to the cash infusion, Optimal's burgeoning bank account soothed her. The black clouds of insolvency withdrew, leaving her light-hearted and joyous. With a spring in her step, she strolled to Bernie and Mike, who were having an earnest sounding conversation.

"Besides," Mike was saying, "I have business connections all over the fucking world. I know every supplier to the big guys. Raytheon, Cessna, even Embraer in Brazil. It won't be long before Optimal is flying on every goddamn airplane in the sky."

"Well, I'm thinking Boeing and Airbus might take more time," Bernie corrected.

"You two plotting the overthrow of the airplane industry?" Lauren quipped.

"You're thinking small, my Dear," Mike said. "We'll take over Exxon and General Electric within the year."

They laughed. Lauren's glance wandered to her husband who was talking with Madison. Wyatt lounged on the arm of the sofa and gestured as he made a point while Madison tossed her head, sweeping a strand of chestnut hair back from her eyes. *Those green eyes. Look at her. Animated. So easy around him. Wyatt seems rapt, captured by her.* She bit her lip, nodded at Mike and Bernie and started toward her husband.

"Great party, Lauren," Marge interrupted, slurring her words. "Sharon, here—I didn't know she's Jennifer's mother—and I are having a ssstupendous chat. We gotta figure a way to fit her into our Sssscrabble parties."

Sharon raised an eyebrow and shrugged.

"Excuse me." Lauren, her jaw clenched, resumed her journey to Wyatt and Madison.

Chapter 44

It was mid-morning when Madison turned her car into a parking spot in front of Optimal. As the engine shuddered to a halt, she twisted the mirror and examined her reflection. She dug into her purse for a brush and stroked her hair, making sure it fell across one eye the way she liked. After freshening her lipstick, she stepped from the car and entered the office of Optimal Aviation Systems.

Wyatt glanced up as Madison settled at her desk. "Wow! You're looking sharp. That outfit must have knocked them dead at this morning's meeting."

"Figured I couldn't go to a big powwow at King dressed in jeans. The V.P. is an old, stuffy guy who hates casual dress, so I thought I'd take advantage of these," she said, crossing her legs. Madison noticed that Wyatt's eyes lingered a moment, more than a moment, on her shapely calves and was pleased.

"How did it go?"

"Wonderful," Madison said. "Vic Flemming had everything set up with the Engineering Veep and the head of Purchasing. Our progress impressed everyone."

"I'd hope so. Finally we have the delta P control working great and you've exterminated all the software bugs."

"Well, most of them."

Wyatt shook his head. "After hundreds of hours spent troubleshooting, testing and redesigning, our work is paying dividends. You done good. High-five?"

They smacked palms and Wyatt laughed. "Maddy, you hit like a girl—floppy wristed."

"Because I'm a girl if you hadn't noticed."

"I did," Wyatt murmured. Madison thought he blushed as he turned aside and fiddled with a handful of papers. "What did they say about our prices?" he asked.

"They were coy, playing the game, but I could tell they liked what they saw. I caught a swallow here, a raised eyebrow there, plus I added a dash of woman's intuition."

"And sneaky feedback from Vic, no doubt," he chided.

"Clandestine, Wyatt, not sneaky. Pros are clandestine."

Wyatt chuckled. "Whatever."

"Well, I did my job this morning. Did you finish the revisions on the quality manual you promised?"

"Nearly. Should wrap it up today—just in time to beat the deadline. It's almost a duplicate of Mike's. A hundred and thirty pages, more or less. Mega-stupid that our micro-company has to write a friggin' tome."

"Tome? Where did you get that word?"

With a sheepish grin, Wyatt replied, "Lauren, of course."

The mention of Lauren's name dragged a cloud over Madison's jubilant mood. She sighed, set an electrical schematic alongside her keyboard and worked on the circuit board for the safety valve. It was a tricky design, and she bit her lip in concentration. Soon, immersed in work, her irritation over Lauren vanished.

Madison was startled to discover that two hours had passed. She stood and stretched, glancing at Wyatt. His head was bent, studying a spreadsheet on his computer. A tiny grin had returned to his lips and his eyes flickered with obvious zeal. *The man is designing again—back in engineer heaven. He'd better get back to that manual.*

A warm, cozy feeling engulfed her as she watched Wyatt work. Madison folded the schematic and remembered how she'd sat side-by-side with him, grinding through the intricate circuits. It was as if their souls intermingled and the memory made her grin. As she returned to her own work, the front door burst open and Lauren whirled into the room.

"Hungry, anyone? I have pizza, cold Cokes and a bowl of nice slaw."

She swept aside a pile of tools, hardware and circuit boards and plopped the boxes and sacks on the workbench. "Dig in."

Wyatt nearly stumbled as he bolted toward the scents of oregano, red pepper and cheese that oozed from the grease-blotched box. "Pepperoni?"

"Of course," Lauren said.

Madison fetched paper plates and plastic cups from a cabinet above the coffee maker. After handing plates to Wyatt and Lauren, she peeled off a small slice of pizza and dropped a dollop of slaw onto hers. Turning, she saw Lauren staring at her.

"Nice outfit," Lauren said in a throaty tone. "Not your usual jeans. Is it prom night?"

Wow! It just got really cold in here. "No," Madison said. "I had an important meeting at King this morning."

Lauren sat next to Wyatt, pecked his cheek and asked, "Did you go to King too, Honey? You're not wearing a suit."

"No. Madison handled it. Ex-employee with a magic touch, you know. I stayed and worked on the quality manual putting the finishing touches on the best manual the FAA will ever see. I'm tired of fighting them." Wyatt took a huge bite of pizza and chewed noisily. He swallowed and said, "Nice surprise, you dropping in with chow. Didn't know I was so hungry."

"I took the afternoon off and decided to surprise you two. Sharon has invited Timmie to a sleepover tonight and will pick her up at after-school care. That gave me time to stay and clean up a few things."

Off to one side, Madison picked at her pizza. She hated pizza. Carbs. Trans-fats. Salt-laced sausage. Grease. She cherished her twenty-four inch waist almost as much as her shimmering hair. She pushed her plate away, leaned back and looked at Wyatt as he guzzled his Coke. *He's a ten-year-old until he puts on his engineering hat; then he's brilliant.* Madison sighed, aching with love for him. She sipped her drink. *Doesn't taste like diet.*

Wyatt belched. "Full," he proclaimed. He gathered the empty pizza box and slaw container and tossed them into the trashcan.

The afternoon passed in a flash with Wyatt sweating over the quality manual and Madison consumed by a complicated algorithm. Lauren busied herself posting the latest bills.

"My headache is killing me," Wyatt complained, rubbing his temples. "It's late and my brain is trashed. Let's call it quits."

Lauren stood, went to Wyatt and massaged his neck. She brushed a wisp of hair back from her brow and looked over her shoulder at Madison. "Oh dear, it *is* late," she sneered. "It's already dark outside."

Madison blushed, suspecting Lauren knew about her fear of the dark.

Wyatt looked out the window. "Sure is. Short days in January." He picked up his coat and went to the door. "Say, Madison, let me walk you to your car."

Chapter 45

"S-Q-U-I-S-H! How's that?" Marge whooped. "I get a double word score to boot! Add it up, Lauren. I might beat you yet."

Lauren chuckled to herself, enjoying her friend's glee. "Ten for the 'Q', plus four and another four. Comes to eighteen. Doubled. Thirty-six. Let's see. Yes, you're ahead of me by seven points."

Marge grinned and took a big gulp of her Bloody Mary. "We'll see who the Scrabble Queen is today."

"I think Lauren can afford to be magnanimous," Betty tittered. "Wouldn't it be nice if we start the New Year with a fresh winner?"

"I'm first in line," giggled Marge. She selected six more tiles, set them in her rack and wrinkled her brows. "Hodge-podge––the Scrabble gods hate me."

Betty re-arranged the letters in her tray. "Say, Lauren, any news on your company?"

"Optimal just had another FAA audit. The inspector came up with more problems, so we're re-writing the quality manual. Wyatt also plans to start an application for a formal patent right away because he's worried about industrial espionage. One of Madison's inventions was stolen two years back because she was slow in filing."

Liza took a sip of wine. "But you have a patent."

"It's just a provisional––good for only a year. Wyatt says if the utility application isn't accepted before the provisional expires, we'll lose protection. We might have to hire a patent attorney to help."

"That could cost a bundle," Liza said.

Lauren shrugged. "Madison knows a lawyer from her work at King Aviation who has connections inside the patent office. He might be able to push our application through quickly. Still, he'll be very expensive. We'll probably pass."

Liza made a play and drew more tiles. "That's the least of your problems if you ask me. It's that Madison woman I'd worry about, flouncing around Wyatt's birthday party like a star attraction. She couldn't keep her eyes off him."

Marge grunted. "Yup, she's a dish. Beautiful eyes and a knockout figure. Enough to give any warm-blooded man a lump in his drawers. I wonder if she dyes her hair."

Lauren tried to dismiss the banter as woman's gossip, but fretted nevertheless. Around Madison, Wyatt always seemed to be his usual self, immersed in his engineering world. *True, Madison stares at him sometimes, but just a look. No harm in that.*

Lauren re-arranged her tiles and couldn't find a word. "Pass."

"Aren't they together right now?" Liza asked.

"Sure," Lauren replied. "At the office—he always works on Scrabble days, just to get out of our hair."

"With Madison?"

"Often. Wyatt grabs any moment he can to work on the pressurization. Sometimes he'll go back to the office after dinner and stay until one in the morning, or longer."

"With Madison?" Liza prodded.

Smothered in Liza's suspicions, Lauren flushed and glared at her mother. Avoiding an embarrassing scene in front of her friends, she quelled her surging anger and vowed to confront her mother later that night by phone. But Liza's words nibbled at her tenuous poise.

Betty looked at Lauren and then Liza. "After all, they're in business together. It seems everything is cool. No need to beat it to death, Liza."

"She's right," Lauren said, "Madison is my husband's business partner. Nothing more. They work together. Nothing more. You know Wyatt; he lives in his engineering fog and wouldn't notice if Madison were nude."

"If Timmie isn't adopted," Marge snickered, "*you* got his attention. At least once."

"More than once. Lots more."

The tension eased. Laughter and smiles settled over the gathering and the tiles clicked once more. Lauren was appreciative that Betty had come to her aid. Once at Starbucks, they'd chatted about marriage and Betty lamented hers had "other woman" troubles. She asked if Wyatt had ever strayed. Lauren laughed and joked on her husband's preoccupation with his profession, but kept her anxiety over Madison to herself.

Lauren fingered the letters in her tray, spelling "skein." She placed the tiles on the board, smiled and tossed Betty a grateful glance. Determined to change the subject, Lauren asked, "Say, Mother, are you planning to go to the Big Sky house again this spring? If school's out, Wyatt and I might bring Timmie for a week."

Liza studied her letters. "I've decided to sell the Montana house––I listed it two weeks ago."

"You what?" Lauren exclaimed. "But you've had it for

centuries. Give up your tennis? Golf at the Arnold Palmer course? Hikes in Yellowstone?"

Liza shuffled her tiles. "It's too much trouble. The grounds keeper is getting old and cranky. Flights into Bozeman are spotty and cramped, not to mention the hour drive to the house. Jordanna, my best friend there, moved back to New York. In view of all that, why bother?"

Lauren shook her head. "You have dozens of friends there. Besides, you usually charter an airplane into Bozeman. A Pilatus or something like that."

"Pilatus? Isn't that an animal from Australia?" Marge said, hiccupping.

"Platypus," Lauren corrected. She studied her mother, whose downcast eyes suggested she wanted to avoid the topic. Lauren remembered Liza had sold her yacht, and now, the Big Sky house. *I wonder if she's ill and keeping it from me.* Lauren resolved to delve into the matter when she phoned later that night.

Dinner dishes were cleared before Lauren found time to call her mother. Liza picked up the receiver on the third ring. "Hello?"

"Hi Mom, it's me. I need to talk over a couple of things." Lauren took a deep breath to steady her nerves. "The first thing; are you okay? I mean, is your health okay?"

"As good as expected for someone in their sixties. Why do you ask?"

"I don't know. It's just strange that you sold the yacht and now the Big Sky house. It's not like you."

"I told you," Liza replied with an edge in her voice.

"They're too much trouble. Why do you keep prying into my business?"

Lauren bristled. "I'm not prying, Mother." She changed the phone to her other hand and continued. "Now that you mention it, you're the one who pries. Your innuendoes aimed at Wyatt today *really* upset me. You're *way* off base."

"Just the truth, Dear. You need to get out of your little velour-lined shell and recognize the obvious."

"Wyatt and I have an extraordinary marriage. We love one another. You just don't understand, Mother. He and I are a perfect duet."

"Duet? Ha! That's not your problem—Madison is the problem. It's obvious she's on the make, but you just can't see it."

"You think I'm blind?" Lauren was near tears. "Sure, Madison is a looker, and thinks a lot of Wyatt. Who wouldn't? I'm a normal woman with normal suspicions and I've watched them. There's nothing going on. Wyatt and I have a joke; he says his mistress is calculus and I believe him."

"Daughter, your world is unraveling," Liza hissed. "Timmie spends more time with me than her father, and it shows. You've hung a big mortgage on your house and dumped your savings into a stupid company with no customers. For what?"

"For Wyatt! For us!" Lauren yelled. "It's *my* decision to do this, not yours! It might sound trite, but we're reaching for the stars. Together. We may fall on our butts, but it will be together."

"You're screaming, Lauren. Calm down."

"One last thing, Mother, don't *ever* embarrass me in

front of my friends again." With tears streaming down her cheeks, Lauren slammed the receiver. The tears felt good, warm and soothing. A single word hovered in her mind, a word that summed up her world.

Together.

Chapter 46

They stood at the window and watched Vic Flemming drive away. Madison's bright smile and sparkling eyes reflected her thrill with their triumphant meeting. Yet she was relieved the grueling morning was finished. She turned to Wyatt and Lauren and said, "No doubt—we have King in our pocket."

"Did we nail it, or what?" Wyatt bubbled. "The airplane gods have smiled on their humble servants. Vic had us doing back-flips, but the pressurization performed perfectly. Can't believe it."

Madison nodded. "Vic took the plots back to analyze at his office He's a careful fellow, that man, especially since they promoted him to manager of King Engineering. I noticed he took lots of notes."

Lauren shook her head. "I'll bet he doesn't look at them. They'll sink to the bottom of his desk drawer as if in a bog."

"You don't know him the way I do," Madison contradicted. "He'll study them under high magnification."

"I'm not convinced," Lauren replied. "He was so excited about the smooth altitude changes that he volunteered to go on the first test flight at Maddox.'"

"My honey has a point, Madison," Wyatt said. "No matter. The day was flawless. The delta P control never wavered and the numbers on the display looked like they were painted on. Same with altitude limiting. Perfect. Everything was perfect."

A flash of irritation poked at Madison, miffed at being contradicted.

Lauren slipped her arm around Wyatt's waist and squeezed. "Nice to see you so happy. This morning you were as tense as Timmie on her first day of school. The pot of coffee you drank didn't help matters either."

"I wish we had a bottle of champagne," Madison said, whirling to the refrigerator. "The only bubbly we have is Coke. It's obvious we're not a serious engineering company."

"Grab the plastic cups and the Coke," Wyatt directed. "Gotta have a toast to the conquest of King Aviation!"

Lauren poured, and they held the red cups in the air.

A serious expression settled across Madison's face. "I want to offer a special toast." Concentrating, she sought befitting words. After a few moments, she brushed back her hair, fixed her gaze on Wyatt and raised her cup. "To a fine man and his elegant design. May we live on the frontier of science forever."

They touched cups and sipped. *How inadequate*, Madison thought. *There are no words for this. Look at him, grinning the way a kid does on Christmas morning; no hint of arrogance or bluster. He draws the world of design around him like a warm blanket on a wintery night.* She took a deep breath to quell a surge of emotion.

Lauren stared at Madison, her eyebrows pushed together creasing her forehead. "Yes. To a fine man."

A strained laugh escaped Madison's lips as she dashed more Coke into the cups. The moment of pain eased, and she felt a smile creep across her face. Wyatt and Lauren leaned back in their chairs, looking tranquil.

"There *is* a cloud," Wyatt said. "Could be a thunderstorm."

"Not now, Honey," Lauren rebuked, shaking her head. "Let's savor our big win, okay?"

"What cloud?" Madison asked.

"Vic confirmed there's another company working on pressurization––wireless, same as ours. I can't shake the idea that somebody has their hand in our pocket."

Madison crossed her arms. "I'm sure it's the same outfit that's talking to Nick Nolan at AirEnvironment."

"Enough, Hon," Lauren said. "It's been an extraordinary day and a long one. Let's go home and pour a glass of wine and light candles."

Wyatt flinched. "Should, I suppose, but Madison and I planned to work late on the FAA problems."

"Can't it wait? It's been ages since we've had our Sunset Ritual. Besides, Madison can stay and work on her stuff. She doesn't need you."

"Well, there's a lot of overlap. We have to clarify the Failure Modes and Effects Analysis," Wyatt explained.

"Whatever in the world that is," Lauren sputtered.

Wyatt grinned. "Airplane talk. Sorry. Bottom line: Optimal is dodging torpedoes until we get this new submittal together. Every day matters."

Madison nodded. She knew her software and his mechanics walked hand-in-hand, so she'd have to work closely with Wyatt to finish the analysis––a pleasant thought.

Lauren stood, crossed her arms and glared. "So you've decided."

Wyatt puckered like he'd bitten into a sour apple. "Yeah. We're pushed into a corner: FAA pounding on us, running out of money, competitor on our heels. It's panic time."

"Wyatt's right, Lauren," Madison said. "It's been three months since the survey and we're close to finishing. Optimal needs the FAA's blessing soon."

Lauren snatched her purse and spun toward the door. "Fine," she growled at Wyatt. "Don't wake me when you come home." As she left, her car tires squealed.

"Dang," groaned Wyatt. "Lauren's sore as heck. Been edgy all day because her boss got mad when she took off work again."

"She'll be okay," Madison said.

"Yeah, I guess. Sometimes I can't figure her out. Oh well, let's get going." Wyatt settled into his chair and opened a folder. On top was the latest letter from the FAA, citing problems with the algorithms and their effects on system reliability.

"Okay, Maddy, let's go through this line by line."

Madison drew up a chair next to Wyatt. *He's all business as usual,* she thought. Even so, his presence warmed her, and she eagerly began analyzing the letter.

"Do you understand their problem with the encryption?" Wyatt asked.

"I'm mystified. We've reviewed the test data and computations several times. They're fine. Why won't they accept the data and let us move on?"

"The FAA doesn't have a stake in our success. They've never handled a wireless pressurization system before and without precedent, they see red flags everywhere." Wyatt pursed his lips. "We'll just have to find a way to convince them our system is safe."

As Madison sat beside him, she could almost feel Wyatt's mental churning. He seemed to radiate determination, which resonated with her own resolve. She wanted to rub his shoulders and caress his cheek to encourage him, but dared not. Madison tried to hold off these thoughts and said, "Let's get busy."

They worked for three hours, struggling to decipher the nuances in the document. As a literal, concrete thinker, Madison was plagued by the vague and shapeless concerns expressed by the FAA. Twice they sprang from their chairs to test electronic communications and valve response, but the data confirmed previous tests. Fatigue crowded her mind and their discussions became labored and halting.

"Can you think of anything else?" Wyatt asked.

"No. First thing in the morning, let's mail everything we have to the Los Angeles ACO one more time."

"And cross our fingers, right?"

"And toes." Madison collected her papers into a neat stack and switched off the computer. "You in big trouble with Lauren?" she asked.

"It'll blow over; it always does." Wyatt latched his brief case and frowned. "I know I'm caught up in my work and Lauren feels pushed aside. I try to get closer to my family, but devil science always takes command. It's a dilemma."

Madison massaged the back of her neck. *He's headed home to Lauren and her anger—he's caught between his wife and work. Which will win?*

Chapter 47

Lauren tugged the collar of her bathrobe, snuggled it around her neck and reflected on last night. It had been past midnight when Wyatt shook her awake and led her by the hand into the living room. There, she found two lit candles and glasses of old vine Zinfandel, her favorite. He'd turned on Pandora, tuned to soft jazz and said, "I'm sorry about tonight. Sometimes my science madness gets between us. No matter what, I love you."

He always did that. Wyatt's occasional blunders hurt her deeply, but every time, he concocted tender, amorous gestures to heal the rift. Lauren had tried to cling to her anger, but couldn't. She basked in the candlelight, sipped wine and yielded to his smile. Like always, hugs and kisses led to urgent passions that swept them into the night.

Lauren set aside her reveries, poured Wyatt a cup of coffee and slid the newspaper to him. "We've been in our new office for a year," she said, "and it's time to renew the lease. I'll write the check right after breakfast. One thing's for sure, the money can't hold up another year. I don't know what we'd do if it weren't for Mike–– his investment will keep us afloat for now."

"It's a good thing. The company is coming together. There's his money, the design work is on track and our test equipment is ready at last."

Lauren brushed a tiny strand of hair back from her cheek. "I'll be late from work tonight. Mother's babysitting this afternoon so I can shop for Timmie's birthday. I was

317

thinking of getting her a book. Maybe it's silly, but I want to share my love of reading with her. Then again, perhaps I'll get another doll. Do you think she's getting too old for dolls?"

"No way. She's only going to be eight."

"I don't know." Lauren tapped her lips with her finger. "Sometimes she's a little lady—seems mature and notices things. For example, she's asked why you work so much and why 'Auntie Madison' is around all the time."

"She's just the same spoiled kid she's always been. I hadn't noticed any big change."

Lauren chuckled. "You never notice *anything*, Honey. Watch out, the next thing you know, you'll be walking her down the aisle."

Wyatt smiled. "You're probably right. The years blast by me like NASA's new ARES launch vehicle." He rose and set his bowl in the sink. "Hey, I'd better get to work. Morales and I have a telecon first thing. I smell an order coming so we're tidying up a few technical details."

"Wouldn't that be great? Lee Wong said his bank and the SBA would give us a loan if we had a real backlog. Don't forget King is in the mix too. Suppose both gave us an order?"

"Now you're dreaming," Wyatt laughed, "but it's a nice dream." He gathered his jacket and briefcase, pecked Lauren on the cheek and left for Optimal.

>< >< ><

Wyatt, pre-occupied with plans for the conference call, was surprised to find Madison already at work when he bustled through Optimal's door. "Boy, you're here early," he said, tossing his jacket on a chair. "What's the deal?"

"Just reviewing a few things. Ed has a way of asking tough questions."

"For sure," Wyatt said. "He seems concerned about pressure drop during ground operations. There are a few minutes yet, so I'll double-check the test data."

Wyatt worried as he booted up his computer. The computations were simple but tedious—easy to make mistakes. The AirEnvironment engineer was fastidious, and a stupid oversight would be costly at this stage of negotiations. There were also complex issues with portions of the software, but Madison, he was sure, was ready. He concentrated and spent the next few minutes grinding through the numbers.

"It's time, Wyatt." Madison collected her notes and laptop, and scooted over to Wyatt's desk. "Are you primed and ready?"

Wyatt grinned, punched the speaker button and jabbed in AirEnvironment's number.

Thirty minutes later, he ended the call. "That was as easy as it gets. We had the answers cold. Dang fine job, Miss McKenzie." Wyatt rubbed his hands with pleasure. "I finally got the flow coefficients right and aced the pressure drop figures."

"We're a team, for sure." Madison smiled and leaned back, crossing her legs. "We're about to sign a deal, but I'm curious. Ed said he wants to come back to California and go through the entire design again."

"Understandable. Wireless data on a critical flight safety system? They'll check and then double-check the checkers. If our telecon is any indication, they won't find any problems and we'll nail down that order." Wyatt bobbed and weaved, throwing phantom punches the way Mike Tyson did in his prime.

The front door swung open and the UPS delivery driver walked in clad in his traditional brown shirt and shorts.

"Hi, Jimmy. Got that package I've been waiting for?" Madison asked.

"Just this envelope. One of you needs to sign," Jimmy said, handing it to Madison.

She dashed her signature on his mini-computer and took the envelope. "Know anything about this?" she asked, looking at the label. "Masterson and Leibnitz, Attorneys at Law?"

"Let me see." Wyatt took the envelope, opened it and extracted a multiple-page letter on embossed letterhead. "What's this? 'Cease and Desist', it says." Wyatt's eyes flicked back and forth as he scanned the letter. "Says we're violating somebody's patent. Tells us to stop development of the cabin pressurization system!"

"Can't be. Let me look." Madison scrutinized the pages, her squint creating crowfoot wrinkles at the corners of her eyes. "I don't understand. Some company called Dynamag Industries claims to have a patent on our design. Not just similar as Ed and Nick said, but nearly identical."

"Impossible," Wyatt sputtered. "There must be a crazy mistake!" Wyatt snatched the letter from Madison and read it once more. "Who's this Dyna…whatever company? Never heard of them. Now we have lawyers shoving their noses into our business!" He kicked the desk leg and winced. "Dang!"

"Just simmer down, okay? I'll Google Dynamag and see what gives." Madison typed in the company's name and her eyes swept across the screen. "Manufacturer of automotive parts. Privately owned. Established 1971 in Trenton New Jersey by Dennis Magana, present owner's father." Madison frowned. "They make car parts, not airplanes. Something's screwy."

"I *got* that," Wyatt said. "This is nuts. I'm not going to cease and desist squat."

"Let's look up Art Weinstein, the patent attorney I worked with at King. I've mentioned him before. Perhaps he could explain all this."

"Cost a fortune. Lawyers are damn vultures feeding off the carrion they've created."

"Hold on a minute. You wouldn't want an engineer to remove your appendix, right? What if Dynamag has the legal power to stop us? We could lose Optimal because of our own stupidity. Let's relax and think through this."

Wyatt scowled, walked to the coffee pot and filled his mug. He gritted his teeth and drew a deep breath. *All right. This is going nowhere. I'm being a jerk and blaming Maddy.* Turning, Wyatt said, "You're right. Let's talk to this lawyer. He's good, you said?"

"Yes. His office is in downtown L.A. Let's call him right now."

Impatiently, Wyatt tapped his foot. He and Madison stood in the marble foyer of a nineteen-twenties era office building on Spring Street in Los Angeles. They waited while the elevator crept downwards, pausing at every floor until at last its brass doors yawned, spitting out half a dozen business people. Stepping in, Wyatt looked at a note he'd dashed on an envelope. "Fourth floor." Wyatt pushed the button and checked his watch. "On the dot," he said, pleased with their punctuality.

The elevator car jerked and then steadied. "Since when," Wyatt said, "does a hotshot lawyer have his office in a hundred-year-old relic?"

The car jerked again and Madison steadied herself by leaning on the wall. "I think it's quaint. Did you see the gorgeous rose marble in the lobby and the wrought iron railing on the balcony?"

"Didn't notice." Wyatt stared at the dial above the doors, monitoring their assent. The car shuddered to a stop, and the doors moaned open. "After you," he said with a sweep of his hand.

They walked into a claustrophobic waiting room where an elderly receptionist pecked at a computer keyboard. The woman looked up, rubbing an arthritis-swollen finger. "Mr. Morgan? Ms. McKenzie?"

Wyatt nodded, startled by her crystal blue eyes.

"Mr. Weinstein is expecting you. Go on in," she said, pointing to an unadorned door.

When they entered, Wyatt saw an older, cherubic-looking man wearing reading glasses that clung to the end of his pudgy nose. His eyes flashed with the same blue twinkle of the receptionist. Light from an ornate floor lamp behind him reflected off his bald head, where a fringe of pure white hair hovered above his ears creating a halo-like glow. He sprang to his feet, extending his hand. "Art Weinstein, at your service."

Wyatt yielded to his impulse to grin at this short, chubby man, a beardless Santa Claus. "Wyatt Morgan. My partner, Madison McKenzie."

"Oh, yes, Ms. McKenzie. I recall we've had a few skirmishes at King Aviation, right? Sit. Sit. Something to drink? Coffee? Soda?"

In unison, Wyatt and Madison replied, "Coffee."

The lawyer picked up his phone, punched the intercom and said, "Mom, want to bring three coffees?"

That explains their eyes, Wyatt thought. He looked around the office. Brown leather chairs, burnished by thousands of worsted wool clad buttocks, exuded confident professionalism. Yet a cluster of family photos perched on a wooden file cabinet and an immense jar of jellybeans softened any hint of stuffiness.

Mom shuffled in with the coffee, her rebellious dentures clacking. With a nod and a smile, she left, pulling the door closed with a click.

"It's nice to see you again," Madison said, crossing her legs. "You represented Maddox Aviation when we worked together on litigation over a software glitch."

Weinstein leaned back in his chair and clasped his hands behind his head. "The folks at Maddox are nice people. I've been doing business with them for years."

"I'm curious," Wyatt said. "How did Maddox, half a country away in Oklahoma, decide to hire you?"

"I guess I speak their language. Originally, I was an engineer. Purdue. I worked awhile at Aero Commander in Oklahoma City. In my late twenties, the law bug bit me, so I went back to school. After graduation, I was recruited by an L.A. firm and moved here. I went out on my own five years later and Maddox picked me up right away because of my experience in general aviation."

Wyatt clapped his hands. "Ah-ha! Finally I've met a lawyer who knows real law––Newton's Third Law."

Madison tapped Wyatt's ankle with her shoe.

Wyatt glanced at her and then his watch, mindful of time hurtling by at $400 per hour. "This is our problem," he said, handing the letter to the attorney. "It's confusing–– full of legalese. We looked into the company, Dynamag, and they're in auto parts. Doesn't make sense."

Weinstein studied the letter for several minutes while jotting notes on a legal pad. "This is peculiar. Tell you what, I'll call Masterson and Leibnitz and see what they're doing. Usually these 'Cease and Desist' edicts are full of holes. Dynamag has a patent pending, not a utility one, which means the Patent Office hasn't investigated the merits of the claim yet, So this letter has little weight. You said you got a provisional six months ago so there might be a conflict with Dynamag's filing." Weinstein caressed the top of his bare head. "I'll know more after I talk to their attorneys."

"Ha. They'll just throw up a big cloud of smoke," Wyatt said.

Madison leaned close to his ear. "Chill."

"It might be a good idea," Weinstein said, "if I reviewed your provisional paperwork to see if everything's in order. You mentioned you've been working on the utility patent. Copy me on what you have. Nowadays, it takes up to two years to process a patent. Any hiccups in the paperwork will push it out further––it can get real messy."

Wyatt leaned forward in his chair. "Mr. Weinstein, can

you find out exactly what Dynamag is up to? Can you get discovery, or whatever you call it?"

"Yes, they have to disclose it. I'll get detailed information and see if we are in actual violation. The technology is key to the whole situation."

It's the key to my friggin' life, thought Wyatt. "Give us a call tomorrow after you talk to those ding-a-lings? I'm ready to grab a machine gun and go looking for lawyers."

Weinstein gave Wyatt a sympathetic smile. "Present company excepted, I presume."

Wyatt blushed. "I didn't mean…"

"I know. Lawyers aren't the world's most popular folks." He folded his hands across his bountiful stomach. "I guess that's it."

Turmoil filled Wyatt. Weinstein was going to bill God-knows how many hours and money was running out fast. He could see Lauren cringing over the cash flow report and telling him, "No way, Hon."

"About your fees," Wyatt stammered. "We're investing every dime we have in product development. Can we work something out?"

The attorney smiled at Wyatt. "I'm aware that start-ups are always short of money. Don't worry––it sounds like you have a case. It's customary in the business that I get paid only when damages are recovered. Besides, fellow engineers have to stick together."

Astonished, Wyatt beamed. "Thanks, Mr. Weinstein. I don't know how to thank you."

"Art, just Art. I'll get to the bottom of this. I have a good friend in the Patent Office and he'll get the skinny. Mom will show you out. Be in touch."

They stepped into the elevator and faced one another as the doors closed.

"Wow," Wyatt exclaimed, with a drawn-out sigh of relief.

Madison chuckled and patted his arm. "There. That wasn't so bad, was it?"

"Running before the wind. Mike and Bernie will be glad to hear."

Chapter 48

Wyatt's euphoria about Weinstein's assurances had faded days ago because the patent was still in limbo. Art had found wording in Dynamag's application remarkably like Optimal's. "The turkeys copied your disclosure," He said. "I've got the noose around their neck."

Despite Art's assurances, nothing concrete had happened. Still, Wyatt had hoped to resolve the problem by the time Ed came to Burbank for the follow-up survey, slated for the next morning. Besides, the Patent Office and the FAA hadn't responded to Optimal's latest submittals.

As Wyatt was printing the part cost breakdown for the meeting with AirEnvironment, he idly checked email and found a message from the FAA. *Now what?* He opened the file and read: "Optimal Aviation Systems' quality assurance manual has been approved." Wyatt gasped. In the pre-dawn stillness, he whooped with joy. Ecstatic, he snatched the phone and called Lauren. Her groggy, sleep-laden croak became a chipper "Honey, that's wonderful!"

"I can't wait to tell Madison—she's not here yet."

"Yes. Do that," Lauren grumbled.

As he hung up, Wyatt thought his wife sounded a little terse, but his elation undiminished, he called Mike at home.

"You know what the fucking time is?"

"It's time to celebrate. The FAA blessed us!"

"No shit," Mike yelled. "That'll grease the skids for AirEnvironment's visit."

"Sure will. Don't forget that Ed wants to check out your

place too. We'll be there first thing in the morning. Be sure to sweep the floor, okay?"

Mike laughed. "Fine, but I'm not putting on a tie. Now go away and let me catch a few zees. It's five-thirty in the morning for Christ's sake."

Wyatt lounged with Ed Morales at the corner table farthest from the door, munching pretzels and sipping drinks. The bar was dark and smelled of leather and bourbon. Because it was early evening, there were few patrons, but their soft voices seeped around the cozy tables. Thick Kelly-green carpet looked inviting and the bartender absently dried cocktail glasses under a flickering Budweiser sign. A lithe, tanned barmaid glided through the cool, dark shadows with a tray balanced lightly on her fingertips.

"There, I just emailed my boss saying I've approved your pressurization system," Ed said, setting his smart phone on the table. "Your design is one of those once-in-a-decade breakthroughs. It'll add a notch on AirEnvironment's gun. Also, Precision Tool impressed me—you have a great resource there. Mike squashed any reservations I had about production. Now that the FAA has given you the green light, you could have a purchase order from Nick tomorrow if we settle on prices and schedule. Providing there are no patent screw-ups, of course. Nick's on business in Jersey somewhere, but is flying in tonight for tomorrow's negotiations." Ed took a swig of beer. "All that aside, you have a damn good system, Wyatt."

Wyatt felt self-conscious and hoped the dim light cloaked his involuntary smile. "Thanks. I appreciate the effort you've put into this. Too bad Madison couldn't be here—her mother is having hip replacement down in Orange County. She'll be back for tomorrow's meeting though."

"Madison's a great engineer with knockers, or should I say an engineer with great knockers," Ed joked. "My software people tell me her encryption code is flawless, even groundbreaking. I hope you realize how incredible it is for AirEnvironment, a big conservative airplane supplier, to give a major program to a three person start-up."

"We do, and we're grateful." Wyatt stifled a grin. *The established suppliers, Randel and Garvey are out of business and Dynamag is under siege. Optimal may be his only choice.*

Ed nodded. "De nada." He turned and waved to the waitress. "Another Corona. Wyatt, a refill on the wine?"

"Come on, Ed, I'm a lightweight. Another glass and I'll spend the night under the table."

"This is near the end of a long business trip," Ed said, raising his glass. "I'm beat, so I plan to do some serious 'relaxing.' The nice thing with hotel bars, it's a short walk to the elevator and my room upstairs." He ran his fingers through his thick hair and his grin gleamed in the dusky light. Although his tie was already loose, he tugged at the knot.

The waitress, on silent, cushioned feet, came to the table and set a foaming beer on a fresh paper napkin. "Thanks," Ed said. "Keep 'em coming, okay?"

"Sure thing, Hon."

Ed guzzled half the beer. "Life's good. Sometimes I feel like a surfer riding the big one. Wasn't it Isaac Newton who said, 'If I have seen further, it is only by standing on the shoulders of giants?'"

Wyatt nodded.

With his chin cradled in his hand Ed said, almost to himself, "Newton may have given me science, but my father gave me this country. He was a wetback. Worked the crops in the San Joaquin Valley. I was born in a shack near Bakersfield and started picking as a kid. Padre showed me how to twist a boll of cotton from its stem and pull tomatoes from the vine without bruising them. He taught me to love work––taught me honor. When I was twelve he died from breathing insecticide––so they said. Wish I could thank him, but I'm forty years too late."

"How did you get off the farms?" Wyatt asked.

"An uncle put me through school. The first to come to 'El Norte,' he got a job, stoop labor, and found work for my parents. Ultimately, he rose to supervision. He was a second father to me."

Wyatt stared at his glass. "Yeah."

Ed jerked upright and swept his hand imitating a teacher erasing a blackboard. "Enough about my life story." He finished his beer and signaled for another. "You and Madison are on a roll. Reminds me of the old days. I'm too young to remember the original founders such as Walter and Olive Ann Beech, Clyde Cessna, Pug Piper and Jimmy Maddox, but I heard the old-timers talk. They were adventurers and wheeler-dealers, putting everything on the line. They inspire me––had a vision, same as you. I fell in love with little airplanes and the people that create them, you know?"

"Odd you say that, Ed. I *do* know. It's not airplanes so

much for me, but engineering itself. It's not what I enjoy, it's what I *am*."

"That's it. *Exactly*." Ed drew a circle in a patch of spilled beer on the table. "In the mornings, design ideas fly through my head while I brush my teeth. I rush through the newspaper because I'm eager to get to work and tackle the latest problems. I still get goose bumps when I see a plane rumble down the runway."

"Yeah, been there. First time we ran our pressurization, I dang near cried. I know how Goddard felt when he launched his first rocket or Doctor Salk when he developed his vaccine. It's depressing to think most people never experience that."

"Are we blessed or cursed?" Ed shrugged. "Sometimes it's a big load to carry. Most people think we live in a bizarre world of mumbo-jumbo—words such as ohms, joules and viscosity." He sipped his beer. "I miss the old days when I cut my teeth on the first Cessna Citation—made serious contributions to the air cycle system. My thinking was more agile back then. So many ideas exploded from my head I couldn't keep track of them." He drained his glass and gazed at the foam lingering on the rim. "Ah, yes." Ed's chin sank to his chest, and he closed his eyes. "Those were the days," he whispered. A tiny tear collected in the corner of his eye and paused like it was afraid to trickle down… afraid to reveal its owner's inner thoughts.

The waitress floated toward their table, but Wyatt waved her away. He realized he'd been given a glimpse into the mind of a passionate man. It was a precious moment, almost religious. Wyatt's throat tightened. He foresaw the day when he, like Ed, would sit in a cloistered bar with a young engineer and get misty over his pressurization system. He'd made a profound advancement in the engineering art and Wyatt knew he'd be compelled to share it someday, not to bolster his ego, but to inspire a fledgling designer. Wyatt, immersed in his own reveries, looked fondly at Ed—troubled he couldn't share his true feelings with this fine man, the son of a wetback.

Chapter 49

The next morning at Optimal, Wyatt slouched at his desk and rubbed his weary eyes. "I can't believe you guys talked me into meeting at this ridiculous hour. It's only seven."

"For once, you're right," Madison joked.

"Sorry about that," Ed Morales said. "I'm not feeling so hot myself. I did too much *relaxing* last night, but we have a noon plane to catch." He set his computer on the desk and fanned out his paperwork. With a weak grin on his face, he said, "I suppose we should thank you two. Nick and I are racking up air miles so fast I have enough points for a first class ticket to Jupiter."

"Nothing personal, Ed, but I hope this meeting is our last for a while," Wyatt laughed. "I've seen more of you than my wife."

Nick Nolan straightened his tie and turned on his laptop. "You're getting a bum deal. I'll bet your wife is a *lot* cuter than Ed."

Ed feigned a laugh. "Let's get going. We finished the tech stuff yesterday, leaving just the schedule and pricing."

"Before we get into that, I've news about the patent situation," Wyatt said. "Late last night, I called our patent attorney for status. He sent this email saying that Dynamag's position is criminal, and Optimal's patent is a slam-dunk. Here's a copy for your file, Nick."

"Good enough," Nick said. He took the copy and stared at the heading. With a frown, he pushed aside his computer and jotted a few notes on a pad of paper. He tore off the sheet and tucked it in his shirt pocket. Then, with a grunt, he scooted his computer closer and entered a few keystrokes. "About non-recurring engineering, you said Optimal would assume the cost of the electronics."

"Yes," Madison said. "Trim templates are simple——we could have them in two weeks."

"And you'd defer production tooling until you have an order for larger quantities?"

"Right," Wyatt nodded. "We're trying to hold down expenses. For now, we'll use stereo-lithography for the casting patterns."

Ed cleared his throat. "If you change tooling, we'll need an analysis proving it won't impact the test results."

"I know," Wyatt said. "Shouldn't be a problem."

Nick gnawed his lip. "Okay. Let's work out prices for the test hardware."

While Ed relaxed in the background, Nick went over costs with Wyatt and Madison. Curiously, Nick didn't press for concessions. After half an hour, they'd agreed on prices.

"Are we ready to talk schedules?" Wyatt asked.

Nick scooted his pudgy body closer to the desk and like a machine-gun, typed "pressurization system schedule" into his computer. The screen blinked and presented a lengthy PERT chart. "You have just four months to come up with the qual test hardware. Tall order."

Wyatt grinned. "I've been working with our machine shop and they've said everything could be completed eight weeks after receipt of order. Leaves plenty of time for assembly and validation work. We'll be ready by mid-September."

"Your supplier may talk a good line, but can he deliver?" Nick asked.

"I'm certain," Wyatt said. "He has an amazing reputation."

Nick clenched his jaw, his cheek muscles working. "Ed, any questions on this?"

"Looks good to me. We know the design is good and my visit to Precision Tool yesterday proves there won't be any manufacturing hitches."

"So that leaves progress payments," Nick said.

Wyatt had gone over Optimal's financial position with Lauren and decided they had to have upfront money from AirEnvironment and monthly progress payments. Money was evaporating at an unbelievable rate, and Lauren insisted the picture was dire.

Nick and Wyatt wrangled for over an hour and finally agreed that AirEnvironment would put up a small initial sum. Progress payments would be based on attaining milestones, not monthly as Wyatt wished. The funds were far less than Lauren wanted, but Wyatt felt he'd done his best. With a resigned feeling, he said, "Give me a moment, okay?" He walked to the back door and called Lauren on his cell phone. In hushed tones, he briefed her on the discussions and after a short back-and-forth, got her concurrence.

Wyatt returned to the table, jiggled his head and tried to clear his mind. "Madison? You okay with this?"

"I don't see any problems." Madison's eyes twinkled as she drummed on the table with her pencil. "We'll be as busy as hummingbirds in a florist shop the next four months."

"Settled?" Nick asked. "Good," he murmured as three hands bobbed up and down. He tapped on his computer. "I'll give you a verbal P.O. number now and follow up with a written one. Remember, everything is contingent on resolution of the patent problem."

"Our provisional patent is still in force," Wyatt reminded Nick.

"Yeah, I know, but it expires in six months," Nick retorted. "Ready to copy?"

Wyatt snatched his pencil, the one that was a gift from Madison, and said, "Ready!"

"A42739. Got it?"

Wyatt nodded.

Ed glanced at his watch. "We gotta get going if we're to catch our plane. Been a good meeting. With a bit of luck, the next time we get together will be to negotiate a big production order."

"One last thing, Wyatt," Nick said. "Be sure to email the cost-breakdown we want. I'll need the exact cost on every major part to satisfy my boss. I know this is unusual, but AirEnvironment has to be very careful committing such a large project to a start-up."

"Will do," Wyatt replied.

"We'll be watching for slippages," Nick cautioned. "Stay on track or we'll cancel. Again, dependent on the patent."

"Gotcha," Wyatt nodded.

They all stood and shook hands, smiling.

Wyatt was euphoric as he watched the men drive away. "Hot damn, Maddy, we did it! An actual purchase order! High five!"

Madison slapped his hand and hugged him, laughing. "We're perfect together. Yesterday, Ed was skeptical as hell, but we blew his worries to pieces, like shooting skeet." She pirouetted, dancing to an imaginary beat. "Hallelujah."

Wyatt sat and put his feet on the desk. "This will give serious ammo to Wong, not to mention the SBA. I'll get with Weinstein and turn up the wick on our formal patent. I'm going to jam this order right up Dynamag's...nostril," he laughed, waving his arms.

Relieved, Wyatt closed his eyes. He had not let his friends down. He was worthy of their trust. Wyatt smiled to himself. *A silly number, A42739, validated the last two and a half years.*

"I can't wait to call Vic over at King and tell him the news," Madison giggled. "'You'd better get on board,' I'll say. 'The train is leaving the station.'"

Wyatt rose and strolled to the coffee pot. He filled his cup and turned to Madison. "To us," he said with a mock toast. "We're at cruising altitude."

"'This merits more than stale coffee my friend," Madison scolded. "I have a bottle of Schramsburg champagne at home. Top-drawer stuff, tiny bubbles, and all that. Let's skip lunch, go to my place and pop the cork!"

Wyatt laughed. "Why not?" It crossed his mind that Lauren might be upset knowing he was going to Madison's for champagne, but dismissed it. *It's just a glass of wine. Hell, we've landed our first order. Thirty, maybe forty-five minutes to celebrate. No big deal.*

Wyatt threaded his way through traffic, following Madison's car. In a mellow mood, he relished the midday sunlight. *Madison is a marvel. We've pulled off some serious science—science that will pay big bucks. Lauren will be proud.*

Madison pulled into a parking spot at her apartment building and Wyatt eased alongside. When he stepped to the front of his car, Madison met him laughing and pointing to his license plate. "*STRIVE1*, indeed. You're something else, Hon." She took his hand and led him into her apartment.

"Here is my friend and confidant," Madison said as a large, dark gray cat ambled over and rubbed her leg. "Wyatt, met Galileo Galilei, the cat of all cats. Friends call him G-G."

Wyatt assumed a solemn look and bent to pet the affectionate feline. "Madison always speaks highly of you, G-G. Pleased to meet you."

"Now for that champagne," Madison exclaimed. "We'll have our celebration."

"Just one glass, Maddy. I'm a cheap drunk."

)( )( )(

It was much later and shadows were getting long. G-G meandered over to the coffee table, sniffed the empty glasses and batted a champagne cork, knocking it to the ground. He found the unresponsive cork boring and resumed his stroll. G-G was miffed to find shoes and a strange smelling shirt on the carpet where he normally lounged in the afternoon sun. Sauntering on, he found a cuddly place on top of familiar embroidered blue jeans tossed on the floor alongside the sofa. With squinty eyes, G-G nuzzled into a denim hollow, yearning for a nap. Then his head snapped erect and his ears swiveled toward the bedroom.

"Oh, Wyatt! Yes! Yes!"

G-G froze, a furry Sphinx, and stared at the open door. Moments passed. A soft rustle. A murmur. Nothing to awaken a cat's curiosity. He stood, turned around and with a huge, toothy yawn, settled in his makeshift nest and dozed.

)( )( )(

An alcohol haze engulfing him, Wyatt tried to clear his head as he clamored into his car. Without looking in either direction, he almost struck a parked pickup as he bolted into traffic. *How in the hell did that happen?* Wyatt agonized. *Damn!* He clutched the steering wheel with both hands, knuckles white with tension. As he drew up to a red light, his eyes dropped to a gaily-wrapped package on the seat. A birthday present for Lauren——her thirty-forth. *Today of all days! I threw away my wedding vows, rutting like a goddamn animal!* "Crap!" he shouted, slapping the dash. Tears welled and trickled down his cheeks, which he gruffly wiped away.

The light turned green and in a stupor, Wyatt drove. He knew he couldn't tell Lauren. Not tonight, not on her birthday. How could he manage cheerful chitchat at the restaurant when the waiter brought the fancy cake he'd ordered? Could he ever tell her? He clenched his jaw.

Madison, what about Madison? He remembered that after she poured champagne, she'd nuzzled him and ran her fingers through his hair. Wyatt just went along, tipsy, numb with joy and too engrossed with the day's events to see the precipice. With bravado, he'd drunk another glass of champagne.

Another tear slithered down and settled in the corner of his mouth.

He anguished over the future of Optimal. How could he keep working with Madison? Smile politely every morning and ask if she slept well? Inquire about G-G's health? Discuss electronic circuitry as if nothing had happened?

Suppose Lauren got suspicious? Then what? His thoughts whirled: Lauren, Madison, Optimal. *Timmie. What about my daughter? If she found out, it would be the end of her trust. Her childhood would disintegrate into little chunks of suspicion. Of hate. Timmie must never know. Never ever.*

He pulled into his drive, reached for the key and hesitated. With a heavy sigh, he switched off the car and picked up the package.

A42739. Look what it's got me into. Crap!

Chapter 50

Madison poured a glass of Chardonnay and stepped out on her balcony overlooking the Verdugo Mountains. The setting sun bathed the craggy canyons and scrub-covered flanks of the ridges with a ruddy radiance. Sharp shadows in the ravines looked stark and menacing. She took a sip of wine and settled into a rattan rocking chair. Slowly, she rocked back and forth, squinting at the deepening twilight and thought about Wyatt.

A warm wave of satisfaction swept from Madison's toes, raced up her body and flooded her mind. *Glorious,* she mused. She felt like a woman again, a woman that Wyatt had conquered. *Maybe it was I who conquered him.* Madison smiled as she replayed their coupling in her mind, his bulk thrusting against her, her legs clamped over his back, the passionate kisses.

Wyatt had shattered Madison's view of him as a single-faceted person, revealing a stranger who flung her on the bed with shameless desire. Although she'd fallen in love with Wyatt because of his sparkling mind, Madison realized that there was something else to love, and giggled at the erotic thought.

Yet hint of regret dampened Madison's joy. She'd vowed never to pursue him, an oath swept away in ardor. Madison drained her glass. Like the wine, her resolve had disappeared. She looked toward the mountains, now cradled in velvet darkness sprinkled with specks of light from scattered homes. With a shudder from the evening chill, she went inside and poured another glass.

Madison curled up on the sofa and propped herself against a large pillow. When G-G leapt on her lap and thrust his nose under her hand, she absently rubbed his shoulders. Uneasiness rose in her like a tide creeping into an estuary: silent, inexorable. Was Wyatt repelled, smothered in guilt and shame, or had she awakened his latent love for her? Was their ecstatic union the harbinger of an enduring bond, or just a tawdry, humiliating episode? Could it be true he was drunk on just three glasses of champagne?

She recalled an awkward moment when Wyatt had dressed and headed for the door. With an odd grin, he stammered something about a birthday dinner-date that night with his wife. The memory made Madison cringe. *I was still naked, and he was talking about Lauren.*

Her worries mounted. What would she say when they met at Optimal in the morning? He say? With the new purchase order, they'd be inundated with work, but they were no longer just business partners; they were lovers. Would they kiss? Should she call him "Honey?" Would he suggest another rendezvous? What if Lauren popped in as she sometimes did?

Madison pushed G-G from her lap, went to the kitchen and poured more wine. She walked to the sliding glass doors leading to the balcony and gazed at the quarter moon hovering over the peaks' silhouette.

Madison's love was rampant, and she hoped Wyatt knew it. She'd convince him this wasn't a casual fling, but the consummation of a romance that had simmered beneath the surface far too long. She'd prove to him that, along with passion, their mutual obsession for science and engineering could become the pillars of an exhilarating partnership in life. He had to understand this and accept her outstretched arms. There was no doubt she'd marry Wyatt. It was destiny.

Madison's pragmatism kicked into high gear. *I must have a plan, a serious down-and-dirty plan.* First, she'd talk with Wyatt, deflect any lingering sentiments for Lauren and redirect his love toward her. She'd assure him that the afternoon's tryst wasn't lust run amok, but an affirmation of their nascent love.

Resolved to go on the offensive, Madison would contrast Lauren's shortcomings with her own striking good looks, outgoing personality and inventive mind. She'd have to torpedo Lauren. Simple.

Timmie, Madison knew, could be a problem. Although she'd felt no affection for the cranky child, Madison decided to cozy up to the kid and win her over. She had to assure Wyatt that his daughter would be embraced and comforted in her new family. Madison's experience in caring for her siblings was cash in the bank.

Finally, Madison decided to hurl herself into and work toward Optimal's fulfillment. She'd capture Wyatt with mutual striving.

The moonlight cast soft shadows on the carpet and Madison stood resolutely, her hands on her hips. *I'll be first lady of a wildly successful partnership with Wyatt. It will be a wonderful life.*

Chapter 51

In the early morning silence of Optimal, Wyatt stared at the computer screen, his immobile fingers poised over the keyboard. His brain was numb and acid rose in his throat as he harked back to last night's dinner. Lauren had bubbled with laughter and spun merry anecdotes about her work, but he couldn't eat, petrified that his joyful façade and strained voice were too obvious.

Frightened that Lauren suspected something, Wyatt had searched for clues, but there was just lighthearted banter. She'd raised a quizzical eyebrow, however, when he declined a glass of wine that would roil his champagne-soaked stomach. Much worse, he was mortified when Lauren winked and wiggled into their bedroom later that night, only to discover he couldn't perform.

"You've been working too many hours, Darling," she consoled. "Get some rest and we'll see how things go tomorrow evening."

Images of champagne glasses, Madison's breasts and the agonizing drive home plagued his sleepless night. Several times he wanted to wake Lauren and explain, but her soft breathing deterred him. In reality, he knew he was too cowardly. The realization he'd carry that burden for the rest of his life sickened him. *No, I'll tell her. Tomorrow.* But he knew his promise was a hollow one. Sleepless, he rose, dressed and went to work.

Madison burst through Optimal's front door, startling Wyatt. Her smile looked confident and the bright sunlight flung highlights into her hair. "Good morning," she sang, whirling into the room. "It's a lovely day." Her glance settled on Wyatt's craggy face. "Say, you look like you've just finished a marathon."

Madison's vibrancy clashed with Wyatt's despondency. "Didn't get much sleep last night."

"Really? I slept like a hibernating bear."

"About yesterday, Madison," Wyatt began. "I don't understand what happened. I must have been drunk."

"Not on two or three glasses of champagne, silly," she said, patting his arm.

"No matter. It makes me sick."

"Seems to me you had a roaring good time," Madison said with a wry grin.

That's the damnable part. A good time? No—a fantastic time. Wyatt drew a deep breath to steady his thoughts. "Maddy, you're a beautiful woman and things got away from me, but that's no excuse. I'm a married man who took a vow of faithfulness. I love Lauren and Timmie and owe them my allegiance—all of it." Wyatt stood and looked at Madison. "No more fooling around, understand? You're an incredible business partner, but we have to forget yesterday and get back to running a business."

Madison shook her head and a lock of hair fell across her eye. She smiled and waved her hand dismissively. "Forget? Sure, Darling, and I suppose you expect me to forget the genius of Faraday or Steve Jobs. I love you. Plain and simple."

"I can't return your love. Lauren is my life, my..." his

voice trailed off. *Look at her—smiling. She doesn't believe me.* Wyatt, his thoughts muddled, struggled to find persuasive words; then lapsed into silence.

Madison swept her hair back and playfully tilted her head. "I understand. Strictly business from now on." With a jaunty grin, she sat and drummed her pencil on the table as her computer came to life.

It became clear to Wyatt that Madison had no intention of confining her affection to Optimal. Grim, he resolved to be vigilant, watch every word and gesture that might encourage her advances. He must not fall prey to Madison's charms again.

The next day Wyatt plopped into the Naugahyde chair opposite Mike's desk. "It's good news/bad news time, Mike," Wyatt began.

"Bad news is against company policy." Mike lit a cigarette, and the smoke swirled about his head. "What's the good news?"

"I thought you quit smoking."

"This?" Mike said, waving the cigarette. "I did. I was clean for a month or two. Fuckin' hard habit to kick, I'll tell you. There's a reason though. I just bought a small powder coating company. Got it cheap—economy was killing him. We signed the deal over a few beers at my favorite bar. The guy smoked like a lathe with a dull tool. What was I to do? Beer and cigs. A match made in heaven. Damn, I *love* these things!"

Wyatt laughed. "Your lungs, my friend. Want the good news first?"

"Fire away."

Wyatt tried to collect his thoughts, but visions of Madison's body and agony about his deceit addled him. He bit his knuckle and said, "Well, there are two things. First, I'll mail my application for the utility patent within a week." Wyatt leaned back in the chair, a thin smile on his lips. "But I have a biggie. I didn't call because I wanted to see your face when I told you. Yesterday we got the order from AirEnvironment; they want three systems for qualification testing by September."

"No shit?" boomed Mike. He leapt from his chair, bolted around his desk and hugged Wyatt. "You're the *man*. Guess you need a bunch of hardware, right?"

"Yeah," Wyatt frowned. "Which brings me to the bad news. Even though your investment in Optimal was generous, we're almost out of money. I can't figure a way to make the payments on the big test equipment."

Mike returned to his chair. "How serious is it?"

"Very. With all the delays, AirEnvironment took much longer than expected to place the order. Still no word from the SBA. Things I can't control."

Mike stubbed out his cigarette and grunted. "Need more cash?"

Wyatt nodded.

Mike kicked his feet up on his desk and lit another Marlboro. He rubbed his chin and scowled.

Wyatt waited, tapping his foot.

"Okay," Mike said. "I'll have to talk to my accountant. Buying that powder coater took a lot of loot. Bad timing, Wyatt. Precision is fucking tapped out, but I'll see what I can do."

A week later, Wyatt was surprised to learn that Mike negotiated a loan from his bank and made another cash deposit into Optimal's account. "Once in, all in," he'd said.

Amused, Wyatt learned that Mike used his unique elocution to convince the foundry to ship castings at a steep discount by the end of July. Wyatt set up a staging area for new parts on two benches while Madison spent her days testing circuitry and watching Wyatt out of the corner of her eye.

In early August, a week late, the foundry delivered castings and Mike scheduled heavy overtime to machine them. His crew, jockeying to integrate the new powder coating operation, strained to keep up. Mill operators squabbled with the grinding guys and supervisors stared red-eyed at their planning sheets, searching for miracles. Mike strode among the workstations, cajoling, pleading and bringing Subway sandwiches to machinists too busy for lunch. One morning, at the start of the day shift, the head inspector found Mike asleep at his desk, head slumped on a stack of Wyatt's blueprints.

Outwardly, Madison kept her word, returning to work with diligence. Wielding her soldering iron behind a cloud of resin smoke, Madison calibrated the PCB's. Her presence made Wyatt nervous like a hang-fire he'd seen on the five-inch gun mount on his destroyer years ago—silent, yet lethal. He avoided sitting next to her, mentioning "that day" or indulging in casual chatter.

Still, Wyatt worried when Lauren worked at Optimal on the weekends. Madison, he decided, could have been awarded an Oscar for her performance depicting an industrious colleague engrossed in electronics, but only in Lauren's presence. When they were alone, there were pats on his arm, silly giggles and coquettish twinkles in her green eyes. His days were queasy, filled with disquieting misgivings.

If not affectionate, Lauren and Madison's relationship once had been civil. But as the days wore on, they often snapped at one another and fussed over trivial things. Wyatt found his thoughts captured in their quarrels. The feverish pace of work failed to sweep his concerns away, but he settled uneasily into his labors. Immersed in the standoff, the pressurization system slowly came together.

September ushered in a scheduling apocalypse and Wyatt felt crushed by the deadline. In desperation, he called Bernie who joined them in the evenings, happily screwing parts together. One Saturday morning, he handed an envelope to Wyatt and went to his bench. Later, when Wyatt got around to opening it, he found a check for another two thousand dollars. The memo line said simply: "Make chips." Later that night when Lauren labored over the books, she entered the sum and said, "Bless him."

With less than two weeks left to deliver qualification hardware, they began system-level tests. The oppressive summer heat became insufferable when the hot air burners were lit, overwhelming the air conditioner. Clothes stuck to their backs, papers adhered to moist palms and sweat dripped from noses onto data sheets. At night, the window was flung open, and the doors propped wide, inviting cool evening breezes and moths that thumped against light fixtures.

And the tests hissed into the night.

From time to time Mike, still in his shop apron and jeans, appeared with a six-pack and pizza and went to work installing test valves or running the pumps.

And the tests hissed into the night.

It was ten in the evening on September fourteenth, D-day minus one. Wyatt tried to swallow his tension as Madison's hand twitched the computer mouse. Behind them, Lauren, Mike, Bernie and even Timmie stared at the computer screen as it scrolled flow data.

"Steady at 5.1," Madison said. "Here we go. Simulated go-around condition, step function to 12.4. Mike, shut that toggle valve, will you?"

Mike walked to the inflow valve stand and flipped a lever. The howl of the hot air by-pass ceased and the display on the computer flashed.

"There's the spike," cried Madison. "I'll graph it; see what we have."

Soon, she'd plotted the change in cabin pressure. "We started at 2,013 feet. Look! It dipped to only 1, 981. Unbelievable!"

"Wah-hooo," bellowed Wyatt. "Fantastic!"

"Is it good, Daddy?" Timmie asked.

"Much better than good, Little One; it's great!" He picked her up and whirled, Timmie's feet carving merry arcs in the air. Her shrill giggle mirrored everyone's joy.

Madison stared at the computer screen and massaged her temples. "At last I got the anticipator right. Thought I'd never get there. Let's shut her down."

As Mike and Bernie shook hands and pounded each

other on the back, Lauren collapsed into a chair and rubbed her eyes. Wyatt put Timmie down and walked over to his wife. He knelt in front of her and took her hands. "We did it, Dear. It's flawless. We'll ship in the morning. On schedule."

Lauren nodded. She heaved a sigh and squeezed Wyatt's hands. "Yes. On schedule. I'll invoice first thing in the morning before leaving for work."

Madison turned and looked at Wyatt and Lauren. Her fists clenched a moment and then she said, "I've been running at high voltage for months. I'm tired—time for sleep." The door slammed behind her as she stormed to her car.

Lauren shrugged.

Chapter 52

"Any word from the Patent Office?" Madison asked.

Wyatt looked up from the workbench where he was installing a thermocouple into a heat exchanger and scowled. "Nothing yet, so I called to follow up this morning. But they insist all communication has to be by letter. Wrote last week and the week before. I'm pounding sand in a rat hole."

Madison was mystified. Right after the provisional had been approved, they'd started working on the formal disclosure. They'd sent in the utility patent paperwork in August, but they hadn't heard back. She understood Wyatt's frustration, yet worried his temper might complicate things, like the way it had at the Building and Safety counter.

Wyatt set down his screwdriver and looked at Madison. "I wonder what Dynamag is doing. Maybe their application crosses over into ours. Maybe they filed first. Maybe they already have their approval."

"Enough of your maybes. Art can't get meaningful information on *our* application, much less theirs. I talked to Ed at AirEnvironment, but he's tight-lipped saying we wouldn't want him giving away our secrets to the other guy. We just have to sit tight."

"I don't sit tight. Not in my genes. *Everything* depends on this patent. If our provisional expires before the utility application is accepted, we're done. I'll write them every day until they respond. Every danged day!"

"Just be polite, my Sweet," Madison admonished.

"Humph."

Two days later, Wyatt stormed into the kitchen after work and growled, "What do you make of this." He slapped a letter on the kitchen counter in front of Lauren.

With a curious look, she picked up the envelope and saw the return address. *United States Patent and Trademark Office.* Lauren's hand shook as she removed the letter and read: "We regret to inform you that the material submitted by Optimal Aviation Systems regarding a utility patent for a Cabin Pressurization System has been found incomplete. In particular, the following items need clarification…"

Lauren's eyes flicked back and forth as she read. "They've listed over a dozen problems. Have you talked with Madison or Art?"

Wyatt's stomach jumped at the mention of Madison's name. After a moment, he composed himself saying, "Called Art, but he was with a client. Madison and I spent over two hours this afternoon trying to dope out the letter. The Patent Office sat on the application for two months and then threw a bunch of trumped-up questions at us."

"What can we do?" Lauren asked.

Wyatt stalked into the living room and flung himself into his chair. "The letter is confusing as one of your Shakespearian sonnets. I'll keep calling Art."

Lauren went to a cabinet, found a bottle of Zinfandel and poured two glasses. "Here, Honey. This will calm you down."

"Thanks. I think we're toddlers in the sprinter's world of patent law." He took a big swig. "Those government goons are like Ronald McDonald questioning Copernicus' theories. Just as bad, the darn paperwork is more complicated than the science."

"There you go, on your soapbox again," Lauren laughed weakly. "We can't just sit around and fuss; let's get Art to help. After all, he's the expert."

"Good idea; too bad we can't afford him."

"Come on, Honey. He said he'd go easy on us. Besides, do you have a better idea?"

"No." Wyatt gazed at his wife and realized how much he relied on Lauren's judgment and steady hand. She buffered him from petty aggravations of the temporal world and freed him to indulge his passions. *I'm a lucky man,* he marveled. *A mighty lucky man.*

"I'll give Art another call in the morning," Wyatt said. "What do we have to lose? We'll find a way around his fees the best we can."

"Fine," said Lauren. "I'll bet he'll take care of this in no time."

Wyatt sighed and resolved, with Art's help, to conquer the patent jerks. But Madison was another problem. She was becoming more and more forward, calling him "Darling" and pressing for long lunches or secretive dinners. Worse, Madison had begun taking shots at Lauren, "She couldn't tell a transistor from an aneroid" or "What's more boring than accounting?" Wyatt was spending more and more time fending off Madison's advances and defending his wife. Wyatt's life had become a giant game of Whack-A-Mole.

Art Weinstein, his collar open and sleeves rolled up, bounced from his chair and shook their hands. "It's great that we *finally* got a response from Washington!"

Wyatt handed the attorney the letter. "As I explained on the phone, the Patent Office has listed a dozen omissions or clarifications. Our provisional will expire soon and Dynamag is still pitching AirEnvironment."

"I know, I know." Art took a few minutes to study the letter. He leaned back in his chair and crossed his legs. "Let me think." He interlaced his fingers, slipped them behind his head and closed his eyes.

It seemed to Wyatt that the minutes crept. He glanced at Madison and shrugged. She gave him a quizzical look and fiddled with her pencil.

"This letter is crazy," Art blurted. "Usually, an application is assigned to a group familiar with the applicable technical issues. Toby, my friend in the Patent Office, knows high-tech stuff and where to look for information. He found out your application wasn't in the queue at all; it had been diverted to an official for some sort of special evaluation." Art shook his head. "I've confirmed that Dynamag continues to pursue their patent, so we have a horse race." He clasped his hands on the desk and leaned forward. "Toby discovered a tidbit––nothing concrete. Do either of you know anything about a Ms. Julie Ann Kelly?"

"Sounds familiar, but I can't place it," Wyatt said. "Why do you ask?"

"Toby ran across a few emails tying Kelly, an official in the Patent Office, to Dynamag. Perhaps just two people hooking up, but that violates protocol. We'll keep digging into it. I know it's frustrating, but there's little more I can do." Art stood and walked to the window, squinting in the bright light. "California autumns are beautiful," he murmured.

Dismayed, Wyatt shifted in his chair, trying to ease his aching back. They'd resolved nothing. He couldn't find the energy to tackle the letter. He couldn't find the energy to rise from his chair or even draw his next breath.

Art, Optimal's last hope, was stumped.

Chapter 53

When the Boeing 737 leveled off at cruising altitude, Wyatt tilted his seat and unlatched the tray table. For the last two weeks he'd fought his lethargy and, with Art's help, toiled re-writing the patent application. Groggy with fatigue, he'd mailed it registered, return receipt, the previous afternoon. He sat back in the cushions and said to Madison, "Now that we've submitted the patent, we've time to concentrate on tomorrow's flight tests. At last we're on our way—be in Oklahoma City around two."

Madison turned her gaze from the window and nodded. "It's too bad that Maddox's air conditioning supplier had problems and delayed us two weeks."

"Well, we're saving a bundle. Ed said by bootlegging our tests with the other guy, there'd be no charges unless we have hiccups. Regardless, we're in the starting blocks now."

Below, diaphanous white clouds speckled tawny patches of desert and a blinding dart of sunlight ricocheted off a car creeping along a razor-straight highway. Madison thrust a tattered airline magazine back into the seat pocket and eyed Wyatt. "We have three, maybe four days together, just you and me. I'm thinking we could have a *fine* time."

Wyatt blanched. He didn't want to be alone with Madison. All he wanted was to test pressurization. "Dang it, Madison. This is business. Let's focus on these tests. Forget that afternoon. It was a mistake, okay?"

Madison reached over and rubbed Wyatt's knee. "I'll wear you down, my Love, like dripping water on a stone."

Wyatt jerked away, grasped a brown paper sack from the floor and opened it. "I'm grabbing lunch. Go back to your magazine or something." Ignoring Madison's steady gaze, he unwrapped a sandwich and took a bite. *Tuna salad and an apple. Lauren's idea of a healthy meal.* When the flight attendant brought a cup of coffee, he asked for a few packets of salt.

Wyatt finished the apple and was about to drop the core into the sack when he noticed a small note written on blue stationery. It read: *Good luck. Love you madly. L.* A postscript followed: *Stay away from that OTHER woman.* Then she'd penned a large happy face. Wyatt crushed the paper and rammed it into the sack, hoping Madison hadn't seen it. *Did Lauren know? No. She couldn't. Stay away? Hard to do sitting next to her in economy.*

He stuffed the wadded sack into the seat-back pocket and tugged his briefcase from under the seat. Wyatt tried to review a few notes, but Madison's presence at his elbow sucked his thoughts like a tornado. He sipped his coffee and realized that without Madison, there was no Optimal. If she bailed, he'd be Pratt without Whitney or Hewlett without Packard. He searched his mind for ways to keep Madison involved with the business while holding her at arm's length. The dilemma troubled him and he grappled with options, but found none.

Frustrated, Wyatt shifted his thoughts. "I researched Maddox Aviation," he said. "Wanted a little background. A few years back, they bought a chunk of the old Aero Commander plant and expanded it. Been hard-hit by the business downturn, but they're hanging tough. I read a news article that Maddox is hell-bent to lower their costs. Guess our price got their attention."

Madison shrugged and an awkward silence settled between them.

After an uneventful flight, the plane landed, jockeyed to the gate and disgorged its passengers. Wyatt hustled along the curved concourse of the Will Rogers World Airport, keeping pace with the tattoo of Madison's clacking high heels. A large wall clock read 2:23 and Wyatt instinctively checked his watch to make sure he'd allowed for the two-hour time zone change.

"Baggage this way," Madison said pointing.

"Humph." Wyatt was miffed that Madison had checked two suitcases while he'd made do with a small carry-on. When changing planes in Vegas, she'd chided him about his "travel trailer," saying, "Mine's checked straight through to Oklahoma. No hassle."

"Good thing," he'd replied. "You must have packed provisions for thirty days. I almost got a hernia lifting them out of the car."

"Poor thing," she'd winked, patting his elbow. "You're such a frail wisp of a man."

Irritated, Wyatt jerked his arm away.

They rented a compact car and drove to their hotel a short distance from the Wiley Post Airport, just west of Oklahoma City.

When Wyatt pulled up to the hotel entrance, Madison got out of the car and walked back to the trunk. "Hernia time."

Wyatt jerked the luggage from the car and waved at his small suitcase. "Take that. I'll schlep yours."

"Ever the gentleman, aren't you?" She fell in step alongside him, pulling his bag. "I know a way to save big money. Interested?"

"Sure."

"We don't need two rooms," she winked. "Thrift can have its advantages."

He frowned. "We're not going there—been through this." Wyatt saw a flash of anger in Madison's eyes.

"I'm not giving up, Honey," she said. "Water dripping on a stone, remember?"

It was early morning and Wyatt found the brisk late September air invigorating. A stout wind blew from the west, whipping dust around their ankles. Shivering, Madison clutched her jacket over her shoulders. They walked across the tarmac to the aircraft where a technician, who'd finished fueling the plane, was removing the grounding cable.

Morales stood by the airstairs, waiting.

"Wow, Ed, does it blow this way all the time?" Madison asked.

"Nope. Like they say in Oklahoma, half the time it blows the other way. Say, I want you to meet a couple of guys. This is Marty Sturgis with Remington Aircraft Corporation and our pilot, Steve Wonder—no relation."

"I hope your flight manual isn't in Braille, Stevie," Wyatt quipped, shaking hands.

The pilot chuckled. "Ah, the Wonder jokes. I suppose you'd want me to name my daughter 'Ima', right?"

Everyone laughed.

"Our test plan," Wonder explained, "calls for ground idle checkouts on Marty's air conditioning. We'll look at pressurization stability and rate of change during descent from maximum altitude. Nothing fancy on the first flight."

"Madison, why don't you ride right seat up front by Steve," Ed suggested. "You can operate the pressurization. The rest of us will be in back where we've installed the data acquisition gear."

After Steve completed his safety briefing, they clambered aboard. The interior of the test airplane was stark. The cabin walls, devoid of paneling, exposed snarls of multi-colored wiring and random lengths of intertwined plumbing. A curious odor, a mixture of hydraulic fluid, wire insulation and solvent nibbled at their nostrils. Rudimentary canvas sling seats promised a utilitarian ride. While they belted themselves in, the pilot spooled up the engines. Wyatt was tense and fidgeted in his seat, fumbling with his laptop. His armpits were damp from nervousness, aggravated by bright sunlight that lanced through the windows, making the cabin stuffy.

Marty turned on a thermocouple recorder and called to Steve, "Turn on the AC." They sat on the ramp for ten minutes, waiting for the cabin temperature to stabilize, but it remained warm. "Sorry," Marty apologized. "Ground operation is always marginal."

Wyatt shrugged. Madison, looking cool and confident helped the pilot program the pressurization system. She peered over her shoulder at Wyatt, flashing a "thumbs-up."

"Cleared to taxi," Steve hollered.

Soon, the engines thundered, pressing Wyatt back in his seat. As the plane gathered speed, he stared at the cabin pressure read-out. *Steady.* The plane rotated and scrambled over the end of the runway. Cabin pressure slowly decayed. *Perfect.*

Engrossed, Wyatt didn't notice that the air conditioning began spewing chilly fog from the Wemacs. Marty, looking pleased, rubbed his hands while Ed hunched over his data display.

Thirty minutes later they were at 41,000 feet and the cabin pressure had settled at 10.91. *Right on.* Wyatt entered the data into his computer while Madison gazed out the windshield, apparently enjoying the view.

For two hours, Steve followed the test plan, throttling back to flight-idle and cruising at select altitudes. The engineers exchanged few words as they jotted notes on their checklists or squinted at laptops, glazed by the sun. Wyatt was surprised when the airplane landed and rolled to its spot in front of the Maddox hanger. "That it?" he asked.

"For now," Ed said. "Let's compare notes in the flight lounge."

They trooped into a brightly lit room where fiberglass and chrome chairs clustered around small Formica tables. Wyatt followed Marty to a counter at the far end of the room where a steaming urn smelled of stale coffee. Wyatt filled a Styrofoam cup and took a sip. "Tastes like brake fluid." He laced it with sugar and creamer and slurped again. "Not much help."

Marty smiled. "Same as yesterday. Fresh or hours old,

it's always the same. There's a rumor it's made from yak scat."

Wyatt grinned.

"Over here, everyone," Ed called. They gathered around a table, their chairs squealing on the vinyl floor. "Let's take the pressurization first. The computer people will download the electronic data on second shift tonight. We'll review it in the morning. Right now, I'm interested in your subjective opinions. Steve, what do you think?"

"Smooth. Damn smooth. My ears hardly popped. Madison showed me how to work the system. Just punched in a setting or two and then it's automatic. Really slick."

"Marty, any comments?"

"I didn't pay any attention until we turned final. Then I noticed that I didn't notice. Has to be the best pressurization I've ever flown with."

"Same for me," Ed said. "Exceptional." He shuffled through his notes and continued. "In the morning, after checking the data, we'll draw up another plan. I'll want to do a simulated landing with an emergency go-around, check altitude limiting and the dump. Does anyone have a cold or trouble with your ears? Dump is mega-ugly on ears."

"Madison and I are go," Wyatt said.

Marty shrugged. "Dump?"

"The pilot can dump the air pressure in case there's a structural problem with the plane," Wyatt explained. "You don't realize it, but pressurization stretches the airplane with a force of around twenty tons—plenty to rip a damaged hull apart."

"You're kidding!"

"Nope."

"No choice, I guess," Marty muttered. "Just give me a warning when you do it."

"Okay. Be here around seven," Ed said. "Steve, can you book a flight around nine?"

Steve nodded.

Ed grinned. "Wyatt, you should treat this lady to a fine dinner to celebrate. It went well. Really well."

Madison gave Wyatt a wide smile. "Sounds good to me."

"Off with you two," Ed commanded. "Okay, Marty, stick around; there's still work to do on the air conditioning pack."

"Level with me, Wyatt. Is IHOP your idea of a celebration?"

"Don't knock it. It's close to the hotel and cheap. We're not rolling in money yet." Wyatt pushed the menu aside. He knew every IHOP offered the same food, and he'd made his choice before being seated.

"I *hate* pancakes," Madison teased.

"So order a steak."

"An IHOP steak? I've heard they're thin as paper and tough as re-treads."

Wyatt chuckled. "A little crabby, are you? Well, *I'm* having steak. You can order your usual salad."

IHOP was his kind of place. No tablecloths or crystal, good coffee and big servings. Tabasco arrayed alongside sticky syrup jars, paper napkins rolled around cheap utensils. Disheveled waitresses with welcoming smiles calling everyone "hon." He felt at home.

Taking care to avoid Madison's feet, he stretched his legs, thrilled the tests had gone well. Although he'd been confident, niggling pre-flight concerns had challenged his chronic optimism. Wyatt smiled, knowing he'd defeated Murphy, this time at least. He'd earned his steak.

The food came and Wyatt salted it without tasting and attacked with vigor while Madison picked at her salad, drizzling smidgeons of vinaigrette dressing on the lettuce between bites. Wyatt filled his coffee cup from the carafe and sighed. "Great day, Madison. I feel invincible, the way Edison must have when he finally got the light bulb to work. Been a long haul." He raised his cup. "Yup, a great day."

Madison laced her fingers and propped her chin on her hands. She looked at Wyatt and a resigned looking smile crossed her lips. "I think your carnal needs have been distilled down to engineering and salty beef." She spread her hands with a helpless gesture. "My loss."

Wyatt shrugged and sliced a hunk of steak. "Hey, think I'll call Lauren. Tell her how our day went." As pulled out his cell phone and punched in his speed-dial number, he saw Madison's scowl. "Hi, Dear. Went great at Maddox. Yeah, we're having dinner. No, no. Nothing fancy. IHOP." Listening, Wyatt frowned. "No. I'm crashing right after we eat. Been an intense day." Wyatt gave Madison a wan grin and then described the flight to Lauren. After a few minutes, he concluded, "Right. I'll call tomorrow. Love you."

While Wyatt was talking, Madison was rapping her spoon on the table. Her face was rigid as if painted by a brush dipped in fury.

Wyatt and Madison spent two more days in Oklahoma as Ed and Steve put the system through its paces. Wyatt waded into the work, enthused and happy.

On the last day, several Maddox engineers, testing other equipment, also flew. Effusive with praise, they shook Wyatt's hand and ogled Madison.

Wyatt was in a buoyant mood as he and Madison boarded the plane for their return to Burbank. Wyatt thumped a thick stack of data that covered his tray table. "Let's go through this, Maddy. It shows how the cabin pressure fluctuated with rapid inflow changes."

"Not now." Madison waved her hand. "I'm not in the mood. Maybe back at the office."

Wyatt was puzzled. They had several hours on the plane, time they could spend productively. "You sure? We could get a lot done."

"Later, I said."

>< >< ><

Lauren, setting the table for dinner, hummed a tune from "All you need is Love" by the Beatles. Things were much different after Wyatt's return from Oklahoma three weeks ago. She remembered him saying that once flight tests began, significant design changes were off the table. Because he had less to do, their weekends blossomed with free time and the Sunset Ritual had been firmly re-established.

Lauren was delighted. It wasn't that Wyatt had been a neglectful husband, but his passion for his craft and focus on the new company sapped his time. It wasn't his conscious decision to prioritize Optimal over the family, she knew; he just struggled to keep a balance. Now, he doted on Lauren. Small things. Wyatt complimented her on a new ravioli recipe, offered ideas on how to deal with a troublesome employee at work and bragged to the neighbor about her accurate bookkeeping. Most importantly, their lovemaking flowered, torrid and impassioned at times, soft and lingering at others. When Wyatt left for work, warm kisses replaced his usual quick pecks.

Even more importantly for Lauren was that Wyatt suddenly seemed to discover his daughter. He played with Timmie, tickled her and one sunny Saturday, trundled her to the beach. The sight of them, frolicking on the sand and evading spent waves, thrilled her. Because soccer season was starting soon, Wyatt joined Timmie, shrieking with joy, to kick the ball around the backyard. When the child became moody, as she sometimes did, he sat with her and offered counsel in a curious "man-to-man" way.

Because he'd escaped the grasp of the new company, Wyatt had become a father.

"Hi, Darlin'," Wyatt called as he came in one evening and set his briefcase on the floor. "Pour the wine and light the candles—I've good news." He wrapped his arms around her, lifted her off the floor and whirled around.

"Wyatt!" Lauren laughed. "You're crazy. Put me down."

With a grin, he pinched her cheek and lit the candles. Lauren joined him in the living room with wine. Timmie sat on the floor between them and jabbed at the buttons of a new Game Boy her grandmother had given her.

"Okay, Hon, what's the news?"

"Had a long talk with Ed Morales today. He's finished the tests and is back in Massachusetts writing the final report. Hopes to submit it to the FAA within a week. We could have certification by Halloween."

"Wyatt, that's fantastic!"

"Darn right, my Love," Wyatt laughed. "Ed said Maddox is still flying our equipment, building hours and gathering endurance data. No problems so far."

"Have you told Mike and Bernie? Do they know?"

"Yup. Called them right away. They're thrilled. Still some work though. I'm going through the drawings, tweaking a few things."

Lauren scowled. "I thought the FAA wouldn't allow any changes."

"They don't, so I have to analyze every change to prove the system function is unaffected. Pain in the butt and tons of paperwork. No matter. We'll snag a production order within four or five weeks. Can you believe?"

Then Wyatt remembered. The provisional patent was expiring in a few days and there was still no word from Art. Soon, they'd have no protection. Not wanting to spoil Lauren's ebullient mood, he decided not to mention it. *I'll call Art again in the morning.*

"It's wonderful, Honey," Lauren said. "Just imagine. My husband...a successful business executive."

"Just an engineer. Much better than an executive."

Lauren pressed her finger to her lips. "Just thinking, once we have the purchase order, I'll try again for the SBA loan. If that fails, I'll bet our own bank, with Lee's help, would lend to us."

"You're fascinating when you do your accountant thing," Wyatt said. "I love every square inch of you. How about dinner before I faint?"

Chapter 54

As Optimal's provisional patent expiration approached, Wyatt grew edgy. Daily calls to Art were useless and his letters to the Patent Office went unanswered. Helplessness infected his mind and he withdrew to his office and fumed.

When nighttime descended on the last day, Wyatt became furious. Days crept by and he couldn't sleep, couldn't concentrate and his temper was worse than a provoked rattlesnake. Timmie and Garfield vanished the moment he walked through the door, but his rage buffeted Lauren who couldn't escape. He assailed Art, anger nearly melting the phone lines. He bellowed when the phone rang interrupting his thoughts of salvaging the company. Even the weekly chore of mowing the grass triggered oaths and vows to tear out the lawn.

Wyatt sat next to Madison scanning the columns of a spreadsheet and tried to focus.

"I hate this," Madison complained. "I can't get my brain around this cost mess."

Irritated, Wyatt grumbled, "We have to do this. With no patent protection, we have to move fast. All Nick wants is justification for our prices. Even an electrical engineer should be able to deal with this."

"Don't be snide," Madison said. "I thought you said Lauren was against giving out a detail price breakdown."

"She is, but what can we do? Lauren's just being her usual accountant self."

Madison shrugged. "Well, let her wallow in the numbers."

Wyatt said nothing and turned his attention to the spreadsheet, plodding through the notes he'd made while assembling the prototype system. His thoughts fragmented and he muttered to himself.

Jimmy the UPS driver, hurried through the door carrying two packages, interrupting them. "Happy Halloween––in a few days," he called.

"I'll bet one of those packages is the new transformer I want to try out," Madison said, taking the parcels as Wyatt signed for them.

"Damn," she whimpered.

"What?"

"Here's another letter from Masterson and Leibnitz, Dynamag's lawyers." Madison handed the envelope to Wyatt. "You open it."

"Can't be good news," Wyatt said as he tore the envelope open and scanned the document. He caught his breath and reread, devouring each word. "Dynamag says they hold patents on our wireless concept and encryption. Somehow they found out we have a production agreement with AirEnvironment and are suing for damages."

Madison looked stunned. She fell into her chair saying, "Impossible. How could they know specifics about our design or hear of AirEnvironment?"

Wyatt wiped his mouth, incredulous. "Somebody's on the take if you ask me."

He handed the letter to Madison who glanced at it and then waved it listlessly. "I... now what? What can we do?"

Wyatt paced back and forth, staring at his shoes. "How in the world do I know? Somebody has to be behind this. It's bizarre that four days after our provisional patent expires, we get sued." Wyatt tried to swallow, but his throat rebelled.

"Is this it? The end?" Madison whispered.

"Not while I'm still kicking," Wyatt growled. He stared at a wastepaper basket, took a step back and kicked it across the room, the clatter making Madison jump. Old papers showered to the floor like a Texas hailstorm and coffee grounds spattered the wall.

"That isn't helping anything, Love."

Wyatt stalked over and set the trash basket right side up. Still shaking with anger, he glared at the debris and the sight diluted his rage.

With a bowed head, he went to his chair and grimaced in thought. "Tell you what––I'll phone Weinstein again. He's supposed to be on top of all this guff."

Madison, looking wan, just nodded.

Wyatt knew Weinstein's number by heart. He picked up the phone and punched in the numbers, vowing to be a little more respectful to the attorney.

After Mrs. Weinstein put the call through, Wyatt said, "Hello, Art, Wyatt Morgan. We have a big problem. No. Not the provisional. Dynamag has sued us." He took a deep breath and read the letter. "So there it is––they claim to have a patent."

Art whistled. "I've been trying for months to pry your application loose, but they kept giving me the run-around.

Just yesterday I followed up with Toby, my friend in the Patent Office. He said your paperwork was still on the desk of the Technical Director, another new position created in response to Congress' new trade laws. Toby said your application had to have extra scrutiny. Well, they scrutinized it to death."

"Damn right," Wyatt growled.

"But I might have something. Are you ready for the juicy part?" Art said. "Toby found out that a Patent Office employee, a Ms. Kelly, is tight with Eric Magana, the president of Dynamag. You don't have to be a mental giant to connect the dots," Art said. "There's more. Kelly, in passing, mentioned she knew Nick Nolan."

"That's nuts," Wyatt gasped. "Is that how Dynamag found out we're working on a production purchase order?"

"Nolan had a direct pipeline into the negotiations. A grade school kid would figure out both Dynamag and AirEnvironment could gain if there was another firm competing with you."

"Yeah," Wyatt said. "It's odd that Nolan kept asking for budgetary pricing. When I gave it to him, he told me I was in good shape."

"Hmmm," murmured Art. "Why would a professional buyer say that? I'd think he'd say your numbers were high; force you lower. He asked for informal prices, huh?"

"More than that." Wyatt sat up in his chair. "I'm working up a detailed cost breakdown for his boss. They want to confirm the margins, or something."

"You're giving him costs on every part? That's never done, except on cost-plus contracts. Don't do it."

"That's what my wife said."

"Well, she's right," Art agreed. "It may be too late, but from now on watch what you say to Nolan. Don't give him the costs. I want you to check your emails and correspondence to see if anything smells."

"Can do," Wyatt responded, feeling reassured. "From the beginning I suspected something was fishy. Now what?"

"Scan the letter and any documents you think pertinent and email them," Art directed. "I'll work out a plan and go to Masterson and Leibnitz's offices if I have to. Mr. Nolan is in my sights."

A tiny smile crept over Wyatt's lips. Weinstein not only knew law, he was tough. It was hard to believe that Nick was a mole, being a colleague of Ed, but it was possible. Big bucks were in play, particularly if Optimal's system became the industry standard. Relieved by the prospect of action, Wyatt's mind cleared and he flexed shoulders like a football lineman taking his stance. *Maybe there's a way through this.*

Later that day, while Wyatt and Madison were scouring their files, the phone rang.

"Hi, Wyatt. Ed Morales."

Wyatt tensed. "Hi, Big Ed. Mind if I put you on the speaker? Madison's here."

"Fine. She should hear this too. There's been a hiccup. Normally, Nick would talk with you, but he's holed up with our legal department. We've received formal notice that a company named Dynamag claims to hold the patents on your design and are taking you to court. Our lawyers tell me we can't issue the production order because of pending litigation. Sorry."

Wyatt was staggered and struggled for words.

"Wyatt? You there?" Ed asked.

"Yeah. I'm here."

"I'm sorry. Nick and the attorneys are trying to hammer something out."

Or to nail it down, thought Wyatt. "How long to clear this up, Ed? A few hours ––a few months?"

"Getting a lawyer to commit to a schedule is like putting your thumb on a tomato seed. There's no way of knowing."

"So I sit on my hands and wait?"

"Guess so. Sorry," Ed muttered. "I keep saying that because I really am."

"Sure. Catch you later." Wyatt pushed the off-button and turned to Madison. "There you are. The other shoe just dropped."

Madison wrung her hands. "We're screwed."

Wyatt closed his eyes and crossed his arms over his chest. What to do? He felt mauled by lawyers and thieves. It didn't matter that his design was perfect, that Madison's software was flawless and that they'd slaved for three years. Everything had come down to this. Hopelessness battled with his intrinsic optimism––a dire contest raging at the bottom of his soul.

He opened his eyes and looked at Madison. "There's one last chance. Call King––they've been interested. Let's find out *how* interested. Optimal is flat out of money. We *must* have an order if there's any chance to grab a loan."

"I'll call Vic right now."

Ten minutes later, Madison hung up, lips puckered and eyebrows knit. "Not yet. Vic says that Engineering has given our proposal the green light, but it's hung up in management. He claims they have too few resources and not enough business to take on anything new."

Wyatt clenched his jaw. "This is bullshit. I'm not sure how, but I guarantee I'll figure something." He stood and picked up his briefcase. "Let's call it a day, Maddy. Before I get home, I gotta work up courage to tell Lauren."

Chapter 55

"Hold still, Timshel," Lauren snapped, fumbling with the child's barrettes. "I wish you'd do your own hair. I have a thousand things to do this morning and I don't need you squirming around." Inundated with problems, Lauren felt unraveled. In normal times, her orderly mind would sort, rank and attack setbacks in a methodical way, but now she was dueling chaos drenched with fatigue.

Wyatt, looking haggard, stepped into the room. "I hope you slept better than I did. Didn't get a wink."

"How do you think I could sleep after yesterday?" Lauren tugged on a rebellious strand of Timmie's hair and snapped the barrette closed. "Done. Now run and get yourself a bowl of cereal. Mommy will be there in a minute."

Lauren stood and faced Wyatt, her nose inches from his. "All last week I fended off creditors. Madison's pushy circuit board supplier calls every day wanting money. Southern California Vacuum Systems is threatening to come and re-possess the big pump. There's no money. Not a cent for Optimal's bills, much less our mortgage payments. You expect me to sleep with that hanging over my head?"

"I know." Wyatt rubbed his swollen eyes. "There's nowhere to turn. I considered going back to Bernie and Mike, but Mike's stretched to the limit and Bernie's so strapped he can't retire." Wyatt hung his head. "They put their trust in me, and I've screwed up everything."

Lauren strode into the kitchen with Wyatt trailing

after her, shoulders drooping. "You're worried about your friends?" she hissed. "What of your family? What will happen to us?"

Her back to Wyatt, Lauren leaned on the counter. "I can't go to work today. I'll call in sick." Her shoulders quivered, and she turned, tears streaming down her cheeks. "Damn it," she whispered, "We were so close."

Timmie, walking from the pantry clutching a cereal box, froze. Her face puckered as if stifling her own tears. "Mommy, why are you crying?"

Lauren knelt and took Timmie in her arms. "It's nothing, Honey. Just silly problems with the business."

Wyatt dropped to his knees and embraced them both. They slowly swayed, linked in sadness. Lauren's jerky gasps changed to soft sighs and Timmie wrestled her arms free to encircle her parent's necks. Garfield crept from beneath a chair, strolled across the floor and rubbed his nose on Lauren's shoe.

"This is nuts!" Wyatt shouted, leaping to his feet. "We're not beaten yet!"

Lauren gasped at his outburst, Timmie jumped and Garfield scampered back to his sanctuary under the chair.

"Here's what we'll do," Wyatt said. "I'll get with Madison and call both AirEnvironment and King. I'll push this up the damn chains of command to their Division Head or CEO if I have to. Next, I'll get Art Weinstein in an arm-lock. No more waiting; he has to get us answers *today*."

Wyatt grasped Lauren's shoulders, drew her up and held her hands. "Darling, you have a great relationship with Wong at the bank. Sit down with him; tell him what's happening. Tell him I'm hoping to have a big order in a day or two. See if you can't finagle a loan directly from him. Blow off the SBA."

Lauren dabbed a wet cheek on the sleeve of her blouse. "I'm not sure I can…"

"Just today, my Love. Let's give it everything we have for just one more day. Please?"

Timmie, her frown easing, held on to Lauren's waist and craned her neck to look at her parents' faces.

"I can't go to the bank. My eyes feel gritty and I bet I look hideous," Lauren lamented.

"Why don't you shower? I'll take Timmie to school."

Lauren knew it was hopeless and her mind wilted like a bouquet in summer heat. She saw Wyatt's eyes probe hers, thirsting for encouragement, seeking her help. There was defiance in his face, a strength that kindled stirrings in her heart.

She sighed. "Well…okay. One last day."

Lauren tried to be optimistic when Lee Wong stood and greeted her with a warm smile. "How nice to see you again, Mrs. Morgan––er Lauren. Please, sit. Coffee? Tea?"

"You know, I'd love a cup of coffee."

"Cream? Sugar?" asked Lee.

"Black. Black's fine."

After getting coffee for Lauren, Lee sat and nudged a large plastic turkey, replete with Day-Glo feathers, an inch to one side. Lee apparently saw Lauren's eyes fall on the ornament and said, "Strategic policy-making by the branch manager. Thanksgiving decorations help set our clients at ease."

"I think you're being facetious, Lee."

"You noticed?" he said, snickering behind his hand. "So, when you called, you mentioned problems. How can I help?"

Lauren wrapped her hands around the cup, drawing in warmth. "Things at our company are taking longer than expected. We've hit a serious cash flow problem. It's obvious the SBA will not come through, so I want to talk over the possibility of a bridge loan from the bank."

Lee prodded his turkey another inch and clasped his manicured hands on the desk. With a thoughtful look, he said, "Perhaps you could tell me more about Optimal—the delays you mentioned and its financial posture."

Lauren launched into a candid explanation of the situation. As she spoke, Lee jotted notes on a pad with his perennial fountain pen. "That's where we are," she concluded. "Wyatt feels certain we'll have the production order within a day or two."

Lee formed a pyramid with his fingers, propped his elbows on the desk and closed his eyes. After a few moments, he said, "I wish I could be more sanguine. We knew from the onset that starting a business in this economy was risky. Now, Optimal has several complicating factors: patent issues, a lawsuit and lack of firm orders. The bank's top management has restricted lending to build reserves in compliance with the new directives from Washington. If you book a big order, the bank might consider a swing loan, but it would be unlikely, even though your integrity is beyond doubt. I'm terribly sorry."

Lauren swallowed and looked into Lee's kind face. She wondered if it had been wise to limit their search for funding to just one bank. *But it's our bank...they know us.* Her stomach churned, and she struggled to keep from weeping. She collected herself and said, "You've been very kind and I appreciate the work you've done. It wasn't long ago that the financial world was sane, and you and I could work together based on the merits of a project. But now, we spend more time fighting onerous regulations and arguing with tax lawyers than we do evaluating business opportunities."

"Ah, yes, I remember you're an accountant. You and I are tilting the same windmill."

"Cervantes. You're well read, Lee," Lauren said with a weak smile. "I guess we're finished." She stood and extended her hand. "Thanks again." Once more, tears welled in her eyes, but she fought them back.

With both hands and a slight bow, Lee shook her hand. "Perhaps you'll get that order soon. We'll talk then."

One last day, he said. Well, the day isn't over. Lauren pointed her car, not toward home, but to Beverly Hills and her mother's house. Wyatt, she suspected, would be furious if he knew her mission, but Lauren was resolute. *Go all out. Just this last day.* She'd stop at nothing to stem Optimal's demise. Nothing, not even her mother.

She took her cell phone from her purse, found Liza in the address book and pushed the call button. "Hello, Mother. Can I drop in? There's something I need to ask. No, right away. I'm in the car now. Fine—I'll be there in about thirty minutes."

The entrance to Liza's home was imposing. Once past

the ivy-covered block walls and wrought-iron entry gate, there was a long driveway bordered by stately elm trees. A marble Koi pond sparkled in the center of the motor court, in turn embraced by two wings of the house. A red Spanish tile roof capped the two-story structure. The massive front door, made of carved teak, had been imported from an old colonial courthouse in French Indochina.

Anxious, Lauren pushed the doorbell. Wong's coffee had made her jittery, adding to her nervousness. Like a bank vault, the door creaked open revealing a withered older woman wearing a black dress with a starched white apron. The maid tilted her head in recognition, saying, "Welcome, Miss Lauren. This way, please."

"Thanks, Emma."

The entry, dominated by a huge spiral travertine staircase, echoed with their footsteps. As they threaded through the rooms, Lauren's eyes darted from the familiar Dali painting to elegant European leather furniture to Murano crystal chandeliers. Everywhere she looked, it seemed money oozed from the walls, and the sight was comforting. Her mother could afford to help.

The maid ushered Lauren into the sunroom, where Liza was thumbing through a catalog from Sotheby's. "Good afternoon, Mother. I see you're shopping at your favorite discount store."

"Humph," Liza grunted, tossing the catalog aside. "Your visit is a surprise. Special occasion?"

"In a way." Lauren gathered her courage, sat and leaned toward her mother. "We're in trouble, Mom." Lauren's composure faltered and words gushed like a broken hydrant. "There has been setback after setback. Now there's another company suing us for patent infringement. This morning Wyatt is meeting with our lawyer to work it out, but it takes time. What I'm saying is, we're out of money. Creditors are beating on our door."

Liza scowled. "I see."

"I need your help, Mom. We need a loan. Maybe $50,000."

Stone-faced, Liza stared at Lauren. "Forgive me if I say I told you so."

"Mother, *please*. You're our last chance. If I can't find the money, we'll have to file bankruptcy. We could lose the house. If there were any other way…"

Liza stood abruptly, walked to the mahogany credenza and poured a stiff drink of brandy from a cut-glass decanter. "I know our relationship is difficult and I can be stubborn. I don't care much for Wyatt, but he's a man of honor and a hard worker. He treats you well if you accept the fact he's an engineer first and then a husband." She clasped her arms as if trying to organize her thoughts and faced Lauren. "Regardless, I'm not a person who'd abandon her daughter and grandchild in need. I simply can't help."

"Can't? You're a wealthy woman, Mother."

"No longer."

"What do you mean?"

Liza returned to her chair and pulled it closer to Lauren. "It's a short tale. When your father's law firm went international, big clients showered us with money. We were awash in luxury. Then, a year or two before he died, I noticed Earl always looked worried. The week after he passed, I found out why: he'd made huge investments in commodities and equity funds. On margin. When the market collapsed, your father lost boatloads of money. He tried to get it back at Vegas and Monte Carlo. My inheritance, Dear, was a portfolio of worthless stocks and a bundle of markers to gamblers. So there you are. If I had the money, I'd lend it."

"Mom; I had no idea!"

"You might had you thought. I sold the yacht and the Montana place to cover my obligations. I wanted to put this house up for sale, but with the mortgage, there's no equity now that the housing market is in the cellar. Worse, I'll have to let Emma go too—after all these years. Terrible." Liza shook her head. "By the way, I wasn't going through the Sotheby's catalog looking to buy, but to get an idea what my paintings and antiques might be worth."

"Oh, Mom," Lauren uttered as she knelt and hugged her mother.

)( )( )(

After Lauren left, Liza paced, her hands clutched behind her. The autumn sun flashed through the windows and caressed the ornate chandelier. Red, green and blue rays, refracted from its crystal droplets, spattered the carpet and Liza's shoulders. The room was warm and bright and a hint of spangled dust clung to the sunbeams.

Liza paced. A scowl reflected the dark mood that engulfed her. Dismayed that Lauren forced her to explain her sudden destitution, Liza poured another brandy. *Goddamned Earl. Fed me to bungling brokers and gamblers, leaving me without a dime.*

Liza paced and recalled that Earl had been a handsome, elegant and ambitious suitor. Their wedding was modest, only 250 guests, but attended by influential schoolmates from Yale Law, where Earl had graduated. The future had beckoned and her love for Earl was consuming. *Yes, I really loved him.*

Liza paced, sipped her brandy and reflected. Lauren seemed steadfast in her love for Wyatt. *As I was for Earl.* Both men were driven by dreams and labored incessantly toward excellence even if it compromised family life. A thin grin creased Liza's face as she saw the similarities between herself and Lauren. Wyatt was stumbling as she'd predicted. *So did Earl at the end.*

Liza paced and her mind scolded her. It had been a big mistake to keep up her lavish lifestyle after Earl died. She'd ignored her finances and squandered what money there was on extravagant trips and posh parties. *I was stupid. In denial.*

Pacing, she remembered how Lauren looked when she left. Crushed. Lifeless. Her daughter had tottered down the sidewalk, her normal easy stride hobbled by an immense burden. Liza felt helpless and agonized over the future of her daughter, grandchild, and even Wyatt.

Liza paced and quaffed the last of her drink. Her lips quivered and her eyes misted. Suddenly, she became nauseated and a blinding headache crushed her thoughts. Dizziness gripped her, and she tripped on the corner of the Oriental rug. Liza caught herself on the arm of the sofa and thought, *Whoa, might want to sit for a moment.* As she eased onto the couch, she rubbed her temple and groaned.

Chapter 56

Dawn on Thanksgiving morning cast a blush on the night as Wyatt slurped tepid coffee and stared through the window at fog creeping through the palm tree. He shuddered. *Optimal is on life support.* Yesterday, he'd struck out with both AirEnvironment and King Aviation. "It's in the hands of lawyers," they'd said. When he called Art Weinstein, the attorney explained that courts, with their immense backlog, blocked any chance for quick resolution to the suit. Now that the holidays had arrived, even further delays could be expected. Wyatt recognized there was little hope, but out of habit, his mind probed for new ideas to save Optimal.

Restless, he went to the kitchen and poured a fresh cup of scalding coffee. He rubbed the back of his neck and flexed his shoulders, trying to subdue the tension. Raising the cup to his lips, his hand shook, spilling coffee on his pant leg.

Last night, lamenting over her failure at the bank and Optimal's demise, Lauren collapsed in the sanctuary of their bed. Worried, Wyatt tiptoed into the bedroom to check on her. Even in the morning chill, she'd cast off her blanket and was sprawled diagonally across the bed, whimpering in her sleep. Wyatt pulled the blanket over her, drew his finger to his pursed lips, and gently pressed a kiss on her shoulder.

Wyatt stole from the bedroom and returned to the living room where he stood, rigid and on edge, cradling his coffee. As he sipped, trying not to spill, he imagined his wife's distraught face rising in the steam of his cup. Startled, he huffed, blowing away her visage.

The phone rang and Wyatt snatched the receiver before another blast could disturb Lauren. "Hello," he whispered.

"Hello, Mr. Morgan. This is Emma, Mrs. Bromwich's maid. I'm afraid I've bad news. Liza may have had a stroke."

"A stroke?" Wyatt set his cup on the end table and sat on the sofa.

"Yes, Mr. Morgan. The ambulance just left."

"Is she okay? I mean, how bad is it?"

"The attendants didn't say. I found her this morning on the floor, unconscious."

"W-where did they take her?" Wyatt stammered.

"Cedars-Sinai."

Wyatt bit his lip, trying to think. "All right. We'll go to the hospital right away. As soon as I hear anything, I'll call you."

"Thanks, Mr. Morgan."

He hung up, strode into the bedroom and sat on the edge of the bed. "Honey?" he said, shaking Lauren.

"Let me sleep. Too tired."

"Lauren, Dear. It's your mother. She's in the hospital."

Lauren sat up, fighting the shackles of sleep. "Mom's in the hospital?"

"Yes. A stroke, they think. That was Emma who called. Said the ambulance just left. We'd better get over there."

"Oh, my God," Lauren cried. She sprang from bed, her eyes searching Wyatt's. "Do you think it's serious?"

"I don't know. Get dressed. Timmie, too."

Lauren scrambled into her clothes and roused Timmie

who rubbed her eyes and fussed. "Timmie. Help me. We're going to the hospital to see Grandma."

"Grandma's sick?"

"Yes, Dear. That's why we have to hurry."

Wyatt hopped into the room, trying to slip into his shoe. "The hospital's thirty minutes away. It's early, so traffic should be light."

"Okay. Let's go," Lauren said.

Thick mist smothered the trees and painted halos around the streetlights. Even though Wyatt drove as fast as he dared in the murk, time seemed to drag. Finally, he saw the street sign, Beverly and George Burns. "This is it. Parking should be around the corner."

Wyatt and Lauren leapt from the car and scurried to the entrance, tugging Timmie by her hands. A weary looking volunteer at the information counter said Liza was still in Emergency and children were not permitted. They followed the signs to the waiting room, which looked forlorn and sterile in the early morning.

"Go on in, Honey," Wyatt said. "I'll stay with Timmie."

Lauren nodded, got permission from the attendant and went through the swinging doors.

She was gone a long time. Wyatt thumbed through a tattered *Woman's Day* magazine and wondered why he'd never seen a waiting room stocked with *Popular Mechanics* or *Scientific American*. A television, perched in a corner near the ceiling, belched a ridiculous talk show, but it kept Timmie occupied until she dozed off.

"Mr. Morgan?" Wyatt's daydreaming was interrupted by a middle age man in a white coat. Lauren was beside him in a wheelchair. Wyatt blinked, shocked by his wife's blanched face.

"I'm doctor Jameson," the man announced. Your wife collapsed when she saw her mother, but she's better now."

Lauren shook her head. "Mom's had a terrible stroke. Doctor Jameson says there's probably permanent brain damage and she may even die. There's nothing we can do but wait."

"That's right, Mr. Morgan. We're doing everything we can for Mrs. Bromwich. It's best for your wife to go home and rest. I've given her a mild sedative so she can sleep." He handed Wyatt a slip of paper. "This is a prescription to cover the next few days."

Wyatt took the paper and woke his daughter. "What's the matter, Mommy?" Timmie asked, looking startled at the sight of the wheelchair.

"It's nothing, Little One. I just got a little dizzy and hospitals always help this way."

With a nod, Timmie put her hand on her mother's arm as an orderly wheeled them to the curb outside.

While driving home, Wyatt maneuvered the car with one hand and cradled Lauren to his side with the other. He felt her shiver and held her closer.

"I wasn't going to tell you," Lauren said, "but I went to see Mother yesterday afternoon. She was fine when I left."

"Why weren't you going to tell me?" Wyatt asked.

"I'll explain later." She dabbed her eyes with a well-used tissue.

They harbored their private thoughts in silence; the only sound was the hiss of the tires on the wet pavement and the smack-smack of the wipers clearing the dew.

Timmie, in the back seat, stared out the window saying nothing.

Even though it was almost ten, the fog still hung heavy when Wyatt helped Lauren into the house. He ushered her to the easy chair, bundled her in an afghan, and went to the kitchen to make hot chocolate. It was a hollow gesture, but he lacked words of comfort and felt compelled to do something. As Wyatt took two mugs of milk from the microwave and stirred in chocolate powder, he noticed a red light blinking on the answering machine. Worried that the hospital had left the message, he jabbed the "play" button and heard Madison's voice saying to call right away. "Important news."

It's Thanksgiving Day, for crying out loud. She can wait.

Lauren gave Wyatt an ashen smile as he set the steaming cup beside her. "Thanks," she whispered.

Wyatt handed the other mug to his daughter and cautioned, "Careful, Timmie. This is hot."

"No marshmallows?"

"I'll get them for you, Sweetie." Wyatt walked to the kitchen and returned with a plastic sack of miniature marshmallows.

Lauren sank in the cushions and with a vacant stare, drew the blanket tightly under her chin. Minutes passed while her hot chocolate grew cold. Then, wraith-like, she stood, crept down the hall and collapsed in bed.

Wyatt felt lost in the empty living room; even Timmie had retreated to her bedroom. There was nothing he could do for his wife, so he picked up the newspaper, read a line, and then flung it to the floor. Restlessness gnawed at him, so he decided to fix an early Thanksgiving dinner for his daughter, figuring Lauren needed to sleep, not cook. He tiptoed around the kitchen, rummaging in the refrigerator and fumbling strange utensils. Although Lauren had purchased a turkey, the naked bird intimidated him. He found a leftover ham in the refrigerator squatting in solidified grease––good enough for Timmie and himself.

After giving Emma an update on the phone, Wyatt microwaved slices of meat and boiled a package of frozen corn. He summoned Timmie and joked about his awkward attempt at cooking, but gloom seeped from his pores, oozed across the table and seemed to smother the child. After a few bites, Timmie said she was tired and stole away.

As he cleared the dishes, still half full, Wyatt once more noticed the blinking answering machine. He pushed aside a persistent headache and dialed Madison. "Glad you called, Wyatt. I've terrible news."

He closed his eyes. *Now what. If bad things come in three's, why am I at twenty and counting?* "Okay, Madison. What is it?"

"Ed Morales called saying one of Maddox's jets in Michigan had a bad fire. Nobody killed, but the plane was badly damaged. The FAA has grounded all Model 750 aircraft pending an investigation."

"So?"

"Remember? Our equipment is installed on a Model 750 test aircraft. It's grounded too."

Wyatt tried to sort out his thoughts. "I don't get the connection."

"The FAA suspects the inflow control valves. There's no real evidence, but the investigators guess that hot bleed air leaked and set the fire."

"But those valves aren't ours," Wyatt said. "Why should they ground our test airplane when the plane that burned had old-style equipment?"

"Because they're not sure why the fire started. Nobody at the FAA will stick out their necks and authorize flights. It's cover-your-ass time. Ed says both the FAA and NTSB have started a joint investigation. Those things go forever and it could be months before we're cleared to fly again. Our whole program is in limbo."

"Not limbo, Madison, more like hell," Wyatt groaned. "This is the final nail in our coffin." He ran his fingers through his hair. "My whole life has turned upside-down. Not only has Optimal gone flat-line, but Lauren's mother had a massive stroke last night. The doctor says she may not make it."

"My God, Wyatt. Is there anything I can do?"

Wyatt rubbed his eyes. "I don't know. I'm bouncing off the walls. Lauren is taking it really hard and has gone to bed. I haven't a clue what to do for her. Timmie seems okay, but she's too young to understand. Somehow I have to get to a drugstore and fill a prescription for Lauren's sedative, but I don't want to leave her. I'm not even sure the drugstores are open today."

"I'm on my way. Don't worry; I'll take care of the prescription," Madison said.

>< >< ><

Madison jumped into her Miata and barreled toward Wyatt's house, ignoring the slippery streets. She grabbed her cell phone. "Hello Mother? I have to cancel dinner. I *know* it's Thanksgiving, but something dreadful has come up. No, it can't wait. Sorry, but this is crucial. I'll call tomorrow. Maybe leftover turkey sandwiches, okay?" Without waiting for an answer, she snapped the phone shut. Madison spanked the car into third gear and accelerated hard through a yellow light. The roadster careened around a corner as she yanked on the wheel to regain control.

After talking with Wyatt, Madison knew he was being sucked into the abyss of his wife's grief—a looming disaster. If she were to comfort Wyatt, she'd have to get him away from Lauren. The Miata's tires, pushed to their limit, skittered in protest.

As she barreled along the streets, Madison tried to visualize her future. Although the downfall of Optimal saddened her, she'd never invested her soul the way Wyatt had. *He* was her altar, not their company. It would be a tragedy to let Optimal crumble, but she had no control over governmental blunders, of espionage or airplane fires. She'd remind Wyatt that his mind remained brilliant and agile, capable of creating an exciting future.

Madison braked heavily and swerved into the Morgan driveway. She switched off the car, took a deep breath and hurried through the fog to Wyatt.

>< >< ><

Lauren reached for a tissue on her bedside table and mopped her runny nose. She paused, thinking she heard a woman's voice coming from the living room. She cocked her head and listened. Nothing. Lauren was ashamed of her weakness and shuddered. *There's nothing I can do for Mom or Optimal. Get a grip.* The carpet felt soft on her bare feet when she went to her dresser mirror. Still in her clothes from that morning, Lauren's Capris and blouse were wrinkled and disheveled. Her hair was snarled and dark circles under her eyes camouflaged her freckles. As she reached into a drawer for a hairbrush, she heard the voice again. There was no mistake. It was Madison.

I've had enough of this woman shouldering into my life—Wyatt's life. With two quick yanks of the brush, Lauren smoothed her hair. She stood up straight, threw back her shoulders and stormed down the hall.

"What are *you* doing here?" Lauren growled, interrupting Madison in mid-sentence.

Startled, Madison stammered, "To help. I came to help. Wyatt said you needed a prescription filled."

Lauren flung an icy glare at her husband. "Leg broken?"

"I didn't want to leave you alone, Darling. Madison and I were on the phone talking about a fire on one of Maddox's airplanes. When I mentioned your mother's illness, she came over to lend a hand. That's all."

"Forget it, Madison. In spite of everything, we're fine. As a matter of fact, I don't need a sedative, so you came for nothing."

Madison squinted, her eyes forming two narrow slits. "You sure? Wyatt said you were on the verge of a breakdown."

Lauren tilted her chin higher. "As you see, we're under control. It's Thanksgiving, and I planned a nice turkey dinner for the family, so I need to get busy. I'm sure you have family obligations tonight, too."

"Ahhh," Madison breathed. "You're right. I'd canceled dinner with my mother, but maybe I can salvage my evening." She reached over and patted Wyatt's arm.

"Maybe another time." Twisting the doorknob, Madison looked back at Wyatt and gave him a resigned look.

As Madison went to the car, Lauren glared at her back and then glanced at her watch—almost one in the afternoon. She went to the kitchen, shoved aside Wyatt's soiled dishes and plopped the turkey in a roasting pan. *Dinner will be very late, but I'm not having Thanksgiving without a turkey.*

The kitchen seemed to take on a rosy glow. Lauren drove off her morning's malaise and replaced it with a newfound vigor, working briskly and decisively. Her back was straight and her hand firm. She remembered reading a passage saying, "The strongest steel is forged in flames." So it was.

Lauren banished any thought of Madison. Free of green eyes and Optimal, Lauren would nurture her family and heal the wounds inflicted on them over the past months. Timmie would bask in the love that surged between her parents and flourish.

Lauren smiled as she closed the oven door. *I'll survive. My family will thrive.*

The next morning Lauren rose early, showered and snatched a piece of toast. "Get Timmie dressed and take her to the park while I go back to the hospital," she instructed Wyatt. "Maybe later, if you can get Sharon to babysit, you can come and see Mom."

"Are you up to it?" Wyatt asked. "Remember the doctor told you to stay home...said he'd call if there were any changes with Liza."

"I'm fine. Mother needs me so I'm not sitting around

waiting for a fool phone call." Lauren gathered her purse and strode out the door.

At the hospital, Lauren learned Liza had been transferred to intensive care. Resolute, Lauren set up housekeeping at her mother's bedside. During the day, she read books that Wyatt had brought. Nighttime found her in fitful sleep on a chair that folded out into a makeshift bed. Although the staff mouthed encouraging words, they shook their heads as they checked the monitors and read Liza's charts. The hours seemed interminable.

Chapter 57

With a whisper, a rain-glistened limousine pulled up to the curb in front of The Blue Gardenia restaurant. The doorman, carrying a large umbrella, leapt to open the rear door. An elegant looking woman emerged onto the slick sidewalk followed by an impeccably dressed man who slid across the seat and stepped under the umbrella. The doorman escorted the couple to the ornate door and into the welcoming warmth of the Beverly Hills restaurant.

"Welcome back, Mr. Magana. Your table is ready," said the portly maître d'. With a slight bow, he nodded to the woman, "Miss Kelly, you're looking beautiful as usual."

Eric Magana chuckled to himself, knowing the maître d' used this well-rehearsed comment for all women, but this time it was true. "Thank you, Eddie; nice to be back. We're celebrating tonight so please send the sommelier to our table." Even though Eric knew the way, the maître d' strutted like a drum major, leading his guests across the opulent room to a quiet corner table.

Eric was forty-five years old and even in the dim room his deep tan glowed. He wore a flawless Savile Row suit and a confident smile beamed from his clean-shaven face. With Julie Ann Kelly on his arm, striking in a chic black dress and four-inch pumps, Eric could pass for a leading man from Hollywood.

The restaurant was decked out for the holidays with a china Santa and elaborate candles decorating each linen clad table. Holly festooned the railings of the mezzanine and Christmas carols whispered in the background.

When the sommelier appeared, Eric ordered, "Champagne, Krug's Clos du Mesnil, ninety-five."

"Excellent choice, sir."

The steward returned cradling the rare champagne as if it were a newborn baby. He uncorked it and poured a small portion for Eric to taste.

After an approving nod from his guest, the waiter filled two crystal flutes and wrung the bottle into an ice bucket. Eric raised his glass in a toast, "To us, lovely lady. After my speech at this morning's big meeting on automotive tort law, I called AirEnvironment. Nick Nolan, their buyer, said he's going to buy fifty pressurization systems from me. The deal is in the bag. Tomorrow, we fly to Boston to sign a very, very profitable contract. Happy you took off a few days to join me in California?"

"Of course," Julie Ann beamed, her perfect teeth peeking between pouty lips. "I'm amazed how naturally you take command. What's your secret?"

Eric shrugged, pretending modesty. "These deals aren't easy, but I've cultivated extremely helpful friends inside the Federal Aviation Administration. And I'm not forgetting you were my pipeline into the Patent Office." He waved at their waiter. "Let's order a nice appetizer."

A year ago, Eric recalled, he'd met with Congressman Jenks in Washington who'd decided to abandon an earmark benefiting his business. Tired of verbal fencing, the congressman abruptly excused himself, leaving Eric pondering the fecklessness of politicians. He decided that Jenks had seen the last of his political contributions and free trips in his jet. Aggravated, he'd set out to find the nearest bar.

He'd ducked out of the blustery autumn wind into The Conference Room, a bar favored by young government employees and an occasional elected official. As his eyes adjusted to the darkness, he saw a gorgeous woman gathering her purse and coat. He strode over and said, "Do you mind?" He smiled warmly. "I've had a bad afternoon with a congressman and could use a drink or two, preferably with a fine young lady. May I?"

She'd hesitated, looking suspicious.

With his most sincere smile he repeated, "Nasty congressman. Bad day." He saw her wavering and finally she said, "Julie Ann."

"*Very* pleased to meet you. I'm Eric," he said, holding her chair.

She set her purse and coat aside, saying, "I was supposed to meet a friend, but she just called to cancel."

"My good luck. Do you like Martinis?" When Julie Ann nodded, Eric snapped his fingers as a barmaid breezed by and he ordered, "Two Gilpin's Westmorland Gin Martinis, very dry, up, stirred, not shaken."

Julie Ann grinned and patted her blond hair.

Eric was accustomed to pretty women and changed them as often as his socks, but he had to admit Julie Ann was stunning. Her beauty buoyed his mood and lubricated his tongue. At first, they chatted about their jobs, marital status––both single––and the weather. Captivated, Eric succumbed to an urge to impress her, just as Tom Sawyer had strutted in front of Becky.

"I own a seventeen hundred man manufacturing firm called Dynamag," Eric boasted. "My father started it forty years ago. Keeps me busy—had to run to New Delhi last week to negotiate a contract with Tata Motors for truck parts. It's a good thing I have my own jet, the way I travel."

Julie Ann cocked her head, looking enthralled. "With the economy so bad, isn't it hard to do business?"

"Things are tough. I had to can a few laggards, but the bottom line is holding up okay."

With a nod, Julie Ann said, "Because I work in the Patent Office, I know good ideas can make a company. I guess you have lots of patents."

Her bright smile and eager eyes enraptured Eric. "Dynamag builds car parts for the big automakers using their drawings—their designs. But I'm looking for my own proprietary items to diversify."

After two rounds of drinks, they ordered a platter of apple slices with Brie and settled into a promising evening surrounded by the soothing ambience of the well to do.

"Just what do you do in the Patent Office, Julie Ann?" Eric inquired.

"I supervise a small group that categorizes incoming applications and sends them to the proper department for evaluation. I'm the gatekeeper, so to speak. Because I majored in physics in college, I can do basic evaluations."

"Physics? Impressive. Still, it sounds like a tedious job."

"It can be exciting. Just the other day, an interesting application came in—a brilliant combination of mechanics and software. I showed my boss who agreed it was a real breakthrough, worthy of special consideration. So he sent it to the Technical Director, a new position congress mandated."

Eric rubbed his chin. "It sounds interesting. How about a little more detail?"

"Oh, I can't reveal specifics on the applications."

"I wouldn't want you to get into trouble. I'm just curious." Eric sipped his martini, thinking. "Perhaps we can connect tomorrow for dinner? Oops. No way. Forgot that I fly to Bermuda in the morning." Eric's brows furrowed and then he grinned. "Here's a thought. Why don't you go with me? It's just the weekend and you wouldn't miss work. Perhaps we might talk about this invention. What do you say?"

Eric's musings were yanked back to the present when the waiter announced, "Medium for the lady and medium-rare for you, sir."

Eric sliced his steak, saw it was just the right shade of reddish-pink and took a bite. "It's not what you know, but who you know. With your help and my connections in Washington, I snatched this deal from that amateur what-ever-his-name."

"True," she said, nibbling a floret of broccoli. "Running your father's company must be challenging."

"It *isn't* my father's company," Eric snapped. "He's dead, and it's mine now. All the while I worked for him, he treated me same as a damn servant. He never liked any of my ideas. Guess what? The company stagnated for years."

"But it's grown a lot since you took over, right?"

"Damn right. I can light fires under people. The old man was hung up on tedious engineering and quality, but never understood that networking and influence were what really mattered. Once he noticed a machinist who'd allowed his milling cutter to wear, and the parts were slightly out of tolerance. What did he do? Grabbed the pieces from the tray and threw them everywhere, yelling 'These are crap!' The workers were all ducking behind their machines. The man was crazy! Those parts could have been used; they were just a tad off." Eric shook his head.

"He sure *sounds* crazy," Julie Ann agreed.

"Well he was. If he could see this contract I'm going to win, maybe he would have realized I'm someone." Eric smoothed the linen napkin in his lap. "Tell you what, after we sign the deal tomorrow, let's fly to Monte Carlo for a little fun." He set his steak knife on the edge of his plate and grinned. "Glad you teamed up with me?"

"Of course." Julie Ann smiled and cut a small piece of filet. Looking up, she saw a young man, dressed in a polo shirt and Dockers, talking with the maître d', who nodded in their direction. The man, looking out of place in the elegant dining room, walked to their table.

"Ms. Kelly?"

"Yes."

"Ms. Julie Ann Kelly?"

"Yes. What do you want?"

He handed her an envelope. "I'm serving you with a subpoena from the Los Angeles Federal Court ordering you to appear at a deposition regarding irregularities in the United States Patent and Trademark Office."

Chapter 58

That same night, in the early winter darkness, a blustery rain hurled itself against the windows setting a gloomy mood. It had been two weeks since Liza died and the house echoed with despair. In past years, the blare of college football accompanied Wyatt as he breezed through the holiday season, but his melancholy left no space for entertainment. It was as if a thick crust had solidified around his mind, insulating him from the outside world. Lauren seemed plagued by the same affliction. The despair was so contagious that Timmie ignored Jenny, preferring to sulk in front of her television. The holiday season had taken the color gray, going on black.

Sequestered in his backroom office, Wyatt shuffled three pieces of paper. The first was a newspaper clipping from the *Burbank Leader,* announcing the collapse of Optimal. Filled with sadness, he read it once more, folded it neatly and tucked it in his pocket. The second was a letter from the mortgage company he received that morning. "This is an official notification of default…" it began. He drew a deep breath, his heart pounding in his ears. With a deliberate motion, he took the letter and wadded it, tighter and tighter until it was no larger than a golf ball. The muscles in his forearm bulged as he compressed the paper and flung it violently against the wall. Then his eyes fell on his birthday card. As usual, he'd forgotten his birthday, but as usual Lauren hadn't. She'd made a cake and invited Mike and Bernie over for a get-together "Just to get your mind off our troubles," she'd said. He'd been relieved when Lauren assured him, "Madison isn't invited."

How can I party after everything that's happened? Wyatt glanced at his watch and saw that their guests were due in an hour. He picked up Marge's vodka bottle, splashed two fingers into a glass, and took a swallow, welcoming the searing heat in his throat. He studied the glass and then raised it in a silent toast. *Here's to me. Happy thirty-sixth. Been one miserable year.* He was surprised that the pint bottle was already half-empty.

A year ago, Wyatt's aspirations were ambitious and full of promise. It was to be the year that Optimal took root—when production orders would solidify their finances and when he'd prove his worth to Lauren, Mike and Bernie. He'd even hoped to impress Liza.

Wyatt took another sip of vodka. A vague haze infiltrated his thinking as he pondered his predicament. While he cherished his ability to focus on technical skills, ignorance of the business environment had crippled him. He had allowed his ideas to be stolen, squandered the family's security and brushed aside his wife. Excitement over a purchase order entangled him in a morass of adultery and self-hatred.

Love for his wife flooded over him and a sudden thought jolted his mind. He sat at his computer and began to type.

)( )( )(

Lauren greeted Bernie and Mike, shivering with the cold, at the front door and ushered them into the house. "Come," she said. "Let me take your coats. There's hot coffee in the kitchen."

"Sorry to hear about your mother," Bernie said.

"Yeah, me too," Mike nodded.

Over the past three years, she'd come to know Bernie well and counted him as a true friend. His easy, genuine smile drew her into his affable world. He wasn't preoccupied the way Wyatt was and Lauren found him engaging. In many ways, he was like a father, but unburdened by the role of disciplinarian.

Lauren was also drawn to Mike, not in a warm, homey way, but as someone who brought excitement into her no-nonsense home. Lauren had finally become acclimated to Mike's lurid vocabulary and enjoyed his exciting, action-oriented lifestyle.

After hanging up their jackets, Lauren called Wyatt to join them in the kitchen where they engaged in small talk. Although she still struggled with the loss of her mother, a counter-current swirled in her mind. She realized that for three years Optimal had been a whirlpool, sucking her time and energies into its vortex. Now the maelstrom was gone, vanquished by a lawyer. Lauren wondered why she secretly looked forward to a renewed family life. Once more, she fantasized about another baby. Lauren felt guilty over her musing, but embraced it.

The doorbell rang, jarring Lauren's thoughts. She went to the front door and found Madison standing there, blowing into her gloved hands.

"Hi," Madison said. "I hope I'm not late for Wyatt's party. I didn't get an invite, but Bernie mentioned it. Guess you forgot."

Flabbergasted, Lauren said, "What are you doing here?"

"I assumed it was an oversight, so here I am."

Fearful that a scene would upset her guests, Lauren waved Madison into the house and returned to the kitchen, leaving her looking for a spot to drop her coat.

Madison has the gall to crash Wyatt's party, the witch. Two weeks ago she intruded on Thanksgiving as if she were part of our family.

"Oh! It's Madison," Wyatt slurred as she walked into the room. He turned his back to her and went to the dinette table where he grimaced as his rheumy eyes fell on the birthday cake.

As Lauren moved to help him, she caught a whiff of vodka. *What in the world?* Then she noticed the glass he held at his side. Puzzled, she lit the solitary candle. "The City of Burbank requires a burn permit if we had thirty-six candles," she joked. "Make a wish."

"I wish for oblivion," he whispered. He blew out the candle, and with Lauren's prodding, sliced the cake.

"Take a big piece, Honey," Lauren said. "You're the honoree, you know."

Wyatt plopped a slice onto a plate, went to the living room and fell into his chair. As he did, Timmie ran from her room and pilfered a slab of cake, heavy with frosting. She squirmed up on Wyatt's lap, balancing her dish.

"Careful, Little One," Wyatt said. "Don't get frosting on me."

Timmie looked up and wrinkled her nose. With a curious expression, she slid to the floor and slipped away to her room.

"Another year shot to hell, Wyatt," Mike said, brushing

cake crumbs from his mustache. "I hope next year will be better."

Wyatt eked out a wry smile, took a bite of cake and puckered. "Too damn sweet. Fights with my vodka." He set the plate aside and sipped from his glass.

"I wish you wouldn't drink. Honey. It's not like you," Lauren said.

Wyatt scowled. An awkward silence settled in the room and everyone fidgeted and nibbled. *This party is a wake, not a celebration,* Lauren thought.

"Say, Madison," Bernie said. "Any luck finding a job?"

"It will take a miracle, not luck," she replied. "King has been laying off people, so there's no chance they'll take me back. I've emailed a hundred résumés, but haven't had a single reply. The news commentators say we're headed for a genuine depression, if we're not there already."

Bernie nodded. "Same at SAC. Last week we canned four shop people and another engineer. Brian walks around like a beaten dog. Everyone has taken a ten-percent pay cut. That put a bullet between the eyes of my retirement plans."

"Business is fucked at Precision too," Mike grumbled. "Rather than lay off people, we've cut back to thirty-hour weeks. I canceled an order for a new machine center and used the money to service the loan I took out for Optimal."

"My job looks okay," Lauren said. "The pay isn't much, but it's better than unemployment." She sipped coffee and stared across the room, ignoring Madison.

Money. Lauren was Liza's sole heir and the mansion, with its contents were hers. Even if the house was mortgaged, the Dali, if genuine, could bring a bundle. Sterling. Statuary. The Bentley. She felt guilty thinking of such things so soon after her mother's death, but resolved to talk to Wyatt later. Lauren noticed everyone was watching her and repeated, "Yes, I still have my job."

Bernie stared at his shoes. "Just because an asshole stole our patent."

"I'm sure Wyatt will come up with an idea even better than pressurization," Madison said. "It's not the end of the world."

Wyatt belched. "Not so sure. Will somebody explain how a company that makes rear-view mirrors came up with a complex airplane system?" He drained his glass and wobbled to the back room. He returned with Marge's bottle, splashed vodka into the glass and drank. "Maybe the goddamn Martians landed and gave them the plans. Maybe God is tormenting us for insane optimism." Red blotches spattered Wyatt's face, and a scowl pulled at his lips, making him look ten years older.

This wasn't the gathering Lauren wanted. She hoped for a cheerful little party but the economy, Optimal's demise and Liza's passing cast a pall on everything. Madison's smug expression suffocated Lauren and even the Christmas decorations she put up the day before looked dismal. Watching Wyatt gulp another slug of vodka, she worried. *His limit is one glass of wine. What's going on?* Unable to follow the conversation and fumbling his words, he was obviously getting drunk. "Honey. Why don't you eat more of your cake?" she said. "You need something in your stomach."

Wyatt waved his glass, sloshing vodka on his shirt. "Clashes with my friend, here."

"Then let me make you a sandwich," Lauren persisted.

Wyatt ignored her. "I wonder what that som-bitch, Dynamag, whatever, is up to. Whatcha t'ink, Mike?"

Mike set his plate on the coffee table and rubbed his chin, "Weinstein has been saying something is fucking bizarre with our patent. I'll bet he's onto something. I've got a feeling I'm going to chow down on Dynamag meat!"

Wyatt poured more vodka and squinted at the nearly empty bottle. Lauren rose and sat by him, slipping her arm around his waist. "I think you've had enough to drink, Hon. Why don't you get some sleep." She looked apologetically at her guests and shook her head.

"Well, Happy birthday, my friend," Bernie muttered, walking over to Wyatt. He shifted his weight from one foot to the other and thrust his hands into his pockets.

Mike stood. "Yup. Bernie's right; I've things to do. Take care of yourself, Wyatt. Thanks, Lauren, I'll be in touch."

"Guess I'll head home too," Madison said. She walked to Wyatt, rubbed his arm and kissed his cheek. "Happy birthday, Wyatt. Be good."

Lauren was thunderstruck. For the first time, she saw that Madison didn't pat Wyatt's arm, but caressed him. It was a kiss, not a peck. Those damned green eyes seemed to blaze with devotion and idolization. Suddenly, Lauren realized: *Madison loves him.* Lauren froze in icy anguish. *She's trying to lure him, trap him. How long has this been happening?*

With her thoughts in turmoil, she escorted everyone to the door, leaving Wyatt staring into his glass. Ignoring Madison as she left, Lauren said, "Thanks for coming. Sorry, guys, Wyatt isn't himself."

"Sure," Bernie nodded, and everyone walked into the rain.

"Come on, Honey," Lauren said, returning to her husband. "Let's get you to bed."

"Look at this. Out of vodka. Need to go to the liquor store. A jug for me and another for Marge. She'll be pissed if she finds I drank all her booze." Wyatt lurched from the sofa and searched his pocket for car keys.

"Wyatt! You're in no condition to drive. Sit down!"

"Naw. I'm fine. Store's real close." He staggered to the door, shouldering Lauren aside. "Right back."

Lauren tried to snatch the keys while following him to the car, her frantic breath hanging in the frigid air. "Wyatt! No! You're too drunk!" He ignored her, slammed the car door and spun out of the drive.

"Wyatt!" Lauren screamed at the taillights of the fleeing car. She clutched her arms across her chest, fending off the cold drizzle and shivered, not from the chill, but from anger and frustration.

Lauren retreated to the warmth of the house, stood at the window and watched the palm tree whip in the rain. *God all mighty, I hope he'll be okay.*

She walked to her chair and fell onto the cushions. Lauren looked at her watch. *I'll give him fifteen minutes to show up before calling the cops.*

As she tried to quell a sense of panic, the image of Madison's kiss returned. Had they slept together? Lauren knew Wyatt possessed a roaring libido and Madison was out-and-out gorgeous. And men often wandered; the hints tossed out at the Scrabble parties were evidence enough, but Wyatt? In all their years together, she'd never seen him drunk. Lauren rubbed her forehead. Tonight was different, Lauren realized. The deluge of problems had overwhelmed him. In design, in science, he was master; but regulations, lawsuits and her mother's death overwhelmed him. He had no tools to deal with these and he foundered.

And there was Madison.

Lauren sighed and looked again at her watch. He's been gone a long time. *Why don't I call him?* She dialed his cell and heard it ring in the next room. *Damn, he didn't take his phone.* Panic set in and her thoughts ricocheted off terrible possibilities. *Did he pass out along the road? Was he arrested for drunk driving? Car wreck?* With a knot in her throat, she dialed the police who had no information. So Lauren called the hospital and close friends, but nobody had seen Wyatt.

She thought of Madison. *Would he go to her?*

Her hand shaking, she picked up the phone and called. "Madison, this is Lauren. Is my husband there?"

"Wyatt? No. What's going on?"

Lauren gasped in relief. Ashamed, she remembered Wyatt was still missing. "He's gone. You saw how he was drinking. He left to get more booze twenty minutes ago."

"Sit tight," Madison commanded. "I'll be right over."

"No. Don't bother. I've called the police and hospitals. It's all taken care of."

"Sit tight, I said. I'm on my way."

"No!" Lauren yelled into the phone as a dial tone buzzed.

Lauren met Madison with a frigid stare. "I thought it was clear that I'm handling this myself."

"I'm in this, too. After all, Wyatt's my partner."

"Partner in *what?* Optimal is dead. We don't need you anymore."

"Well, I think you do." Madison pushed past Lauren into the house. "Have you called the police?"

"Like I told you. I gave them the license plate number and the description of the car. Called friends and the hospital, too."

"You said he was going for more liquor," Madison said. "Do you know where the store is? We could go there."

"There's several."

"Get the phone book. We'll look them up." Madison flung her coat on the sofa and sat in Wyatt's chair. "Let's hope he's pulled over—sleeping it off or holed up in a bar somewhere," Madison suggested. "He's under terrible stress. You can't imagine."

Lauren stood motionless, staring at Madison. "Are you crazy? I'm his wife. Of *course* I know! He fought the government and lawyers but the only thing he couldn't deal with was *you*. You flounce around, patting him, cooing in his ear, tempting him. You've slept with him, haven't you?"

"He told you?"

Lauren flinched, shattered by her suspicion's confirmation. "He didn't have to. I see him clam up when I mention your name. I see your talons reaching for him." Lauren stood, feet apart, in front of Madison. With her hands on her hips, she hissed, "Understand this: he's mine. Forever. Now that Optimal is finished, you have no business in my house. Not in my life. Not in Wyatt's life." She thrust her arm and pointed to the door. "So get out. Now!"

Madison stood and tossed her head. "You're dead

wrong. Wyatt and I have connected in a way you never could. We love each other. While you stagnate in your petty accounting world, we party in the glories of science and engineering. You'll *never* understand him. Pretend he's coming back to you if you want, but he's mine. I'll search this town until I find him. The next time you call my apartment, you can ask for Wyatt; he'll be there."

A red haze of fury blurred Lauren's sight, and she slapped Madison––hard. "Get out!" she screamed.

Madison recoiled and rubbed her cheek, then snatched her coat and stormed out the door.

Lauren breathed a sigh of relief, collapsed in her chair and tried to steady her nerves. As she sat, Lauren noticed Wyatt had left the light on in his office. Out of habit, she trudged down the hall to turn it off and noticed he'd also left the computer on. She was about to turn it off when she saw a letter addressed to her on the screen. She sat and read.

"Dearest Lauren: I'm so ashamed of my failure as your huband. I have let my vanity and ambition ruin our marriage and future. I don't know how to fix things. I only know I'm despirate for your love. If you decid to take Timmie and leave me, I'd understand, but the idea that you might kills me. The past months have prove I'm half a man. Without you I'm empty. I've tried to figure out ways to save us, to save the house, to be a father for Timmie, but I be scuttled. I sit hear and beg I wish you just hold me. Can I survive? forgive…"

Tears streamed down Lauren's cheeks as she read Wyatt's lament, a dirge. In a vodka stupor, Wyatt had reached out and her heart swelled with compassion. Her vision of Wyatt as a rock softened with the realization that her strength was crucial to him. *You're wrong, Miss Electrical Engineer. He's much more than science; Wyatt's a Gestalt, a word you probably don't know. Sure, he's quirky, but they're pieces of a man at his pinnacle. Yes, I do know him and he'll shake off his troubles.*

With purposeful steps, Lauren went to kitchen and spooned fragrant coffee grounds into the coffeemaker. *No word from police or hospitals, so he must be safe, He'll be home soon and want coffee. Now that Optimal is finished, we'll have time for our Sunset Rituals. We'll be a family once more. No matter his past transgressions—we'll find a way to repair our marriage. We must for Timmie's sake. We must for us. I will forgive him.*

As the year's first rain pattered on the roof, Lauren lit the candles and waited anxiously.

)( )( )(

Glossary

ACO: Aircraft Certification Office. Regional FAA organizations that oversee certification of aircraft.

AQMD: South Coast Air Quality Management District. A government agency that sets and enforces air quality regulations in portions of Southern California.

AYSO: American Youth Soccer Organization

CAD: Computer-Aided Design. A computer system to assist the creation, modification, analysis, or optimization of a design.

CDR: Critical Design Review. A meeting where all aspects of a design are examined.

DCMA: Defense Contract Management Agency. A government agency that oversees federal acquisition programs by monitoring delivery schedules, costs and conformance to design specifications.

Delta P: Differential Pressure between the aircraft cabin and outside. Usually expressed as PSI or PSID (pounds per square inch or pounds per square inch differential).

EMT: Emergency Medical Technician

EPA: Environmental Protection Agency. An agency of the U.S. federal government for the purpose of protecting human health and the environment by writing and enforcing regulations based on laws passed by Congress.

ER: Emergency Room

GPA: Gone Prior to Arrival. A police term.

HR: Human Resources. A department within a company that administers company policy, processes hiring and firing paperwork and manages company provided insurance.

IMTS: International Manufacturing Technology Show.

ISO: International Organization for Standardization. Develops and publishes international quality standards to harmonize activities that are international in nature; aircraft design and operation being typical.

LAPD: Los Angeles Police Department

LLC:	Limited Liability Company. An LLC is a legal structure of a firm that provides limited liability to its owners.
MRB:	Material Review Board. A typical Material Review Board consists of representatives from design engineering, manufacturing engineering, quality assurance and purchasing. Only the Material Review Board can decide what to do with discrepant material: scrap, rework, use-as-is, etc.
NCMR:	Non-Conforming Material Report. A formal document that describes parts which do not conform to engineering drawings or specifications.
NTSB:	National Transportation and Safety Board. A federal agency that investigates transportation accidents to establish probable cause.
O.D.:	Outside diameter
OSHA:	Occupational Safety and Health Administration. A federal organization, OSHA's mission is to assure safe and healthful working conditions by setting and enforcing standards.
PCB:	Printed Circuit Board. A non-conductive card clad with copper foil that has been

chemically etched to form electrical paths and electronic component mounting pads.

PERT: Program Evaluation Review Technique. A project management tool used to schedule, organize, and coordinate tasks within a project.

P.O.:   Purchase Order

SBA: Small Business Administration. A government agency which serves small businesses by guaranteeing loans from private lenders.

SOW: Statement of Work. A document that lists, in detail, work to be done.

Wemac: A registered name for an adjustable air outlet used in aircraft. Similar to those found in automobiles.